# Lifesign

Carl Goodman is from Surrey. He likes hard-hitting, contemporary stories with dark and unusual themes and is currently working on more DI Eva Harris novels.

# Also by Carl Goodman

## The DI Eva Harris detective series

*20/20*
*Lifesign*

# CARL GOODMAN

# LIFESIGN

**hera**

First published in the United Kingdom in 2022 by

Hera Books
Unit 9 (Canelo), 5th Floor
Cargo Works, 1-2 Hatfields
London SE1 9PG
United Kingdom

A CIP catalogue record for this book is available from the British Library.

Print ISBN 978 1 80436 024 8
Ebook ISBN 978 1 80436 910 4

This book is a work of fiction. Names, characters, businesses, organizations, places and events are either the product of the author's imagination or are used fictitiously. Any resemblance to actual persons, living or dead, events or locales is entirely coincidental.

Look for more great books at www.herabooks.com

Printed and bound in Great Britain by Clays Ltd, Elcograf S.p.A.

I

*For Cheryl and Ross*

# *Prologue*

Kyle ran.

Cold night air burned his lungs, trainers almost silent as he pelted over rolling swathes of fractured concrete. They were behind him. He could hear them. A pack of five. Three on foot, two on bikes, all carrying. Knives, and that weird-shit hook thing the fat kid had waved in his face before he slapped him a good one. Bastards would cut him, he knew that. One of them would stick him too.

A carving knife in the gut. A rusty blade someone had used for hacking up Sunday roast, shoved into his belly while they all watched, goading each other on. Metal and flesh. He could almost feel it coming.

Kyle Shaw. Fifteen years old, lean build, mellow skin and tight curly hair, long strides, sure-footed. A good-looking kid, everybody said so. His mum said so. She said he took after his dad, but Kyle didn't believe she knew who that was. The girls at school said so too, with sly glances and dirty giggles. Sadie said so, which was where the problem started. Sadie said so in no uncertain terms.

Sadie had said so in the lift, when she pushed the emergency stop button. She was in the year below him, but that didn't count for much. All the girls were up for it. All you had to do was ask, except Sadie had asked first. Not asked, Kyle thought as he jumped a metal bar. Sadie had demanded.

So what could he do? It wasn't like she wasn't fit. Best-looking girl in her year, she knew make-up and fashion, she looked the part even in her uniform. So when she pushed the button and started taking everything off, Kyle had thought: yeah, all right then.

He had given her one right there, up on the seventh floor of her block of flats, just down the road from school. The lifts were dodgy. Everyone knew that, so nobody would have given a second thought to one getting stuck again. All metal mirrors and fluorescent lights, Kyle got his kit off too and pushed her up against the aluminium doors. It had been great, a bunch of fun. Only problem was, Sadie had made a Gif.

He knew there would be trouble as soon as he saw it. She only shared it with a few friends, but then one of them posted it. He thought he looked pretty good with Sadie's legs wrapped round him and that expression on her face, he thought he looked fit too. It was only a pity her boyfriend didn't agree.

Kyle kept running. Over a tangle of junk and rubble just high enough to stop the bikes in their tracks, under a metal gate that would fall if anyone put weight on it. Down an alley, a narrow gap between two breeze block walls. Into sudden darkness.

A dead end. Kyle spat fear. He could hear them behind him. He only had a few seconds before they boxed him in. There was only one way out.

Up.

He checked his stride before he hit the wall. Two sliding steps, then hands over the top. For one gut-wrenching moment he thought he wouldn't make it, his trainers slipped and scraped on rough breeze blocks, but then his foot caught in the corner and he gained traction. Kyle heaved, clawed, and dragged himself up.

He had to roll over razor wire, coils and braids that scratched his skin and snagged his jeans. He pushed down on it with his leather jacket, used his weight to flatten it, arched his back, kicked his legs.

One by one the five skidded to a halt beneath him. They screamed. Sadie's boyfriend flipped a knife, sent it spinning at him. Kyle flinched, felt the blade scrape his knee, saw it tumble off into the darkness. Somewhere in shadows it clattered to the ground. Kyle rolled over. He fell.

He dropped to the floor on the other side of the wall but managed to land more or less feet first. Hard concrete took the breath from him, but then with a stagger, he stood. From beyond the wall there came a furious, frustrated yelping of pack animals that knew they had lost their prey. 'You're a dead boy,' Sadie's boyfriend screamed. 'I'm gonna cut your *fucking* knob off.'

Maybe he would, Kyle thought as he stared back up at the wall and remembered where he was. Maybe they would catch up with him tomorrow, but now he knew they were coming. Tonight though, he thought as he looked behind him at the concrete landscape lit only by the moon, for a few hours he was safe.

Right?

—

Moonlight cast sharp shadows. In a couple of hundred metres the wall became high steel railings topped with spikes, and a hundred metres beyond that the railings ran into another stretch of vertical concrete. The railings there were twisted, bent out of shape where some piece of heavy machinery had reversed into them, probably years ago now. He could squeeze through the gap, creep out of the site and make his way home through the darkened lanes and silent alleys. Just not yet.

Not until Sadie's boyfriend and his band of psychos got bored of hanging around and left, because he knew they would not follow him in. He knew they didn't have the balls for that.

Kyle wandered away from the breeze-block wall and strolled towards the building.

It stood like a monolith lit from above by an inconstant moon, a pearl-white disk crossed with tendrils of cloud. Once, the building had been part of the water treatment plant, a pump-house filled with steam engines and filtration tanks. Then electricity had replaced steam and the engines had become smaller. The building was no longer needed, but the council had put a preservation order on it, so it could be used but not torn down. For a while a storage company had filled it with containers and lockups. Over the years, though, the cost of upkeep became too great, and the storage company had found cheaper premises. Now it was abandoned, a chamfered stone block no one knew what to do with. It didn't matter. Kyle thought the building looked incredible.

Dangerous though, he knew that too, which was why Sadie's boyfriend wouldn't venture in. The stone tanks lay open and some of them were deep; deep and unguarded. Fall into one and you wouldn't need to worry about clambering out. Just a splash on concrete, brains and blood and broken bones. Inside though, there would be brilliant places to climb.

A castle, Kyle thought. His castle, lit by shafts of moonlight. Lined with metal frames and steel gantries, suspended walkways that once stretched between stacked containers. Like a movie set, where aliens lurked around every corner. He'd been in the building before. Tonight, hiding from Sadie's boyfriend and his dog-faced crew, Kyle felt like going deeper.

–

It took him twenty minutes to find the racks. He wasn't looking for them, but then he wasn't really looking for anything at all. They stood in a storage area he hadn't seen before, set on a mezzanine deck atop a stone plinth some eight stories high, placing it not far below the ceiling in the huge volume of what would have once been the pump room. A narrow gantry led to it. He tested it, hesitantly at first. There was no reason to expect it would still take his weight, but after a couple of steps he figured it probably would.

High metal shelves with boxes stacked on them lined the outside edge of the platform. When Kyle touched them, he felt the difference immediately. No dust. Everything else in the building was covered with it, coarse grains of stone and concrete, but in this area everything felt new. Somebody had been here recently. When he looked around, dark-adapted eyes probing the shadows, he found he could make out tables covered with what looked like equipment. His foot brushed something. A metal pole; a tripod. And on top of the tripod, a light.

He followed the cable. The power to the building had been switched off long ago, so if there were lights then somebody must have brought their own electricity. It only took him a minute to find the battery pack. It took him half that again to find the switch.

Cold white LEDs flooded the space. Four lights on tripods formed a square that encompassed the tables. Kyle stood. Looked around.

Wished, with every fibre of his being, that he had not.

–

She stared back at him from behind green-tinged glass. Skin bloated, eyes as dark as hell, wisps of hair floating and coiling in some unseen current. A face, drawn, contorted and flayed, pared from its skull like orange peel. Someone had removed her face and her scalp, stretched them over a metal frame and then suspended the frame in liquid. And the trouble with that, Kyle realised as he felt bile erupt in the back of his throat, was that tank of liquid was just one of many.

Despite himself he looked up at the racks. They were not empty. When Kyle started screaming, he found he could not stop.

# Part I

## Natural Selection

# Chapter One

Three rounds from a semi-automatic rifle tore the air and ripped the crate next to her to shreds. Burst mode, Detective Inspector Eva Harris thought, as a police officer in black body armour grabbed her by the neck and dragged her behind a concrete column. She had not expected either of those things.

Jacks, she remembered as he forced her to the floor and all but knelt on her, his name was Jacks. A grey-haired fifty-something who had exuded quiet competence at the operational briefing. A Counter-Terrorism Specialist Firearms Officer with some sort of military background, given the job of babysitting unarmed Detective Officers on a raid that absolutely should not have involved anyone firing actual shots. *Well*, Eva thought as she struggled to breathe, *just shows how wrong you can be.*

More gunfire. Eva covered her head with her hands and stayed down as Jacks intended. She felt him move. A moment later the metallic scream of his assault rifle slapped her ears. From across the other side of the warehouse she heard another gun discharge, more staccato drumming as one of the other SFOs joined Jacks in the process of neutralising the threat. Such a clinical term, Eva thought as she tried to make out which of the other three firearms officers had also started firing. A euphemism, given that in this context neutralisation meant shooting someone dead.

When she stepped outside of the moment what struck her most was how calm she felt, given the operation had just gone catastrophically wrong. Initial surveillance had identified four individuals, but as soon as they entered the warehouse Eva counted six. Kitson, the SFO's bronze commander, had changed deployment immediately and suddenly it was the fire-arms officers taking point, not simply supporting the DOs. Jacks had shoved her behind him. He didn't strike her as the kind of officer who had much trouble with insubordination.

'Two up above us,' Jacks barked at his mike as she edged around the column. 'The walkway is metal.'

'On it.' Eva heard the response through static. A handful of seconds later a pair of concussion grenades tumbled through the air and detonated on the walkway. Light seared behind her eyes. The sound of the blast hurt like steel shards stabbing in her ears, so whoever was on the walkway must have really felt it. They had. Someone screamed. Jacks ran.

Up half a flight of stairs, he dropped where the landing turned a dogleg, and fired two bursts of three rounds. More screams, but this time she could hear pain. Somebody else shouted, incoherent and almost hysterical. It took a second for her to realise. They were trying to give themselves up. 'Support,' she heard Jacks bark. 'Two hostiles wounded. Looking to disarm.'

Eva knew then why she had taken an immediate liking to Jacks. He could have shot them dead, killed them on the spot and the internal enquiry would have exonerated him in minutes. Instead he had taken a calculated risk. Three SFOs formed a phalanx and advanced towards the stairs. Kitson and the other team members were still outside with the hostiles they had already disarmed.

She took a moment to look around her. The location of the warehouse had come from a previous investigation, from a hoard of material a local criminal named Warren Muir had collected, over the course of half a dozen years. He'd kept it in a metal case as an insurance policy, to protect himself from capricious masters. Muir was a whale of a man, middle-aged with a scrapy ponytail and thinning hair, waistline ballooned by the beer his shabby pub served. A facilitator who worked for lowlife, some local and some more distant, purveyor of brute force and ignorance to those whose businesses required it. One of Muir's thugs had tried to ram her through a crash-barrier on the A3 with a scaffolding lorry and in the process killed an innocent bystander. Eva had chased Muir around his dingy premises, following the sound of his laboured breathing, until she found him prostrate on a stained linoleum floor, desperately trying to destroy the evidence he had squirreled away for his own security. *Funny*, she thought as she watched the firearms officers surround the stairs. *Who knew Pandora's box was made of tin?*

Eva stood. A tall woman with closely cropped blonde hair, her movements were lithe and poised. She moved like a dancer. She took her weight on the balls of her feet and scrutinised the scene in front of her through suspicious green eyes set below black, arcing brows. Young for a DI, she had already seen more than her fair share of trouble. She knew about violence. She had come to understand it at a visceral level. And she knew when it was not over.

Eva was about to step out from behind the concrete pillar when something made her stop. A sudden gnawing realisation chewed at her gut, and this time she felt her short hair lift from her scalp. Two on the gantry, one by the door, two knocked to the floor as the firearms officers stormed the room. She crouched down, inched her head around the edge of the column and yelled, 'SFOs! We're missing one hostile!'

The words had barely left her lips when something sailed out of the darkness. There were too many places to hide. The men in the warehouse were far better prepared than surveillance had led them to believe. Something bright, flickering. It tumbled as it flew, struck the ground and shattered. A split second later another petrol bomb burst on the floor, then two more. A lake of flame spread over polished concrete. Whoever was in the shadows threw another. This time it erupted above the entrance and a curtain of burning liquid poured down. Shouts from outside. Nobody was going in or out through that door, Eva realised.

Two of the SFOs fired shots into the back of the warehouse. Sparks flew in darkness. She heard the screech of metal striking metal as the rounds ricocheted off the side of a storage container. *Too bloody organised*, she thought as the lake of flames seeped towards her. For a moment terror paralysed her. Then heat forced her to move.

Eva crouched and ran, kept behind packing cases where she could and glanced at the SFOs when she thought it was safe. On the gantry above the screaming grew, became more hysterical. A realisation came to her from nowhere. *You weren't part of the plan*, she thought as she crawled the last few metres to the corner of the warehouse. A couple of seconds later that idea felt as though it had been confirmed. Whoever was behind the storage container lobbed a petrol bomb up onto the gantry. The wounded men kept screaming. In another few moments, they stopped.

She didn't know what to do. She couldn't do anything to help the SFOs, she couldn't see a way out of the warehouse. *All you can do is try not to die*, Eva thought as she shielded her eyes against the light of the flames. She saw Jacks run down the stairs and sprint into the darkness behind the storage container. He fired as he ran. A few moments later he came back out and stood in the middle of the warehouse while the pool of fire seeped over stacked boxes and turned them to fuel. Jacks lowered his weapon. Guns covering the corners of the warehouse, the SFOs clustered around him. Eva took a chance and joined them.

Four SFOs, one DI and a fire that was rapidly consuming the warehouse. Dense black smoke broiled and churned over the ceiling. Looking up at it was like staring at the underside of a turbulent sea. It would drop soon, Eva knew. Some law of fluid dynamics would reach thermal equilibrium and the acrid clouds would fall like a curtain on a stage, choking them all.

'There's an exit,' Jacks said, 'behind the container, but he's blocked it.'

'We won't get through that.' One of the other firearms officers waved at the flames that engulfed the entrance.

Eva nodded at the gantry. 'What about the hostiles?'

Jacks shook his head. 'This whole op was a trap and they weren't supposed to get out either. Two birds, one stone. I reckon we've got about three minutes before the heat gets too much. Any ideas?' He didn't direct the question at anyone in particular.

One of the SFOs barked a question. 'Can they clear the door from outside?'

Jacks shrugged and tapped his radio. 'Yes. There were a couple of racks filled with junk by that exit. I think he brought them down somehow. From what I remember it'll take five to ten minutes.'

'Shit,' Eva snarled. 'How the hell did he get past the team at the back?'

'Don't know,' Jacks snapped, 'and now's not the time. Ma'am,' he added. Slightly pointless under the circumstances, Eva thought. The pool of flame edged towards them.

'And that's the only way out?'

Jacks glanced around. 'Entrance we came in through is too hot to exit, roller door at far end will be jammed closed. There was an exit to the roof but we wouldn't get up the gantry now. That's the last way out.'

Eva looked around what remained of the warehouse. 'Could we open it with a forklift?'

Jacks followed her gaze and saw the orange-and-black machine she was staring at. He shook his head. 'Too big. Wouldn't get it round the storage container.

She kept staring. What did she know? What scrap of knowledge from her past might actually prove useful? There weren't any computers in the warehouse so she sure as hell wasn't about to hack her way out. Something about the industrial vehicle had caught her attention though. Despite the flames she found she couldn't look way. Finally, it struck her. Eva blurted, 'What makes a forklift move?'

Jacks froze for a moment. Then he swore. 'Oh, Christ. Maybe.'

One of the other SFOs yelled. 'What?'

'Forklifts use LPG,' Eva told him. 'Liquid petroleum gas. Comes in reusable cylinders.' Jacks was already moving.

Heat seared her skin and smoke scorched the back of her throat, but she followed Jacks. The red cylinder sat on the back of the truck. Eva unclipped the gas hose and Jacks struggled as he lifted it to the ground. One of the other SFOs caught the other end. Together they dragged it towards the exit.

'Get everyone away from the back door,' Jacks yelled at her. She didn't need telling twice.

Eva screamed into her radio. 'Clear the area! Hundred-metre perimeter *at least* in next thirty seconds.' She clicked off the button, thought for a moment and clicked on again. 'Then get on the ground. We're going to try to open the back door.'

One of the SFOs heard her. 'This is fucking insane.'

She could only agree. 'Yes. Any better ideas?' He didn't answer. Flames consumed the racking. Jacks and the other SFO dumped the red container against the barricaded door. She couldn't see how close it was until Jacks turned the light on his phone on and placed it in the neck of the cylinder as a target. Then they ran.

Behind them, something fell. The fire had reached the ceiling on the side of the building where the entrance had been. The roof would collapse soon, Eva realised. She wondered if it would take the force of the blast. Looking up she doubted it, but maybe it would hold for the ten seconds or so it would take them to run across the floor of the warehouse. It didn't make any difference, she decided. They were way beyond the point of risk assessments now.

The five of them huddled behind one of the concrete columns that stretched from the floor to the ceiling, fifteen metres above them. 'Two right, two left,' Jacks instructed the SFOs. 'One up, one down. Full auto. You,' he glanced down at where Eva squatted with her back to the column. 'Cover your head. Be ready to move. You lot,' he nodded at the other SFOs, 'that's a forty-seven-kilo bottle of LPG and it's going to be a fuck-off big bang. Keep behind the concrete. Give it five seconds after it blows then run like hell.' A burning pile of boxes fell across the floor. She could feel the heat of it on the back of her hands. 'On three,' Jacks said.

Four automatic rifles emptied their magazines into the darkness. Eva counted seconds. She had not even reached two when the cylinder exploded. Air seemed to be sucked out of the room only to return nanoseconds later to crush her from all sides. It felt like a car crash, like falling off a building, like hitting the ground, being hit by a train, like being blown up. An SFO tumbled over her, tossed like a rag doll by the blast. The world was bright and blurred. A booming in her ears, subsonic, hypersonic and then monotone silence as though her eardrums had burst. Shrapnel flew past, buried itself in the wall. Then like a light being switched off, the force of the blast was gone and only the flames remained.

She tried to get to her feet, but Jacks already had her by the scruff of the neck and was dragging her. His mouth moved but she couldn't hear what he said. She couldn't hear anything at all. The two other SFOs grabbed the third that had tumbled past her. He moved, but his foot pointed the wrong way. Jacks bellowed silence as he dragged her towards the gaping hole where the door had been. Eva managed to twist and stagger forward, so Jacks stopped dragging and started pushing. She didn't need the hint. Out, across the pulverised sheet of the metal door now forming a twisted ramp over racking that had fallen behind the exit. Something sliced the side of her hand. She felt the stickiness of blood, but she kept going. Behind her she saw Jacks and the other two, half dragging, half carrying the last of the SFOs through the gaping hole in the breeze-block wall where the doorframe had once been. They were ten metres from the building when the ceiling caved in. Inside, metal girders fell to the floor and crushed everything. Smoke and dust burst from the building like a pyroclastic flow. She saw the SFOs flinch as the cloud engulfed them, but they were far enough away from the building by then.

Eva closed her eyes, covered her mouth and let the cloud of smoke and dust envelop her. All it could do was cover her now.

–

She dozed at the hospital. After ten minutes the silence in her head had become a monotone note, and ten minutes after that she could hear voices, although she couldn't distinguish individual words. One of the paramedics who arrived at the scene shoved a light in her ears. Eva couldn't hear her speak but by the way she nodded she guessed the news was not bad. She had sat in the ambulance and let another paramedic clean and tape her hand. After half an hour she could understand what was being said.

Jacks stopped by her cubicle. Most of his body armour was off now. There was a calmness about him Eva thought, quiet and contemplative. He must have seen violence many times before to be able to switch off so completely once it was over. 'Any damage?' Jacks asked.

Eva shook her head. 'No. They're keeping any eye on me to make sure I haven't got concussion, but I haven't. I could tell them that, but I'm letting them get on with their jobs.'

Jacks nodded, then pulled a chair from next to the bed and sat down. 'That was a lunatic idea, but it saved all our necks. Nicely done.'

Eva beamed. 'Rule one of digging yourself out the shit. Work with the tools you've got, not the ones you wish you had.'

He laughed. Deep lines crinkled around his eyes. She noticed scar tissue buried in amongst them. 'So,' he said after a moment, 'what exactly was that all about?'

She sighed and laid her head back against the pillow. Jacks had almost died too, and now he was asking her a perfectly reasonable question. 'I guess ultimately it's about a man called Semion Razin. To the best of our knowledge Razin has never set foot in the UK, in fact the closest he's ever got to Europe is probably St Petersburg.' Eva had never met Razin and doubted she ever would. She had seen photos of the tall, slightly stooped individual with thin wire glasses, goatee beard, long grey coat and homburg hat who styled himself as some intellectual from the Russian revolution, but the chances of their paths ever actually crossing seemed almost infinitesimally small to her. She knew that Semion Razin was a Ukrainian by birth, had spent his life in the apparatus of the Russian criminal underworld and the kleptocracy that supported it, and seldom left their protection. And yet, she thought as she tried to convey to Jacks the influence the man exerted, Razin's actions had affected herself, officers around her and criminals and their victims across the whole of Western Europe. 'He syndicates, franchises, sets up divisions and focuses on specialities,' she told Jacks. 'Razin's empire is structured more like a diversified multinational than an Organised Crime Group.'

'What's his connection with Surrey?'

Eva shrugged. Her neck ached when she did. 'It's just another market. It's a rich county and there are a lot of wealthy foreign nationals willing to do illegal business, not to mention avaricious locals. That's an opportunity, but it requires infrastructure. Razin has that. Somebody called DCI Jeffrey Cowan was involved for a number of years.' She knew Jacks would be familiar with the name. Everyone remembered a bent cop. 'Cowan turned out to be the fixer for Razin's organisation in the county. He made evidence go away and quietly dropped spanners into a number of investigations that caused them to fail. He took some hefty backhanders from Razin's people in the process.'

Jacks nodded when he heard the name. 'Cowan led you to this?'

She shook her head. 'A guy called Warren Muir. He worked for Cowan. Now he's doing twelve years in HMP Frankland, in a secure unit for his own protection. Muir had a pub on the Allen Estate and provided thugs for the bottom end of Razin's local businesses. He was smart enough to know he needed an insurance policy, but stupid enough to keep it in a tin box in his wardrobe. That box has been the gift that keeps on giving. It's going to take us a year to follow up on everything Muir kept tabs on.'

'And Razin knows this?'

Eva ran her fingers through her cropped hair. 'Doubtful. I wouldn't imagine Razin could even find Surrey on a map. His local organisation must know though. Cowan might have been the facilitator inside the police who protected Razin's business interests, but he didn't run things. There's another layer of management, far more entrenched. And there's a senior manager too,' she added.

Jacks let the words tumble around inside his head for a moment. Then he asked: 'Do you know who that is?'

She hoped her face didn't betray her. 'Maybe.'

He sat in silence for another few seconds, as the implications of what she had not said resolved themselves inside his mind. 'Do you have firearms training?' he asked eventually.

The change of tack surprised her. 'I've done the NPFTC.' She meant the National Police Firearms Training Curriculum. 'I'm qualified with Glock-17s.'

'Any good?'

She didn't understand. 'I got pass marks.'

Jacks nodded. 'So maybe you should make some time and come out to Pirbright.' He meant the Army Training Centre that Surrey police used for firearms instruction. 'I do advanced weapons and CQB courses there.'

Eva laughed. 'Bloody hell, I'm not planning on joining SCO19 any time soon. Close-quarter battle's not really my thing. I was with cybercrime before I came to Surrey. I'm lethal with JavaScript and a relational database.'

Jacks stood. He looked down on her and smiled. 'Well you know,' he told her quietly, 'sometimes you've got to work with what you've got.

## Chapter Two

A doctor discharged her not long after that. Eva hitched a ride back to the station in a patrol car and collected her own vehicle from there. Two in the morning, and the Kingston one-way system was as quiet as the grave. Only traffic lights flickered in amongst the pools of light cast by streetlamps, the only movement was the shadows of urban foxes, hunting in amongst discarded burger and sushi cartons for scraps of food to drag back to their dens by the river. In the privacy of her car she let out a long, shuddering sigh, as she allowed a slow realisation to finally seep into her mind. She had nearly died that night.

No wonder Jacks had been worried. The operation should have been a routine bust, not a firefight. Somebody had known they were coming, and the implications of that chilled her to the core. Information leaks should have stopped when retired DCI Jeffrey Cowan washed down a couple of packets of paracetamol with a bottle of Danflou Cognac vintage 1865, which would have set him back almost seven thousand quid. *Talk about keeping it for a special occasion*, Eva thought as she pulled into the car park underneath her apartment. Jacks thought she needed advanced firearms training. Should she take him up on that?

Half the lights in the car park were off, but she eased into her parking space without any problem. The car park filled the entire basement underneath the block of flats where she rented. An awkward ramp sloped down, the corners were tight and square, concrete columns held the scraped evidence of where less cautious drivers had misjudged them. The usual stench of petrol and river-damp that stank like urine clung close to the ground. One of the old fluorescent tubes flickered constantly, signifying that soon it would be dead. Eva slammed the car door and squeezed the key fob, and amber lights flared in the gloom. She had taken almost a dozen steps towards the angled stairway that led up to the entrance hall before she realised she was not alone.

A figure crouched behind one of the other cars. She heard a rustle. She couldn't see any details, but it had moved slightly when she was about halfway across the car park. Eva turned; walked a few paces backwards. The door to the lift and stairwell was only a handful of steps behind her. She could make it through before whoever was behind the car caught up with her, but she didn't feel inclined to do that just yet. Perhaps it was some sort of adrenalin hangover, or maybe she was just pissed off. She simply didn't feel like backing away again that evening.

'Oi,' she snapped at the figure behind the car. 'This is a private car park and I'm a police officer. I suggest you get your arse out of here before I have you forcibly removed. That's the emphasis on forcibly.'

She heard a sigh and another noise, as though whoever was behind the car was dragging themselves to their feet. If she'd had to put a description to the sound, the word she would have chosen was: reluctant.

A hooded figure stood up slowly. 'I know you're a cop,' it told her. 'That's why I've been waiting for you. Been waiting bloody hours.' The figure pulled the hood down. 'I'm Kyle. I live with my mum on the eighth floor. What is it with you cops, you party all night or something?'

Eva swore quietly. 'I've been working. What's up? If you've got a problem, you could've just gone to the station.'

'No,' Kyle told her, 'I couldn't.' About fifteen, Eva guessed, mixed race, short black hair and around five-nine, about as tall as she was. She was fairly certain she had seen him before, around the flats. And worried, Eva saw when she stared at his face. More than that. She thought he looked afraid.

She knew she sounded exasperated and more than a little irascible. 'Look. I've had a really bad day at the office and I just want to go to sleep. If you've got something to say, make it quick.'

To emphasise the point Eva started walking away. Kyle blurted. 'I've found a dead body.' Well, it was enough to stop her leaving the car park at least. She turned back to face him. 'Anyway, I think I have. It's at the waterworks in Hampton. I was climbing. There's all this gear there, it's brand new. It shouldn't be there. Then I turned on the lights,' he stopped. She saw him shudder. 'It's wrong, I tell you, it's so *fucking* wrong.'

'You want me to send a patrol car over there to take a look?'

'They won't find it, not without showing.' He spread his hands. 'You're a proper detective, right? My mum said that. I could show you.'

Eva rocked her head back and stared at the ceiling. 'Kyle. I've just been discharged from hospital. I feel like shit. I want a bath and I want to go to bed.'

Kyle pleaded. 'It'd take ten minutes to get there at this time of night. Five minutes to show you. That's it. If it's nothing you'd be back here inside half an hour and I dunno, I'll wash your car for a year, okay?'

He sounded almost hysterical, she thought. He was right though; it wouldn't take long. Maybe he had found the body of a vagrant, or a drug user who had chosen an empty building to expire in. If he had, she could call in uniform and leave it to them.

She pressed the button on her key fob and the car lights flashed again. 'Okay,' Eva told him, 'but you'd better not be messing me around.'

He shook his head as they drove away. 'Swear to God, I'm not,' he said. Then he said: 'If there is a God.' Eva stared at him, but he hid beneath his hood. Kyle sat in silence with his arms folded as they headed back into the one-way system.

The building sat in darkness, silhouette obscuring a thin haze that filled the softly glowing sky. Moonlight glinted on scaffolding and shone on Victorian roof tiles. Eva shuddered. She couldn't help it. It reminded her of a night two years ago, the very first time someone had tried to kill her. Her first encounter with a murderer; one who had butchered police officers before and taken pleasure in doing so. On paper he had succeeded, but it no longer felt there was any point in splitting hairs. Colin Lynch, drug dealer and all-round twisted bastard, was dead, and that was an end to it. Perhaps.

Kyle showed her where to find a gap in the high steel fence that surrounded the site. She parked the car and they got out. It was a struggle, but she managed to force her way between the twisted railings and a concrete wall. When they were through the fence Kyle stopped and turned to face her.

'Listen. I know you're a cop and all, but I want you to stay behind me. Just walk where I walk. It's all solid, but there's the old water tanks. They're deep and there ain't no railings round them. I know where they are, okay? Follow me and it won't be a problem.'

He sounded earnest she thought, as though he was taking responsibility. Despite her irascible mood Eva found she liked that. 'Okay Kyle,' she said. 'You lead the way. I'm trusting you.'

They walked towards the building, single file. 'It was a pump house years ago,' Kyle told her. 'Then it was used for storage, then they abandoned it. Don't know why they did that. Now nobody uses it and it's just falling down. Seems stupid to me. A waste, y'know?'

'Can't argue,' Eva agreed. The concrete underfoot was cracked and broken. 'Any reason you were here tonight?'

In the darkness she had to imagine the shrug. 'Nothing special,' he said. Eva thought he sounded a little evasive, but she ignored that. 'I just came here. Been here a couple of times before, thought I'd take another look around.' He glanced over his shoulder. 'Nothing wrong with that, is there?'

'What, apart from trespass and the fact the premises are downright dangerous? Nothing at all. But if you've dragged me here for nothing that picture may change.' She said it with a quiet laugh though.

'Wait and see,' Kyle muttered. The attempt at humour had not changed his mood at all.

They walked through a half-open door, through an ante-room no more than a dozen paces long, then out into a cavernous space. Small pieces of debris lay everywhere. Chunks of broken concrete, crumbling stone fragments, fractured glass from shattered panes, broken slats from discarded palettes. Dust permeated the air. Every breath and footstep echoed, as though they had stepped into a concert hall, long after the audience had left.

'This used to be the pump room,' Kyle said. 'The storage company had it filled with metal containers and walkways. Got your phone? Use the torch.' Kyle pointed towards the ceiling. 'We're going up there.'

She had a moment of reluctance when they started to climb the stone stairs. Suppose this was one of Razin's tricks, using a kid to lure her to a disused building and then having one of his thugs chuck her off the roof? After a handful of steps, she dismissed the thought. At this level Razin's people were just not that subtle, and in any event, she simply was not important enough to warrant a sophisticated ploy.

She counted eight flights. The ceiling was still ten metres above them. Broken skylights gave her a clear view of the moon. When they reached the top, Kyle led them to another walkway. Eva paused. 'Is that safe?'

'Yeah. I've been across it twice. I think someone's dragged some heavy gear over it recently too.'

'Why do you think that?'

'Coz it's on the other side?'

She sniffed the air. If there were a corpse on the platform in front of them, if it had been there for a while, she would have expected to smell the subtle signs of decomposition by now. Then again, she thought as she put one foot carefully in front of the other, the space was well ventilated. 'Where did you find the body?'

'Over here.'

'What, was it lying down, sat up, leant against the wall?'

'Best if I just show you.'

They reached the platform. It was part of the pump house structure Eva realised, almost a balcony on the top of a column that was probably fifty paces long and twenty deep. Ornate Victorian wrought-iron railings guarded the edge, but modern metal racking filled the space. It felt smooth to her touch.

'I'm going to turn the lights on now,' Kyle warned her. Eva appreciated his thoughtfulness, even though it was unnecessary.

'It's okay,' she told him. 'I've seen dead bodies before.'

'Yeah, right,' Kyle said. She heard him press a switch.

Light flooded the space. It took a moment for her eyes to adjust. When they did, she gasped. 'Oh my good God.'

'So, did I waste your time?' Kyle demanded, in a tone lost somewhere between fear and indignation.

Smug little bastard already knew the answer to that, she thought.

'No,' Eva admitted testily. Her hand shook as she opened the contacts book on her phone. 'Now keep quiet while I call in a scene of crime team.'

–

Forensic pathologist Judy Wren stood with her fists on her hips and stared at the racks, mouth open. 'Please tell me you haven't touched anything.'

'Do I look like I want to touch anything?' An hour and a half later Eva watched as SOCOs began the laborious process of cataloguing the crime scene. 'The kid's had exclusion prints taken and a DNA swab. I got victim support to look after him because I couldn't get hold of social services at this time of night.'

'I would imagine they're still in bed. Like all sensible people,' Wren added as she pulled a white polythene hood over her iron-grey hair. 'But nonetheless, you had to call me.'

Eva jerked her thumb over her shoulder at the racks. 'Would you have forgiven me if I hadn't?'

'There is that,' Wren conceded. As she spoke more lights came on. The SOCOs had set up extra battery packs. 'What on earth have you found here, DI Harris?' They walked slowly between the racks.

'I think it's your job to tell me,' Eva said. 'What the hell is this?'

'There must be close on a hundred tanks,' Wren shone a flashlight into the recesses in the racks, 'and at first glance, it seems every one contains a body part.'

They stopped in front of one of the glass tanks. Two rows of racks stood facing each other. The top shelves looked about two and a half metres off the ground. Each rack had five shelves. Each row had five bays. One tank sat on each shelf in each bay, the bays faced inwards and outwards on the racks. Not quite all of the bays were filled but a few had two or three smaller tanks. The tanks varied in size. Eva guessed the average would hold about a hundred litres of liquid, so the racks had to be sturdy. Some were smaller, a few were round; all of them were filled and most of them held what were obviously human organs. A few of the pieces of organic material she found harder to identify. They all bobbed and drifted the way a dead fish might. A few of the tanks were considerably larger. A couple contained what appeared to be intact human corpses.

The tank they stopped in front of sat at shoulder height on a shelf on one of the black metal racks. A pale green liquid completely filled it. Inside the tank, floating as though with neutral buoyancy, was a severed human arm.

'Seems?' Eva asked.

Wren shrugged. 'I don't actually think there's much doubt, but I'm a bit curious about how neatly they've all been laid out. I'll need to examine them all before I pronounce them as human.'

'What's stopping you?'

Wren tapped the glass. 'The liquid. Chances are its form-aldehyde, which is not particularly good for your health. I've sent for a fume hood. I'll wait for that to arrive before opening anything up.'

Eva stopped and looked up and down the racks once again. She saw organs, dismembered limbs, torsos, as well as the item that had clearly disturbed Kyle most. A flayed face and scalp complete with long dark hair, stretched out over a metal frame. Eva forced herself to stare at the face. Something about the way it had been positioned seemed significant, as though it had been given pride of place. Like a piece of work of which somebody was especially pleased or proud. It was extraordinary; she had to admit that to herself, however reluctantly. Like a map of the world unwrapped from a globe, the face and scalp had been severed with utmost care. There were no rips as far as she could see. The skin had been sliced along the edge of the face, in front of the ears and along the line of the jaw. It must have been prised from the muscle behind it. The eyelids were intact and open, long dark lashes surrounded them, again undamaged as best she could tell. The scalp had been removed in the same cut, then folded over a metal bar so it sat at right angles to the face, like two sides of a cube. The skin had been stretched. Somebody had inserted metal eyelets along the line of the jaw, and black thread drew the face taught. The frame the face was attached to looked like chrome; it glistened in the white light that now permeated the liquid. Despite her best efforts not to, Eva shuddered. The display seemed so grotesquely meticulous.

It was then another thought struck to her. It crept in slowly, like a spider crawling on to her scalp. She felt it wriggling in the recesses of her mind, picking away at her brain, struggling to dig its way through. She felt a sudden clamminess on her skin as the limbic system in her own brain pushed fear pheromones into her sweat and told her: now is the time to be afraid. There was, she realised as she looked along the racks, something horrifyingly familiar about the way in which the tanks had been arranged.

Eva straightened up and moved away from the tank with a sharp, awkward step. She hoped to God Wren had not noticed her momentary panic attack. She struggled to bring herself back under control and tried to hide her reaction by burying her hands in her pockets. 'Formaldehyde is used in embalming,' she managed to say. 'Is there any chance these are old bodies?'

'I don't think so.' Wren turned and walked back down the racks. She apparently had not noticed Eva's momentary loss of control. Wren shone her flashlight into a tank where the arm floated. Eva took a deep breath and looked at where Wren was pointing. She saw a small, moderately elaborate tattoo.

'Roman numerals,' Wren said.

'This year's date,' Eva agreed.

# Chapter Three

Eva's team arrived over the next half-hour. First on the scene was Detective Sergeant Raj Chakrabati. Through the broken skylight she could see the signs of dawn approaching. I've got to get some sleep soon, Eva thought.

'Okay,' Raj said when he saw the contents of the racks, 'I was going to offer to go and get breakfast, but I don't think it would stay down.' Even at that time of the morning Raj's appearance was fastidious, thanks to the attention of his designer wife. Apart from his dark, tangled hair, over which she had no control, and through which Raj frequently brushed his fingers. He was doing it now Eva noted, as he stared almost dumbstruck at the racks in front of them. A nervous habit she assumed, one that surfaced in times of stress. She hardly felt she could comment.

Eva leant on a railing, looked over the edge of the stone column into the abyss below and moved away from that sharply too. 'Are Newton and Flynn on their way?'

'Parking up, they'll be here in a moment.' Raj looked around at the rest of the building. 'What have we got?'

As Eva started to explain, Rebecca Flynn and Jamie Newton reached the top of the stairs. Flynn, tall as Eva and with hair permanently scraped back into a ponytail, swore. Newton, taller still and distinctively good looking, simply stopped and stared. 'Come on over,' Eva told them. 'SOCOs have confirmed the walkway is safe.'

They stepped across hesitantly. 'Are these for real?' Flynn demanded. Not the kind of person afraid to speak her mind, the look on her hard face conveyed the incredulity they were all feeling.

'Judy Wren thinks so. She's waiting for a fume hood before she starts opening the tanks up but yes,' Eva nodded. 'I think we've got our work cut out for us.'

They stood in silence for a while as the three detective sergeants absorbed the scene in front of them. The balcony, platform, whatever it might have once been that the racks stood on, was now an oasis of light in mottled gloom. It had a surreal quality to it, Eva thought. Bright white LED lights on slender stands dotted in-between monolithic racks. SOCOs in white polythene suits measured and recorded, cameras flashed, every now and then she caught the green glint of a laser tape measure. And in amongst it all, God alone knew how many bodies.

'How did the raid go?' Newton asked eventually. About Eva's age, Newton's good looks and gentle charm were reinforced by a soft northern accent, and the sound of his voice snapped Eva out of her reverie. She must have been awake for more than twenty hours now, and although that would not have normally counted for much, getting blown up in the middle of the night had probably thrown her off her game.

They would not have heard yet, Eva realised. Newton, Flynn and Chakrabati had worked later than usual the night before tracking down more leads from Warren Muir's box. They had left the station around eight, about the time Eva was preparing to go on the raid. With support from uniform, three DOs from drugs and organised crime, as well as Specialist Firearms Officers and even a couple of PCSOs, she hadn't felt the need to waste her teams' evening. They would have been there if she had thought she needed them, Eva knew that for a certainty, and at some point, one of them would cover for her on another late shift. It had seemed like a sensible use of resources. *Hindsight*, she thought as she stared across at the racks, *is a wonderful thing.*

'Badly enough that you'll probably see it on the news,' she said with a sigh. 'It was a total set-up. There was a firefight, one of our guys got his leg banged up and two of theirs got toasted. Not by our people either,' she added. 'Somebody wanted them out of the picture.' Through the haze of tiredness a thought finally managed to seep into her mind. It had been a set-up. But who exactly had been set up?

Flynn stared at her. 'And you came straight on to this?'

'Bloody kid lives in my flats,' Eva said. 'Little sod looked upset. And he promised to clean my car if he was wasting my time.' She gazed at the racks again. 'I think I lost the bet.'

'I'd say so.' Jamie Newton turned back to look at her. 'Have you actually had any sleep?'

'Not actually,' Eva admitted.

Newton glanced at the others. 'Then go,' he told her. 'We've got this now.'

–

She needed to think before she could sleep. Eva knew if she didn't clear her mind, she would only lay listening as the town drew itself into wakefulness. And so, she ran a bath, opened a bottle of ice-cold beer and sipped it as she soaked.

At twenty-seven she was one of the youngest serving DIs in the Home Counties. It would have been unusual, except that cybercrime divisions across the country had been looking for people with the most up-to-date skillsets to tackle a tidal wave of digital crime that threatened to swamp traditional policing. Eva had fitted that bill. A computer science graduate who started as a trainee analyst at the Metropolitan Police Cyber Crime Unit, she had moved into regular police work four years earlier as part of a fast-track programme. By now she should have been heading a team of young officers with technical backgrounds, investigating online fraud, money-laundering, drug networks and cyber terrorism, but during a two-year secondment gaining non-cyber-related policing experience, Eva had encountered Colin Lynch.

A vicious man, thick-set and brutish, Lynch had masqueraded as a scrap metal merchant with a yard filled with broken cars and heavy machines, but in reality he was one of the most prolific drug dealers in the south-west of the country. Black eyed and grey skinned, face usually covered with untidy stubble and hands that could crush a windpipe, she'd seen him on CCTV, long lank hair brushing his shoulders as he manipulated the controls of a mechanical digger, the same one he'd used to cut a police officer in half when she'd found a pile of drugs in one of his vans. Lynch's operation appeared from nowhere when a chance investigation uncovered it. It would not have touched her personally, but on a surveillance operation Lynch had tried to kill Eva too.

He had smashed her car. Pulverised it with her in it. She had been left dangling head-down in a stream while blood loss from a cut in her femoral artery sent her into hypovolemic shock. Her heart had stopped for eight minutes. Technically, she had died. Perhaps it was a meaningless distinction now science had kept pigs' brains alive in suspension long after decapitation, but it felt important to her. She had always been fit, but now she trained relentlessly. Surgeons had shaved her head to attach sensors to look for damage or errant electrical signals in her brain. Now Eva kept her hair close-cropped because she liked the way it felt. More than anything else though, she had found within her an insatiable yearning for revenge.

Her darkest secret. When Eva discovered Colin Lynch and his drug distribution network was being run as an unofficially sanctioned 'lesser of two evils' operation between Serious Crime and the Security Services with the intention of undermining Semion Razin's businesses, and that he would probably never be brought to justice, she found herself unable to cope. Something else had snapped inside her mind, and the yearning for revenge had become overwhelming, calculating and cryogenically cold.

Lynch had to die, that was all there was to it. Muir was a common or garden thug, but Lynch was a monster. She could remember the metallic flavour of the thought, the acrid piquancy that accompanied the decision to act. She couldn't kill Lynch, she had realised, but she could orchestrate his death. And who better to serve as executioners than Semion Razin's organisation? Eva knew they wanted Lynch dead. Lynch was competition. Not on anywhere near the scale of Razin's multinational operation, but as far as his franchises in the UK were concerned Lynch was a drain on resources. Ergo, Lynch had to go. Everybody knew that. Eva had simply provided the means.

On a cloudless evening two years earlier, Colin Lynch had visited an old stone house on the edge of the New Forest at a place called Winter's Gate Farm, flipped a light switch and set off a bomb; location, timing and even paperwork for commercial explosives furnished by then Detective Sergeant Eva Harris. Razin's people never knew who had provided the documents to secure authorised nitro-glycerine from a quarry. They were curious, but they didn't really care. All that mattered was Lynch was gone and a competitor had been eliminated. Somebody else had cared though. Superintendent Alastair Hadley, instigator of the unofficial operation. Hadley had cared. And Hadley had worked it all out.

Eva pulled the plug, grabbed a towel, padded through into the kitchen and dropped the beer bottle into the bin marked recycling. She slumped onto her sofa, ran her fingers over wet hair and watched the distant lights of aircraft queuing up to land at Heathrow. Hadley had thought he owned her, an asset he could do with as he pleased. Gaunt, with a sneering manner and contemptuous gaze, a seemingly permanent curl to his lip only emphasised by a thin moustache, it was Hadley who had pushed through her promotion to DI. It was also Hadley who had diverted her from her intended career path into a role for which she seemed spectacularly unsuited; one that would have ultimately crushed her. Poor Hadley, Eva thought as she stared at the broiling stacks of cumulonimbus forming on the horizon. He had misunderstood everything. Technically, Eva had died.

How did Alastair Hadley ever imagine he could compete with that?

She felt her eyelids start to droop. Before she fell asleep on the sofa she moved to her bed, turned off her phone and covered her head with her duvet. Hadley had failed. Hadley had wanted to keep control, even after she revealed Jeffrey Cowan was Razin's man inside Kingston station, but Eva was cunning. She had found Lynch's encrypted communications with Hadley, and with painstaking attention to detail decrypted them. They were enough to incriminate him, to put him behind bars for a decade, but Eva didn't want that. What she wanted most was to be free again, to have Lynch and Hadley consigned to her personal book of history. She could have broken him. Instead she told Hadley to go to hell.

Her investigation into Cowan was only a few months old, but still it felt like the distant past. Warren Muir's magical box kept giving out its gifts, and slowly but surely Eva and her team were putting significant dents into Semion Razin's operations within the affluent Home County. All should have been good.

And it would have been, except for an operation that had almost gone catastrophically wrong and everything that implied, and a pump house filled with dissected body parts that had a flavour to them she did not want to recollect.

As Eva drifted, another name violated the precincts of her dreams. It brought with it a face she wanted to forget, but which stared back at her from beyond a curtain of obscuring blackness none-the-less. She cried out in her sleep. It was a whining, keening sound. She heard it through a fog of nightmares.

It made her think of the whimper of whipped dogs.

## Chapter Four

She slept until after midday. Once she had dressed, she left her apartment and walked to Kingston police station. On the way, she picked up a vegan burger from a stall in the old market. Eva was not strictly a vegetarian, but she knew the food at all the stalls was excellent, and the spicy lentil burger had become a favourite. On the way to the station she passed the Coronation Stone, after which the town had been named well over a thousand years before. A Sarsen stone, probably from Salisbury plain, it might have been cut from the same quarry as the heel stones of Stonehenge. Something ancient, she thought as she passed the stubby megalith; something that would still be here long after she was dead and buried.

What the hell was up with her? It was not just the shock of being shot at, she thought as she walked towards the station, nor was it the discovery of dozens if not a hundred body parts suspended in formaldehyde, although either of those things on their own would have been enough to ruin her day. There was something else, a disturbingly familiar cadence to her nightmares that she couldn't dismiss as simple paranoia.

The gates to the station loomed in front of her, but as she approached them, she felt a sense of dread she couldn't ignore. Not paranoia, Eva thought as she touched her security card to the lock, pattern recognition. A deep-seated phenomenon sometimes called a sixth sense, although she knew there was nothing mystical about it. Just the secondary and tertiary levels of processing the brain performed to allow it to act on incomplete data, a fundamental defence mechanism that probably predated humanity. Not just that, she thought as she buzzed in at the back door of the station, but a complexity of data-manipulation that computer hardware designers would also give pieces of their anatomy to understand. Her thoughts were filled with body parts today, Eva reflected as she trudged up the stone stairs to her office. Not just limbs and organs in tanks, she thought as she nudged the door with her shoulder, but the way in which those tanks had been arranged, neatly and aesthetically.

She could be wrong. She knew that. She doubted she was.

–

She was barely halfway through her burger when there was a knock at her door. The door was closed, which was unusual enough to signify she wanted to be alone, and yet somebody had seen fit to disturb her. A one in four probability, she calculated. It might be Raj Chakrabati, Jamie Newton, Rebecca Flynn or Will Moresby, a hulking uniform sergeant who, like Jacks, exuded quiet competence. Eva made a guess based purely on the sound of the knock and took a chance. 'Come in, Jamie,' she said.

Jamie Newton peered around the door, a puzzled frown on his face. She didn't bother to explain. A really stupid game, Eva told herself, but it amused her ever so slightly that she had been right.

'Got a sec?' Newton asked.

'For the bearer of bad tidings? Yeah, have a seat. I'm going to eat though,' she told him. 'Let me know what you've found while I munch.'

Newton dropped into a chair and stared. 'Are you all right?'

Eva shrugged. 'You tell me. I'm sure you're going to.' He kept staring, so she had to give him something of an explanation. 'There was just something about those racks wasn't there? They were so bloody neat.'

Newton had a sheaf of papers in his hand. He chucked them on her desk. 'So it wasn't just me.'

'No. Did Raj notice? More importantly, did Becks?'

'If they did, they didn't say anything.'

She nodded as she chewed. Both actions were slow and methodical. 'I was standing with Judy thinking that I was looking at a whole load of dismembered body parts when something else struck me.'

'How aesthetic they were,' Newton laced his fingers together and rocked back in his chair, 'as if they had been arranged.' About the same age as her, Newton was painfully good-looking and principled almost to a fault. Lean and well built, he had the unconscious style of a fashion model who would always inadvertently fall into a pose. Even relaxing in his chair, she could almost imagine someone with a camera framing him for a magazine cover. 'It struck me too. For a moment I thought I was in an exhibition. Don't know, maybe I was. It was just a bit too well laid out. It made me think of Damien Hurst.'

'Carved-up cows in cases,' Eva nodded. Chilli sauce oozed and dripped from the lentil burger. 'Or sharks, or sheep, or whatever it was; dissected bodies on display for the entire world to see. Except it wasn't. It was more like a private collection.'

'There was a fair bit of gear there too,' Newton said, eyes inevitably drawn to the mess she was making of the burger, 'and some of it was pretty expensive. It got Judy Wren's attention.'

Eva frowned and licked her fingers. 'What kind of gear?'

'Scientific,' Newton said. He pulled out his phone and swiped through a couple of badly framed photos. 'A top-of-the-range microscope,' he checked his notes, 'a centrifuge, electronic balances and a,' he paused, checked his notes again, 'spectrophotometer. Judy took a stab and reckoned there was around twenty grand's worth of kit on the bench.'

She put the burger down, closed the cardboard packet and dropped it into her bin. The dripping sauce did not sit well with the photos. 'So what was it, somebody's private lab or an art exhibit?' Eva wondered aloud, not expecting Newton to have an answer.

'It looked like both to me. We found more lights, on the shelves. Just little LEDs, but when they came on the racks looked like something out of a museum. Everything was lit up.' He showed her another photo.

'Christ. How did you get away without putting the wind up Raj and Becks?'

Newton shrugged. 'I said I'd do some digging on the storage company that used to rent the space. I think Becks thought I was just skiving.'

'Good,' Eva muttered. 'What have you got?'

Newton picked up the sheaf of papers he had dropped on her desk. 'Metal Box Storage look like an ordinary, legitimate company, and I'm pretty sure that's actually what they are. Raj has the best eye for P&L accounts, but I'm okay too. The patterns of trade look plausible, and they broadly match what was going on in the outside market over the past six or seven years. It's not Metal Box. It's one of their customers.'

'At a storage facility?'

'Lots of companies use them. Often it's just to keep financial paperwork for the statutory seven years. Sometimes it's just old crap that nobody can bring themselves to chuck out. I checked Metal Box's accounts, then I checked the customer list.'

'So who used them? I mean I think I've guessed, but I need to see it in black and white.'

Jamie Newton opened the file and turned a page towards her. A number of lines were highlighted in yellow marker. When she ran her finger across to the client column Eva saw they all had the same name: New Thought.

Detective Chief Inspector Corrine Sutton was not an especially tall woman. Thin faced, with dark hair and a sharp fringe that only served to emphasise the severity of her features, Sutton was an old-school officer with a tongue and temper she rarely troubled to rein in. Sutton could make your life a living hell, Eva thought as she waited for her to respond. By the same token, when Sutton was on your side it felt as though you were bulletproof.

'I'm so hoping you're going to tell me this is a mistake.' Sutton pointed at the chair in front of her desk. Eva took the hint and sat. 'Or an administrative error. Or a coincidence.' Sutton glared. Eva waited. 'Or just a bloody nightmare,' Sutton added.

'We have racks full of body parts artistically arranged in what was once a storage facility used, by amongst others, the New Thought Transcendentalist Church,' Eva said. 'I mean it could be a coincidence.'

Sutton only grunted. 'I'd very much hoped the case against Mathew Harred and New Thought was well and truly closed.'

'I couldn't say that. It's true the case against Harred is airtight, or at least it will be once it actually goes to trial.'

'If it goes to trial.'

'It will at some point, ma'am. It's got to.' Sutton raised an eyebrow but didn't comment.

There was no doubt whatsoever that Mathew Harred was a murderer. Over the space of four years he had killed at least seven people, one of whom Eva had actually witnessed when Harred bludgeoned Jeremy Odie to death with a mallet. Whether he was sane and competent to stand trial was another matter.

'Harred thought of his actions as art,' Sutton said eventually.

'I think it was a lot more than that, ma'am. Harred's paintings were remarkable. The psychiatric assessment team brought in an expert to offer an opinion on the fresco at New Thought, and she all but raved about it in her report. His paintings were an extension of the church's transcendentalist philosophies, although to what extent the church itself was involved in his crimes is still impossible to say.'

'He's proving a challenge for the shrinks.'

'Yes.' Eva received progress reports from the prosecution team on a bi-weekly basis. She made a point of reading them at least twice. 'He scores top in narcissistic personality disorder on the Psychopathy Checklist assessment. The factor analysis basically says he's a lethally dangerous nut-job, which doesn't actually come as any surprise. That's not the problem. Harred claimed he was freeing his victims from the constraints of their existence, that in a sense he was liberating them. You saw the fresco at New Thought.' Everybody involved with the case had seen it, Eva knew that, and they had been overwhelmed by it too. A vast painting on the wall of the church that Harred had spent years working on. A masterpiece in the Pre-Raphaelite style that depicted Harred's view of the afterlife, or hyperspace, or the multiverse, or some other nihilistic view of existence that only Harred could truly understand. 'Harred really believed that it would be unsafe to try him for murder.'

'In one sense it doesn't matter,' Sutton told her. 'Harred is locked up and whether it's murder or insanity, nobody is ever going to let him out. It doesn't make any difference.'

'It does to the families of his victim's, ma'am,' Eva reminded her. She spoke softly when she did so. 'They deserve to see Harred tried for his crimes.'

Sutton almost managed a smile. 'He will be. Just be patient.' Then she frowned. 'Is Mathew Harred responsible for the body parts your boy discovered?'

There was no way Kyle could reasonably be described as her boy, but Eva let it slide. 'I don't think so.' Sutton raised an eyebrow. 'Harred is a painter. That's his obsession. It's true, something about the arrangement of the tanks did remind me of Harred, there was just an aesthetic that had a sort of "school of Mathew Harred" flavour about it. But we all know he's bloody good in a style that dates back to the 1850s. He's not going to suddenly turn into some Young British Artist and start working on creative arrangements of dismembered limbs.'

'Which means what?'

'New Thought were patrons of art. They imagined themselves as Medicis to Harred's Michelangelo. They sponsored Mathew Harred. The real question is, who else did they sponsor?'

## Chapter Five

Naomi Gray woke for the third time, but this time the room was dark. There had been lights before, the diffuse glow of bulbs on stands hidden behind polythene sheets suspended from metal poles, but now all she could see was the blinking of the equipment he had placed on the bench. She could hear though. She had heard him before when he called her by her name. 'Naomi,' she heard him say, 'you're not supposed to be awake.'

A soothing voice, calming and kind. She distrusted it instantly. The surface on which she lay was padded slightly; she could feel a cotton sheet underneath her. She had managed to raise her head a little, which was when she saw where she was.

Was it a warehouse? It felt like a room within a room, a region delineated by polythene walls that hid the space beyond. It made her think of quarantine, of the plastic tents she had seen in Africa where outbreaks of Ebola had erupted. She half expected him to be clad in some sort of biohazard suit, whoever it was that worked at the benches. He wasn't though. The lights from outside the space rendered him as a silhouette, but she could see he was dressed normally.

Her head hurt and her throat felt tight and dry. What had happened? She struggled to think back. The last thing she could remember was going for a run. Early evening, an hour before sunset, she'd had time to get home, shower and change before going to dinner with friends from work. The Swiss marketing guys were over. Despite their national reputation they'd turned out to be a lively bunch, so she had been looking forward to the meal. She had parked her car in Bushy Park and started on her usual route, a loop along Chestnut Avenue under the shade of lines of trees, around the Diana Fountain and then back towards the Pheasantry. By the time she made it to her car again she was hot. Sweat ran down her neck, she felt good. She remembered going to open the door. Then she remembered the pain.

Sharp, sudden, excruciating. In the back of her leg, the upper part. For a terrifying moment she thought she must have torn her hamstring. Naomi had grabbed at her leg, but then she felt something she didn't understand. Long and sharp, a metal shaft ending in what felt like a soft clump of nylon feathers. Shock and pain. Then warmth. Like a soft pervasive radiance that seeped into her muscles and sapped all strength from them, spread gently through her body until it reached her head and sought to hide even her own thoughts from her. Time began to drift slowly to a halt.

Naomi had tried to scream, but there was no one near to scream at. The car park was almost empty. It usually was. That was why she liked it. She grabbed at her phone and tried to key the emergency combination, but after three presses the buttons seemed too hard. Before she collapsed, she had found only one question that could echo in the sudden emptiness of her mind: why?

The first time she woke he noticed almost straight away. He purred at her, did something above her head, and darkness descended once again. The second time she awakened more slowly. She had time to think. She kept her breathing shallow and slow, her eyelids closed. She had listened. She could hear him working. She heard the familiar clink of test tubes and the swirl of a glass pipette. Slowly, a hair's width at a time, she half opened her eyes.

The same room, space, whatever it was. He had his back to her. He sat on a stool at a bench, hunched forward, studying a laptop screen. Light from an anglepoise lamp kept him in silhouette. Where was she?

It had all the equipment of a medical facility, but it felt makeshift, as though someone had set up in some place that just happened to be available. Why would you do that? Her thoughts returned to quarantine, to her brief and terrifying exposure to drugs trials in the Democratic Republic of Congo, but she quickly dismissed the idea. She had been abducted.

Air blew gently through the space, warm air, blown from a heater somewhere. She felt it drift over her. Naomi looked down. She almost screamed.

Naked, but it was not that. Laid out on a hospital trolley, a lamp shining down on her, a dozen or more tubes and wires protruding from her body. Clear polythene hoses that carried blood, her blood, from her arms and legs, two lines from each limb segment, another from her abdomen, one above it in her stomach. Thin tubes, a trickle of blood as if to a dialysis machine, but this was no procedure she had ever heard of. And wires, electrodes, most of them small, slender cables that suggested sensors as though for an ECG, but too many for that. They covered her torso. She felt clips on the ends of her fingers, maybe to measure blood oxygenation or possibly galvanic skin response. Two pads, one above her right breast and one below her left armpit, defibrillator paddles in stereo-apical position. 'What the hell,' Naomi murmured. 'What the hell are you doing to me?'

He jumped up from his stool, spun on his heel and stomped to where she lay. He snarled. She couldn't see his face. 'I said you're supposed to be asleep.' He must have pressed a button, because she heard the whine of a small electric pump. Then the drugs hit her and everything turned black.

The third time she woke she lay completely still. The drugs were meant to keep her asleep, but he must have been using the smallest possible dose on her. Maybe he didn't want to contaminate her blood, or perhaps her body was becoming tolerant to them. Either way, when she awoke this time she didn't feel as dazed and senseless as she had before. This time she planned to escape.

Darkness, and the flicker of LEDs as the equipment did whatever it was supposed to do. Perhaps it was night-time. Maybe he was asleep. Naomi took a breath and tried to lift herself from the trolley.

Christ, it was difficult. Her limbs felt like lead. She must have been lying still for days. Weakness, pain and nausea threatened to push her back down again, but she struggled to sit up. She paused for a minute, maybe two, before she started trying to remove the lines from her body by touch.

Her fingers were numb. She could hardly grasp the tubes, let alone pull the tape away. If she could stand, perhaps she would regain some of her strength. She swung her legs carefully over the side of the trolley and put her foot to the floor. She felt cold, hard concrete. Naomi tried to drag herself upright. She failed. The wires and tubes caught. They dragged another trolley, something clattered to the ground. She had to hang on to something. Lights flickered into life in the space outside.

He burst through a gap in the polythene curtains. Strode towards her, lights behind him, fists clenched, hands raised. She thought he was going to punch her. He grabbed her by the throat. 'What the *hell* do you think you're doing?' She couldn't form an answer. He yelled, 'I've had enough of this. You're wasting my bloody time. You haven't had the treatment, have you? Have you?' he screamed at her again. She wanted to ask what on earth he was talking about, but her throat was so dry it had all but closed. He grabbed her jaw. 'Has Anna? Has Anna had it?' Fear mixed with bewilderment. She didn't understand. He could see that in her face, it seemed, because he let go of her and stormed away. 'I don't have time for this,' he spat as he turned towards one of the tables, 'and I don't have time for you.'

It hit her the instant he threw the switch, a paralysing shock that wracked her body. She arched backwards, shot up on the balls of her feet, twitched and spasmed, felt her hair rising from her scalp. She thought he would make it stop. He did not.

The last thing Naomi ever sensed was the smell. The acrid stench of burning insulation, from wires that were starting to combust. It was not a design flaw, she thought as her brain shut down. It was just they had never been intended to carry that amount of voltage.

## Chapter Six

Eva sent a couple of emails, dropped a message to her team telling them she was going to be out of the office for a few hours, and then shut her laptop down. It was her line of enquiry, she reminded herself as she walked away from the station. Sutton had not twisted her arm. In fact she had questioned the wisdom of the approach when Eva suggested it. There was not really any ambiguity. Her specific words had been: *are you bloody serious?*

*The decision to act.* The phrase tumbled out of the past and into her head. She thought she might struggle to remember where she first read it, but it only took her a moment to recall. At university, during some random search or other she stumbled on a quote by Amelia Earhart, the first female aviator to cross the Atlantic. *The most difficult thing is the decision to act, the rest is merely tenacity. The fears are paper tigers. You can do anything you decide to do. You can act to change and control your life; and the procedure, the process is its own reward.* They had helped her make her final decision to quit university and join MPCCU. Eva wondered why they had pushed their way into her thoughts once more, but it didn't take much to work it out. She hoped her own fears were in fact paper tigers. Earhart, she reminded herself, had disappeared, presumed dead, over the Pacific Ocean in 1937.

Eva should have brought her car to work, but her flat was only ten minutes' walk and she had needed food and fresh air. She collected it from where she had parked it the night before, did a search on her phone, put a postcode into her sat-nav and drove away.

She drove for an hour. Motorway traffic moved in fits and starts, so she left the motorway as soon as she could, then followed an A-road towards a village called Crowthorne in the county of Berkshire. She headed north along a road that ran through open countryside, although dense woodland along the A-road hid the scenery from view. After a few miles she turned off onto another road, named after a Royal Engineer born in the eighteenth century. Soon she found she was following a high red-brick wall that snaked alongside that road. The wall seemed both impenetrable and un-scalable in itself, but Eva knew it was only an outer perimeter. Inside the wall, and separated from it by a swathe of open ground monitored by CCTV and thermal cameras, was a fence, higher than the wall but hidden from the road, and topped with razor wire. Inside that was a labyrinth of smaller steel chain-link fences that subdivided the site, each of them monitored and alarmed.

She had to show her warrant card to even reach the car park. She sat in front of a security gate while the guard on duty checked her authorisation. A white sign with a blue logo stood next to the security gate. The sign read: Broadmoor Psychiatric Hospital.

–

Martin Harding's office looked like any other office, except for the discreet steel grill that protected the glass and the high-security fence that stood beyond it. It faced north, Eva noted. The light that entered the room was cool and blue. Perhaps Doctor Harding had realised this, because on his desk and in the corner of the room lamps lit by tungsten bulbs made warm pools that fought to keep the cold at bay.

'I have to admit I was surprised, and more than a little concerned, when you said you wanted to interview Mathew yourself.' Harding leant forward across his desk. His arms were open and he looked her directly in the eye, although the desk came between them. A combination of openness and distance, she realised, making him seem amenable, but from his side of a carefully positioned barrier. It was unlikely to be an accidental statement, coming as it did from the head of psychology at a mental institution.

If Harding had a colour, then it was sandy brown. His hair was English blond and slightly unkempt, he wore a fawn jacket and tawny-rimmed glasses that must have had the mildest of prescriptions, because he kept taking them off to toy with them like a priest fiddling with a rosary. Early forties and with a voice as mild as his prescription. A reasonable man, Eva thought, or at least as reasonable as any man could be who acted as guardian and gatekeeper to a hospital preoccupied with insanity.

'Mathew Harred is still under investigation. The circumstances surrounding his involvement with New Thought are far from clear. It can't be that much of a surprise the police would want to interview him again?'

'I'm not referring to the police,' Harding said. 'I'm referring to you.' He sat for a moment, waiting for her to respond, intending for her to fill the gap in the conversation and reveal her intentions, but Eva knew the trick. After the crash, after Colin Lynch had tried to bury her headfirst in pig shit and slurry, once the surgeons had examined her for signs of physical brain damage, then the psychiatrists had looked for mental scarring. Over time she had come to recognise all their ploys. She didn't hate Harding for playing his games, but she did need to make him understand that they would no longer work on her. Eva drew her silence around her like a cloak and waited for him to realise. Eventually, he did. He put his glasses down. 'You do know you're something of an obsession for Mathew?'

'How does that,' she sought for a word she imagined he might relate to, 'manifest itself?'

'In paintings and drawings, as you might expect.'

She couldn't keep the incredulity from her face. 'You actually let him paint?'

'A difficult decision,' Harding agreed. 'Consider the alternative. If we'd prevented Mathew from painting, there's little chance he would have engaged with us at all. We would have had to put him in a cell and give up on him completely.'

She frowned. 'I'm not sure the families of his victims would consider that a bad outcome,' Eva suggested carefully.

Harding shook his head, a small gesture but one that conveyed the depth of his disagreement. 'I think they would if it meant they never got to the truth. What is Mathew Harred? Is he mad, perverted, deluded, or a brilliant liar? Does he believe in the extraordinary universe he created or is he simply a talented illustrator who's fooling us all? We could lock Harred up in prison. If we were somewhere else we might sentence him to death. Where does that get us? Revenge is fine for a week, a month, or a year. It's satisfying for a while, but at some point we're left with the question: why? If we really want justice for Harred's victims and their families, we have to understand Harred. We have to quantify him, dissect him.'

An interesting choice of words, Eva thought, but she was as sure as she reasonably could be that Martin Harding's assertion had been a coincidence. 'What does he paint?'

Harding's face clouded. 'Well, he paints you for a start. In part that's why I said I was concerned that you wanted to interview him.'

She waved a hand as though to dismiss the idea. 'He's painted me before. So what is it, lurid? Has he drifted into comic book pornography? Whatever it is, it doesn't bother me. If he has me being gang-raped by demons or whatever I'm afraid I'll just be disappointed. He has a talent. If he's let it slide into gaudy Manga salaciousness I'm only going to feel let down.'

'It's not that. To some extent it's the opposite of that. It's more akin to apotheosis, the glorification of a subject to divine level. Hero worship,' Harding added, and watched for her reaction.

Eva shook her head, slowly. 'I don't understand that. I do know he became interested when he found out about my background. I had an accident.'

49

'I know,' Harding said. 'Mathew told me. More than once.'

She hated the cross-examination, but she knew Harding was only doing his job. 'I don't know what to tell you. There's been another discovery and we need to establish whether Mathew knows anything about it. It may not directly relate to him, but we cannot take the chance. I have to interview Mathew. I don't believe he would lie to me, not about this. He has no reason to,' she added. She knew she sounded as though she was trying to convince herself.

Harding shrugged. 'I could refuse an interview but frankly my reasons for doing so would be based on guesswork. I don't understand Mathew yet, so I don't know how this will affect our examination of him. I think something will change, but I have no idea what. So yes Detective Inspector, I will give you permission to meet with Mathew today, with all the usual provisos.' A reasonable man, Eva thought. At least, as reasonable as he could afford to be. He frowned though. 'Perhaps you could help me with one question first.'

'What?'

Harding put his glasses back on, laced his fingers and stared at her. 'Why does Mathew insist on calling you "destroyer"?'

–

Two orderlies flanked her as she walked along a windowless corridor lit by fluorescent tubes. For the most part Broadmoor tried hard to look like an ordinary hospital. New buildings that were well lit and open contrasted with the Victorian edifice, which served as a reminder of the way attitudes to mental health had changed. The Broadmoor Criminal Lunatic Asylum had become an NHS trust, with a 'highly structured and well-staffed therapeutic living environment'. Eva knew that for the most part people here were treated as patients, not prisoners, the intention being to return them to the outside world as soon as it was safe to do so. There were, she reminded herself as the corridor reached its end, always exceptions.

He sat at a table in a room with a single window made from reinforced glass. The table, Eva noticed as she entered, was bolted to the floor. The chair on which he sat was entirely plastic. Two more orderlies stood beyond a windowed partition. She had wondered if he would be restrained in some way, handcuffs or a straitjacket, but Mathew Harred was exactly as she remembered him. Grey-green T-shirt and jeans, powerful build, closely cropped hair flecked with grey, trace of stubble on his chin, sardonic smile on a face that, given his crimes, was worryingly handsome. Being charged as a serial killer and locked up in the UK's most secure psychiatric unit had not changed him one iota.

Harred grinned when she entered the room. The orderlies who had accompanied her stood at the back, ready to protect her if needed. The other two were ready to restrain Harred if he became violent, although she knew he would not. That would be too predictable.

'Eva,' Harred almost purred as she sat down. 'How lovely to see you again. To what do I owe the pleasure?'

Sarcastic bastard. She wanted to slap his face at the very least. Maybe gouge his damned eyes out. Instead she put on a beatific smile and laced her fingers in her lap. 'Mathew. Are they treating you well?' His expression changed to a look of mild surprise. So we're going to play games, Eva thought. Let's play games.

'It's actually very peaceful here. The light's quite good too. A bit brighter than I'd normally like, but not bad. They let me paint.'

'So I've heard.' Silence settled over the table. Eva didn't bother to take the same approach she had with Harding. Mathew Harred could probably sit and wait until the sun went out before feeling the need to speak, so there was no point. 'What do you paint?'

Harred shrugged. 'Reflections on the transience of life, our extended existence in the multiverse, the triumph of perception over recursive realities, the baseless and illusory nature of death. The usual stuff.'

'I'm sure Fredrick Huss would approve.'

'I'm sure he would. How is Fredrick?'

She did not miss a beat. 'I was hoping you could tell me.'

He raised an eyebrow, but she couldn't tell anything from the gesture. 'You're still looking for Fredrick then. Is this what you're here to talk to me about, Eva?'

Fredrick Huss, so-called pastor of the New Thought Transcendentalist Church in Virginia Water, had disappeared during her investigation of Harred. She had met Huss only once, then he simply vanished. Silver hair and mellow voice, he'd appeared gentle and urbane, but that had not been a million miles away from her first impression of Mathew Harred either. Harred had mutilated his victims with carefully cut slices, striations that ran the length of their bodies and split the skin like furrows in a field. Then he had punctured their eyes. The patterns made sense to Harred, but only to Harred, it seemed. Whether Huss was victim or accomplice she still had no idea. 'No,' Eva told him, voice flat and uncompromising.

Harred chuckled, quiet and dark. 'I thought I was supposed to be the obstructive psychopath in the room. Mind you, I'm not saying I'm alone in that.' She didn't know exactly how to respond, but he brushed it to one side. 'Okay, never mind. You gave me what I asked for.' He meant when Eva had found him at New Thought church with DS Rebecca Flynn crucified on scaffolding with a catheter in her carotid artery. She had told him a secret then, her secret, in return for Flynn's life. She damn well knew why Harred called her 'destroyer.' It was because he understood her far too well. 'You've looked for Fredrick, but you haven't found him.' It was not a question.

'Yes,' she said, 'and no. We do know he never left the country.'

'No.' Harred shook his head emphatically. 'You do not. You know someone calling themselves Fredrick Huss didn't leave the country, but as for the real Fredrick Huss, if that's even his name, you know nothing.' Before she could ask the obvious question Harred carried on. 'What do you actually know about New Thought?'

'It's a church, or at least a charitable institution, established in the state of Colorado.'

'So nothing.'

'Enlighten me.'

'What do I get?'

She didn't want to ask the next question, but the perverse cadence of the conversation made it inescapable. 'What do you want?'

His teeth were bared. 'Pose for me. I want to paint you.'

She knew she flinched. 'I'll have to think about that.' The thought that he might want to use her as an actual live model hadn't occurred to her, not even when Harding had talked about his drawings. The prospect suddenly horrified her.

Harred kept grinning. 'Then think. I'll give you some free stuff in the meantime to whet your appetite.' He leant back and looked totally relaxed, completely in control. The urge to kill him returned. 'Thelema,' he said.

Eva shook her head. 'I don't know what that is.'

'Transcendentalism is the polite façade. Thelema is a philosophy that comes out of Western esotericism. The fundamental axiom is: "Do what thou wilt shall be the whole of the Law." Aleister Crowley said of it: "Pure will, un-assuaged of purpose, delivered from the lust of result, is every way perfect." Crowley believed himself to be the Prophet of the Aeon of Horus, incidentally.'

'I have no idea what you're talking about,' Eva said. Then she frowned. 'Wasn't Aleister Crowley a Satanist?'

'So you do actually have some idea of what I'm talking about,' Harred complained, 'and no. Not exactly.' She waited in silence again, but she didn't have to wait long. 'New Thought claims transcendentalism was its starting point, not its destination. At least, the Heart claims that. The governing council,' he said before she could ask, 'board of directors, I don't know what you might call it. Fredrick spoke of them.'

'You never met them?'

'I may have met one of them.' He rubbed a long finger over his chin for a moment. 'There was a visitor, a couple of years ago now. I don't know his name but Fredrick was, I guess you'd say, deferential. The visitor acted as though he expected to be deferred to.'

Eva frowned. 'For New Thought, what does that involve? Bowing and scraping? Acknowledging Lords and Masters, oaths of fealty and the like?'

Harred scowled. 'Don't be dull. This isn't some outmoded secret society left over from the dark ages. These people are sophisticated, single-minded. They have their eyes on infinity.'

She couldn't decide whether he was trying to be helpful or was just being obstructive and hiding facts in plain sight. 'What does that actually mean?' she asked him.

'Ah. If you mean in the sense of what do they specifically hope to achieve, as in what's their purpose, then I don't know. You'll have to find that out for yourself.' He shrugged. 'But maybe that's a naïve question too. What does any religion hope to achieve? Converts, I suppose, validation through numbers, reinforcements to quell any self-doubt. I don't think New Thought really cares about those sorts of things.'

As ever with Harred, the truth was caught up in his own unique view of the universe. It was beginning to frustrate her. Eva tried a different tack. 'Did Fredrick Huss know about your activities? Did he know you killed Kelly Gibson, Olivia Russell and Grace Lloyd?'

'Freed them,' Harred insisted, predatory once more.

She waved a hand, trying to gloss over his obsessions. 'Let's not get caught up in semantics. Did Huss know?'

'Oh, let's,' Harred purred. 'What do you mean by "know"?'

She had anticipated that any conversation with Harred was going to be difficult, but she hadn't realised how bloody fractious it would be. Eva let out a long, disappointed sigh and didn't attempt to hide her impatience. 'Am I going to get anywhere with this?' she demanded.

He shook his head, as though he didn't feel responsible for her frustration. 'You still haven't said why you came here. Except it wasn't really to talk about Fredrick.'

'I'm interested in where Huss is now. I'd like to know if he knew about your actions concerning Gibson, Russell and Lloyd, and how this Heart or whatever it is of New Thought connects with that.'

'If in fact it does, and I've told you my price for that information.' He sounded reasonable, conciliatory almost, but then, like a switch being flipped, he changed. She had started to wonder whether his madness was really just an act, but in that moment, she became certain it was not. 'Come on,' Harred roared, arms crossed, suddenly enraged, furiously impatient although not making any move towards her. The orderlies tensed but didn't approach either.

His anger didn't frighten her. If he wanted to provoke a fight-or-flight reaction, then flight was not the option she would have chosen. If he attacked her then the orderlies would restrain him, and she was pretty damned sure she could at least gouge her fingers into his eyes before they realised he was not the real threat. He did nothing though, apart from glare, and she could glare too.

'All right,' Eva snapped. 'Do you know a company called Metal Box Storage?'

'No.'

'They used part of the old waterworks at Hampton to keep lock-ups and containers. We know New Thought rented storage space from them.'

'Still no.'

'The company gave up the site a few years ago. It's abandoned now.' He shrugged and pulled a face. 'We found tanks of formaldehyde with around a hundred dismembered body parts in them.' Eva watched as a sense of surprise Harred could not disguise settled on his face. She felt the urge to dig deeper. 'It was a remarkable presentation,' she all but purred. 'Quite a beautiful concept, very *modern*, if you know what I mean. A contemporary aesthetic, a long way from dusty representations. In its own way – exhilarating.'

She could see his lip curl. 'Well maybe, if you think cutting a cow in half is art,' he sneered. 'Personally, I think you're confusing creativity with novelty.' Then he shrugged as though he didn't really care, as if he was secure enough in his own delusions to ignore the slight. 'What condition were they in?'

Perhaps there was no point in trying to provoke him. 'Expertly removed and preserved. There was scientific equipment there too. We can't make up our minds whether it's supposed to be a laboratory or an art installation.'

'And you want me to do your job for you?'

It was her turn to shrug. 'That would be nice.' It was the only way to deal with Harred, she knew that. Be as brusque and blasé as he was, keep pushing, take more.

'Well,' he said, pulling at his bottom lip. 'It's nothing to do with me.'

She scowled at him. 'I didn't think it was. Not directly anyway.'

He sat and thought for several seconds. 'It's nothing to do with me,' he repeated, 'so I suppose it doesn't matter if I help a little. How's my painting?' He meant the fresco, the vast work that adorned the wall of New Thought's church.

Eva blinked. 'It's fine. It's locked away; the church is closed but nobody's touched it.'

Harred nodded, seemingly reassured. 'Just as well, because you're going to have to take another look at it. I did paint someone, again a couple of years ago. It was a request from Fredrick. I never met him. Fredrick gave me photos. I didn't think anything of it at the time. Fredrick asked me to add a symbol. I thought it was going to be the Unicursal Hexagram, one of the symbols of Thelema. It wasn't. I don't know what the significance of it was. You'll have to look at the painting though.' Harred beamed. His face practically glowed with some inner light. 'All the answers are in the painting.'

The painting was huge, and she had counted over two hundred figures in it. 'How do I find him?'

'Look for the last constellation, my little fox. He stands underneath it.'

He had just called her a vixen; she had no idea why. The urge to slap him came over her again. Eva stood to leave. 'Nothing else you can tell me?'

'Probably lots of things,' Harred laughed. 'Maybe there's something else. If I remember it correctly.'

'What?' She was almost at the door.

'A name,' Harred said. 'Derzelas.'

## Chapter Seven

Despite Harred's information, Eva couldn't afford to let the investigation into Muir's legacy slip. There was too much pressure from Sutton and above to allow that to happen, but this time at least it felt as though a raid was going to plan.

Eva followed Moresby into the shop the day after she interviewed Harred. No Armed Response Unit, nobody carrying weapons, only Moresby and half a dozen of his uniforms with DS Rebecca Flynn providing the verbal aggro. Eva watched, wry smile on her face, as Flynn bellowed at staff and customers alike. About the same height as Eva, with scraped-back hair and an almost permanently disgruntled expression, on a bad day Flynn had all the charm of a kick in the teeth. She was also fiercely loyal; Eva that knew for a fact. Rank did not impress her, but Flynn was the kind of person who would go to hell and back for a friend.

Another tip-off from Muir's insurance policy. The shop stood at the wrong end of the town centre, where Clarence Street looped back into the one-way system and ran past nightclubs and a cinema complex on one side, and a row of buildings ripe for redevelopment on the other. It was not a prime location, Eva thought as she looked around the shop. It was the kind of place you had to go looking for.

Red-painted panels lined the walls. In front of them she counted a dozen glass cases, and in each of the cases she saw second-hand electronic equipment. Mobile phones, tablets, laptops, games consoles, a couple of VR headsets, a few cameras. In the middle of the store were racks filled with

DVDs. Some were movies, some computer games. You could bring in pretty much anything electronic and exchange it for cash. Everything was taken at face value. Which was why, she thought as she scanned the shelves, Warren Muir had employed this place to dispose of Jeffrey Cowan's used goods.

'What do you want to go through?' Flynn asked. 'It'll take days to sort this lot.'

'I don't think we need to,' Eva told her. 'Anything on the shelves is probably worthless. It will have had a basic wipe done, but I doubt there was much of use on any of it. I'm more interested in finding out what they've got in the back office.'

Flynn watched her face. 'Why do I think you know what you're looking for?'

'Because I do,' Eva admitted. 'This is what I trained in. These clowns think they know cyber and digital, they think they've erased everything from this crap, but the truth is you can never get rid of data, not really. Not unless you systematically destroy the media it's stored on, and that gets expensive.'

Eva stalked through a door at the back of the shop, and Flynn followed her. Two of Moresby's men were already dismantling the place. She saw three tables, a desk, a coffee machine and a safe. The safe had a digital lock with a standard keypad: one through nine plus zero, star and hash.

For a moment she wondered if she was going to have to break the lock. She had done teardowns on similar safes at MPCCU, so she was certain that she could. The safe had a model number on it, which meant she would be able to get the specifications from the manufacturer's website. It would take a bit of brute force, the kind Moresby could provide, but she knew that once the cover plate to the keypad had been removed she would be able to get at the electronics of the safe through an old-school RS-232 connection and a cable to her laptop. Then it was only a matter of time, and not very much time at that. Except, Eva thought as she checked the messages on her phone, she couldn't be bothered to make even that effort.

'Where's the manager?' she asked Flynn. A few moments later a gangly young man whose appearance fitted the shop's decor sloped into the back office. Eva stood beside the safe and waited. The young man shuffled uncomfortably as she stared, first at it, then at him. 'It's your choice,' Eva told him, voice almost laconic. She let the rest of the implications hang.

The young man was not an idiot. Apart from anything else, he must have known the safe was a long way from being impregnable and getting on the wrong side of the police at this stage would be a stupid thing to do. With a few muttered expletives he knelt down and tapped in a six-digit combination, and the safe opened. When it did, Eva nodded at the door through which he had just come. One of Moresby's men led him away.

Eva pulled the safe door. Inside, amongst bundles of files and a few hundred pounds in cash, she found a laptop.

'Is that what you expected to find?' Flynn asked.

'Hoped,' Eva said. It should have been a routine raid, and this time it had been. Despite the fact that things had merely gone according to plan, the sense of relief that washed over her felt like a cool, fresh shower. 'It'll have been wiped,' she told Flynn and Moresby, 'or so they think. This is where the real fun starts.'

Later that morning she sat at her desk with both her laptop and the computer taken from the safe in the exchange store open in front of her. Cables linked the two machines. Eva had thought about ripping the hard drive out of the computer from the shop, but that would probably be her last step. The machine had been wiped, she knew that already, but somebody had most likely used a low-cost application bought from the Internet to clean data from the disk. That was good enough to erase personal information and leave it in a state where it could be resold, but it was not enough to protect it from the kind of deep-diving tools MPCCU employed. She wouldn't get everything back, she knew that. Perhaps she would get enough. It had taken over two months of sifting through Warren Muir's files before she recognised a pattern, but when she did it had fallen on her like a collapsing building.

She knew Semion Razin's organisation used Surrey to both sell drugs in and launder money through. A prosperous county filled with affluent towns, it was an easy place in which to move large sums. It was also conveniently outside of the City of London, where so much attention was being paid to electronic money laundering. Eva knew Razin's people were cleaning tens, if not hundreds of millions of pounds through the county every year. She just didn't know how.

Muir's ledgers had given her the clue. Maybe ledgers were a grandiose term; scrappy notebooks would have been closer to the truth. For all his untidiness though, Warren Muir had an eye for detail. She had found a list of seven- and eight-figure transactions on one page of his notebooks that referenced deals done with individuals named only by their nationalities: Chinese, Russians and Saudi Arabians. It wasn't the nationalities that had caught her eye though. It was the amounts.

Had Muir rounded them up? She had read one million three hundred and seventy-five thousand, one million five hundred and ninety-five thousand and other similar sums. If he had known the exact numbers, and presumably he had, why would Muir have rounded them up or down?

Before she started, she re-read a couple of presentations from information security sites. 'Reconstruct the world from vanished shadows,' one was titled. Another read, 'Recovering deleted VSS snapshots.' Next she went to GitHub, a website popular with programmers for sharing source-code online, and cloned a repository called Lib-vee-shadow to her computer. It felt good, she thought as she watched the main branch build itself on her machine. It felt comfortable. She had first learnt to code when she was fifteen, for the simple reason that she found she enjoyed it. It turned out she was also damned good at it.

As the files were downloading, another thought came to her. What had Harred meant when he said 'last constellation'? And why had he called her his 'little fox'? It didn't make sense. It wasn't part of the mythology Harred had assigned to her. It didn't relate to Pallas Athena, it had nothing to do with the destroyer, so why had he suddenly switched narratives? Was it just further evidence of his supposed insanity, or was he trying to tell her something else?

She had been working for about half an hour when Raj Chakrabati poked his head around her door. 'Somebody said you'd gone all black-hat on us.' He meant she was using malicious hacker tools, which was not actually true. 'Mind if I watch and learn?' Raj was stocky and not tall, with long, dark hair and pristine shirt and trousers. Eva knew he owed his immaculate clothes to his wife, even if he himself always appeared a little untidy. She had met Chandra three times, and on each occasion had been staggered by the elegance of the saris she wore. It had come as little surprise to discover she was a fashion designer.

'Pull up a chair.' She angled her screen towards him when he sat. 'I'm using VSS Carver to restore the catalogue data from the disk image. I reckon I know where this laptop came from, but I need confirmation.'

'You didn't say anything?'

'Too tenuous,' Eva admitted. 'If I'm honest, it's a hunch. Muir mentioned a name a couple of times, and the amounts he'd listed in overseas transactions caught my eye.'

'Seems like a coincidence the laptop would just happen to be in the safe when we raided it?'

Eva shook her head and stroked a couple of keys to make sure the processes she had set running were all still going. 'Actually, I don't think so. I think there's a fairly regular supply of laptops from this source, all of them sent for wiping in case the fraud squad should ever come knocking. I think they upgrade their computers every month or so to conceal data.'

Raj frowned. 'That sounds like an expensive way of doing business?'

'It's an on-cost. It gets charged to the transaction and the transaction makes it seem like a drop in the ocean. It's actually a pretty smart way of doing things if the deal is good enough.'

'So the exchange sells the laptop for a knockdown price, but there's always an audit trail to hide behind. I sort of see how that could work. But what's the deal?'

Eva checked a progress bar buried under several windows. It was nearly done. 'Razin's people work all the way around the globe, right? They need legitimate businesses where large chunks of money can be cleaned.' On the screen of her laptop a crude button graphic blinked from red to green. Eva opened the files that had been returned from the erased hard-drive. They were still fairly shredded, but at least she had something. The names were just hexadecimal gibberish, so she ran another tool that scanned the original headers for file type and added the correct extension to them. Then she sorted them by extension. The file names she was looking for all ended in 'JPG'.

'It's both amount and frequency they need,' Raj said. 'There aren't that many industries that meet the criteria.' He looked at the list. 'Will it have got everything back?'

'There's one,' Eva said. 'And no, it won't. The JPEGs will be degraded; it'll have brought back maybe one pixel in twenty. That should be enough though.' She started opening the images. As she expected, they were blocky and pixelated, but it was obvious what they were.

Raj understood immediately. 'Houses.'

'Yes,' Eva agreed. 'Whoever is running Razin's businesses in the county is an estate agent.'

## Chapter Eight

The text from Judy Wren didn't come as much of a surprise. *Need to talk*, was all it said. Wren would have been working non-stop on the material retrieved from the disused waterworks, splitting shifts with her team to find answers as quickly as possible. Eva knew better than to hassle Wren. The older woman was remorselessly efficient, and pestering her would only slow the process down.

She looked completely shattered, Eva thought as she opened the door to her office. Papers were strewn everywhere. She saw whiteboards on the wall covered in notes written in blue and red marker. Wren usually kept them clean. Realisation dawned on her when she looked back at Wren. 'Have you actually slept since we turned up that lot?'

'A few hours,' Wren admitted. 'We took turns on a z-bed in the theatre.' Wren nodded through the window at a dark-skinned man and an Asian woman who worked in the room beyond. 'It's surprisingly peaceful when you haven't got customers in.'

What passed for collective humour in the forensic scientist world, Eva assumed. By customers, she meant bodies in need of examination.

'You need to get some proper rest soon.'

'Tell me something I don't know.' Wren stifled a yawn. 'I need to show you what we've found first. And no, you're not going to like it.'

She hadn't expected she would. Eva cleared papers off a chair and sat down. 'Is it New Thought?'

'How could I possibly know that? It's not like they've got labels attached to them. I can tell you that there are ninety-six containers, all filled with formaldehyde and bodily remains, and at least seventy-three of those containers hold organic tissue that is human. We've still got to examine the rest, so all I'm saying about those is we haven't looked at them yet.'

'I didn't really think there was animal tissue involved.'

Wren shuffled prints from photographs. 'No. But you live in hope, don't you? In any event we've got a breakdown of organs and other parts. We've found multiple hearts, lungs, livers, kidneys, brains as well as completely and partially severed limbs, plus a couple of bodies that are externally intact. Internals are a different question. We've been trying to match them up. It's been a bloody nightmare.'

She could see the strain on Wren's face. 'Any luck?'

'An odd way of putting it. I suppose the answer is yes, in the sense of discovery. We've been able to notionally reconstruct five bodies so far, three female and two male, all fairly young. By that I mean most likely early to late twenties. All of them gave us viable DNA samples, meaning that they hadn't been chemically impaired.' Wren saw Eva frown. 'Formaldehyde causes lesions in DNA by damaging free nucleotides. It reacts with nucleic acids, free bases and aromatic amines.' Eva shook her head. 'Over time it puts sodding great holes in the DNA strands,' Wren explained.

'But not these?'

'But not these,' Wren agreed. 'Because they haven't been immersed for long enough. Which is why we were able to get a viable DNA sample from this little beauty.' She held up a print of the dissected face. 'Much as it pains me to say it, it's something of a work of art.'

Eva shuddered. 'Give me Rembrandt any day. Why art?'

'In the sense of extremely well done. Meticulous. The crafts-manship is not inconsiderable. I wonder if Amanda Tyler's parents will admire it?'

She felt the hair crawl on her scalp. 'Oh, Christ.'

Wren glared. Darkness seemed to surround her, and it was not simply lack of sleep, Eva realised. 'I could not have put it better myself, Detective Inspector. Amanda Tyler, age twenty-two, promising career at some local multinational apparently, went missing around three months ago. Because of an almost certainly unrelated incident involving a friend and a few tabs of ecstasy picked up at a party on a Saturday night, Ms Tyler's DNA happened to be on the police database. Reported as a mis-per by her mum and dad, because although Amanda didn't mind getting a tiny bit wasted at the weekend they said she never let it get out of hand. A good girl, that's what they called her.' Wren tossed the print on her desk. 'I wonder how they'll like her now?'

Eva leant forward and rested her head in her hands. 'And the others?'

'Nothing yet, but the DNA all seems intact, which suggests they too haven't been in formaldehyde for very long. No, I can't give you dates,' she added. 'That's going to get extremely complicated and take a while. But I strongly suspect there are going to be more Amanda Tylers in our files very soon.'

She let the implications sink in slowly. 'So somebody has recently killed at least five people and then dissected them.'

'Seems that way,' Wren said. She almost sounded cheerful. Perhaps it was because she had finally been able to unburden. 'Thing is there was that load of technical gear set up near the tanks, so I can't figure out if this is some twisted bastard's idea of art or science.'

'How do you mean?' Eva demanded.

Wren's face grew dark again. 'I don't know about the New Thought angle, because although the crime scene looks like an art gallery from the samples and the equipment set up on the benches it's pretty clear the bodies were experimented on, both before and after dissection.'

Moresby drove. He had signed out a patrol car from the pool and met Eva in the station yard. 'Don't take this the wrong way,' he said as they skirted the one-way system and crossed Kingston Bridge, 'but you look bloody awful.'

'Mathew Harred has that effect,' she admitted as they slipped between the 'walls', the dark Tudor brick divides that separated the road from two royal parks. 'What's worse is I think the bastard was actually being helpful.'

'He has reason to lie,' Moresby pointed out. 'If the shrinks say he's deluded then he gets to do his time in a cosy mental institution somewhere. If not, he gets to spend the rest of his life in jail.'

'I actually don't think he cares, so long as he can paint. It's a genuine obsession, which I suppose lends credence to the insanity argument.' Eva hesitated, and then told Moresby about Harred's latest demand.

'Jesus Christ,' Moresby gasped. 'You're not going to, are you?'

'It might come to that if we can't get anything more on New Thought. The disappearance of Fredrick Huss is a real worry. It suggests somebody at least suspected Harred's involvement in the killings and was several steps ahead. And now this thing in the waterworks.' Eva gazed out of the window as they crossed back over the river at Hampton Court. 'New Thought is more than just some crackpot cult. They're powerful, influential and they act with impunity because they're practically invisible. You open the door and they disappear, which is exactly what Huss did.'

Half an hour later Moresby drove into a car park in Virginia Water. Everywhere around them Eva saw signs of affluence. The roads were lined with trees and gated drives. The houses were spacious and well maintained. She knew the average cost of a property here was comfortably in excess of a million pounds. The top end of the market could be ten times that. New Thought had chosen to place their church in the middle of it all, taking an ancient Norman structure, restoring it and extending it. Mathew Harred's canvas had stretched over two hundred feet long, and almost a hundred high.

The fresco had done its job, Eva reflected as she climbed out of the patrol car. It had acted as an object of curiosity and fascination for the wealthy and inquisitive, luring them into New Thought's orbit. That, and the parties Berta Nicholson had thrown. Berta too was inquisitive and wealthy; her money had come from her family. Eva doubted she had ever worked. Berta had single-handedly funded Mathew Harred's painting, and watched its progress intently every day. That wasn't all, Eva recalled.

With her partner Lily Yu, Berta Nicholson had hosted lavish gatherings where unbridled hedonists indulged themselves in what might have been viewed as depravity, except Eva had never thought of Berta as depraved. Merely adventurous. But to what end? At first it had seemed that lifestyle and accumulation of wealth was a motive in itself, but now she was less certain. Berta and Lily had also ended up as victims of Harred's delusions, dead at the bottom of the swimming pool where guests at her parties had inevitably congregated, in a continuous and open exchange of partners and permutations. Anything went at Berta's parties – anything except anyone getting hurt. That fate had ultimately been reserved for Berta and Lily themselves.

'Any sign of the lawyers giving way?' Moresby took a bunch of keys from his pocket. They each had tags on. The doors at the front of the church were crossed with blue-and-white tape.

'I have no idea,' Eva said as she stared up at the building. 'I don't think anything will happen until Harred's evaluation is finished, and if I understood his psychiatrist correctly, that could take a while. Everybody is waiting for somebody else to make the first move.'

Moresby opened the door. New Thought had seemingly forsaken the building, even though they still owned it. Fredrick

Huss hadn't been replaced as pastor; presumably whoever made such appointments was waiting to see if Huss was implicated or exonerated. In the meantime, the church was in limbo – not quite a crime scene and not quite abandoned. The keys had ended up being kept in the evidence locker at Kingston station by default.

Eva found the lights. A panel by the door had neatly printed labels on it, but she ignored them and just turned on everything. Light flooded the building. It seeped out from under the double doors that led to the main hall. Eva took a breath, pushed them open and forced herself to go in.

'I know he's a serial-killing nut job,' Moresby growled as he followed her, 'but this thing is just bloody incredible.'

She couldn't argue. The scaffolding towers Harred had used to paint the fresco had been pushed back against the far wall once more – the same towers on which he had crucified Rebecca Flynn, dangled her over a seventy-foot drop and jammed a catheter into her neck to drain her blood, just to taunt Eva. Harred's intention had been to goad Eva, remind her of her shortcomings in hunting down Jeremy Odie, an ophthalmic surgeon responsible for multiple deaths while attempting to cover up the failings of a lucrative medical implant. For Odie, the only way to conceal evidence had been to drain the victims' blood and remove their eyes. Harred had yet again found an aesthetic in the grotesque. Eva avoided mentioning Harred and that night around Flynn. Becks was tough, both physically and mentally, but everyone had their limits.

The painting though. That was something else entirely. It covered the whole north wall of the cavernous extension. Carefully positioned spotlights illuminated it with an even glow. Harred had arranged walkways over the floor of the church to control the view of the painting. In-between them he had placed black fabric laced with tiny LEDs to give the illusion of stars, both below and above the fresco. The painting glowed. Eva suspected Harred had added something slightly fluorescent to the oil paint to give it the unexpected intensity she saw. The colours seemed more saturated than reality; the shadows were darker and the highlights were brighter than real life. It was, she had to admit, overwhelming.

'What exactly are we looking for?' Moresby asked.

She wondered that herself. 'Harred said that all the answers are in the painting. I don't know if he was just being mystical. He could have been, but I think he meant something specific.' Eva started walking along the length of the fresco. In front of and above her she saw a tableau, Harred's tunnel vision that stretched towards infinity like a wormhole universe. Dotted around it were stars and planets, nebulae and asteroids, as well as shapes and structures she knew were supposed to represent concepts at the bleeding edge of physics. Calabi-Yau manifolds, Ricci curvatures, Euclidean hypersurfaces and holographic spaces: she knew the names but the algebra meant nothing to her. They were the mystery that Harred intended. In amongst them all though, scattered on physical objects and ethereal scenes that blended with the rest of the painting, were people.

Like a mourner at a funeral, Eva first paid her respects to the dead. Kelly Gibson, Olivia Russell, Grace Lloyd and Alicia Khan stood together, reading from a scroll. Ordinary women, students who had come to observe Harred's great work in progress, but who instead became his victims. She could look them in the eye. They were life-size, and so real that she expected their silken robes to rustle in some unfelt breeze. They stared back at her with an expression on their faces that seemed to say: we know something you don't. Next she came to Berta Nicholson and Lily Yu, basking in the light of an alien sun, razor-sharp shadows cast over their faces. Irrespective of logic and sense, Eva still considered their deaths to be a personal failure on her part. She hadn't seen that, when Harred had completed his masterpiece, he would turn on his benefactors. 'But what are we looking for?' Moresby repeated. Eva sighed, and dragged herself out of her reverie.

'Harred said something I didn't understand.' She stopped herself. Then she admitted. 'He says a lot of things I don't understand, it's part of the delusion. He said, "look for the last constellation, my little fox". I thought he was calling me a fox; I had no idea why. He wasn't though.' She walked along the painting again.

'Then what?' Moresby asked.

Eva gazed upwards. 'It turns out there are eighty-eight constellations recognised by the International Astronomical Union. They cover the whole of the sky, both northern and southern hemispheres. They have a map. It's an equirectangular plot of declination versus right ascension, apparently.'

'Of course they have,' Moresby grumbled. 'Maybe they have it in English too?'

'They also have a list. That's just alphabetical. And the last constellation on the list is Vulpecula. It's a Latin name. It means fox.' She pointed. Halfway up the painting there were six stars linked together by a tenuous line in a shape that looked like nothing more than a zigzag.

'How is that a fox?' Moresby demanded. 'And what the hell is that supposed to be?'

She couldn't see. There was a figure standing underneath the stars, but it was too high up to get a clear view. Eva glanced over her shoulder. 'We need scaffolding,' she told Moresby.

Together they rolled the smallest of the towers away from the wall and dragged it around the walkways. Eva steered. Moresby pushed. 'Can you get one of the forensics photographers down here to take detailed shots of this thing? I don't want to have to keep coming back to this damn place just in case there's anything else we've missed. Get them to do them square on so I can stitch them together in Photoshop.'

'They might have already done that,' Moresby said. 'I'll ask the question though.' When they had manoeuvred the tower in front of the painting Eva started to climb the ladder. Moresby followed her.

The platform stood about thirty feet above the ground. It put them on eye level with the figure standing beneath the pattern of stars Harred had called the last constellation. It seemed unlike the other figures arranged around the painting, Eva thought. There was something especially cold in its stare, shadows cast over its face, a look she didn't understand. Perhaps a frailness to it as well, a pallor that seemed unhealthy, but she couldn't be certain.

'And what's that?' Moresby demanded. The figure was holding something in its hands. It looked a little like a DNA strand, Eva thought. In some way the person holding the object was different, but for a moment she couldn't work out quite how. Then she realised. Modern attire. Unlike all the other figures, he was neither naked nor draped in a neo-classical style. He stood apart from Harred's view of creation, as though offering an alternate infinity, some other branch of his multiverse. For a moment she thought she might understand the difference, the reason he didn't seem to fit. Whatever she thought of it, whether she liked it or not, Harred's imaginary domain seemed to her essentially spiritual. This figure, and the object he grasped, was a representation of something entirely more scientific.

In the middle of the object, which the figure held as though it were offering it to her, there was a symbol, which she also didn't recognise.

'I think his name is Derzelas,' Eva told Moresby. 'Either that or Derzelas is what he's holding. But as to what it means, I have absolutely no idea.'

'Would Harred?'

The question hung in the air while she tried to imagine an answer. 'I actually don't think so,' Eva said eventually. 'If he knew he would have said more.' She felt her shoulders sag a little then. 'I could have asked Berta Nicholson. She might not have known, but she would have given an honest answer.'

'Damn shame,' Moresby agreed.

It came to her then as she stared at the strangely out-of-place figure. 'I can't ask Berta,' Eva said, 'but she might still be able to help.'

# Chapter Nine

When she returned to the station she found Jamie Newton and Raj Chakrabati waiting for her. 'Got a match,' Raj blurted as soon as he saw her.

'Certainly have,' Newton agreed as they followed her into her office. 'Webb County Partners, the MD is Duncan Webb. The photos all matched properties on their website. I mean they're pixelated but it's still obvious the shots are the same. Webb County are into all the usual stuff, residential sales and lettings as well as business properties, but they also have an international network. They've got sales agents in Dubai, St Petersburg and Shanghai, which is why they've been able to grow so quickly. They specialise in acquiring UK properties for foreign investors.'

Eva put her phone on her desk. Raj and Jamie's news quietly thrilled her, but the photos she had taken of the figure at New Thought would not leave her mind either.

'Financials are interesting,' Raj said. 'They're doing well. Every aspect looks squeaky clean at first, until you get on to the details of who their clients are. It's roughly a seventy-thirty split between domestic and foreign in terms of numbers of sales, but value is a totally different picture. Webb County's international sales outstrip domestic by almost ten to one. They put almost three hundred million quid in residential property through their books last year, and most of it went overseas.'

Eva frowned. 'I didn't know there was that much property sold in Surrey in a year?'

'It's not just Surrey,' Newton said. 'They're also marketing developments in Nine Elms and further into the city, zones one and two. Any one of those new tower blocks going up is a hundred million quid outlay.'

'It's a nice business,' Raj added. 'You get a foreign investor with collateral that secures a loan from an international bank to buy the property. They let the flats out and use the income to service the loan. The tenants may actually be subsidiaries of their own companies, which all then sub-let. They leave it a few years while the value of the apartments goes up, usually outstripping any other legitimate investment they could make. By the time they sell to the next company they've not only cleaned a fortune in dodgy money and actually grown it, they've also given their business a legitimate track record in property financing.'

'That sounds like it would take a fair bit of management?'

'Yeah,' Raj agreed, 'especially as Webb County Partners sometimes create new companies to market specific properties. It's a calculation, I think. Can they make the paper trail sufficiently complex so that HMRC can't afford the resources to follow it? Everything is weighted in their favour.'

She could see that. It made complete sense, depressing as that felt. 'So you can just be too expensive for the system to take you on, or that's what they're betting on.'

'Pretty much,' Raj agreed, 'although a lot of this is conjecture,' he admitted.

'I know,' Eva conceded, 'but I'm sure you're right. It's not just the property connection. I think Duncan Webb will be more than that. I think he'll be the local manager for Razin's operations in the county. I keep seeing references to someone who fits that description in Muir's notebooks, and the way so many money trails stop just short is too much of a coincidence.'

'We can't prove any of that,' Raj said, although the way he said it made the point sound like an annoying detail.

'I know that too. If it is Webb, then he's competent and careful. Webb needs to think there's been a mistake, that there's

75

something he's missed. It needs to be enough to make him worried, to cause him to go back and check any precautions he's put in place to cover his tracks. It can't be something he's done himself because he'll be too confident in his own measures. It's got to come from left field. Webb needs to think somebody has done something stupid and it's potentially exposed his activities to police scrutiny.'

'I mean, I see where you're going,' Newton said, face drawn down in a look of concern, 'but that's got a serious issue. If we do convince Webb somebody's stuffed up, and if he really is running Razin's local organisation, then whoever we point the finger at stands a good chance of winding up dead.'

'True,' Eva agreed. 'But that's not necessarily a problem.'

–

Eva sent one more email. She had to dig through case files to find the address, but the files were recent and the email was most likely current. If it was not she would have to go hunting, but even if she did she doubted she would find it hard to track down the contact she was looking for. Charlotte Savini was not the kind of person who made herself difficult to find.

She had first met Savini at one of Berta Nicholson's parties. Almost her first glimpse of her had been Savini naked, sand-wiched between two men in Nicholson's swimming pool, although that particular combination had changed several times. When Eva had interviewed her as a potential witness to Harred's crimes though, she had been unable to find anything to dislike about the woman. Savini was intelligent, confident, extremely good-looking and highly successful. She too had been outraged by Berta and Lily's murders. They had spoken at length. Eva found they had more in common than she would ever have imagined.

When she composed the email, she tried to make it as pleasant and unofficial as she could, because Savini had no reason to cooperate with the police. There would be no animosity, but there would at least be inconvenience. Eva didn't hold out much hope.

She had just closed the lid of her computer when her phone vibrated. Eva glanced at the screen. Despite her low expectations Savini had responded almost immediately. 'Yes,' the email read, 'of course. Let me check my diary and suggest times. Regards.'

Eva put the phone away, a little more satisfied. Despite everything else, perhaps two things had actually gone right that day.

## Chapter Ten

Lewis Ashley bellowed like a thing possessed. He screamed and shouted, swore and spat, threw his arms around and strained at the restraints, lashed out where he could. Fear and anger, confusion and pain. *You bastard*. Words in his mouth and in his head; half the time he could not tell which was which. *What the fuck are you doing to me?*

The room spun. He had been drugged, that much was obvious. When he had awoken, he had found himself upright, strapped to a frame, bound by nylon ties at the wrists and ankles. Tubes connected to his arms and legs, two in the upper arm, two in the lower, same pattern in the legs, two into the centre of his torso. Cables covered his chest and groin. He could see his blood in the tubes but knew enough to realise it was just a trickle. The tubes snaked away. Somebody was taking his body fluids for examination.

The man standing in front of him didn't flinch. White coat, scrubs maybe, ordinary clothes, hair covered by a net, face covered with a surgical mask. Average height, average weight, just nothing remarkable about him, Lewis thought. Except that the *bastard* had darted him near his house and strung him up here, wherever here was, naked and trussed up like a biology experiment.

The man stared. He waited while Lewis wore himself out. 'I want to ask you about the treatment,' he said once Lewis sagged in the restraints.

*What the fuck are you talking about?*

'I think you know. You've worked with Anna. She must have confided in you or let something slip. You can't keep a secret that big, nobody can. Things leak, information seeps out. I want to know what you know.'

*I don't understand? Why am I here?*

'I just told you. You're here because you work with Anna and because I want to know about the treatment. Are you going to waste more of my time, or can we just get to the facts?'

*Facts? Anna who?*

A hiss of breath. 'Please don't do that. Don't insult my intelligence. I can put you back to sleep again and wake you in another day or so, but every time I do that the chances of heart failure or a stroke increase, even in someone as young as you. I told you that last time. I know you worked as a research associate for Anna. I know you must know about the treatment.'

Realisation dawned. *Anna? That Anna? No, I worked for Colby. Just for a few months. I barely saw Anna.*

'So you admit you know her?'

*Of course I know her. Everybody knows her, by sight anyway. I didn't work for her, not directly. What's Anna got to do with this?*

Another hiss. 'You're really starting to try my patience. I don't believe you. I don't believe any of it. I want to know the results of the treatment. I want to know who's had it, and what the effects have been.' He took a step closer. 'I'm willing to use force if necessary.'

*I'll show you force. Let me out of these straps and I'll give you fucking force. I don't know what the hell you're going on about; I don't know what treatment you mean. You're bloody mental; you need to be locked up.* Lewis bucked and strained at the restraints again. Somewhere, a machine started beeping.

The man turned away. He walked over to a table where equipment sat, humming quietly. A printer came to life. A single sheet of paper rolled its way out of it. The man in the white coat picked it up and read. After a while he put the paper down. 'You haven't had the treatment.'

*What treatment? I haven't had any fucking treatment!*

'There's signs of necrotic cell death in your blood samples. In response to alkylating DNA damage cells undergo necrosis as a self-determined cell fate. That wouldn't happen with the treatment. So you haven't had the treatment. Do you understand what that means?'

*I said I haven't had any treatment. I don't know what that means.*

The man in the white coat took something from a drawer. A gun, Lewis realised. A dart gun. He started to shake, to strain at his restraints again. 'It means you're of no use to me.' He snapped a dart into the gun. The dart had a cluster of nylon feathers at the end of it. The feathers were black, Lewis saw. The man shot him.

The dart buried itself in Lewis's chest. Batrachotoxin R, Lewis guessed, because he knew about that sort of thing. Panic swept over him, tempered by a sense of inevitability now. There was no antidote. He also knew he would expire in under a minute. It must have been a large dose, because barely thirty seconds later Lewis went into sudden, paroxysmal, cardiac arrest.

When Lewis was dead the man in the white coat pulled his mask down and sighed. Such a waste of effort. All these false leads, even though he knew he was getting closer. And yet the time squandered and energy misspent seemed inexcusable. What did he have to show for it? He was no closer to Anna. He stared at Lewis, slumped and slack-jawed, hanging limp in his restraints. The only upside to the exercise was it had resulted in another healthy body, another source of fecund organs to continue testing on. He could take some solace in that at least.

Picking up a scalpel, the man in the white coat walked over to where Lewis's body hung and proceeded to castrate him.

# Chapter Eleven

Two cars drew up in front of a red-brick Elizabethan building in the county town of Guildford. Eva halted under a sign that gave information about parking restrictions and ignored it. Rebecca Flynn stopped behind her and parked at the kind of angle that said: I do not give a toss.

Newton and Chakrabati followed. The four of them marched up the quarter flight of stone stairs that led to a pair of wood-and-glass doors. Eva shoved them. Raj deliberately caught one with his shoe, so it shuddered noisily. They spread out through the entrance hall of Webb County Partners and started looking around, all except for Eva. She stood over the woman sitting at reception, who had an expression of alarm painted across her face, and glared.

'Can I help you?' The woman asked the question reflexively as Newton, Flynn and Chakrabati commenced a search of the hall. Newton picked up items and turned them over. Raj took photos on his phone of the posters of property developments that hung on the walls. Flynn went through the racks of brochures and selected one of each. Eva ignored them.

'We're here to see Duncan Webb.'

The woman was flustered. 'Do you have an appointment?'

Eva produced her warrant card. 'DI Harris, Surrey police, this isn't a casual visit so no, we don't have an appointment. I know Webb is in. Where is he?'

Two minutes later Eva pushed her way into Duncan Webb's office. Newton and Flynn followed her and began looking around, as though conducting a threat assessment. Raj blocked the doorway. Duncan Webb looked venomous.

He stood at the window, behind his desk. Early fifties, Eva decided, Webb looked like he played tennis or squash, something energetic anyway. He had a tan. Savile Row suit, or if not from there then somewhere in the same postcode. Dark tie with regimental stripes, gold tie-clip, pale-blue shirt with gold cufflinks. Eva hated him on sight. 'I assume you're going to explain what the hell this is all about,' Webb snarled.

Eva dropped into the chair in front of his desk without being asked. 'We're investigating dealings between Webb County Partners,' she paused, 'and Detective Chief Inspector Jeffrey Cowan, retired and deceased. Apart from fraud and misconduct in a public office, Cowan is being investigated posthumously for several counts of murder and attempted murder. We believe Cowan invested misappropriated funds with your company. Those funds were acquired as a result of homicides, which means the directors of this company are potentially accomplices.' Flynn and Newton stood behind her and studied him. 'Sit down,' Eva told Webb.

Webb sat, more out of surprise than anything else. 'I'm not sure I know the name?' he said.

Eva raised her eyebrows. 'Not Delta V Funds and Equity? They're the principal investors in Burnham Properties. You market apartments in four of their buildings as well as owning a percentage of them.'

'Of course I know Delta V,' Webb snapped.

'Cowan was an investor.'

Webb's jaw dropped. 'Impossible,' he spat.

'HMRC has proof. Not in his name but through an intermediary. The money that Jeffrey Cowan put into Delta V, which went into Burnham and then into Webb County, came from the proceeds of crime. And that crime involved murder and attempted murder.'

She could almost see the wheels turning inside his head. 'I know all the investors in Delta V,' Webb insisted. 'Cowan is not amongst them.'

'Not directly, but monies have been traced back to him. Cowan put eighty thousand pounds into Delta V.'

Eva saw the doubt on his face. 'Delta V is a six-hundred-million-pound fund,' he said. 'Eighty thousand is the kind of sum that gets lost in small change.'

'Doesn't matter. Not when several people died in the process of acquiring it.'

She had him questioning himself, she could tell. 'I don't know any Jeffrey Cowan,' Webb said eventually.

'Yes, you do. You sold him his house.'

'Do you have any idea how many houses this company sells?'

Eva flicked her hand. 'We know exactly. We also know you, personally, were involved in that sale.' She leant forward. 'We have sources,' she added before he could ask.

'Well, I'm struggling to remember,' Webb insisted. Then he frowned. 'If this is about money laundering why aren't HMRC here?'

'They will be,' Eva promised, 'but it isn't. Not today. They know Cowan was in the employ of Semion Razin, a criminal sometimes based in the Russian Federation.' Webb didn't blink, so she continued. 'But Cowan also made two attempts on the life of a police officer. We believe he had associates. The officer is pursuing the matter vigorously.'

Realisation slowly dawned. 'Who is that officer?' Webb asked. He already knew the answer.

'Me.' Eva stood and leaned across his desk. 'I'm here to warn you. HMRC will be sending a team to go through every transaction your company has made in the past five years. Make sure the required information is available. Don't show them any wiped laptops, because I have to tell you the guys you use for cleaning your computers are not very good.' This time he did blink. 'But that's just the start of it,' Eva said. 'I'm investigating a murder and two attempted murders. If I find there's a connection with any of your businesses then you are in trouble of a different order of magnitude. I will investigate every aspect of your life. Home, social connections, business. I will be that Harpy. Cowan knew what I can do.' She didn't know whether to use the next words. She didn't know if it was going too far. She spoke them anyway. 'That's why he killed himself.'

She saw the look on Webb's face change then. It cooled from anger to pure hatred. Enough, Eva thought. She stood up straight. 'I want everything you have on your dealings with Jeffrey Cowan,' she told him. Webb remained silent. 'I want them on my desk within forty-eight hours. Do this voluntarily. If you don't, I'm coming back with a warrant and I will rip this place apart.' She didn't wait for an answer. Eva turned and headed for the door. Newton and Flynn stepped aside, and then followed her.

'Nice going,' Raj said as they marched back to the cars. 'Do you think you did enough?'

Eva glanced up at the window at the front of the building, but she couldn't see Webb. Right now, he would be searching records of minor holdings in Delta V Funds and Equity for any sign of Jeffrey Cowan. He wouldn't find them. Eva knew that. The whole thing had been a lie to unsettle him. The look of hatred on his face had told her she had succeeded.

'I reckon so,' she said as she climbed into the car.

Somewhere in the back of her mind Mathew Harred laughed and spoke. *Destroyer*, was all he said.

## Chapter Twelve

Eva took the DLR to where Charlotte Savini worked. She got on at Canary Wharf and got off at South Quay Plaza, in a development of shiny new tower blocks. Savini had given her instructions. *I'm really happy to talk*, she'd said, *but I'd prefer not to do so in the office.* This didn't surprise Eva, and it didn't make any difference either. She had almost nothing on New Thought, and there was a fair chance Savini knew that, so the fact she was prepared to meet at all seemed like a gesture of goodwill. Eva knew she couldn't afford to take advantage.

She did know that Savini worked in finance; that she traded derivatives for a hedge fund. This in itself meant she was no lightweight. Eva had seen the maths involved in formulas such as the Black-Scholes Merton model; the differential equation used to calculate option prices, and knew it to be complex. Savini herself would only be providing the inputs, and a spreadsheet would be doing the rest, but Eva also knew you had to have at least an understanding of the model to be sure the data you were inputting made sense. That meant Savini was smart, as well as good-looking and successful. She was intrigued to know what specifically had drawn her to Berta Nicholson and Lily Yu.

Savini breezed into the coffee shop an entirely predictable five minutes late. She greeted Eva with a broad smile made from flawless teeth. 'I'm so pleased to see you again,' she told her as she pecked at both cheeks and dropped into a chair, 'even though I don't imagine I'm going to like whatever the reason for your visit is.'

It didn't seem like the time to sugar the truth. 'Sorry,' Eva said. 'I feel as though I'm hassling you because you were good enough to help before. That's not the intention, but we need some information about New Thought.'

Savini glanced at a waiter, who scurried over to the table and took her order for a coffee. Eva's had already been served. Not exactly Starbucks, Eva thought as she sipped her Yirgacheffe. Not exactly Starbuck's prices either. 'I have to ask why, but I suppose you won't be able to tell me,' Savini said.

Eva had been concerned about this ever since Savini had agreed to meet. 'I don't think there's any point in concealing the background,' Eva told her. 'I could end up asking wrong questions and you might give me wrong answers just because I didn't give you all the facts.'

Eva watched Savini's reaction as she processed her words. 'Wow. That's very logical of you,' she said once she had understood. 'So you're going to tell me what this is about?'

Eva kept her gaze on Savini. She made certain she looked the woman in the eye. 'If you're okay with that,' she told her, doing her utmost to make the implications clear.

'Ah,' Savini said after a moment. 'I think I understand. I'm really not going to like this, am I?'

Eva shrugged. Then she told Savini about the body parts and her interview with Mathew Harred. She watched as Savini's perfect smile faded slowly from her face.

'Jesus,' Savini said when Eva had finished. 'I don't know what to say. You think Harred has something to do with these cut-up bodies too?'

'Not directly,' Eva admitted. 'Did you ever meet Harred? I know he never came to Berta's parties.'

'I met him once,' Savini said, 'at New Thought. Berta and Lily wanted to show off his painting. I could understand why, it was amazing. Harred though,' she shook her head slightly and frowned, 'Harred made me feel nervous. I'm not sure exactly what it was. He was never threatening or overbearing, but I felt that could have easily changed.' She glanced at Eva as though making an admission. 'I'm glad he never came to Berta's parties.'

Eva knew she needed to be delicate. 'Why did you go? I mean I guess I could see the appeal, but you don't seem like you'd need to try very hard to find partners on your own.'

Savini toyed with her spoon. 'It's not that. Berta's parties were safe. Everyone there wanted the same things. Nobody was in a position to judge. You could get mildly wasted and do what the hell you liked, secure in the knowledge that everyone else was doing that too. Your reputation was never at risk. Nobody was going to boast or brag, because that would have broken trust, and they wouldn't have been invited again, which would have been crap. Berta was a brilliant judge of character. If she didn't like you, you didn't get in.'

'She didn't get Mathew Harred right though.'

'No,' Savini agreed, 'she was blind to Mathew. It was the painting, of course. It was the distraction that kept everyone from looking too closely at the painter.'

'He never painted you?'

'He asked. I managed to avoid it.'

Eva tapped her finger. 'What about Fredrick Huss?'

'Fredrick came to Berta's parties, but not that often. I think they made him nervous. Fredrick was a transcendentalist.'

Eva didn't understand why Savini needed to point that out. 'New Thought is a transcendentalist church?'

'It is,' Savini said, 'but not exclusively. New Thought is more like a collection of philosophies loosely grouped under one so-called church. Did Harred say anything about Thelema?' Eva nodded. 'I mean I don't actually know if that's at the heart of it, or if anything really is. They call themselves transcendentalist for convenience as much as anything else. Berta's group were some-times called hedonists, but that was just a label. There are plenty of other groups, and some are a bit weird. There's a bunch of Gaia worshippers on the west coast of the US who advocate a return to not just pre-industrial but pretty much stone-age society. You don't necessarily have to subscribe though. New Thought is the proverbial broad church.'

'You said "Heart." Harred said that too.'

'Yes.' Savini brushed her long blonde hair back. A complex woman, Eva thought, and probably not without her own demons, but when it came down to making the final, simplistic judgement of whom Eva liked and whom she didn't, Savini fell into the former category. 'They're sometimes called that. I hear it said in different ways. Sometimes it's like people are talking about the deadly secret innermost circle of Freemasonry, and sometimes it's like the parish council that organises the church fete. I don't know what the truth is,' she shrugged again. 'Maybe Fredrick does.'

Back to Huss, Eva thought, which was getting her precisely nowhere. Not Savini's fault, she realised. She was just not asking the right questions.

'Harred told me about a figure in the painting. He said it might have something to do with the body parts, but he didn't claim to be sure.' Savini looked as though the information meant nothing to her, so Eva took out her phone. 'Does this mean anything to you?'

Savini took the phone from her. 'The face doesn't,' she said after a moment, 'but then it probably doesn't mean anything to Harred either.'

'Why do you say that?'

She turned the screen of the phone towards Eva and pointed at the object the figure held. 'Because he's got this wrong. He's made it one symbol when in fact it's two characters, and it's much simpler.'

Eva frowned. 'Why would he do that?'

'I wouldn't imagine it was intentional. My guess would be he was painting someone he'd only heard about or seen photos of because they were from a different sect within New Thought, one that didn't have much contact with Huss's church. He just got the symbol wrong, and for whatever reason Huss didn't see fit to correct him.'

'Would Huss have known?'

Savini thought for a moment. 'Yes.'

When she too stopped to think, Eva realised her understanding of New Thought had also changed. From a straightforward if bizarre transcendentalist church, she now knew them to be something more complex, an amalgam of Thelema cultists, transcendentalists, hedonists, Gaians and god – or gods – only knew how many other sects, all co-existing under the banner of New Thought. What she didn't know was to which one the person or object Harred referred to as 'Derzelas' belonged.

'I'm not sure how much I should say.' Savini seemed suddenly reluctant. 'I just don't want to mislead you. I knew this sect existed, but nobody talked about them much. Some of them seemed, well, pretty wild, but then some of them had reason to be. I do know one of them.' She seemed wistful, almost regretful. 'He's been through a lot. I admire him. I don't claim to understand him.'

Eva didn't understand either. 'Is there any chance of meeting him?'

Another, much longer, hesitation. 'Maybe,' Savini said eventually. 'Let me do some emails. It won't be straightforward. These people value privacy more than most.'

She couldn't ask any more than that. Except, Eva realised, that Savini seemed to know what the symbol should look like, and it wasn't the shape Harred had painted.

'It's a lower case "h" with a plus sign next to it,' Savini told her when asked, though not without awkward reluctance. 'The symbol isn't theirs as such. It was invented by a guy called Fereidoun Esfandiary, an Iranian-American born in 1930, although he later changed his name.' She saw the look on Eva's face. 'Yes, I know. I'm good with names, and this story just had a bizarre fascination to it. Esfandiary started his own movement, one that had many points of similarity with the transcendentalists, which is why they were able to sit together under the New Thought umbrella.' Eva waited. 'h-plus is the symbol of the transhumanists. They believe in transforming the human condition through any artificial means possible.'

## Chapter Thirteen

Eva changed at Canary Wharf DLR station and took the Jubilee line back to Waterloo. The underground carriage was half empty, and she took a seat. For a while she just sat. The drone of the tube train was soporific, and it left her happy to let thoughts tumble around inside her head on the off-chance they might rearrange themselves into coherent ideas.

Body parts suspended in formaldehyde and Warren Muir's legacy. They were the binary star system around which her world currently revolved. Savini had been helpful, but Eva knew that with gentle pressure she could do more. Transcendentalism and now transhumanism. She knew she would have to get down to some serious research on those subjects if she hoped to make any connection between dissected bodies and New Thought, but at least that could wait for a few hours. Savini clearly had a contact, somebody she might even feel protective of. Why? Wren believed there were at least five complete bodies in amongst the insipid green tanks – five people who had died fairly recently, judging by the state of their DNA. The only real connection with New Thought was via Metal Box Storage, which made it a tenuous correspondence at best, and yet the aesthetic of the scene had immediately resonated with her. It just looked like something New Thought might have imagined. The more rational flip side of that argument was how implausible it would be for an unconnected killer to have rocked up at the same storage company used by Mathew Harred's patrons. When she ran those odds in her mind the picture became very different.

Park it, the voice in her head told her; put it on a shelf. Savini will do what she can because whatever else she is, she's a decent human being. The immediate problem isn't Savini or body parts. The immediate problem is what will Duncan Webb do now you've set up this story about Jeffrey Cowan. Is Webb going to take it lying down, or is he going to try and do something about it?

The train drew into Waterloo. When she thought about it in those terms it felt like a bloody stupid question.

—

The idea she might have just done something incredibly foolish stayed with her as the overground train trundled towards Kingston. Who was Duncan Webb? Was he just the guy who funnelled Semion Razin's money into convenient investments and left it squeaky clean? Webb might be simply the detergent of choice. Muir had led her to Webb though, as Muir had also indirectly led her to Jeffrey Cowan. Muir's notebooks pointed to someone who sat above Cowan in Razin's local organisation, another level of management that might even communicate directly with the *Bratva* in St Petersburg. It felt like the tasseography of tea leaves or divination of chicken bones cast in a fire, but if that was the case then Eva was convinced that the manager was Duncan Webb. So how good an idea had it been for her to get in Webb's face?

—

She found herself looking around her as she made her way back to Kingston. On the train she checked the carriage and changed seats twice. When she left the train at the overground she stood for a moment and stared at the street. Nothing. Not a sign. She turned and walked through side-streets back towards her car.

She walked up Richmond Road, past Acre Road and East Road, to where the lanes split, and the traffic became two-way once again. She had wanted to park near the station that morning, but the closest she had been able to get was a residential side-street with single yellow lines and permit-holder restrictions. She had put her Surrey Police badge on the dashboard as a talisman to ward off traffic wardens.

What would Webb do? Would he bide his time and wait to see how her supposed investigation played out? Unlikely, Eva decided as she walked. He would understand the danger of inaction. Whatever he decided to do, Webb would move quickly.

He would try to disrupt the investigation. She didn't know how. She doubted it would involve any legal challenge, although his lawyers could still be obstructive. If she was right that Webb worked for Razin, if he really was the Manager, then he would probably try something more direct. Jeffrey Cowan had taken that approach when he tried to run her car into the crash barrier on the A3 and then set fire to her apartment. Would Webb be any subtler?

She needed to cross Richmond Road then. Eva stepped between two parked cars and started to walk, but glanced at a movement to her right. A lorry, filthy, white cab, maybe five tonnes, a tipper back that you might dump builders' rubble into, steel bull bars welded around the grill. She could probably get over in time, but she didn't feel the need to exert herself, and so Eva waited for it while it headed along Richmond Road. Half a dozen metres away, though, it slowed, as if the driver had just spotted her. She waited for a moment. Perhaps he thought she was going to step out?

She half expected him to do something crass then. It wouldn't have been the first time a builder wolf-whistled her in the street. The lorry almost stopped, as though the driver was making up his mind. Unexpectedly, it accelerated.

Prat, she thought irritably as she watched it quickly pick up speed. It wasn't exactly a vehicle built for boy racers to show off in. Eva stepped back from the road a little. The lorry kept accelerating. Then it swerved towards her.

She didn't have time to scream. She jumped back just as it rammed the car on her right. Metal twisted and screeched. Even with its handbrake on the vehicle careened into the car that had been on her left. Windscreens exploded. Glass fragments filled the air. Eva threw her hands over her eyes. The first car shunted under the boot of the second, bodywork shredded. If she hadn't moved, the impact would have ripped her legs off at the knees. Eva staggered back, shaken. The lorry reversed. Then it came at her again.

She didn't think. She just ran. He sideswiped another car, half shoving it up onto the pavement. Terror made her swift. She sprinted, flat shoes pounding on paving stones, but he accelerated past her. Then he swerved again. Another ear-splitting crash as the lorry smashed a two-seater, pulverised it, and threw its mangled remains in front of her.

Eva skidded to a halt before she hit it. Her mind was numb. It couldn't be happening, not on a street, not in broad daylight. She gasped, started running the other way, but whoever was in the lorry had anticipated that. He backed up, slewed around and came at her like a locomotive.

Another crash. She looked over her shoulder and saw the wing he had taken off a car coming from the opposite direction. He rammed a motorbike parked by the side of the road, caught it at an angle, sent it flying towards her. She felt shards of fractured plastic hit the back of her coat. She ran harder, pumped her legs as fast as she could. Her chest started to ache. She couldn't breathe. Eva heard him accelerate again.

A boom. A sound like an explosion. She swerved left into an alleyway between houses just as the wreckage of another small car slammed into a brick wall to the side of her. Eva ducked, threw her hands over her head as stone fragments sliced the air. Heard the lorry turn, and saw it drive straight at her. She pelted towards a wooden gate that blocked her path, threw her body at it and prayed the lock wouldn't hold. For a split second she glanced back. The lorry was hurtling up the path towards her, pulverising bushes and fences and decorations. Ceramic fragments flew like shrapnel. She kicked as she ran. Wood splintered as the force of her impact ripped the rusted bolt from the gate. She heard the screech of brakes as the driver realised the gap was too narrow, and she was beyond his reach.

Eva ran. Kept running. Through another garden, she clambered over its fence into the road beyond. She chose a direction at random, turned right and kept sprinting. Then she saw something that made her think miracles could still happen. A black cab, amber light glowing, trundling out of Richmond Park.

Eva ran at it, jumped inside and pulled her warrant card out. 'Just drive,' she snarled at the driver. 'And keep the for-hire light on.' He went to question her but she slammed the window that divided him from the passenger compartment shut. Then she crouched down in the back and peered out.

She saw it after a minute or so. Pulverised front, broken glass, prowling like a wounded animal, heading in the opposite direction. The driver would abandon the lorry soon, that much was obvious. The lorry slowed to a halt beside the wrought-iron gates that led to the park. Eva saw someone get out, but at that distance she couldn't see any details.

*Dear God*, Eva thought as she watched the driver disappear into the park. *It's happening again.*

# Chapter Fourteen

Moresby's people cordoned off the lorry. A SOCO dusted the cab for prints, but Eva was certain there wouldn't be any. Whoever had been driving the lorry had intended to kill her. They would not have come unprepared.

Blue-and-white tape flapped and twisted in a light breeze. A couple of patrol cars had slewed to a halt and blocked the main road while more of Moresby's officers directed traffic towards side streets. 'What a bloody mess,' Moresby reflected as he surveyed the scene. Eva couldn't disagree. Parts of vehicles lay scattered around. The amount of damage the lorry had done was remarkable. The insurance claims were going to cause a few raised eyebrows, she suspected.

'I had just realised that if Webb is the Manager then it might have been a stupid idea to provoke him,' Eva told Moresby. 'I think I might have been right.'

Moresby jammed his fists on his hips and stared. 'Are you actually okay? This wasn't half-hearted. Some bastard tried to make you part of the pavement. I wouldn't want to think you're getting used to people trying to top you.'

She let out a long sigh. She felt herself shudder when she did so. 'Truth is I'm kicking myself because I should have known. Any time we go near Razin's people, it all gets out of hand.'

Eva was about to say more when a car she recognised literally screeched to a halt. Flynn was driving, she assumed. She was correct. Flynn, Newton and Chakrabati piled out of the car. 'What,' Flynn bellowed as she stormed towards them, 'the fuck?' Eva didn't know what to say. The three of them surrounded her, made sure she was intact, then Newton and Chakrabati backed off a little to give Flynn space. 'This was Webb, right?' Flynn demanded. Eva shrugged, and then nodded. 'We need SFOs and SOCOs,' Flynn barked at Moresby. 'We're going to go into his place and rip the fucking building to shreds. Then we break his arms and legs.' Jamie and Raj looked as though they were up for that too. Moresby just smiled.

'We're not going to do that, Becks,' Eva said, glad to have the distraction of needing to calm Flynn down. As she spoke the words another thought came to her. 'In fact, we're going to do exactly the opposite of that.'

Raj grunted. 'I like her plan better.'

Eva ignored him. 'We brush it off. We show Webb he can't intimidate us. We go back over his dealings with Cowan and then we demand more. We get HMRC and the Serious Fraud Office to pay him separate visits too.' They didn't look completely convinced, so she pressed her point. 'I'm all right,' Eva insisted, 'so he screwed up. Let him know we know he screwed up. I don't want to kick him in the balls. I want to put his balls in a vice and crush them till they burst.'

Newton still seemed sceptical. 'You think you can get HMRC and SFO on his back?'

She opened her mouth to speak but then she closed it again. *Careful*, she told herself. *You know you can make that happen, but they don't need to know how.* 'With a little help from the DCI,' Eva said after a moment. Raj said nothing. Newton barely blinked. She was damn sure he had just guessed, but he too kept his mouth shut.

Flynn had joined a completely different set of dots. 'He's going to try again.'

Eva nodded. 'I know that too. Next time I'll be ready.' Flynn also didn't look convinced, but Eva had explained all she was going to explain. 'Go on, back to the station,' she told them. 'I'll be ten minutes behind you.' Not without reluctance, they turned and left.

Moresby stood beside her as she watched the car disappear. 'You think I'm wrong,' Eva said.

'About what? Squeezing Webb till he pops? No,' Moresby said. 'It's totally logical. Make the bastard sweat and give him nowhere to turn. Stuff HMRC down his throat and SFO up his arse and wait till they meet in the middle. Makes perfect sense.' He put his hands behind his back and rocked up on the balls of his feet slightly, the policeman's stance from time immemorial. She knew he was taking the piss.

'So what then?' Eva demanded.

'I'm with Raj,' Moresby smiled again. He made her think of a bear, in the moment before it ripped your head off. 'I liked Flynn's plan better.'

–

Sutton paced, slowly and methodically. Eva sat and waited. 'If it was Webb,' the DCI mused after a moment, 'you must have really got to him. I don't think an investigation on its own would provoke him into doing something like that.' She turned to stare at Eva. 'So what else did you say?'

There was no point in lying. 'I told him I painted Jeffrey Cowan into a corner, which is why he killed himself. It's not the truth. I kind of embellished it.'

'To see if Webb would bite,' Sutton agreed. 'Well, he did.'

'I didn't think his first move would be attempted murder.'

Sutton turned to gaze out of the window. She seemed unusually reflective, Eva thought. The initial rage on learning someone had tried to pulverise one of her officers had subsided. It was a pattern she had seen in the Detective Chief Inspector before: fury followed by cryogenic calm and analysis. She admired it. She also recognised it in herself. 'Then you didn't think it through.'

'Ma'am?'

The DCI finally decided to sit. 'It's the mistake we all keep making with Razin's people. We expect them to act like ordinary criminals or even businesspeople because Razin's operation is organised that way. Everything is franchised. But at the end of the day Razin is Russian Mafia, and he enforces order accordingly. You just told his local manager you effectively killed one of his senior people. Whether or not that's true, word gets out. You stood up to Razin. Not simply Surrey police but you, DI Eva Harris. That's how it'll look anyway. It's not surprising Webb moved quickly. Anything else would have made him seem weak.'

Eva shuffled uncomfortably. 'I said it in his office, and only said it to him.'

'So? He'll have assumed you were saying it in other places too. He couldn't take the chance. He had to deal with you. He still has to.'

She was right, Eva had already realised that. She'd wanted to provoke a response and she had done so. Now Webb had no choice but to retaliate. 'Well, at least we know it's him.' It seemed like small consolation. She knew exactly how Sutton would respond.

'Knowing it and proving it are two totally different things, which you know full well. Do you think you can actually get HMRC and the SFO to start an investigation? That might be enough to keep him away from you for the time being.'

Another awkward subject. 'I've been in touch with some former colleagues at MPCCU.' She kept a careful eye out for Sutton's reaction as she spoke. 'He markets enough properties in their area to warrant their involvement in an investigation. Money laundering through high-value property is a significant issue for the Met too. MPCCU is in close contact with the National Cyber Crime Unit and the National Cyber Security Centre. That's the business-friendly part of GCHQ.' She paused. Sutton had not reacted. 'They're also in touch with GCHQ directly.'

'You're planning to hack Duncan Webb.'

'It's not really hacking,' Eva insisted. 'The tech-hub lead at MPCCU is just going to use the resources she has available to open his emails, texts and messages. Then she'll gain access to his laptop and mobile devices so we can examine his records. And his company's records. And his employees' records too.'

Sutton glared. 'And you have legal authority to do this?'

Eva's expression didn't change. 'I don't need it, ma'am. MPCCU will obtain that. They may argue there's a national security angle.'

'Christ's sake,' Sutton snapped, 'we're supposed to be enforcing the law, not circumventing it. It's not enough to win. We have to look like the good guys too, otherwise what's the point?'

Eva closed her eyes and pursed her lips. She knew, she damned well knew, that Sutton was right. 'It's asymmetric,' she agreed when she opened her eyes again. 'But then it's been that way for too long, and it's not been in our favour. We know the tactics groups like Razin's use to evade prosecution. We piddle around picking up low-level drug dealers while the big money gets funnelled through ostensibly legitimate pseudo-businesses we can't afford to pursue. They screw us over, time after time.' *Christ*, she thought as she spoke, *I'm starting to sound like Alastair Hadley.*

'So we start using tactics like theirs?'

'It's different,' Eva insisted. 'We dig. If there's nothing there to find, we stop digging. They keep selling and dealing and pimping and murdering. Where do you draw the line?'

Sutton looked like a Sphinx. 'Where the law says you draw it. It may be fashionable to undervalue that, but at the end of the day it's all we've got. I know Webb and the like keep coming up with ever more sophisticated scams, but if we sink to their level there's nothing left.'

'Webb just tried to kill me,' Eva reminded her. Sutton nodded.

'Prove it,' she told Eva. Not a muscle moved in her face. 'Then arrest him for it.'

The incident room seemed especially quiet when Eva walked in. Jamie and Raj's desks were empty. She assumed they were out following up on information, but apart from the brief discussion on Richmond Road she hadn't spoken with them since the evening before. Flynn was there though. She sat in front of her computer screen and frowned.

'Working late?' Eva asked.

Flynn glanced at the clock in the corner of her screen. 'Not sure. I wasn't planning to, but something just came in.'

Eva looked over her shoulder. 'Is this to do with Webb?'

Flynn rearranged windows on her desktop. 'No. I've been following up on the body parts in the old waterworks.'

The board for that investigation looked sparse, Eva thought. There was only a single photo on the board with a name written under it in blue marker. 'What have you got?'

'I pulled the info on the body Wren identified,' Flynn said. Amanda Tyler, Eva thought as she looked at the solitary photo. Victim support had been in contact with her parents. They lived in Sussex, so a local DI had picked up the horrendous job of breaking the news. 'She didn't seem particularly interesting, I'm sorry to say. She worked for a company out near Dorking, and aside from an unlucky bust there's nothing unusual about her. First thought was a sexual motive, but that doesn't come close to explaining the body parts.'

'It doesn't,' Eva agreed.

'So I tried a different tack. Wren said the spectrophotometer was worth a few quid, so I thought I'd see if I could trace it by its serial number. I tracked down the manufacturer and then the distributor. They knew all about it because they keep a record of them for servicing.' She checked her notes. 'It was something called a double beam spectrophotometer, and list price is about eight grand. They're used to identify substances by analysing the light reflected from them. Wren says they're pretty much standard equipment in any lab.'

It was a good line of enquiry, Eva thought. 'Did the distributor have a name?'

'Yes. It was sold to a pharmaceutical company for one of their research facilities. They use a number of them, which isn't unusual apparently. The end user is Swiss, but it has some of its R&D in the UK.' Flynn read from her screen. 'So Seifert Pharmaceutical does a number of prescription painkillers as bread and butter business, and more complex drugs for cancer, HIV, neurodegenerative diseases, heart disease and various vaccines.'

'Do they know if they've had one of these machines nicked?'

Flynn shook her head. 'I haven't been in touch yet; I only just got Seifert's name. I did a really quick scan of records, but it doesn't look like anybody has reported any kind of lab equipment stolen in the past couple of years, so I'm guessing not.'

Eva pulled at her lip. She couldn't see the connection. 'It doesn't exactly sound promising,' she told Flynn.

'It didn't,' Flynn agreed. 'Until I found out that Seifert is the company where Amanda Tyler was working when she disappeared.'

–

The text from Savini pinged on her phone a little after three in the morning. She was awake anyway. The picture of Amanda Tyler had permeated into her brain, and refused to go away. This was the picture on the whiteboard in the incident room thankfully, Eva thought as she stared at the ceiling, which had been taken from the missing person's report filed by her parents. Not the image of the dissected face suspended in formaldehyde. She supposed she had to be grateful for small mercies.

New Thought, Metal Box Storage, Amanda Tyler, now Seifert Pharmaceutical. Four almost disconnected data points attached only by the most tenuous of threads. She imagined Venn diagrams drawn on the ceiling of her bedroom, or network graphs with pitifully few nodes and links. Eva understood the logic though. When you turned the probabilities on their head, the chances of those data-points appearing in the same investigation and not being connected became vanishingly small.

She rolled out of bed, padded into the kitchen and opened the fridge door. She found a carton of milk, took several large gulps from it and then walked through to her living room, to slump on the sofa and watch the world beyond the window. Nothing moved. In the sky outside there were no planes. The one-way system was empty, and the only change in an otherwise static landscape was a traffic light cycling inexorably through its three-colour spectrum.

*Ping.* It was the low-frequency sound of a sonar beacon from a movie, the sound effect she had for no particular reason chosen as the tone for text message alerts. She could ignore it, she supposed as she slouched on the sofa and stared out the window. It could wait until morning. A text at this time of night was not usual though; otherwise she would have set her phone to silent. Eva stomped back into her bedroom and picked up the glowing screen. Savini, she saw.

*I've had a reply*, the message read. *He'll talk to you, but we have to meet on his terms. I'll get my office to book flights. We only get one chance. Can you leave today?*

It took her several seconds to process the text. Why the urgency? So Savini had a contact. Was it significant? Did it warrant getting on a plane to somewhere and talking to someone who couldn't be bothered to get their arse down to a police station for a formal interview? For a moment it annoyed her. Then Eva thought about Savini again. She wasn't stupid. She wouldn't waste police time intentionally. Eva thumb-typed a response. *Where?*

Three grey dots animated in the bottom left of the screen. Savini was typing. When she saw the reply she felt instantly awake. Another circle in her Venn diagram, an additional data-point in her graph. A coincidence in itself perhaps, but when put beside the few sparse facts she already had it looked too similar. It seemed like synaesthesia, she imagined as she re-read the message. It had almost the same flavour.

*We'll fly into Lucerne,* Savini wrote, *then get a taxi. Falkenblick is a two-hour drive. Pack for a couple of days. Have you ever been to Switzerland?*

## Chapter Fifteen

The man almost shook with excitement. The printout in his hand showed a summary, but he had needed to read it four times before the implications sank in. The DNA methylation levels in the CpG sites, where cytosine nucleotides were followed by a guanine nucleotide in a linear sequence of bases, all corresponded. The presence of recombinant human growth hormone had been detected. The biological age tests were positive. He had measured 'Horvath's clock', the 353 markers that recorded DNA methylation of those CpG dinucleotides, and they were out. The GrimAge and DNAm PhenoAge analysis matched, and they were wrong. Chronological age, he thought as he stared down at the bound and naked figure of Michael Conroy, didn't correspond with epigenetic age. Ergo, he thought as he prised the tape from Conroy's mouth, he had received the treatment.

He had been looking in the wrong place. Of course he had, it was obvious now. The subjects he had suspected, Naomi Gray, Lewis Ashley and all the others, had been young, fit and healthy. He had imagined they would be likely candidates because of proximity, favouritism, nepotism, wealth, promise, sex or some other social factor. How naïve that assumption had been; he saw that now. Conroy was fifty-five years old, of Afro-Caribbean descent with greying hair and a medical history of back problems. Of course he was a more likely candidate, he thought as held the printout under the light. The effects of the treatment would be more obvious in him. The summary had a conclusion. It was a simple table, containing only four cells.

Known chronological age, the header in the first column read. Under that was a number, 55, as expected. Epigenetic age, the second column said. Under that was a different number: 43.

*Forty-three.* There was no way Conroy, a moderately unfit individual with a family history of heart disease, could possibly have a biological age twelve years younger than his chronological age. He simply could not be that healthy. He had been given the treatment. It was the only explanation. More than that. The treatment had worked.

'You've been taking drugs,' he told Conroy. 'You've been given drugs,' he corrected himself. 'Don't deny it.'

Conroy seemed confused. Confused by sedatives, he assumed. He could hardly blame him for that. 'Why should I deny it?' Conroy slurred. 'I'm at high risk of atherosclerosis, there's a genetic predisposition. I'm working with the biotech team. It's a clinical trial.'

Rage surged within him. For a moment he felt the urge to smash Conroy's face, to tell him not to lie, to jam electrodes into his balls and hear him scream himself to death, but he forced himself to stop. It was possible, he thought, conceivable, that he might be telling the truth, from his perspective anyway. With hindsight Conroy seemed like an ideal test subject, and better than that, he had a reason to volunteer. Would she have concealed the truth from him? Would she have kept the true nature of the treatment to herself? The more he thought about it, the more likely, and predictably underhand, the idea seemed.

'What drugs do you take?'

'Why do you want to know? Why am I here? It's a trial for atherosclerosis for Christ's sake. It's never going to be worth that much. It sure as hell isn't worth kidnapping anyone for.'

He thought he had kidnapped him because of a medical treatment for atherosclerosis. How ridiculous that would have been. If Conroy was lying, he admitted to himself, then he was good at it, because the sedatives alone would have loosened his tongue. 'Just tell me,' he insisted. He kept his voice quiet and reasonable though. Perhaps he was a little in awe. Michael Conroy was unique.

'Recombinant human growth hormone,' Conroy said. 'A bunch of others, I can't remember them. Three times a week.'

'How long for?'

'Six months.'

*Six months!* If he had to bet, if he had been forced to place money, he would have wagered Conroy's starting genetic age was closer to sixty than fifty-five. A seventeen-year reduction in epigenetic age in six *bloody* months. He could hardly believe it. And yet the evidence was right in front of him.

Was Conroy lying? He doubted it. Conroy was a scientist, but it would be simple enough to mislead him if information was falsified in a consistent manner. Did it matter? Probably not, he thought as he checked the printout again. How far had she gone? How many others were there like Conroy? Was he phase two? Had she completed the proof of concept? Was she now commercialising the treatment? He shivered with excitement then; he could not stop himself, even though he knew Conroy was watching him. That must be her plan. The first stage anyway, where she sold the treatment to those able to pay millions for it. She needed people like Conroy to test on, to prove that it worked. And it did. He had the proof in his hand.

'We're not getting any younger,' he muttered to himself. Except, it would appear, that for Michael Conroy this was no longer true. Reversal of epigenetic ageing through recombinant hormone therapy, in order to slow down and even reverse the rate of cellular decay in the body. Another thought occurred to him. Perhaps it was not a complete lie. Perhaps that would also have a positive impact on atherosclerosis.

It didn't matter, he thought as he set the printouts down next to the scanner; it made no difference. He had been right all along. And Michael Conroy was one of the very few human beings in the history of the species who actually was getting younger.

He did feel awe. It was an incredible achievement, even if she wanted to keep it only for herself and those like her. Conroy was almost unique.

It was with the greatest of respect that he picked up a scalpel, lifted Conroy's chin, and cut his throat.

# Part II

*Gilgamesh Syndrome*

# Chapter Sixteen

*Ten hours later*

The road crossed Lake Lucerne at Stansstad and continued to wind through the Alps. She knew, because Savini had told her, that their destination lay near Andermatt in the Usurn Valley. 'It's on Nätschen,' Savini had said, referring to a mountain, 'but it's only at about eighteen-hundred metres.'

Eva had raised her eyebrows. 'Does this involve skiing?'

Savini had smiled. 'No. Just a taxi.'

The flight from London City had taken an hour and a half. When Eva had told Sutton about Savini's contact, the DCI had seemed almost relieved. 'So this takes you out of the country for a couple of days?'

'It will do,' she had admitted. She hadn't anticipated Sutton's response.

'That'll keep you off Webb's radar for a bit.' Eva had opened her mouth. Then she had shut it again.

Savini had arranged everything, or at least her office had. Eva turned up at London City on a DLR train in trainers with a rucksack. Savini had valet parking for her Porsche. She had glanced at Eva's clothes when she met her at security. 'Don't worry,' Savini had said. 'It's Switzerland.' Eva had no clue what that was supposed to mean, but it didn't seem the time to ask.

The flight was with an independent operator that Savini's company used. You couldn't book direct through the usual sites, Eva had discovered after a cursory search. Everything else was funnelled through Zurich. She counted around a dozen other people on the small jet. When she went to ask Savini a question about their destination, though, Savini had simply put a finger to her lips.

'This is going on expenses,' Savini explained when they had left the airport in the back of a large black Mercedes. 'My boss won't care.'

'Surrey police don't have to pay for this?'

Savini shrugged. 'My company makes a great deal of money. It's about time we gave a little back.' That was the end of the matter, it appeared, because Savini refused to discuss it again.

Eva glanced at the back of the driver's head. He didn't appear to speak English. 'So why are we here?'

This was something else Savini had not wanted to discuss on the plane, where there was a chance they might have been overheard. 'If all goes well, you're here to meet Jonathon Crane. I'm going to leave him to tell you about himself.' She glanced at Eva, but now she wasn't smiling. 'I wouldn't do him justice. It wouldn't be helpful.' Then she added, 'and it wouldn't be right.'

'So what does Crane know?'

'He knows about the transhumanist sect within New Thought. He's a part of that, inasmuch as he's a part of anything. Maybe it's more accurate to say he's sympathetic to them.' Savini shrugged again. A look of dejection settled on her. 'I don't know how he copes with it, I really don't. I don't think I could. It must take real strength.' She shook her head. 'Sorry, I'm getting ahead of things. Like I said, I'll let Crane tell you.'

The car glided south. The Alps were all around them, as far as Eva could see, picture-postcard mountains that encompassed the landscape and formed a seemingly impenetrable wall against the horizon. Eighteen hundred metres was nothing, she knew that. The mountain they were going to topped out a kilometre higher, but there were dozens whose peaks passed through the four-thousand-metre line. In the distance she could see banks of cloud wrapped around necks of summits white with snow. A clear blue sky arched over them all.

Crystal clear air. That was the first thing she had noticed when they left the city. The Swiss were obsessed with it. They had stopped briefly on the road for Savini to rescue a pair of designer sunglasses from her hand luggage, and Eva had stood by the car for a moment to take in the view. Even the silence had seemed pristine.

'Crane will be at this place, Falkenblick?'

Savini nodded. 'Kind of. Falkenblick is a spa, for the most part. It has a huge range of therapies and a fantastic location. You'll love it,' she assured Eva, 'but that's not the point. They also have workshops. They do actual research on-site, into healthcare and all sorts of medical things. That's why Crane comes here. He gets involved; he's as much a researcher as he is a patient.'

The fragments of information were starting to annoy Eva, but she knew Savini was only trying to keep her facts straight. She assumed she would get the whole picture when she finally met this Jonathon Crane, of whom Savini seemed almost reverential. 'What kind of spa does research?'

'In Switzerland? A few. I mean, they do the real R&D in proper laboratories, but all the big cosmetic firms try out their most important new products on spa customers first, once they're past the clinical trial stage. Anti-ageing creams, top-of-the-line moisturisers, that kind of thing. It's basically market research. They check out customer reactions, price-point, all the usual stuff. It's done really tastefully though; it's not as if you're a guinea pig or anything like that.'

Eva chewed that over for a few moments. 'So Falkenblick is run by a cosmetics firm?'

Savini shook her head. 'Drug company. They're more into health products than cosmetics.'

She felt a slight tingling along the line of her neck. It might have been the unnecessary air-conditioning in the car. 'A drug company?'

'They've got offices in the UK,' Savini told her. 'They're called Seifert Pharmaceutical.'

Her first view of Falkenblick took her by surprise, which was clearly the intention. She supposed she had been expecting a blocky pastiche of a Bauhaus building jammed like a bunker into the mountainside, or perhaps some sloping-roofed Swiss chateau perched like a cuckoo clock overlooking the valley below. Eva only supposed that, because when she came to think about it she realised she'd had no expectations whatsoever. Whatever she might have imagined, though, it would not have included a cluster of intermeshed geodesic shapes growing limpet-like from the side of the mountain, overlapping and intertwined until they melded in to one chaotic whole. Afternoon sunshine sparked and flared on mirrored glass. The spa looked either like an outpost on another planet, the work of a mad architect or some vast crystal formation; Eva couldn't make up her mind. One thing it certainly looked was expensive.

The car drew to a halt in front of a slate reception area, protected from the world outside by thick walls made of glass. When she stepped from the car, Eva realised the walls were placed in diagonals that protected the entrance from the freezing Alpine wind. A stone awning hung over them. Though it couldn't actually be stone, she thought as the driver carried their hand luggage through the glass divide, because the weight would have been incredible. Rainbows shimmered in the air. Slate above and below, and the rest of it felt like walking through the middle of a prism.

'This place is insane.'

Savini nodded. 'Icelandic architect. He actually did go mad not long after he finished it. If you think this is crazy wait until you see the pool.'

–

She didn't see how her case got from reception to her room before she did. Maybe it just teleported, she thought as the door

113

closed behind her. It sat on a rack at the foot of a vast bed, an untidy lump of black plastic in an otherwise white room. Eva had to ignore it. The view of the mountains from the faceted glass wall behind her bed took her breath away.

When she eventually stopped staring, the next thing she did was phone the incident room at the station. It felt like making a direct-dial call from another planet. Flynn answered. 'Good hotel?'

'Not bad.' It didn't seem fair to tell her just how good. 'Something you need to know though. Apparently, this place is owned by Seifert Pharmaceutical.'

She heard the intake of breath. 'Christ. I knew drug companies made shed-loads of money, but that's crazy.'

'It's not a hotel, not as such. They call it a spa and I don't think they're just being coy. I've been told they use it to try out new treatments on guests prepared to pay top prices for them. That's not the point.'

'It's Seifert again,' Flynn agreed.

'What have you got?'

She heard Flynn shuffling files, both physical and digital. 'Nothing you couldn't find on the Internet or in an annual Report and Accounts. Seifert was originally a Swiss pharmaceutical company, but they have the usual network of subsidiaries dotted all over the place now. The corporate headquarters is still in Geneva, but that's just like the registered office. Sales and marketing is in the US for the most part, but product development is split between Switzerland and the UK. I did a search,' Flynn told her, although that much was obvious. 'Seifert come in at number thirty in the list of the most valuable pharmaceutical companies in the world. Their turnover is around seven and a half billion US dollars. By comparison the number one's turnover was seventy billion. But do you know, out of the entire list I only recognised two or three names. I added them all up. It comes to about three quarters of a *trillion* dollars turnover every year, and I didn't know most of them even existed.'

'It's crazy,' Eva agreed, 'all the stuff that's hidden in plain sight. Anything obviously dodgy?'

Flynn scoffed. 'These companies are so big that's like asking if there's anything obviously dodgy in Scotland. You could probably find anything you liked.'

She had realised how futile the question was almost as soon as she asked it. 'Keep digging please,' Eva told Flynn. 'Focus on Seifert's UK business and the office Amanda Tyler worked at. Grab Raj or Jamie and go take a look. Don't piss them off, not yet,' she added. 'It might just be coincidence.'

Eva heard the scepticism in Flynn's voice. 'Really?'

'Not really,' she agreed, 'but they may not be the guilty party. To say this is looking complicated is an understatement. Let's just keep an open mind, okay?'

Flynn acquiesced. 'Okay,' she said. 'What are you going to do?'

'I'm going to look around here, see what I can find out.' She knew she sounded evasive.

'In a spa.' Flynn observed. 'In Switzerland.'

'I'll bring you back some essential oils,' Eva promised.

'Thank you so much,' Flynn said. Her voice was flat and toneless. Eva could imagine the other phrases that were tumbling through her mind. 'By the way,' she said before Eva could hang up, 'I did find out one other thing about Seifert from their website.'

'Go on?'

'It's a publicly listed company, but the majority shareholder is still the founder. Arnaud Seifert is still chairman.'

'Okay,' Eva said. It was interesting, but it didn't seem especially relevant. 'Chairman is sometimes something of an honorary position. Who actually runs the company?'

There was a brief pause. 'That would be his daughter,' Flynn said. 'The Managing Director is Anna Seifert.'

## Chapter Seventeen

Eva met Savini in an ethereal corridor that bridged two geodesic domes, glass walls lit by a reflection of virgin snow that covered the ground ten metres beneath them. 'Crane will see you first thing tomorrow,' Savini told her as she stared out at fir trees covered by a pristine, fractal blanket. 'He'll be in touch.'

'You're not coming?' She frowned at Savini. The ubiquitous white light chased shadows from the corridor and from their faces.

'I'm not invited,' Savini said. 'Don't worry. That's not unusual and it's not Crane being difficult. He's just extremely focused.' She didn't know what to say to that, but Savini didn't seem concerned. 'In the meantime,' Savini said, taking her by the elbow, 'we should enjoy some of what Falkenblick has to offer.'

That didn't feel as though it was going to be a hardship. 'Such as?'

'There's a progressive level of therapies. It starts with the usual aromatherapy and whole-body massage.' Savini paused. 'Then there are the more advanced treatments. Plasmapheresis, for example.' Eva watched Savini's face. 'Blood filtering,' Savini explained. 'Basically, extracting the blood from the body and filtering it to remove toxins that contribute to ageing.'

She had to let that sink in. 'You do that voluntarily? Isn't that like elective surgery?'

Savini laughed. 'So there are needles involved, sure, but they put you under a sun lamp at the same time. It's very relaxing and you feel great afterwards.'

Eva wasn't convinced. 'It doesn't sound relaxing to me.'

'Sure, small steps to begin with,' Savini told her. 'I guess we'll just start with the spa then.'

She led Eva to a cedar-wood counter that stood at the entrance to what she assumed was a changing room. From behind the counter an elegant blonde woman with her hair swept up in a bun furnished them with towels. Savini led the way into the changing room. More wood, Eva noticed. On the walls, on the lockers, the benches, everything blended. She sniffed the air. The scent of pine was everywhere. Savini dropped her towel next to a locker and started to undress.

She suddenly realised the problem. 'I didn't bring a swim-suit,' Eva told her. 'Can I buy one?' The thought of not being able to experience the spa suddenly disappointed her more than she had expected. Savini laughed.

'Darling,' she said as she put her clothes into a locker and stood naked in the middle of the changing room, 'it's Switzer-land. Swimsuits aren't merely frowned upon, they're positively verboten.'

–

She didn't know why she felt uncomfortable. Savini took her by the elbow and they walked through the door at the end of the changing room into another corridor, this time one with a number of glass-walled chambers leading from it. The rooms were filled with steam. Eva draped her towel over her shoulder and clenched her jaw. God's sake, it wasn't as if she had anything to be embarrassed about. She worked out, she knew she had a dancer's physique, the only blemish on her was the scar that ran from her groin almost to her knee, but even that had faded a little over the past couple of years. Perhaps she was more concerned about the social etiquette of nudity. If you met someone, was it rude to stare? For a moment she thought she was going to laugh, but then Savini directed her into one of the glass chambers and the urge evaporated.

The heat was stifling. Steam took her breath away; she felt dizzy and needed to sit. The scent of eucalyptus almost overwhelmed her. Her skin erupted in sweat. Savini sat next to her, but the initial effect didn't last long. After a few moments Eva realised they weren't alone.

In amongst the clouds of steam she counted seven other people in the chamber, men and women, all naked and all uninterested by this fact. With their slim, athletic builds and toned bodies, they reminded her of Savini and her carefully manicured perfection. She caught a man staring at her through the clouds of steam. She stared right back. When she did he smiled and nodded his head, almost as if he was an acquaintance she had just passed on a street. He was not, Eva thought as she tore her eyes away and gazed at the other people in the room. Unhandsome, none of them were.

They sat for ten minutes. People came and went; nobody spoke. After ten minutes Savini stretched, flicked sweat from her body and said she was going to take a shower. Eva followed. She couldn't decide if she felt like a lost puppy or a stranger in a strange land, but whatever she was she didn't yet feel confident enough to explore the spa on her own. She knew Savini's tastes. She had seen them before. God alone knew what she might run in to.

The showers were mixed, but she was beginning to get used to that. After the initial shock, the impact of seeing so many naked people was beginning to subside. Three other women and two men came into the shower room. They smiled and nodded politely, washed themselves and then moved on.

Eva caught Savini watching her, a curious smile on her face. 'How are you finding it?' she asked.

'It's fine,' Eva told her. 'I guess my British prudishness doesn't run as deep as I imagined. Is the whole spa like this?'

'The spa is,' Savini said as she rinsed soap from her hair, 'but the treatment centres aren't. Those are more like medical facilities. You can get your blood cleaned while lying on a sun lounger, but you can also go for whole-body scans and other diagnostic tests. They'll do everything from check your amount of body fat to sequence your DNA for genetic disorders.'

'And Seifert Pharmaceutical do all this?'

'Seifert Biotech,' Savini corrected her. 'It's the research and development subsidiary.'

–

The spa complex was spectacular; that was the only way she could describe it to herself. After a while, wandering naked in amongst so many other good-looking, well-toned and equally naked people became passé. What she was not able to feel unimpressed by, and what held a particular fascination for her, was the pool.

She had noticed Savini watching her again as they walked into the dome that held the pool, obviously in anticipation of a reaction. Eva didn't think she disappointed. She felt her jaw drop as she realised the body of water that seemed almost to hang in the air was in fact made from glass walls and a glass floor that looked out and down over the mountain's edge.

'Is that safe?' she blurted at Savini as she stared into the water.

Savini laughed. 'Everybody asks that. They tell you the walls are twenty centimetres thick and the supports could hold up a skyscraper. It's perfectly safe. It's amazing, isn't it?'

Eva couldn't argue. The water was the temperature of blood. When she dived under the surface it was like flying into some other space, a fluid domain that brought back memories that even now she didn't feel ready to explore. What, she wondered as she stared out at the shapes of mountains beyond the water, would Mathew Harred make of this?

She swam, skirted the bottom, watched the world outside and the aquiline shapes of swimmers as they too dived to take in the view. Eva stayed in the pool far longer than she had intended. When she finally climbed out she dried herself, slung her towel over her shoulder and went looking for Savini.

Eva found her on a lounger, sunglasses on, basking in the late afternoon sun. She was about to ask where they could go next when she noticed tubes running from needles in each arm. The tubes ran to a machine next to the lounger, and a nurse stood nearby in discreet attendance. Blood filled the tubes. Savini lay with eyes closed, and a slight smile on her face.

-

They met for dinner in a restaurant with faceted windows that reached far above them. A crescent moon focused its light on jagged peaks outside. Savini looked elegant. She wore a blue silk dress. Eva had on a black T-shirt, jogging bottoms and trainers. Some people had dressed the way she had; others wore outfits that were more like Savini's. Nobody cared. They wore what suited their mood. It was the kind of confidence that came with affluence, Eva realised. She had no idea how much a suite at Falkenblick might cost, and she suspected she would be horrified if she ever found out, but it was obvious that, for the people here, money was not their primary concern. The thought made her uncomfortable. It made the police officer in her wake up and pay attention once again.

'So tell me about Seifert,' she asked Savini while they munched on something vegan.

'I don't know a lot. I've met Arnaud a couple of times. He's the founder and the chairman. He's a very clever man, but you could work that out for yourself.'

'Is he connected to New Thought?'

Savini nodded. 'Yes, but I think it's more an alignment of interests with the transhumanists than a specific involvement. A lot of what Seifert does, and Seifert Biotech in particular, is exactly the sort of thing they're interested in.'

'Which is?'

'God,' Savini said, 'it's quite a list. Anti-senescence, cognitive enhancement, mechanical implants, nanotechnology, interfacing with artificial intelligence – and that's just some of the more mundane concepts. Biohacking is a big one; anything involving altering DNA to prevent ageing, or changing the folding of proteins to prevent disease, or gene editing to prevent synapse loss and neurodegeneration. So is the idea of backing up your consciousness to hardware in some way.'

'It sounds,' Eva ventured, 'a bit far-fetched?'

'Of course it is,' Savini agreed. She reached into her pocket and put her top-of-the-range smartphone on the table. 'How far-fetched would that have seemed to someone in 1999?' She had a point. Eva knew about technology S-curves and how new developments could explode into the market, seemingly from nowhere. 'Fereidoun M. Esfandiary was an early proponent. He changed his name to FM-2030 in the mid-1970s, but died in 2000. They deep-froze his body. It's in a facility in Arizona somewhere apparently, waiting for the day his brain patterns can be scanned and imprinted into a clone.' She kept a completely straight face as she spoke.

'Right,' Eva said after several moments' silence. 'Are you going to have your body deep frozen when you die?'

Savini couldn't maintain the pretence any longer, and burst out laughing. 'What, and have somebody shove a stick up my arse and use me for a lollipop? Hell no. I plan to live a long, debauched life and exit at the proper time.'

Eva licked her lips. 'You were doing that blood-cleaning thing though.'

'Sure. But biotechnology is about health-span nowadays, not lifespan. Stay fit and healthy until you croak it, not stuck in some old people's home with a nurse wiping your backside. It's becoming big business, and Seifert are on the leading edge.' Eva caught another note in her voice then, and she saw another side to Savini. Not a hedonist or a transhumanist, although she doubted Savini was that, but a hard-nosed businesswoman seeking alpha.

The food was excellent, as she had expected, and broadly devoid of calories. They sat in a bar afterwards. Eva sipped on a glass of full-fat Pinot Grigio; Savini had vodka with Diet Coke. 'And Crane?'

'Crane is,' Savini said, as the alcohol loosened her tongue, 'different. He's both a patient and a brilliant researcher, which is why Seifert values his work. Don't let him scare you,' she said as she swirled her second drink. 'Deep down, he's a sweetie.'

There didn't seem any point in asking any more questions. She could tell Savini would only continue to be evasive, and in any event she would have her answers in just a few hours. Scratch that, Eva thought. There was just one other obvious question she needed to ask. 'How do I find him?'

'Somebody will take you to the Research Centre,' Savini said. 'Don't worry about it. He'll find you.' She tossed back her drink, set her glass on the table and stood up. 'I'm going for a quick swim before bed,' she told Eva. 'Coming?'

Eva knew where it was leading, but an almost insatiable curiosity overcame her. She followed Savini back to the spa. There was no attendant on duty, but the pile of fresh towels seemed limitless. They walked through into the changing room, undressed and then wandered into the corridor.

Savini had downed two large vodka and Cokes in fairly short order. Eva had only managed to get halfway through her glass of wine. She watched Savini prowl. She stalked between the steam rooms as though hunting, which, Eva thought, she almost certainly was. And if she was, she thought as she followed her, she seemed to have come to the right place.

There were fewer people in the spa at that time of the evening. The attendants stopped working at ten, but the pool, the saunas and the steam room were accessible right through the night, which seemed like tacit permission. The guests obviously took it as such. It wasn't long before she saw a couple up against the glass of one of the steam rooms, arms and legs wrapped around each other, screwing slowly in the broiling clouds.

They weren't alone. They found three more couples in the sauna, sweating and slick, bodies entangled. Savini grinned. She seemed almost feral, as though her mind had switched off and she was completely under the control of her body chemistry. The couples in the steam room didn't seem to interest her especially. She kept hunting.

It was as if sex was the inexorable consequence of the place, Eva thought. Good-looking people in close, intimate proximity; the outcome seemed inevitable. And who would not want to, in such luxurious surroundings? The spa was deliberately enticing, the environment intentionally sensual, and the invitation open. Once the staff have gone, it seemed to imply, feel free to do what you like.

By the pool it seemed Savini had found what she was looking for. A group of a dozen strangers enjoying each other in gradually shifting permutations on the edge of, and in, the water. Savini walked slowly up to them, lowered herself into the pool and put one arm around a man's neck, the other around a woman. Eva saw her shudder, like a heroin addict taking a long-overdue hit. The three of them moved together. Savini kissed them both on the mouths, and then lowered her head. She stopped for a moment then, as if belatedly remembering Eva, and looked up again. The expression on her face was unambiguous. *Come and join us*, it said.

She had to admit it to herself. She was tempted. The desire to drop into the water and stop thinking, to give in to whatever urges came over her was something she didn't know if she could resist. And did she need to resist? For Christ's sake, nobody but Savini would ever know. Savini, who was currently fucking her first couple and who didn't look like she was about to stop any time soon; of all people, her secret would be safe with Savini. She almost convinced herself. Eva also found herself walking slowly towards the pool.

One of the other women slipped under the water, just for a moment. When she looked down, Eva saw her face, eyes closed, and a mass of dark hair drifting in the current. She had to close her own eyes then as the puritanical streak in her conscience seemed to wake up. It wasn't sex that had awakened it, not even Savini's unbridled, almost desperate, promiscuity. It was the work ethic in her. The image of Amanda Tyler would not disappear.

*You're here to do a job,* she told herself, as the woman broke the surface and immediately slipped into the arms of a new partner. *That's all. Anything else is a betrayal.*

With almost painful reluctance, Eva turned her back and walked away.

# Chapter Eighteen

She woke to a tapping on her door. The room was dark, almost pitch black. When she remembered where she was she coughed and told the room's voice assistant to clear the windows. Liquid crystal panels on faceted panes faded slowly from black to transparency, and like an incoming tide, morning sunlight flooded in.

Eva dragged a sheet around her and stumbled to the door. A pleasant-faced Swiss woman delivered room service, a prescribed healthy breakfast that came with a note. '8am,' it read. 'Research Centre.' It was signed: 'Crane'.

She sat on the side of her bed, half wrapped in her sheet, and sipped black coffee. She wondered if Savini had made it back to her room. The woman was clearly driven, had an overwhelming need. Her lust had seemed nothing short of insatiable. And yet it was not simply about sex with Savini, Eva thought as she took in the heavy, dark aroma. It was something more communal than that. About being part of a group, both a centre of attention and anonymous at the same time. What drove her? Were the demons in her childhood or in her present? Was it the ennui of a woman who was so successful in her own right she found it hard to meet equals, at least ones she liked, or was it a reaction against that success? Was it simply mindless distraction, animalistic gratification as a counterpoint to the constant, sly manoeuvring and positioning of complex trading? A way of letting off steam with like-minded people in yet another safe environment? And if it was, Eva thought, what did that say about her?

Last night she had been tempted. The truth was she had never thought of herself as anything other than uncomplicated, but last night, and for that matter at Berta Nicholson's party, she had felt an almost overwhelming urge to connect with anyone, in whatever physical combination was available. She was not prejudiced in any way, but there were certain tropes she had just not seen herself fitting in to. Was she wrong? Was it just a combination of stress and dazzling surroundings, and being surrounded by dazzling people? The sight of the woman underwater, whose drifting hair had so reminded her of the flayed face of Amanda Tyler, was all that had stopped her. Should it have? Should she have given in? Was the excuse that she was here on work just that, a pretence to prevent her from engaging in actions she was by no means certain she was ready for? It seemed academic now. The opportunity was hours in the past.

Eva bared her teeth and ripped the end off a gluten-free croissant. Seven-forty, her phone told her. She just about had time. Dumping the tray on the bed, she stalked off towards the shower. *Better make it cold*, she thought as she dropped the sheet on the floor.

—

Eva asked about the Research Centre at reception. Almost instantly a man appeared like a be-suited genie and indicated she should follow him. Forty-something, medium height, medium build, he didn't speak but led her on a brisk walk through sections of the spa where elegant people sat, talked and admired the view from panoramic windows. At the back of the inter-linked domes he took her to a door that opened with an eight-digit pin code. Behind the door lay a corridor that was over fifty metres long, snaking, featureless, and lit by regularly placed globes of light. At the end of it was another door and another eight-digit pin code. When she looked back Eva noticed black glass disks that concealed CCTV cameras.

She stepped through the door. The area she found herself in seemed a complete contrast to the spa. It was functional, utilitarian. The only thing the two spaces had in common was scale.

The man left her there. She stood alone in a space the size of a sports hall, with racks and tables placed in seemingly random locations around it. There were rooms off the central hall. Some of them looked like more traditional laboratories, or clean environments at least. One had the appearance of an operating theatre, the kind of place where minor outpatient procedures might be performed. The rooms all had glass windows that opened onto the hall, but a few of them had blinds drawn down over them. There were people in the rooms, only three or four, and they all seemed engaged in quiet, solitary activities.

Eva walked slowly across the hall, absorbing each detail of the space. When she reached the far end she found a screened-off area that looked like a small gym. There, in amongst the weights, she found Jonathan Crane.

She must have gasped, albeit quietly. In that moment she fully understood Savini's reticence. Crane was complicated. That much was immediately obvious.

He stood in the middle of the screened-off area, a gymnasium weight held in his left arm. Even from a dozen paces away she could read the markings. Crane appeared to be holding a hundred and fifty kilos in the air with no obvious effort. That was both unsurprising and confusing, because the arm that held the weight was completely artificial. As, Eva noted, was a substantial part of Crane's body.

He wore only a black singlet and a pair of black shorts. Close to two metres tall, his torso, right arm and upper legs were powerfully muscled, as though he spent much of his time lifting weights. The rest of him though. Eva had seen accident victims and amputees before, but Crane seemed unique.

The left arm was prosthetic from the shoulder, and so were his legs from below the knees. Part of his scalp was shaved.

There seemed to be a metal plate that covered a section of the left side of his skull. Scar tissue, everywhere. The result of burns and lesions, she had to assume. Rough stubble covered his chin, and the hair that remained was thick and dark. Crane was in his mid-thirties, she guessed. She wondered if that number still held any meaning for him.

It was the prostheses that surprised her most though. It wasn't only his artificial limbs, there were other attachments, cables and hoists that entangled him. When she absorbed the rest of the space, she saw that not all of the equipment was from a gym. Some of it was mechanical, the kind of machinery she associated with industrial robots. As she watched, Crane swung the weight, slowly. A mechanical arm as tall as he was, painted green with the manufacturers' name emblazoned on its side, took the weight from him, rotated through a hundred and eighty degrees, and set it down on a spot on the floor marked out by yellow-and-black hazard tape. Crane lowered his arm. It was only then he seemed to notice her.

He turned his head slightly and gave her a brief, sideways glance. 'Royal Engineers,' he told her. His voice was deep and terse. 'Afghan, IED, all the usual stuff. Any other questions?'

Plenty, Eva thought. After the initial shock, the sight of Crane filled her with immediate fascination. What was she looking at? What was he doing? The combination of gym equipment and industrial machinery set the tone straight away. Crane seemed to be testing the limits of his own strength, but why the robot arm? He was obviously expecting some well-meaning but ultimately vacuous comment, perhaps pointless sympathy for his condition. That would plainly have irritated him; she could tell that from the barely tolerant sideways glance. Which was fine, Eva thought. It didn't interest her either. Whereas the detail of what she was seeing certainly did. 'Yes,' she said, as she moved closer to him. She jabbed a finger at the shoulder joint of his prosthetic arm. 'How the hell does that not sheer off?'

A trace of a smile flickered on his face. 'Good question,' he conceded. She knew it was. She was no mechanical engineer, but Eva knew a single point of failure when she saw one. 'The weight's about enough to tear the arm off,' he told her as he started unclipping cables from his left arm, 'hence the frame.' He pointed to the support struts she now saw clipped to the prosthetic. 'It connects to the legs and transfers most of the force into the floor. It's clumsy,' he told her, 'and it's not ready for use in the field, but it basically works.'

Now she was closer she could see the details in the construction of his arm. It was unlike any prosthetic limb she had ever seen. The pneumatic rams looked as though they came from another piece of industrial machinery. It was clearly not a practical piece of equipment. She also recognised a three-phase electrical cable that ran from the top of his arm to a transformer in the corner of the screened-off area. 'And this?' Eva said, walking towards the robot arm.

'Wait,' Crane told her, voice suddenly sharp. 'Let me take this off.' He reached up with his right hand and pulled a plastic strap from his forehead. When he did so the robot arm sagged to the ground.

It took her a moment to understand, but when she did so she felt sudden, almost childish excitement. 'Is that actually BCI?' Eva demanded.

Crane nodded, peered at the back of the slender headset and powered it down. A Brain-Computer Interface. She had read about them but never seen one. Eva knew the headset would read electrical patterns near the surface of the brain and convert some of them into actions.

'It's crude,' Crane told her. 'It's a bit like pushing a mouse with your nose, but it works.' He passed her the headset. It felt light; most of it would sit on the left side of the head, and sensors on curved arms reached out to touch the forehead and three other locations around the skull. 'The robot is intended to be a collaborative system. I'm looking at whether you can augment that with workers using prosthetics. Like a third arm.'

'So you're not telling the robot what to do,' she ventured, 'you're just using BCI to trigger sequences?'

He nodded, a slow and grave gesture. 'Exactly. It's like pressing the "now pick up this" button, but without needing to use your hands.'

God, she wanted to know more. 'Did you code the interface yourself?'

Crane nodded. 'It's not the most efficient.' He waited.

She couldn't resist. 'I could take a look. I'm good with design patterns.'

'A cop who codes,' Crane said. 'Charlotte said you were unusual.' He carried on unclipping his arm. When it was detached, he set it down on a workbench and picked up a more normal-looking prosthetic. 'My design, 3D printed,' he told her. He gave her that sideways look again, but this time it came with a twisted, mischievous grin. 'You've probably noticed I'm into body-building.'

## Chapter Nineteen

They sat in front of a screen in one of the rooms that led from the hall. Crane's programming wasn't bad, but Eva could see plenty of ways to improve it. He watched her as she cut, pasted and annotated his code. There were a few thousand lines of it when she started. With care, and through paying attention to the rigidly methodical way in which she had been taught to structure objects and classes, she thought she should be able to halve that.

'You're here for a reason,' Crane said after a while.

Eva nodded as she refactored his work. 'Savini said you were loosely connected to New Thought. Did you ever meet Mathew Harred?'

'Loosely,' Crane agreed. 'And no. I only heard about him after he was arrested. Why do you want to know?'

She told him about the body parts in the disused building as she typed, how they had been found, how they were laid out and, perhaps of most importance, how they were lit. Crane listened in silence, motionless, brow furrowed. Even though his face gave nothing away, she could tell he understood the reason for her visit was not trivial. 'Savini spoke about the transhumanists, and Harred mentioned a name,' she said once she had told him everything else she could think of. 'Derzelas.'

Crane kept frowning. 'Did Harred say what it meant?'

'Nothing,' Eva admitted. 'He only gave me the name.'

'But you think the transhumanist sect within New Thought has something to do with these body parts?'

She glanced at him. 'It's an obvious conclusion, isn't it? I'm not saying that makes it right, but it's a line of inquiry that needs following at least.'

He sat quietly for a while longer, watching her code. 'And?' he said eventually. He had already worked out there had to be more.

'One of the bodies, the only one we have a positive ID on so far, was an employee of Seifert Pharmaceutical.'

Crane tapped a finger of his right hand quietly on the desk. His left hand lay in his lap, as inert as the rest of his arm now. 'What do you know about the transhumanists?'

'Virtually nothing,' she told him. 'Savini, Charlotte, mentioned them to me only a few days ago. I'd never heard of them before, not even outside of the context of New Thought. I was hoping you could help with that.'

He pulled himself to his feet, stood, wavering very slightly, and looked out of the window at the hall. 'It's a philosophy,' he told her. 'One I can sympathise with, to some extent at least. Some of those who get involved are damaged, either physically or mentally. Others think of themselves as pioneers.' Crane held his prosthetic arm in his real one, as though to support the weight a little. She noticed him rubbing his fingers along the metal. For some reason it seemed like an intimate gesture, almost affectionate. Or perhaps, she thought, it was just making contact with something he now simply felt reconciled with.

'I came across them after Afghanistan. More correctly, New Thought put me in touch. I was at Queen Elizabeth's Foundation in Leatherhead at the time; they'd scraped up the pieces and put me back together. I had an invite to go to Virginia Water, but for some reason I never did. I don't think I was ready.'

'But you became involved with New Thought?'

'They have an online presence. They're very persuasive, although transcendentalism always seemed that bit too far out there for me. Transhumanism I could get my head around. By that point a lot of it just seemed like common sense. I guess in a way I was already experiencing it.' Crane held his arm up to stare at it. 'I'd started printing my own prosthetics by then. They were pretty basic, but they were mine. The engineering part of it was second nature; I wished I'd had 3D printers when I was out in the field. Over time they got more sophisticated and I started sending descriptions to a bunch of journals. That's where New Thought got really interested. Seifert too,' he added.

'New Thought and Seifert are connected?'

'Along with others. They have some common interests. I started talking with some of the transhumanists group. They communicate. I mean, in the sense of exchanging ideas. New Thought facilitates that through meetings and closed forums. They had some fairly radical perspectives. They view nature as just a work in progress, a system that allows a species to evolve to the point at which it can "take it from here". That implies the ability to increase lifespan, intellectual capacity, body functionality and what they call sensory modalities. North sense is a weird little example of that – having a sensor implanted in you that pulses whenever you face north. Maybe you could have sensors in your hand that detect electrical fields or adapt your eyes for night vision. They think in terms of that kind of implant surgery becoming commonplace. Right now, it's at an early stage. A lot of what they do is fairly crude, like the first researcher who put chips in himself to unlock doors in his office, but even that's changing. There are pretty sophisticated control systems you can implant now.'

'Brain-Computer Interface?'

'I was thinking just about the chips. BCI is at a very early stage. It'll get there, but it's not there yet.'

Eva paused before choosing her next question to give herself time to absorb the information Crane had given her. She did not, she decided, have the flavour of it yet. 'What are they like? The transhumanists you met, what were they like as people?'

Crane shrugged. A gesture that made his left arm creak a little. 'Just people, but with their own agendas. As I said, some of them were physically damaged, some were or had been ill, others had psychological scars. But some of them were what you would call completely normal, whatever that means. They were just into it, into trying to see what comes next. If you're looking for an identikit transhumanist profile, you're not going to find one.'

'Are they all into,' she decided to use his phrase, 'body-building?'

'No, not all of them. Quite a lot of the group view it in the abstract. They only talk about transhumanism and debate its merits. A few like to take a more practical approach.' Crane turned to face her once again. 'There are some who take risks. They experiment. On themselves mostly, but they try things out. Biohacking, augmentation, implants, what you might loosely call cybernetics. Some of them use drugs to stimulate cognition, allegedly. I know a couple who are into experimental gene sequencing.'

Eva frowned. 'Isn't that dangerous?'

'What,' Crane scoffed, 'using CRISPR-Cas9 to alter DNA and then inject it into yourself piggy-backed on a virus? What could possibly go wrong?' She could imagine plenty of possibilities, which Crane too had almost certainly thought of. 'It's the same with all these things. It's not about the group, it's about the individual.'

'Derzelas?'

'Maybe,' Crane agreed, 'although I've not heard that particular name before. And Seifert.'

She heard the hesitation in his voice. 'What do you think about them?'

He didn't answer immediately. 'I think they're a hard-nosed commercial company, but that they don't preclude the possibility of doing some good. Anna Seifert has sometimes made decisions that surprised me. She's shown generosity where she didn't need to. That doesn't make her a saint.'

'Who is?' Eva wondered.

'Exactly. But I can't imagine Seifert being involved with displaying body parts like an art exhibition.'

'Seifert is a large company,' Eva pointed out. She swept her hand around the room, alluding to the hall and the spa beyond. 'Just look at this place. How many thousand people does Seifert employ worldwide? It's also about the individual, not the company.'

He didn't seem ready to argue with that. 'And Derzelas?' he asked.

'You tell me.'

Crane looked about to say something more when Eva's phone rang. She scowled. The call was from Flynn. 'Sorry,' she told him. 'They wouldn't disturb me unless it was urgent.' Crane seemed to understand. Eva thumbed the graphic and waited for the call to connect. Crane watched. On a whim, she put the call onto speaker so he could hear it too. She had come a long way to talk to him, and she could understand his reluctance to get involved. As with Savini, keeping information from him felt counterproductive.

'I'm really sorry boss,' Flynn told her, 'but the DCI wants you back here yesterday.'

'Got something?' Eva asked, although the answer to the question seemed obvious.

'Loads,' Flynn said. 'Me and Jamie went to Seifert about the same time Wren came back with some more DNA matches. We're still trying to cross reference, but all of the organs in the racks look like they came from people who had been employed by Seifert at one time or another.'

She caught the look of surprise on Crane's face too. 'Christ,' Eva swore, barely able to believe what she was hearing.

'It gets worse,' Flynn assured her. 'If we haven't double-counted, there are at least six more missing persons that have disappeared from the company in the last sixteen months.'

–

Savini stared, eyes narrow. 'Tell me honestly. Is this because of last night?'

'It is not,' Eva insisted. She hesitated. 'Truth be told I'm still trying to figure out how I feel about that.'

'You left early.' The suspicion didn't leave her voice, so Eva had to explain about the woman in the water. Savini still didn't appear completely convinced when she finished, but she did at least seem less prickly. 'Is that just an excuse?'

'It might be,' Eva admitted, 'but the fact is I'm not sure. What I saw was a bunch of people enjoying themselves and not hurting anyone else. I've got to say that didn't feel unappealing, but one thing remains true. I'm here to work. This place is incredible, but I'm not here for pleasure.'

That, it seemed, was something Savini could understand. 'Have your people had a breakthrough then?' she asked.

It was not the noun she would have immediately employed. 'No,' Eva said, as a sudden wave of dejection brought by the implications of Flynn's phone call washed over her, 'I think it might be exactly the opposite of that.'

–

The three of them stood in a sheltered area at the end of a narrow road that ended up at the research centre. Eva supposed that externally it would have better resembled her expectations of Falkenblick if she'd had any in advance. Broadly featureless, it hid behind the spa, which seemed like a metaphor in itself. Crane and Savini stood with her and waited for a taxi.

Crane seemed sanguine. Eva sent a copy of his code to herself via a cloud-based file-transfer service and promised she would keep looking at it. 'You may be busy,' Crane pointed out.

'In the short term,' Eva agreed, 'but honestly, this is the kind of stuff I do to wind down. I like coding, it feels comfortable. I'm really keen to help.'

He seemed to appreciate that. 'We didn't really talk about Derzelas.'

'We didn't,' she agreed. 'Is there anything you can tell me?'

'I might be able to find out,' Crane admitted, 'but after that call I need to do some fact-checking before I start talking out of turn. This could be important, right? But don't worry,' he continued, right hand raised, 'I'll keep in contact. Let me get you information I'm certain of, not just cultist hearsay.' He hesitated. 'There may be more I can do. There are other people I can ask questions of. No promises of course, but I'll be in touch.'

She couldn't ask for more than that. After only a few minutes, the taxi appeared from the direction of the spa. Eva passed her bag to the driver. Savini seemed more relaxed when Eva thanked her for her help. Crane, she thought, was less so.

'Tread carefully,' he told her as she sat in the back seat of the black Mercedes. 'If somebody is targeting Seifert's staff, they're not going to appreciate police interference.' Crane glared. It wasn't anger, she realised after a moment. It was the inevitable intuition of someone who had already experienced the worst of all possible outcomes. The index finger of his prosthetic hand uncurled, and he aimed it at her to emphasise his point. 'Do not end up as a subject in your own investigation, DI Harris,' Crane told her. 'Watch your back.'

–

Eva reflected on Crane's warning on the flight back to London City, but it seemed difficult to absorb. Sat in a comfortable chair in the narrow fuselage of the aircraft as it drifted over a featureless landscape formed from pristine white clouds, even the violence of Webb's attempt on her life seemed distant. What, she reflected as she stared out the window at the diffuse line where white blended into blue, had she achieved? On the face of it very little, except that she was now convinced her meeting with Crane would bear dividends. He was so serious and quietly intense. Eva wondered if that had been his demeanour before whatever piece of improvised barbarism had ripped him to shreds in some equally distant war. When she sought a word to sum up her impression of Crane, *purposeful* was the adjective that came immediately to mind. It was not as if helping him with the programming for his interface would be a hardship. Sharing in that purpose, albeit in a small way, was something she believed she could relish.

Not today though, she thought as the plane descended into the white clouds and the view outside darkened to ubiquitous grey. Flynn's call had dispelled any illusion of coincidence. Somebody was targeting employees of Seifert Pharmaceutical, or Biotech, or whatever division the multinational had conjured up to please its shareholders and befuddle the taxman. Was it another Mathew Harred; an unhinged artist with manifold, incomprehensible obsessions, or was there some more practical perversity in the racks of dissected body parts?

The prospect of hunting another psychopath like Harred weighed down on her, because she knew exactly what that meant. Even now, were there other Amanda Tylers trapped somewhere, waiting for someone to end their lives? And why? Harred's reasons had been unfathomable, lost in his own inter-pretation of mysticism and art. Would this new killer be any less incomprehensible?

One thing was different, she thought as turbulence made the aircraft tremble. Harred's fresco was a work of art, but it was no more than that. The bodies in the waterworks, however aesthet-ically arranged, had also been experimented on. Wren had found needle marks and incisions. There had been equipment there too, laboratory grade. Did that suggest a more specific purpose than Harred's, something more tangible and therefore something that could be discovered?

She would wait for Crane's email. She believed him impli-citly when he said he would find out what he could. In the meantime, she would set her team loose on Seifert Pharma-ceutical.

With a jolt, the plane set down at London City.

# Chapter Twenty

An hour and a half later she collected her car from the car park and drove straight to Seifert Pharmaceutical. The sat-nav plotted her a route through Esher and on towards Leatherhead. The first part of her journey was along busy suburban roads lined with trees that had over the course of decades churned up the tarmac footpaths, the second part along relatively quiet country lanes. On the way she called the incident room.

Newton picked up. After a couple of seconds he put the phone on speaker so Flynn and Chakrabati could join in the conversation.

'How are they behaving?' Eva asked first. She meant Seifert in general. She didn't yet know which individuals they were dealing with.

'Co-operating,' Raj told her. 'I think they're in shock. The people on the list didn't all work at this location, and some of the staff seem to move around a lot because of their jobs. They act as though they hadn't put the pieces together.'

'They probably hadn't,' Flynn chipped in. 'I mean, they employ a lot of people worldwide. We're not imagining this company is collectively disappearing employees, right? If there's a connection then it's down to an individual or a small group.' It didn't seem like an unreasonable assumption, Eva thought, but she reminded herself to check it all the same.

'They're hiding something,' Jamie Newton said. He said it with such flat certainty that even Eva was surprised. 'No, I don't know what,' Newton admitted, voice made harsh by the speaker, 'but I'll put money on it.'

'It's a pharmaceutical company,' she pointed out. 'Commercial secrets are part of their business.'

'I know,' Newton agreed, 'but nevertheless.' Eva made a mental note to sit down and talk with him when she was back in the station. Newton rarely made pronouncements as bald as that, so to do so he must have had something specific on his mind.

Two kilometres from the town of Dorking, on a site that had once been farmland, Eva followed a lane that led to a security gate in an area protected by unobtrusive surveillance. An open fence, low and made from cleft chestnut posts and rails, was all that defined the perimeter of the site. Beyond the fence, copses of trees and re-wilded scrubland edged by denser woodland hid whatever structures had been built on the fields. A small, unobtrusive sign made from carved stone with the company name embossed into it stood opposite the gate. As she approached, an older man in a uniform stepped from a kiosk to block her way. When she stopped, he examined her warrant card, phoned ahead to reception and after a few seconds' delay raised the barrier to let her pass. As she drove on, she noticed discreet cameras hidden in trees that monitored the gate and the lane beyond it. When she paid attention to them she realised there were a surprising number of cameras. Very little would be able to cross the fields without being observed. Eva adhered to the strict speed limit as she drove.

After a minute or so the lane divided. Visitors' parking, a sign told her, was to the left. Rows of birch and conifers lined the lane and blocked her view, so when she turned into the car park and finally saw her destination, the familiarity of it stunned her.

It must have been designed by the same architect who had created Falkenblick. The building was another collection of geodesic domes, interspersed with sharp crystalline shapes that delineated a chaotic whole. Both metal and organic in a range of muted hues, like the spa it reminded her of the salt crystals she had once grown in a school science class.

She parked, then followed signs to the reception area. The entrance felt similar to Falkenblick's, but instead of the mass of slate that had buttressed the Swiss location Eva saw awnings of rough-hewn rock from Portland. The reception desk sat in the middle of a three-storey atrium, the glass of which cast rainbow patterns onto the warm stone floor. When she announced herself at the reception desk, she was told that Arnaud would see her shortly.

Arnaud Seifert, chairman of the board. Not 'the chairman', not 'Mister Seifert', but 'Arnaud'. Was the familiarity fake? Realistically, did anyone get to be the chairman of a company as large as Seifert without being hard-nosed and a completely remorseless bastard? The receptionist seemed relaxed enough; efficient but not overly deferential. Could Seifert Pharmaceutical really be one big, happy family? If they were, how did they feel about the fact that some of their people had been sliced into pieces and stored in noxious chemicals? Not enough information, Eva concluded as she stood waiting. She would just have to reserve judgement and observe.

She waited in reception for five minutes exactly. Eva noted both the time at which the woman on the front desk picked up the phone to inform Arnaud Seifert he had a visitor, and the time at which a smart brunette woman in a dark blue suit emerged from a chrome lift. Five minutes, almost to the second. It felt like someone's idea of etiquette, Eva thought as the chrome elevator rose five floors to what she assumed Americans would call the C-suite. Perhaps it was simply the cliché of Swiss precision.

Arnaud Seifert sat at an oval table in a room made of glass and screens. The boardroom perhaps; certainly a meeting or presentation suite. Beyond tinted windows, the Surrey landscape filled the horizon with fields almost uninterrupted by buildings. The screens were large, translucent and glowed with data. She saw business intelligence dashboards that reflected products, production, market trends, research and other statistics she didn't immediately recognise. On the one hand it was impressive, Eva thought as she shook Arnaud Seifert's hand. On the other, it was simply the business of business.

Seifert was closer to seventy than sixty. A tall, overweight man with silver-grey hair and thin spectacles wearing an immaculately tailored fawn suit that looked as though it could have been hand-made that morning, he nodded his head slightly as he took Eva's hand. Not quite a court bow, she thought as she turned to face the other occupant of the room, but formally polite nonetheless. There was an engaging warmth to him that reflected the comfort his role brought with it. *I am the chairman*, his body language said, *which is, of course, how it should be.* Anna Seifert's demeanour, on the other hand, seemed almost cryogenic by comparison.

Eva found she could not be certain of Anna's age. She would have guessed mid-thirties but she made yet another mental note to check that detail later. She was almost certainly older than she looked, Eva thought as she turned her attention to Seifert's managing director. When she shook her hand, she found her grip to be firm, yet surprisingly cool.

Anna wore an almost featureless grey suit that contrasted with Arnaud's opulent jacket. Pocket-less and with a mandarin collar, everything about it said: work. Her straight blonde hair was tied in a ponytail at the nape of her neck, and when Eva stood in front of her she found she was looking directly into the other woman's eyes. It didn't feel precisely confrontational, she thought as she released her hand and sat in the chair offered, but it would have been no surprise at all to suddenly find a chessboard on the table in-between them.

'We are, of course,' Arnaud Seifert began in a deep voice that rumbled slightly, 'shocked, confused, horrified and appalled. This has come completely out of the blue for us.' An apology, perhaps, Eva thought. Although in all probability, she had to concede, none of it was even remotely Seifert's fault.

'How did you discover this?' Anna Seifert's tone was impressively neutral, with only a hint of an accent.

'By accident,' Eva told her. 'A young man, being where he should not have been.' She watched the two of them. 'May I ask, does the name New Thought mean anything to you?'

Anna stiffened slightly, as though the question was unexpected. Arnaud did not. 'Yes,' he said without hesitation, 'but not, if I'm honest, a great deal. We have had some minor involvement with them over the years, through various communities and organisations. I imagine you're referring to their interest in transhumanism? It is simply that, I think.'

'Did you deal with them in the UK or overseas?'

'Both. I spoke with Fredrick Huss here, only briefly, but he seemed very pleasant. We dealt with Dominic Vance in the United States. I believe he is quite senior, although I don't pretend to understand their hierarchies.'

The name meant absolutely nothing to her. 'And Jonathon Crane?'

'Crane is a friend,' Anna interjected. Quite stridently, Eva thought. 'There is absolutely no way in which he could be involved.'

It was something she needed to make clear. 'There is no suggestion whatsoever of that,' she told Anna, looking her in the eye. She couldn't be certain, but she had the impression that assurance counted for something.

'Detective Inspector,' Arnaud said, bringing the conversation back under his control, 'our company employs over fifteen thousand people in forty different locations around the world, six of which are in the United Kingdom. Can you be certain Seifert is the only connection between the human remains and these disappearances?'

'No,' Eva admitted, 'but it is a connection. Can you think why there seem to be so many missing persons' cases involving people at your company?'

'Between one hundred and eighty thousand and two hundred thousand people go missing in the United Kingdom every year,' Anna Seifert said. 'I'm not even certain the numbers you are talking about are statistically anomalous.'

She was about to bite Anna's head off when she realised she might, just possibly, have a point. 'I won't argue with you until we've done further analysis,' Eva told her, 'but you can't deny that it *is* statistically anomalous that at least five of those missing persons turned up as body parts preserved in formaldehyde in a disused waterworks.' The look Anna gave her was not readable, but she was unable to disagree.

Eva stood in awkward silence for a moment. The visit to Seifert was as much as anything else a courtesy; a formality required to smooth the way for further investigations that would require Seifert's cooperation. Show your face, press the flesh. Sometimes it had to be done. Where next? Perhaps all she needed to do at that point was seek assurances of cooperation, and to promise reasonable treatment and minimal disruption from the police in return. It was probably the best she could hope for, but leaving so soon felt lame. Eva was about to seek those assurances and make the polite noises when, from nowhere, another thought struck her.

She didn't know where it came from. Something about the remorseless march of numbers across the translucent business intelligence screens, or the stylised logos depicting idealised figures that came and went as products were individually highlighted. Eva found herself asking the question almost before the thought was fully formed. 'Does Seifert conduct experiments on human cadavers?'

Arnaud Seifert looked genuinely surprised. 'Of course we do,' he said after a moment. 'The MHRA requires that medicines, pharmaceutical devices and blood products are assessed in human tissue prior to being marketed. It is indirectly a legal requirement.'

Of course it was, Eva realised. The thought persisted, the idea that was struggling to manifest itself as a coherent hypothesis. She turned her attention to Anna. 'So you do use cadavers and body parts? Where do you conduct these experiments? Do any of them take place here?'

Anna's expression remained unreadable. She stared back at Eva, and although her face gave nothing away, Eva couldn't help but have the impression that the question angered her.

'Yes,' was all that Anna said.

## Chapter Twenty-One

Anna led the way. Arnaud Seifert didn't feel the need to accompany them. The temperature in the lift felt suddenly glacial as it descended to the basement levels of Seifert Pharmaceutical. Another question struck Eva then. 'What is the difference between Seifert Pharma and Seifert Biotech?'

Anna seemed bored by the inquiry, as though it had been asked many times before. 'It's only a matter of risk. Seifert Pharma is the company that owns the older, more established products. We have everything from cancer treatments to flu vaccines under that name. Biotech is more unpredictable, and so higher risk. Some years it makes a profit. Some years it needs further investment. Carefully managed, of course,' she added with a glance. 'Not everything Biotech does will work, and so we ring-fence it. It's a standard business practice.'

Eva knew it was, but the distinction seemed significant. 'And is it Pharma or Biotech that conducts experiments on human cadavers?'

'In fact,' Anna said as the doors slid open, 'both. We're required to provide information to demonstrate new products are safe to use in humans. That means implanting and checking for reactions, which is a separate issue to clinical trials. We are also required to demonstrate safety standards are being maintained and manufacturing quality is consistent. Testing on cadavers is the most straightforward way to prove that consistency.'

There seemed to be a self-evident flaw in the argument. Eva needed to ask the obvious question, but then again, she didn't want to sound flippant. 'Does the fact that the test subjects are dead make a difference?'

The corridor down which they walked had clinical, white-painted walls. LED panels in the ceiling chased shadows away. The environment seemed sterile, as she supposed it actually was. There were warning notices everywhere. On the doors that led to what she assumed were individual research labs, instruction graphics indicated what level of biosecurity was maintained within the rooms, who the primary contacts were, what hazardous materials were in use and what procedures to employ in the event of a fire or other emergency. It didn't seem sinister, but it did seem as though Seifert took biosecurity seriously.

'"Cadaveric tissue" is the technical term,' Anna told her. 'And no, not for certain categories of test, providing the components are preserved correctly. That's more complicated than it sounds,' she said as they approached a pair of locked doors, 'but the benefits can be significant. The percentage success of drugs trialled at early stages with cadaveric tissue is significantly higher than those conducted on, say, mice. And with medical devices it's far easier to identify undesirable reactions with human body parts.'

The doors opened. Eva didn't see what Anna did, but somehow she unlocked them without appearing to touch or swipe near any sort of sensor. Perhaps someone was watching, she thought as she followed Anna inside.

At the end of a short corridor was another pair of double doors. Biosecurity everywhere Eva thought; the doors at the end wouldn't open until those behind them had closed. When the second set of doors opened, the cold hit her.

It was like stepping into a chiller cabinet, which Eva assumed it actually was. She shivered. The room was high ceilinged and less brightly lit than the corridors outside, and the lights here had a slight bluish tinge, as though they also emitted some ultraviolet component. Perhaps thirty metres square, walls lined with metal lockers and rectangular metal panels. Although there had been no obvious sign on the outside doors, she knew immediately she was in a morgue.

Anna ignored her discomfort. 'The temperature in here is kept at a constant three degrees Celsius,' she told Eva as she led the way to the console that oversaw the environment. 'Any higher than that and the bodies would begin to decompose, any lower and we run the risk of causing cell damage. If the water within them freezes, human cells rupture,' she added.

'Getting hold of bodies in exactly the right condition must be something of a challenge,' Eva said.

'It is,' Anna agreed, 'and we pay a premium for the best product. Seifert uses a range of suppliers to ensure we always have a stock of high-quality and well-preserved cadaveric tissue.' She anticipated Eva's next question. 'And yes, I will provide you with their names.'

Eva gazed around the room as Anna momentarily looked away. Everything was organised, everything had its place. It had a neatness to it, an *aesthetic* that for a fraction of a second felt disturbingly familiar. Why would that be, she wondered? Perhaps it was the lighting. There were rows of small LED lights that lit the hidden corners of the space. In places they had almost the feel of emergency floor lighting in an airliner. The purpose of the lights here was to illuminate the space without having an impact on temperature; she could work that out for herself. Perhaps all modern morgues looked this way.

And it was an undeniably modern space that made full use of available technology. In the corner, quiet and incongruous, she saw an industrial robot waiting at a charger — a forklift device used by staff for transporting heavy weights, Eva assumed. From a technical perspective it interested her. Above the forks she noticed a pair of arms like those Crane had been working with, the type of machinery found on thousands of production lines around the world but attached to a movable platform. She saw a pair of stereo cameras on an extendable brace. That told her the robot was equipped with a machine-vision, so it was clearly capable of more nuanced tasks. The large forks at the front of the robot kept her attention though. It depressed her to think what they might be used for.

Anna had turned her attention to a screen. The console had a keyboard and track-pad that sat underneath a large screen, one that could be seen from any point in the morgue. The top-level graphic showed temperature and had two rows of ten rectangles numbered from left to right laid out underneath it. Most of the rectangles glowed pale blue, and two or three were empty. Underneath the display she read a single word: Locked. As she watched, that changed. Unlocked, it told her now. It gave the exact time and then said: Anna Seifert.

'Is that facial recognition?'

Anna shook her head slightly. 'No. Security in the complex is tied to RFID chips, for some of us anyway. The passkeys on the chips are several orders of magnitude more complex than face ID algorithms.'

It took a moment for the implications of that to sink in. 'You have an RFID chip implanted inside you?'

'I have several devices,' Anna admitted. 'Some for security, some that carry personal data. Medical, financial and so on.' She swept through screens on the console. 'A few others.'

Eva had heard of people implanting chips into their bodies before, Crane had also mentioned it, but Anna hadn't seemed the type to experiment with herself in that way. Clearly, she needed to re-evaluate the woman. A number of other questions leapt into her mind though. 'What's to stop the chip triggering something just through proximity? Suppose you hadn't wanted to open that door?'

Anna gave her the same kind of sideways glance Crane had used, as though she too was re-evaluating. She raised the index finger of her right hand. 'The processors won't do anything unless they're told to. There's a sensor in the tip of my finger, it's minute. All it does is act as a switch. If I touch one of the chips with it, it activates.' To make the point she stroked the back of her left hand. Suddenly, all around them, the panels in the walls began to open.

A hiss, as hermetic seals were broken, and even cooler air drifted into the room. Still above freezing, Eva assumed, but enough of a differential to cause soft tendrils of mist to slip from the drawers. One by one, racks on pneumatic rams delivered bodies into the room.

'As you can see,' Anna said as she walked over to the first drawer, 'everything is meticulously labelled. We literally barcode every component.' Eva looked down on the body that lay between them. A young man, in his twenties perhaps, stomach and rib cage open and major organs removed. Just as Anna had claimed, strips of white plastic bearing barcodes adhered to his limbs and torso. 'I always have mixed feelings in here,' she admitted as Eva watched her unlock the much smaller screen that lay next to the body. 'We try to obtain younger tissue samples because there's less chance of cellular damage through environmental factors. Drink, drugs, pollution, sunlight, exposure to viruses, sexually transmitted diseases, lack of exercise, food contaminants, they all build up over time. So we try to get younger people, late teens, early twenties, that sort of age range.'

'Mixed feelings?' Perhaps it was just her accent. Her first impression of Anna had been that she seemed the diametric opposite of emotional. Was that true?

'About the waste, of course.' She tapped the screen and personal information concerning the body appeared. Name, age, date of birth, date of death, name of GP, consent of next of kin, and then more detailed information. Height, weight, blood type, medical history, chronological age, epigenetic age, body adiposity index, ethnicity based on DNA analysis, exposure to communicable diseases, vaccines received, the data went on and on. 'Dead before their time, isn't that the popular expression? Although if they are dead, presumably it was their time.' Anna closed down the screen and wandered over to another drawer. 'Whatever "their time" might mean.'

Eva didn't feel the urge to enlighten her. In the next drawer she saw a more fully dissected corpse. A woman, once, little more than her torso left intact. 'I mean,' Anna admitted, 'it's tragic, right? Who can deny it? What could these people have done with fifty, sixty more years of life? We can't know, of course. We like to imagine they would have been something wonderful, something significant, but that's pure sentimentality on our part. Perhaps this one would have been a rapist, that one a poisoner. Isn't that what you police often encounter?'

'Not as frequently as you might imagine,' Eva said. In that moment, try as she might, she could make no sense whatsoever of Anna Seifert.

'And perhaps they would have simply been ordinary,' Anna continued, seemingly oblivious. 'Let's face it, most of us are. We can't all expect to be a Marie Curie or a Rosalind Franklin, can we? But perhaps in death they can do more than they would have in their ordinary lives.' A third drawer. A seemingly random collection of organs, all barcoded as meticulously as the first. 'It's possible. Perhaps it will be one of these people who will finally give us a cure for cancer. Or Alzheimer's. Or congenital heart disease. Or Ebola, or baldness, or obesity, or God help us, even just the common cold. Look at them, Detective Inspector,' Anna waved her hands as she walked between rows of meticulously preserved bodies. 'Don't you see? Together, we have so much work to do.'

The tone jarred, but Eva couldn't tell if that was only again her reaction to Anna's trace of an accent. Was it psychopathy or fatalism? Perhaps it was simply regret at lives lost. 'Did you know Amanda Tyler?' Eva asked after a few seconds.

Again, that unreadable expression. 'I know the name,' Anna told her as she stared at the console, 'I just seem unable to picture her face.' Eva felt her mouth open slightly. Was that a coincidence too? She was positive neither Wren nor her team would have given out any specific details concerning the body parts found in the waterworks, certainly none of them would have mentioned the flayed face drawn taught over a metal frame. Would Anna have used that turn of phrase if she had known? 'Presumably you have a list of other victims?' Anna asked as she checked notes from another drawer. Another man, body intact but the top of his head removed. Eva could see the empty space where the brain had once been.

'We have,' she said as she looked around at the contents of the rest of the drawers. Twenty racks, seventeen occupied by bodies in increasing states of dissection. 'I can't say any more until next of kin have been contacted.'

'Of course not,' Anna agreed. 'We all understand the procedures.' A moment later she sighed and made a gesture in the air with her hand. From vents on the side of the room, diaphanous plumes of vapour drifted down and coiled around the floor. 'An anti-bacterial solution,' she told Eva as she stepped into one of the plumes. 'It's just a precaution.'

Eva did the same. The vapour smelled of menthol. They stood across the room from one another as it washed over them, the walls between them lined with dead bodies. A bizarre scene, Eva thought as she watched Anna, sinister, almost necrophilic. Anna stared back at her with her unreadable expression.

'As important as it is, I do hope this investigation won't disrupt the work Seifert conducts. I know it is imperative that you apprehend whoever is responsible for these abductions, but please bear in mind: the medicines developed here will save hundreds, if not thousands of lives. I simply ask that you be mindful of that as you proceed.'

Was it a threat? Standing there in a room filled with corpses, being lectured to by a woman who controlled her environment through electronic implants, it certainly felt that way. And yet Anna hadn't asked for anything other than cognisance. If it was in fact a threat, Eva thought as she stepped out of the cascade of vapour, it was a mild one.

'I'll bear that in mind,' Eva told her as she walked towards the exit.

–

When the time came to leave it was Arnaud who escorted her back to the elevator. He limped a little, as though excess weight played on his hip joint. Affable though, Eva thought as they walked. The staff all smiled and nodded. Arnaud smiled and nodded back. Everything seemed well in the house of Seifert. Except, Eva thought as she stood waiting for the lift, at least eleven people employed by the company had disappeared in less than a year and a half, and five of those were certainly dead.

'I'm sorry we meet under such difficult circumstances,' Arnaud said as he waited with her. 'I hope you are able to obtain some clarity very soon.'

Another interesting choice of words, Eva thought, but probably of no more significance than Anna's. The older man was simply trying to be precise, she reasoned. Again, she had to stop herself. Arnaud Seifert's grandfatherly appeal was misleading. This was a man who had started a multi-billion-Euro company on his own.

One last question. 'Is there anything else you can say about your contact with New Thought?'

Arnaud shoved his hands in his pockets and looked thoughtful. 'They are a curious organisation,' he admitted after a while. 'When we go looking for financial partners for this project or that, especially in the US, their name seems to crop up more frequently than others. I think you're aware that some of our development work is focused on anti-senescence. Ageing is both an inconvenience and an indignity, I can assure you of that personally. It doesn't necessarily need to be that way though, or so our scientists believe. We are just now on the cusp of making significant steps forward in increasing not only lifespan but health-span.' He took his glasses off and polished them. It seemed like a practiced gesture. 'These are exciting times, but of course such research costs money and we cannot take all the risk. In this area, with some of the people we speak with, sometimes,' Arnaud frowned a little and put his glasses back on, 'sometimes it feels as though they are seeking New Thought's approval. Not consent,' he added as the lift arrived, 'more – approbation.'

Eva stood between the doors of the lift. They wouldn't close while she was there. 'Do you get it?'

'Usually. Occasionally not. Sometimes I have the impression New Thought have their own road map. The people we ask to invest look to them to decide whether a given product fits their, ah, philosophy, vision, I don't know what exactly. If it does, they invest. If not, they pass. It's all very amicable,' he added as he shook Eva's hand, 'but it's also very deliberate.'

The lift descended. In the reception area, people were now milling around. Maybe twenty or thirty, in small groups discussing whatever it was that people who worked for a company like Seifert might discuss, and others who stood alone, as though waiting for their colleagues to arrive. She didn't think any more of it until she was in her car and driving away; it didn't strike her until she reached the end of the lane and she was preparing to turn left onto the main road. That was when the subconscious processes that were replaying the interviews in the back of her head suddenly pinged. Pattern recognition, she realised as she put her foot down and accelerated away; that most powerful of human cognitive skills. Pity it didn't work a bit bloody quicker.

Was it significant? She wanted to dismiss it as coincidence, but some nagging suspicion stopped her. It seemed almost irrelevant. Almost, but not quite.

It was only an impression, but something about way the bodies in the morgue had been laid out echoed the arrangement of the glass containers in the waterworks.

# Chapter Twenty-Two

Sutton caught her before any of her team could. 'Having fun?' she snapped. The sense of displeasure was palpable. Eva armed herself against the inevitable tirade.

'The contact in Switzerland may still be useful ma'am,' she told Sutton. After months working for her Eva had become used to giving progress reports in corridors, canteens, or anywhere else Sutton chose. 'He's agreed to do some digging amongst the transhumanist community, and right now I think they're the most plausible line of enquiry. Seifert are sending staff and patient records as we speak. They're being helpful, but I think there's going to be a lot of data to sift through.'

Sutton blinked. 'Patient records?'

'They test on human cadavers. They have their own morgue.'

'Jesus.' Sutton shook her head. 'Harris, I have the sense this is getting out of hand. I know we're running to catch up and we wouldn't even be at this point except for that kid of yours, but we need to move faster. Are all your team working on this?'

Eva took a breath, but then shook her head. 'No, ma'am. We're at a fairly crucial stage with Webb County. I've got Raj on that, Becks on this and Jamie split between the two.'

Sutton swore, long and hard. 'Put Jamie on this full time and see if Raj can split his workload. No,' she said before Eva could complain, 'I'm not trying to micro-manage. I've just had a call from Borough.' Eva felt the hair on the back of her neck start to rise. 'A missing person report filed by a bloke in Slough. Seems his girlfriend went out two days ago and hasn't been seen since.' Eva didn't need to ask, but Sutton told her anyway. 'And yes, she worked for Seifert Biotech.' The air in the corridor suddenly seemed unusually cold. 'If we've got our numbers right, then that's twelve,' Sutton said.

-

The missing person report sat on her desk. Eva was about to open it when a text from Judy Wren pinged on her phone. *Need to talk*, it read.

Again?, Eva thought, but she knew Wren wouldn't be wasting her time. *Shall I come to you?* she replied.

*Too late*, Wren wrote. *I'm already here.*

Wren paced. The whiteboard in the incident room was filled with faces now. It felt as though the investigation had gone from tenuous at best to suddenly being inundated with information. She saw names carefully stencilled under photos in Flynn's respectful longhand. Amanda Tyler, Michael Conroy, Naomi Gray, Lewis Ashley, the list went on. Tyler had worked as an intern, Conroy was a researcher, Gray had been in the field, Ashley was a pharmacologist. Nothing tied them together, Eva thought as she stared at the collection of photos; not age, sex, gender or ethnicity. There was seemingly no common link between them. Apart, she reminded herself, from the fact that they all worked or had worked for Seifert. She dropped into a chair. Perhaps Wren would be able to offer some new information, Eva thought.

Flynn, Newton and Chakrabati sat with Eva and watched the forensic examiner.

'Judy,' Eva asked eventually. 'What's wrong?'

Wren stopped pacing. Her phone was connected to one of the screens in the interview room and she was waiting for images to download. 'A deficit of data and a surfeit of hypothesis,' she said as a blue line marched inexorably from left to right. She looked up, stared at the faces gazing back at her and seemingly realised that none of them had a clue what she was talking about. 'I'm guessing,' she admitted finally. 'Problem is, I'm also pretty certain I'm right.'

'Take us through it,' Eva suggested.

Finally, the first of the images loaded. 'Ninety-six containers, comprising components of five dissected bodies. Okay, about seven containers have still got question marks hanging over them, but I'm not expecting there to be any blinding revelations. This is what we've got. Limbs and organs show signs of testing, and most of that testing has been conducted in a fairly rigorous, scientific fashion.'

'And yet the body parts were arranged like an art exhibit,' Jamie Newton pointed out.

'I know,' Wren agreed, 'a detail that is not consistent with the other observed facts. I mean, maybe it is. Maybe it's just one of those psychopathic traits that reveal themselves over time. Kill someone, cut them up, do fairly particular experiments on them and then decide the human body is a work of art after all. It's possible, right? Problem is, it doesn't tell us anything.'

'What kind of experiments?' Flynn asked.

'The kind that pays particular attention to blood and tissue samples. Kidney, bone marrow, liver, brain-stem, all of those organs in the tanks show signs of having sections taken from them. Thin slices,' she added, by way of explanation. As she spoke, she flicked images on to the screen. *Pieces of meat*, Eva thought as the various body parts were displayed. *When it comes down to it, that's all we are.*

'So our perpetrator isn't some kind of necrophiliac,' Eva suggested.

Wren seemed uncomfortable. 'I have no direct evidence of that either way.' She looked for a whiteboard. 'It might be an idea to try and make a common timeline. It's going to be a bit vague, but I think there are five distinct points that can inform us.' She picked up a marker and drew a horizontal line. Along it Wren made a series of crosses. 'Let's start at the end. Post-mortem testing, I've just told you about that. The point before that is dissection. He cuts them up when they're dead. Some organs he removes with a scalpel, some limbs with a bone saw. There may be other methods, but the marks are ambiguous. Before that is method of death, and it's hard to tell but my thinking is, this varies. I can't be certain,' she emphasised, 'but I think some of them died quickly, some not so. Go back a step. This is where it gets interesting.'

'He tests on them when they're alive,' Flynn said, not even trying to keep the disgust from her voice.

'He does,' Wren agreed. 'It's very hard to identify and nowhere near as conclusive as I'd like, but there are cuts and lesions consistent with taking minimally invasive samples. So he's testing them *for* something.'

Eva's voice was suddenly sharp. 'What?'

'Not a damned clue,' Wren admitted. 'There's just a huge range of possibilities. Park that,' she said as she pointed at her timeline. 'Let's go back one step. I guess the first stage is what you might call "acquisition". I'm assuming these people aren't volunteering, so how do you persuade a dozen people to come quietly to be experimented on?' She only let the question hang for a moment. 'I think I have an idea. No, I can't prove it; I just have a theory and a scrap of evidence to support it. Look,' Wren said, flipping through a series of images, each of which had a small feature highlighted. 'I found this mark five times, all on lower extremities. It's just a bit too big for a syringe, too small for something like a cigarette burn. I couldn't think what it might be, but Antony Naeku, one of the pathology interns, said it looked familiar. He's Kenyan.' Wren took a breath. 'He's worked with wildlife preservation groups. He thinks the wound might have been caused by a veterinary dart, the kind they use to tranquillise animals for tagging.'

Eva stared at the images. It was hard to deny that Wren's timeline seemed to make sense. 'So you shoot these things with a rifle?' she asked.

'That's the thing,' Wren said. 'You *can* shoot them with an air rifle or pistol, but there are plenty of other ways of delivering them too. Antony said he had seen rangers who used a small crossbow, and there are $CO_2$ air systems as well as jab sticks. There's another thing, which is of course, what do you inject? There are a whole list of products and doses depending on the capture, but one product caught my eye.' Eva felt her jaw start to drop once again. 'Seifert Xanazipan,' Wren said.

'That's ironic,' Newton muttered.

Eva could not disagree. She was about to comment when she noticed the look on Wren's face. 'Go on, Judy,' Eva told her.

Wren hesitated. Uncertainty was clearly weighing on her. 'Look,' she said, and Eva heard a slight tremble in her voice, 'this is supposition on my part, okay? But if he is darting them then he needs them alive and sedated, for whatever reason. And,' she looked around the faces in the room, 'I think he's keeping them that way too. Right up until the moment he kills them. Either sedated or possibly restrained, I think he keeps them that way for days, but more likely weeks. No,' she added hurriedly, 'I can't prove it right now, but I would bet money that that latest missing person, and probably several like her, are still alive somewhere.'

## Chapter Twenty-Three

Dusk. The Land Rover drew to a halt outside of a single-storey, utilitarian building constructed from concrete and metal, and painted dull, army green. Dark blinds covered triple-glazed windows. In the distance, the maniacal howling of dogs echoed over empty hills.

The man turned off the headlights. After a moment two security lamps flickered and lit the spot where he had parked. He exited the car and stepped into the light. As he did so an electric motor whirred into life and a pair of double doors on the side of the building started to slowly open. More light spilled out from the building's interior. He waited for the doors to fully open and then walked into the building. A few moments later he exited it again. This time he dragged a trolley behind him. He waited for a moment, made certain that everything was as it should be, and then turned the trolley and pushed it around to the back of the Land Rover.

It wasn't an urban vehicle. Darkest green so as to be almost black, with metal bars front and back as well as impact panels welded to its side, it was the kind of 4x4 that might be used in shrub or on the savannah; anywhere where there was a high risk of collision. The lock on the back door was manual, not controlled by any central locking system. He unlocked it with a key. The door swung wide. He pushed the trolley against the back of the Land Rover. Then he used a lever to lower it until the top of the trolley sat a centimetre beneath the vehicle's lip.

The contents of the black plastic sack were heavy. He estimated sixty kilos. The sack itself was thick and strong, the kind you would use to take away builders' rubble. It was sealed. He had closed it with a line of industrial adhesive so that its contents had no chance of falling out. He grabbed the sack by its side and dragged.

It moved awkwardly, catching on the edge of the door, so he had to reach in and twist it around. It took a minute, but with some effort he was able to ease the sack onto the trolley. He pushed the trolley towards the building but stopped before he entered, went back and closed the back of the Land Rover and locked it. Everything in the right order, he told himself as he tapped the switch that would shut the double doors. Mistakes were always fatal.

When the doors had locked, he pushed the trolley through the building. His path was lit by a series of lamps in metal shades that hung suspended by black cables from the apex of the sloping roof. Beyond the path, in the darkness where the light did not reach, the other occupants of the building made their noises, grunted and hissed, tasted the air and watched him as he laboured. After thirty paces he came to another pair of doors, flaps really, made from heavy strips of translucent PVC. He pushed the trolley against them and they curled under its weight.

The area he stopped in was not large; no more than four metres square. The lighting here was different though; six fluorescent strips flooded the space with the colour of daylight. A bench with a stainless-steel worktop shone in the glow of the neon tubes. It was clean, sterile. He knew that. He had polished the surface himself.

From a dish on the work surface he selected a scalpel. Swan and Morton 10A, non-sterile blade, his preferred tool. He liked the blade's straight edge. It always felt more precise than the curve of the regular 10. He took the blade to the plastic sack, and cut it open.

The woman inside the sack wore a suit. Not expensive, an everyday suit, the sort you would wear to work when nobody important was there. Dark blue and practical; he found he could respect that. He used the scalpel to cut it off her.

The first thing he did, as she lay naked on the trolley, was weigh her. Sixty kilos, he had estimated, whereas in reality she was sixty-two point three. The trolley had been rolled onto industrial scales, and he already knew the trolley's exact weight. Getting a specific weight was important. He needed to know it to calculate the precise dosage of sedative to keep her asleep.

Next he wheeled out the frame that held the monitors that would track vital signs, as well as the electric pumps that controlled the flow of all the liquids he needed to keep her alive, and attached it to the trolley. When that was done, and he was sure the woman was still deeply unconscious, he went to work.

Needles into the veins and arteries that carried blood to and from the heart. Feeding tubes straight into the stomach, another to take away accumulated waste. He catheterised her, then attached the sensors that would ensure the pump that supplied liquid to keep her hydrated knew how much to inject. Finally electrodes, to monitor brain activity, galvanic skin response and the involuntary signals that controlled extremities. When he was satisfied, he connected the data feed that would record every change in her body chemistry as he conducted his experiments. Every last breath would be recorded, right up until her very last breath.

He pushed the trolley through another set of PVC flaps, into the area he thought of as 'the ward'. A row of large cubicles, divided by polythene sheets, each containing a subject similarly monitored and sedated. A ward with a capacity of five. The problem was that now, with the arrival of this new woman, he had six patients to attend to.

It didn't matter, he decided as he checked his records. Patient number three had given him as much as she was going to, in her current state at least. In the early days this part of the procedure had caused him difficulties, but his system was more efficient now. The syringe was ready. He had the precise dosage. All he needed to do was turn the lock and push and wait for the vital signs to fall to zero.

It only took a minute. When he was finished, he wheeled Jennifer Collins out of her cubicle and pushed Michelle Barnes in, to take her place. Her profile was that much closer to Michael Conroy's. He expected to find solid evidence of the treatment in her too. Collins would be useful enough, once he had extracted the necessary material, but in her current state she was simply taking up room.

Once Michelle Barnes was settled, he went to check the battery charge on his various tools, the drills, the carvers and the circular saws. It was going to be, he thought as he pushed Jennifer Collins's body back to the room with the stainless-steel work surface, a long night.

## Chapter Twenty-Four

Too much bloody information, Eva thought as she sifted through the folders of files that had arrived by motorcycle courier stored on an encrypted hard drive from Seifert. They had been as good as their word. They had supplied every record from the past sixteen months that might even possibly pertain to the abductions, although how exactly one would sort allegedly pertinent information from spurious was something Eva was still guessing about. At the very least, though, she had been able to put a ring-fence around the files that concerned experiments on human bodies.

She had needed to do some background research even before she dived into the material. The governing legislation was the Human Tissue Act 2004. The governing body was the Human Tissue Authority. They had a website, Eva discovered, but then everybody had a website. What was perhaps a little disturbing was just how cheerful the website seemed.

A pale-blue banner identified them as the regulator for the use of human tissues and organs. The content beneath read like a newsletter, with sections featuring information for both professionals and the general public. There were even social media feeds. She spent almost half an hour perusing the site. By the end of it she felt it also had given her too much information.

At least she felt she had a grasp of the structure of the legislation now though, and the roles of the various actors who were required to play their part. Designated Individuals were held responsible for maintaining compliance with the legislation, and Research Ethics Committees made the decision as to whether experiments on human cadavers were actually justified. Facilities such as Seifert's morgue were referred to, somewhat euphemistically, as 'tissue banks'. Providers of human tissue required licences, although, paradoxically, storage of tissue didn't always need the same licencing. Enough, she thought as she turned away from her web browser. Time to sink her teeth into Seifert's data.

She read through those files for an hour and a half. Seifert really had included every last detail. She had the identities of the bodies in their tissue bank for the corresponding sixteen-month period over which she now thought abductions had been taking place. There were causes of death, consent of next of kin, details of organs and limbs used in research as well as descriptions of the various drugs being trialled, although at this point they were only series names, not the fancy brand descriptions they would eventually receive if any of them got to market.

The sky outside her window began to darken. She could hear soft rain falling on the streets and pattering on the glass. She would need to eat soon. Perhaps she would stop at a market stall on the way home and pick up something that didn't need cooking. Eva was about to shut down her laptop when one more folder caught her eye. It was labelled, quite simply, Third Parties.

It took her a few minutes to understand why. When she did, she realised that Seifert also conducted tissue experiments on a paid basis for other companies. It was not a large business, and as she read through the notes in the folder, she began to realise that the main purpose of the activity was not to make money but to support what might be viewed as strategic alliances, mostly with small start-up companies. An endpoint of potential acquisition was clearly the objective.

She could see how it worked. Company A might come to Seifert with a product they were developing; a new form of hip joint, for example. If Seifert thought the design had something novel about it, they would initiate trials in human cadavers on a reduced-fee basis to help Company A get over its first regulatory hurdle. If subsequent clinical trials were successful then Seifert had an inside track on the technology, and at the most advantageous point would make Company A an offer. If, however, the clinical trials were unsuccessful, Seifert would still have covered its costs. It felt like a shrewd way of gaining information, Eva thought. Harsh but essentially equitable, or so it seemed. Eight companies had used the service in the past year. Most were for medical devices of one sort or another; three were for drug trials, or at least trials of more advanced drug-delivery systems. Only one stood out. She bit her lip. Did it warrant further investigation? The trials had stopped several months ago, which seemed curious in itself. 'Not suitable for further investment,' the note on the file read. It was signed: Anna Seifert.

Which was curious, Eva thought, given that Anna Seifert had allowed the company, which went by the name of BioHeuristics, to implant Radio Frequency ID chips in her own body.

–

Eva passed the incident room on the way out. The lights were still on. Flynn and Newton had left for the evening, but Raj Chakrabati sat in front of his computer.

'You planning to be here all night?'

Raj looked up and grinned. 'Not bloody likely,' he said as he did a quick save on a spreadsheet. 'I'm about to mail a bundle of files to HMRC. I'm just being paranoid. I don't want to make any obvious cockups with those buggers – you know what they're like. I think I've got my ducks in a row, but I'm just summoning up the courage to hit send.'

She laughed. 'I know that feeling. They'll rip every last number to shreds. But if they agree there's grounds for investigation, they'll pour fire on Duncan Webb. That'd be worth having.'

'Yeah,' Raj agreed. Then he shook his head. 'Except it's not true. It's just a fishing expedition, right? Delta V is a beast of an investment fund. Fact of it is I'd almost be afraid if there was any danger we might actually bring it down. Lots of legitimate investors would take a serious haircut. If Webb had used funny money to build it up the amount of damage it'd cause if it collapsed would be horrendous, but I can't believe he'd be mad enough to do that. We know Webb is bent, but he's not stupid. Investigating Delta V is a ploy to gain open access to other areas of his business. It's just shaking the tree.'

She wondered what he was telling her. 'Is that any reason not to do it?'

Raj shook his head. 'No. But we just need to be aware of the consequences.' He hesitated. 'To be honest boss, it's no surprise Webb tried to knock you off. Delta V is like the crown jewels. He really can't afford for it to come under suspicion.'

'Webb said it was a six-hundred-million-pound fund?'

'Which isn't unusual in itself,' Raj told her, 'but the way stakes in these funds get bundled up and re-sold always magnifies the value. The cumulative market worth is in the billions. I don't know,' he complained as he closed down his spreadsheets. 'There comes a point where all this high-finance shit feels too much like anti-gravity or perpetual motion to me. It's all two-plus-two-equals-seven; it's like pulling money from thin air.'

'It is,' Eva agreed. 'Whoever said money doesn't grow on trees was dead wrong.' She wondered if she should introduce Raj to Savini, but then she also wondered what the consequences of that action might be. 'Are you good to go?'

'I am,' Raj said finally, and to illustrate the point hit 'send' on the email. 'Cry havoc and let the dogs out or something. I dunno, "bombs away" might be better.'

She laughed again. 'Let's hope HMRC agrees,' she told him.

'Yeah,' Raj said. 'Let's hope.'

The next morning Eva joined the rush-hour throng and took the train to Waterloo Station. She could not get a seat. She stood for forty minutes on the Overground, squeezed in-between a man watching videos on his phone and a woman who spent the entire journey putting on make-up. At Waterloo, the crowd carried her along. The Northern line was jammed. Damp, sweaty bodies crushed against her. She changed and exited the Underground at Oxford Circus. Fine, light, cold rain fell and soaked her hair. She ran her hand through it as she walked and stayed close to the overhangs of shops and department stores. She cut up Holles Street and edged around Cavendish Square Gardens before reaching Harley Street. There, she went looking for, and found, a Regency townhouse with a brass plaque next to the front door. A small black logo read: BioHeuristics. The clinic bore the name: Aaron Rose.

'My first patient is at ten,' Rose told her after his assistant introduced her, 'I hope we can be finished by then?' It didn't seem like an unreasonable request, Eva thought as she walked into Rose's consulting room, given that he had just received a completely unexpected visit from the police.

Rose was probably in his late forties, she estimated as he settled in behind his desk. Average height and weight and balding over the middle of his head. What hair he had left was brown and untidy. His suit made up for that. It wasn't as extravagant as Arnaud Seifert's, but it was presentable nonetheless; the kind of suit one might imagine a Harley Street consultant would wear. Rose seemed worried, Eva thought as he studied her through gold-rimmed glasses, but he struck her as the kind of person who might always seem worried. Perhaps it was part of his demeanour.

'I don't think this will take very long,' Eva assured Rose. 'I'm investigating a number of murders and the name BioHeuristics has come up in connection with them, but the link is somewhat tenuous. I'm only here to clarify what it is you do.'

'Ah,' Rose sighed, seeming visibly relieved. 'I think I understand. Have you discovered tags?'

She frowned. 'Tags?'

'Chips,' Rose said. 'Embedded in the bodies. I'm assuming that's the connection?'

'Not precisely,' Eva told him. 'Why exactly would it be?'

'It's a fairly large part of my business,' Rose admitted. 'Micro-processors embedded under the skin or sometimes deeper to help with the identification of bodies in the event of kidnap and murder. I have an overseas clientele. They come here from all around the world to be tagged. Sometimes I embed personally identifying information, sometimes it's financial data or medical details. There's an Italian gentleman,' Rose hesitated. Eva raised an eyebrow. 'Well, I won't divulge any confidential details, but suffice it to say he has something of a history. He's written that history down and the file that contains it is on a chip now safely buried, quite deep, inside his body. In the event of his death that chip would become accessible following a post-mortem. It's an insurance policy, if you will. I get quite a few requests for that type of work.'

'Your main line of business is embedding data in human bodies?'

'It's *a* line of business,' Rose said. 'I also get involved in access control and functional systems. Multi-function implant-able systems are an exciting area to be working in right now; they're the first step towards practical cybernetics.'

'Transhumanism?' Eva asked.

Rose's shoulders rose and fell. 'I suppose it depends on your definition. I tend to think of what I do simply as implantable technology; it isn't augmenting the human condition in the transhumanist sense. If there's a piece of functionality you need on a regular basis, rigorous security for financial transactions for example, and that functionality can be attached to a processor and embedded inside you, why not? Phone security is good and getting better, but it's still possible to copy a thumbprint or fake facial identification. Multi-part sub-dermal processors are so much more secure.'

169

Eva made a mental note to ask Wren if any of the incisions in the body parts she had examined were consistent with chips being removed from under the skin, or deeper. 'And you use Seifert Biotech for validation for the Human Tissue Authority?'

'Medicine and Healthcare Products Regulatory Agency,' Rose corrected her. 'Did. We had a business disagreement. It ended.' He shrugged again. 'These things happen.'

'But you had already implanted chips into Anna Seifert.'

He looked uncomfortable. 'Detective Inspector, that really is rather confidential. I shouldn't really talk about specific patients without their say-so.'

Rose had technically already broken the law by admitting Anna Seifert was a patient, but she wasn't about to labour the point. 'Hypothetically then, what kind of systems might someone consider implanting?'

He seemed more comfortable with a generalised question. 'Storage, location and activation, primarily. Storage is up to you. I can implant up to a terabyte SSD with surface-contact access ports. You can read and write to it with a device that only has to touch the skin above it to connect. Data transfer is a little slow, but the data is verifiably safe. Location is a popular one, especially anti-kidnap systems that connect to phone networks. And someone we know,' he said salaciously, leaning forward and lowering his voice, 'has the most sophisticated set of activation systems currently implanted in anyone. Sensors in the back of the hand and forearm and a trigger in the fingertip. It's like using a numeric keypad for devices with Bluetooth. I was very proud of that particular piece of work,' Rose admitted.

Eva had to sit for a moment and absorb what Rose was telling her. 'How many different types of devices do you implant?'

'About fifty if you count the various storage capacities of chips. Some are just sub-dermal, meaning they slide into a tiny flap cut in the skin. Some are set deeper. I can embed processors in bone, in the skull or upper and lower limbs. The active chips charge wirelessly.'

She thought for a while. 'And Seifert? How many people from that company have you implanted chips into?'

Rose shook his head. 'A difficult question. I hope my answer won't be held against me.' The only response she could give him was a slight shake of the head. 'Ah well,' Rose conceded. 'The individual you mentioned is so far the only employee of the Seifert company I have, to the best of my knowledge, worked with.'

–

She kept to her side of the agreement. Eva left Rose's consulting room just before ten. During that time, he showed her both his catalogue and videos of procedures, some of which seemed little more invasive than getting a tattoo, while others looked more akin to keyhole surgery. *We put chips into cats and dogs*, Eva thought as she watched Rose's handiwork.

She didn't feel she had learned anything. It seemed the journey was a few hours wasted. *Process of elimination*, she tried to convince herself as she walked back to the waiting room. The thought infuriated her. Somewhere, if Wren's conjecture was right, at least some of the abductees were still alive, and here she was screwing around with random leads. And yet what else could she do, except follow those leads and eliminate them one by one? She needed to step back and try to imagine some bigger picture, one broad enough to contain abducted victims and dissected body parts, as well as New Thought and Seifert Pharmaceutical. Right now, nothing was making sense.

There were four people in the waiting room. Three men, two heavy and unshaven, one thin and sallow faced, and a woman, mid-twenties, long dark hair and Eastern European face. They sat apart from each other and ignored Eva as she walked through. They didn't look like heiresses in danger of kidnap, or Mafia bosses seeking insurance against assassination. In fact, they didn't look as though they could even afford Rose's not-inexpensive services. Odd, Eva thought as she opened the front door and stepped out into the light rain that fell on Harley Street. Not odd enough to worry about though.

She took the spurious impression and filed it in the back of her mind.

# Chapter Twenty-Five

The incident room had been transformed. Flynn and Newton had printed out every scrap of information they could find on the missing persons and pasted it onto whiteboards in a series of concentric circles that eventually reduced down to a single name: Seifert. Raj had retreated to a solitary corner where his lonely board held information pertaining to Webb County Partners and Delta V investments. He had more deadlines from HMRC and their specialist investigative team, but he chipped in whenever he felt he could contribute.

Twelve missing people abducted over sixteen months – if the data from Seifert was to be believed. Twelve people who had missing person reports filed against them that recorded their employer as either Seifert Pharmaceutical or Seifert Biotech, five of whom were now confirmed dead. Eva stared at the photos. Why had it taken so long to make the connections? As she read through the profiles of the victims though, both confirmed and assumed, she began to understand. The ages of the victims ranged from twenty-two to mid-fifties; they were male, female, black and white. On the face of it there was no connection, except for the fact that they all worked for either Seifert Pharmaceutical or Seifert Biotech; but even that one detail was hard to make fit the facts. Michael Conroy was a scientist, Amanda Tyler a marketing intern, Naomi Gray a field researcher, Lewis Ashley a pharmacologist. There was a very good chance, she realised as she stared at the photos, that, despite working for the same company, none of the victims had ever even met each other. If there was a common point of reference even within Seifert, it was going to be a nightmare to track down. Flynn and Newton were on that now.

Eva gazed at them as she turned away from the boards. Heads down and silent, reading through the piles of paper and digital records that had been extracted from the information Seifert had supplied. Most of it would be irrelevant; she knew that. But it all had to be catalogued and indexed anyway.

'I'm working on extra resources.' Eva turned and saw Corinne Sutton standing in the doorway. At least she understood the complexity of the task, Eva thought as she nodded gratitude to her DCI. 'It's going to take a couple of days unfortunately,' Sutton continued, 'but Area are aware that they need to step up on this one.'

'A couple of days is probably good, ma'am,' Eva said quietly, so as not to disturb Flynn and Newton. 'We're just putting information into categories right now, trying to find some useful groupings. It's when we start on the next level that we'll really need more hands.'

Sutton stared. 'Still no connection?'

'Apart from Seifert? Not so far. Anna Seifert said something that almost had me convinced for a second. She said that around two hundred thousand people in the UK go missing each year, so was it even statistically anomalous that twelve had gone missing from Seifert?' Sutton glared, so she tried to explain. 'Two hundred thousand from a population of seventy million is one in three hundred and fifty. Seifert employs fifteen thousand people, nine thousand in the UK. For them to have the national average of missing persons we'd be looking at around twenty-five mis-pers. It's not helpful,' she added, 'but it does explain why nobody joined the dots.'

Sutton stood in front of the whiteboard and kept staring. 'How did they get the tanks and the racks up there?' She meant to the top of the stone plinth that hung below the ceiling in the waterworks. It was a bloody good question, Eva thought. She and Wren had debated that one themselves.

'It's possible they were able to power the freight lifts at the back of the building; they run to the top. That would give them direct access to the mezzanine level, but it's still a pretty sizeable job to move a hundred tanks from the lift to the racks. And were they filled before or after they were moved? Either way that's a hell of a lot of formaldehyde that needs moving.'

'And expensive too,' Newton chipped in. 'A couple of hundred quid for twenty-five litres. Got to be a few grand's worth of chemicals there.'

Eva glanced at him. 'Does Seifert manufacture formaldehyde?'

'No,' Jamie Newton said, unable to suppress a wry grin, 'but one of their subsidiaries, Seifert Chemicals, lists it as available for bulk delivery. I don't know if they're acting as manufacturers or wholesalers though.'

'Jesus Christ,' Sutton snapped, 'every bloody line of enquiry leads back to Seifert but then the leads just stop. Are they hiding something? Is someone withholding information? What the hell is going on at that place?'

She had not yet grilled Jamie Newton on his suspicions, Eva remembered as Sutton ranted, but then they both had been inundated by material from Seifert. 'If they're hiding something then they're hiding it in plain sight,' she told Sutton. 'We're swamped with reports and files, as you can see. There's no obvious overlap between the victims, despite them working for the same company.'

'Well,' Newton ventured, 'there is one, boss.' Eva turned to stare at him. He flicked up a pile of paper. 'Just looking through this stuff, they might not have had much contact with each other, but there is one person they all interacted with fairly regularly.'

She could see where he was going. Sutton could not. 'Who?' the DCI demanded.

'Anna Seifert.'

The one thing for some reason she felt bizarrely certain about was that Crane would not let her down. There was just something about the man, an air of unimpeachable reliability that, like Savini's intrinsic decency, she simply felt she could rely on. Neither of them was without flaws. Eva had witnessed Savini's in lurid detail, and she was reasonably sure Crane could be an awkward bastard when he wanted to, but both of them seemed to have one thing in common. If they said they were going to do something, then they would do their damnedest to actually do it.

She had not expected Crane's text though. *Derzelas*, he started, as though halfway through a conversation. *I've spoken to someone who thinks they know something. Do you want to meet them?*

It felt like a rhetorical question. *Damn right*, Eva messaged back. *When and where?*

*That's where it gets tricky*, Crane wrote. *Tonight is the only chance you'll get.*

Sooner rather than later. That had to be a good thing, didn't it? *I can do tonight*, she messaged back. *Where do I need to go?*

*That's the catch*, Crane told her. *You better get moving. They're in Berlin. I'll meet you there.*

–

Sutton didn't seem delighted. 'You think this Crane guy is reliable?'

'It's gut instinct,' Eva admitted, keeping one eye on the clock on her phone, 'but yes. I believe he understands how important this is and I don't think he would waste my time. He's an ex-soldier,' she added as Sutton waited for something that would actually convince her, 'he definitely understands this is a life-or-death matter.'

'But you don't know anything else.'

'I do not. But if there's even a chance that somebody knows something about this Derzelas thing or person then I think it's worth following up. We need to know what connects the victims, because it's not just about Seifert. I still think New Thought have played a part in this somewhere along the line. Arnaud was completely open about the fact that they had had contact.' Sutton still didn't seem persuaded. 'We need a break, ma'am,' Eva all but pleaded. 'I know it's a long shot, but I just don't think Crane would set up a meet unless he really believed there was a good reason for it.'

She knew it would take a moment or two for Sutton to run through all of the options in her head. 'And you think you can be back in the office tomorrow?'

'Late tomorrow ma'am,' Eva said, 'I'm pretty sure I can be back here inside twenty-four hours.'

Another pause. 'Okay,' Sutton said eventually, 'run with it and we'll see what happens.' Eva put her phone back into her pocket and went to leave. 'But Harris?' Eva had known there would be a sting in the tail. Sutton glared as she spoke. 'If this doesn't do it,' she said as soon as Eva was through the door to her office, 'if this doesn't clarify who or what Derzelas is or what the New Thought connection might be, then I'm closing down this line of enquiry completely.'

—

A cab dropped her at Heathrow. She had booked her flights on her phone as they drove. Talk about travelling light, Eva thought as she stalked through the entrance to Terminal 2. She had her phone, wallet and passport, and that was it.

Crane messaged her after she made it through security. *This is important*, he told her. *Dress down*.

What the hell did that mean? Eva checked her phone. She had forty minutes before she needed to board, just about enough time to pick up something scruffy from the airport shops. Luckily she had changed into trainers when she stopped home to grab her passport, and she picked up a pair of slashed jeans and a black off-the-shoulder T-shirt and put them on her credit card. *Why?* She had messaged back as she paid. *Nightclub*, was all Crane said.

Urban camouflage, she assumed. On a whim she grabbed make-up and hair gel from a chemist and a cheap nylon rucksack from a luggage shop. Beyond the window, rain had begun to fall on grey runways. Eva went back to the luggage shop and bought a black cagoule that could roll up into a tiny nylon bag. It was the diametric opposite of fashionable, but at least it was functional. Then she boarded the plane.

Just over two hours later she exited the terminal at Berlin Tegel and used an app on her phone to find a cab. A polite city on the face of it, Eva thought as she watched the towers of Potsdamer Platz drift past, but so drenched in history it felt as though it might suffocate her if she really paid attention. Forty minutes after she left the airport, she found a hotel near Heinrich-Heine-Straße U-Bahn station. A small room with a single bed, long net curtains on the windows and only a chair and writing desk beside it, shower and toilet in a cubicle the size of a wardrobe. Not the smart end of the city, she thought as she closed the door, but if all went well she would only be there for a few hours.

Crane emailed her soon after. 'I'll text you nearer the time,' he said, 'but so long as we're there for around midnight it'll be fine. If you got a room at the hotel then it's only a ten-minute walk. So we're going to meet two people, they'll be together. It's a nightclub like I said. They do theme nights like all nightclubs. This one they do once every few months and people come from a long way for it. I did some digging with the transhumanists I know, but they pointed me a bit further along. These people know New Thought, but I don't know if they're directly connected. They say they know about Derzelas and I've got no reason to disbelieve them.' His email ended there.

The next email came a few minutes later. 'This is kind of an extreme gig,' Crane said. She had the impression he was trying to tell her something. 'Don't be surprised, but whatever you do just don't look like a cop. I've been here before. It takes a bit of getting used to but I just need to emphasise it's really important to play it cool tonight. Try and look like you're into serious clubbing. Don't worry about going over the top because trust me, whatever you do, nobody is going to notice.' He sent a URL with the mail.

A nightclub in Berlin. She sort of knew the reputation. She had heard of clubs with dark rooms where anything went, and some where sex on the dance floor was an every-night occurrence. Eva had been expecting something like that as soon as Crane had said 'nightclub', so why was he labouring the point? She clicked the link at the bottom of the email. It took a couple of seconds, but the website for the club loaded and then skipped straight to the page for the theme night.

When she saw it she swore out loud, even though there was no one in the room to hear her.

# Chapter Twenty-Six

Soft rain had followed her from London. Either that, or it had been here all along. When she saw the link Crane sent she had understood the cryptic nature of his email. *Don't look conspicuous*, he was telling her. In fact, the only way not to look conspicuous seemed to be to do exactly the opposite, but how the hell was she going to manage that?

In the end she resorted to going at the jeans and T-shirt she bought at the airport with a pair of scissors. By the time she finished there seemed to be more designer slash than fabric, but that was okay. She smeared mascara around her eyes and waxed her hair, then summoned up the courage to look at herself in the mirror. Somewhere between zombie-apocalypse and heroin-chic, she decided as she adjusted the cuts she had made in the T-shirt to let as much skin show through as possible. It would have to do.

Eva threw the cagoule over her shoulders and pulled up the hood. If needs be she could dump it when they got near to the club. On the street, the same soft rain soaked the pavement.

When she finally found Jonathon Crane, he was standing in the doorway of an empty building on Köpenicker Straße, dressed in a coat that reached down to his ankles and with a hood pulled over his head. 'I'm sorry this has all turned out a bit weird,' he apologised as he took her hand, 'but some people I talked to knew about Derzelas, the name at least. This is the last night these people are in Berlin; they're back to wherever it is they live tomorrow.'

They walked in the rain. 'You don't know where that is?'

'They keep it to themselves. You can kind of understand why.'

She could, at that. What she could not do was contain her incredulity. 'Is this stuff actually for real?'

'Oh yes,' Crane assured her. She couldn't see his face under the hood of his coat, but she could hear the certainty in his voice. 'It's about as extreme as it gets. I mean, I get the transhumanists. I understand them. I know what it is they're looking for and why they're looking for it. Modders though,' Eva saw the shoulders of his coat move in a pronounced shrug, 'they're another story.'

It had certainly seemed that way from the website. 'Is it permanent?'

'Yes,' he assured her, 'or most of it is. And the reasons for doing it are as varied as you can imagine. Look,' Crane said, and when he turned to face her, she could see the scars on his jaw but not his eyes, 'the two I'm going to introduce you to, they're okay. Weird, even by my standards, but the fact is they're actually lovely people. For that matter so are most of the people here, no matter what they look like. A few though,' he pulled his coat over his shoulders, 'are head-cases. They're basically Ultras who work for Eastern European gangs and do this stuff to terrorise. You'll know them when you see them, so do not get on the wrong side of them. If they knew you were a cop it would not end well.'

He could have mentioned that before she left London. 'I'll bear that in mind,' Eva told him. The club was ahead of them. She could see the queue. 'What happens now?'

'Now,' Crane told her as they crossed Köpenicker Straße, 'we immerse ourselves in the wonderful world of body modification.'

–

*Dark They Were, and Golden-Eyed.* Eva knew the name, but she had to dig back through her mental filing cabinet to retrieve the source of it. It was the title of a Ray Bradbury story, she remembered as she followed Crane towards the end of the queue, about colonists to Mars escaping a nuclear war on Earth and gradually transforming into Martians. It seemed an apt name for the club, or it did on this particular night. The transformation theme stuck her as especially relevant.

She assumed they were going to join the end of the queue, but Crane kept walking. There were maybe a couple of hundred people sheltering under awnings or umbrellas. A few, a small number anyway, were dressed like Crane and hid in the shadows; Eva didn't understand why, and didn't have the chance to think about them, because Crane marched right up to the front of the queue with her in tow. People stared, but nobody complained. Three bouncers stood in front of the door, heavy-set men, well over a hundred kilos each, one shaven-headed, one with a thick beard and the last who somehow fitted in-between the two. Crane stopped in front of them. Then, with a flourish, he took off his coat.

Even Eva gasped. The prosthetics Crane had selected for the evening were polished chrome, or so they appeared. An intricate array of coils and Celtic knots, presumably designed and manufactured by him, shimmered in the streetlights. All 3D-printed, the dark metal plate that protected part of the side of his skull had been covered with a brilliant outer layer, traced with more knots and ridged with horns. Pure theatrics, Eva thought as she took a step back to admire the effect. Behind her, in the queue, she heard a couple of complimentary whistles and a smattering of applause.

Even the bouncers nodded their approval. The rope at the front of the queue was lifted, and Crane stepped through. Eva walked behind him, but the rope came back down. Crane turned to her and frowned, so she pulled off her cagoule and bundled it into a ball. The bouncers now seemed less certain, but still they hesitated. Crane stepped forward, lifted the rope and put out his silver arm for Eva to grasp. 'She's with me,' he told them. It was all that was needed, Eva saw. Together, they walked into the club.

'That was probably the flashiest entrance I've ever actually seen,' Eva admitted as Crane led her towards the cloakroom.

'I should damn well hope so,' Crane told her as he folded his cloak, 'I printed this arm especially.' He draped his cloak over the silver limb. 'Keep your eyes open though,' he warned her, 'because now things are going to get seriously weird.'

—

The woman behind the cloakroom desk was naked, but Eva had been half expecting that, because by now she had read stories. What she had not expected were the golden contact lenses and intricate tattoos that covered every part of her, including her face. Pixie ears, Eva noted as she turned her head, surgically adjusted to an elfin shape. When she smiled, her forked tongue flicked the air. Her feet appeared to be cloven hooves, but when Eva peered, she realised that they at least were only cleverly made-up boots.

And that was probably the only faked modification she saw from then on. The club was spread across four floors, three above ground and one at basement level. Berlin club culture was as hedonistic as Berta Nicholson's parties, but here an undercurrent of threat pervaded the air. She followed Crane through to the ground level, which had the largest dance floor and the stage shows. It felt, as the heat and stench of sweat hit her, like walking into some outer circle of hell. Her eyes struggled to adapt for a moment. When they did, she was still not certain what she was looking at.

There were people here, hundreds of them, and for the most part they looked like normal human beings. Drunk, stoned, half-naked or dressed in outrageous costumes, but people, nonetheless. In amongst them though. Something else.

Body modification. The very idea horrified her, not only because it was intrusive, but because it seemed so permanent.

The first person she literally walked into looked like a lurid comic-book demon from a Manga universe. Tall, bulging muscles, wearing only tattered trousers, tattoos over every inch of his skin, but that skin was distended. Ridges on his forehead, shaved scalp, a row of chrome spike piercings ran over the centre of his head where a Mohican should have been. More metal in his face than she had ever seen. She stepped backwards, but he only turned and grinned at her. When he did so she saw his teeth were filed into sharp points, and, like the girl on the counter, his tongue had also been split. Reflective contact lenses and an actual tattoo on the white of his eye. She must have looked shocked, because he gave her a lascivious leer. 'Bienvenue,' he growled, voice traced with sarcasm. She pulled herself together after that.

She saw more modifications scattered around the dance floor and the lounges that surrounded it. A woman with what she now knew was corset piercing walked between tables; studs ran the length of her back on either side of the torso, black lace threaded between them. A man passed her with what appeared to be hideous facial deformities, but the manic searching she had done on her phone before she met Crane had told her this was a bagel head, caused by an injection of medical-grade saline into the forehead. It would fade within twelve hours she now knew, and leave virtually no trace behind.

Amongst hundreds of people she saw dozens of modders, all showing off their bodies. Some were grotesque, like a hulking lizard man who stalked the dance floor flicking his forked, extended tongue at dancers, while others were bizarrely beautiful and artistic. Eva saw two women who had presumably come together, an angel and demon pairing whose tattoos and carefully contrived implants were little short of exquisite. A crystal man whose skin was peppered with hard, mirrored plates stood under a spotlight and shimmered in its glow. The room spun. The scent of marijuana filled the air. Eva shook her head and tried to bring herself back to reality. She needed to focus on the job in hand, not stand around gawping like a backpacker on an alien planet. She turned around, scanned the dance floor and went looking for Crane.

'Where are they?' she demanded when she caught up.

'Not sure,' he admitted as he too glanced around the dance floor. 'Let's try the next level.'

It didn't help that she didn't know who or what they were looking for. On the next floor they found bars and smaller rooms, some of which had floor-to-ceiling video screens showing Japanese anime to quietly stoned audiences. There were darker rooms too. A few couples disappeared into them, their intentions obvious. Other rooms, lit by lurid neon, showed re-runs of football matches. Crane shied away from those. Eva could see why. Well-built men with vicious spikes protruding from knuckles and forearms congregated there and yelled at the screens, drank shots and snorted coke. Ultras, Eva guessed; tattoos that emulated everything from Bratva to Yakuza to LA gang signs. Some had scarification; raised skin in intricate patterns caused by branding. One of them looked out of the room, and for an instant, he caught her eye. A cold stare made of mirror lenses and sharpened teeth, for a moment it almost seemed as though he recognised her. That was impossible, she thought as she looked away before she too was caught staring, wasn't it? When she turned, she saw that Crane too had noticed the exchange, but after a moment he turned his back on her and carried on.

'Here for one reason only,' Eva muttered under her breath as she followed Crane deeper into the club.

–

It took Crane almost twenty minutes to find what he was looking for. Another side room, darkened, a dozen tables dotted around it. In the centre of the room Eva saw a podium, not high, scattered with cushions and strips of material. The people at the tables seemed more relaxed than some of the frenetic crowd outside; they sat in twos and threes and were getting quietly drunk or high. Savini would like it here, Eva thought as Crane led her to an empty table. She sat, then looked up at him, but he didn't join her.

'What's going on?'

'I have to meet some friends,' he said. 'I won't be far. I'll catch up with you afterwards, just stay here and wait for me.'

She felt suddenly bewildered. 'What?'

'Watch the show,' he told her. 'Stay behind. They'll come to you.' With that, he was gone.

She took a drink so as not to look conspicuous, a scotch and soda served by a waitress with completely black eyes and elfin ears. Eva waited. After five minutes the lights dimmed even further.

Two figures emerged from the darkest shadows, a man and a woman. She couldn't see the extent of their modifications, but they were wrapped in what looked like silk gowns. She could sense anticipation growing amongst the small crowd. In the dim light, she saw the couple pick up tall glasses and drink the contents down. They danced, slowly. Soon after, they started laconically peeling the gowns from each other and running their hands over their bodies.

She thought she knew what would come next, but what Eva had not expected was the effect the liquid had on their skin. Slowly, helped by the beam of a soft ultraviolet lamp, they began to glow.

For a moment Eva didn't understand what was going on, but then realisation struck her. Both body modders and transhumanists, she guessed. She had seen articles about genes being injected into mice that caused them to become phosphorescent in the same way fireflies glowed at night. Whatever it was they had drunk was causing their skin to emit light.

It wasn't bright, but it was noticeable. She heard appreciative murmurs from the tables around her, and the pair on stage responded to that. Moving more quickly now, they knelt down on the plinth, leant on the cushions and began to fuck.

She was glad it was dark. Somehow, the idea of sitting at a table on her own watching a sex show was not one that had occurred to her when she woke that morning. What made it worse was that, by the sound of it, some of the people around her in the dark were starting to have sex too.

Where the hell was Crane? What did he mean when he said he had to meet some friends? All she could do was slide down in her seat and watch the couple, whom she presumed she was going to have to interview, run through positions on stage in front of an audience who were clearly heavily into watching. More than that, Eva saw as the couple twisted and writhed, she was going to have to sit with them having seen the intimate body modifications they were now displaying.

She didn't know the names. There were piercings everywhere, as well as bizarrely shaped implants, ribs and protrusions she wasn't certain she knew how to describe. Around her she heard the sounds of grunts and moans, building in time with the couple on stage.

*Christ*, Eva thought as she waited for the show to finish. *Just… Christ.*

# Chapter Twenty-Seven

It took nearly half an hour for the two of them to come to her table. By then the room was almost empty. Eva guessed there would be another show in a few hours, but for now there was more going on in the rest of the club to distract punters. That suited her fine, but she was left wondering when Crane would return.

They sat opposite her, still loosely wrapped in the silk gowns they had worn at the start of the show. 'You're Crane's friend,' the woman said as they sat. Eva nodded. 'Tal,' the woman said, pointing at the man. 'Gala,' she said, pointing at herself.

'Eva,' Eva said. She didn't feel as though she could dive straight into the reason for her visit; there had to be some preamble. Luckily Gala seemed to be thinking the same way.

'Did you like the show?' She asked the question with a slight, sarcastic smile. Both of them were completely covered in tattoos, and up close Eva could admire the intricacy of them. Even the sclera of Gala's eyes was blue. The effect was disturbing, but strangely aesthetic.

'It was,' Eva fished for suitable a word, 'awesome.' Then she asked: 'How did you achieve the glow?'

Tal smiled at her. His teeth were razor sharp. 'It's called messenger RNA. It's based on the trials that were done in mice a few years ago. Maybe you saw it?'

She had. 'Isn't that heavyweight biochemistry though? That's not the kind of stuff you mix up in your back bedroom?'

'Well, it is,' Tal said, 'if you know how.' He glanced at Gala. 'We know somebody who knows how. Which is kind of why you're here, isn't it?'

Eva took a chance, although it didn't seem too much of a guess. 'Derzelas.'

'Derzelas,' Tal agreed. 'What do you know about it?'

'Precisely nothing.'

'Join the club,' Gala said. Her English was flawless, as was Tal's. If she had to put a nationality on them she would have guessed Scandinavian of some sort, but it would have been just that, a guess.

'Meaning we don't know his real name, even if it's him that's actually Derzelas,' Tal explained, 'but we do know what he can do.'

Gala produced an electronic cigarette from somewhere. 'God,' she emphasised as she drew down a menthol cloud and then exhaled it, 'do we.'

'You mean the phosphorescence?'

Tal frowned and shook his head. 'No. I mean yes, but that's just a trick. We were talking one night, he was looking at new ways of identifying chromosomal damage without needing to take samples, and realised in a few cases that the technique of delivering mRNA could be used to produce a colour reaction to certain deficiencies. We offered to act as guinea pigs.' Tal glanced at Gala once again. 'It was the least we could do.'

'You sound like you have a background in science,' Eva said.

Tal smiled. 'You're not going to find out,' he assured her. 'We don't generally approve of cops, but Crane assures us you're an exception.'

Eva pressed the point. 'Do you work for Seifert, then?'

'No.'

She wasn't going to get any further by going down that route. 'What do you mean, it was the least you could do?'

Gala gave her a broad smile filled with extraordinary sadness. 'Tal was dying,' she said.

'Slowly,' Tal said, 'and quite painfully. I had an adult form of Sandhoff disease, a neurodegenerative disorder. I was wasting away. I have to tell you, it's a really shit way to live, or to die.'

She felt the hair on the back of her neck rise, just a little. Somehow, she knew she had just made the first connection. 'What happened?'

'I was part of New Thought,' Gala admitted. 'I'm not going to tell you about that either, but you must know they are very well connected. They helped, or at least they tried to. They put out some feelers. That's when we met Derzelas.'

'Is that his name?'

Tal shook his head. 'No. And no, I'm not keeping it from you. I don't know his real name. As I said, I don't even know if he called himself Derzelas. It's a code name but I never understood whether it's for him or what he does.'

Eva waited. She knew intuitively that it was crucial not to rush them. 'He's a scientist, obviously,' Gala told her. 'A researcher involved in genetics. He worked on attempted cures for a number of genetic disorders, but there was something different about him, something that set him apart. He's prepared to trial drugs on humans well before it's legal to do so. He knows the diseases are worse than the consequences of failure.'

'I was dying,' Tal reiterated. 'He gave me one chance in four. He said: this will either work, or it will speed up the degeneration, or it will kill you in a couple of days, or it will do nothing at all. It's your choice. He didn't sugar the medicine. I absolutely knew the risk I was taking.'

'What,' Eva asked as she let the information sink in, 'did he do?'

'Technically? An unregulated CRISPR–Cas9 intervention that delivered messenger RNA to cellular polymerase via a modified virus, in my case e-coli.' Tal shrugged. 'What can I tell you? Gene therapy, it's not rocket science. It's a damned sight harder.'

She tried to understand. 'So he could, what, be struck off for this? Disbarred or something?'

'I think there are those who would try to frame his work as criminal. Would that be you, Detective Inspector?' Gala asked. The implied sneer annoyed her.

'If that work involves abducting people, killing them and then dissecting their bodies, then yeah, I'd count myself amongst them.'

Gala hissed. 'Don't be ridiculous. He saves lives, he doesn't kill people.'

'This is why you're here?' Tal snarled.

Perhaps she had gone too far. 'I'm not claiming it's Derzelas, if that's even his name. To be honest if I could eliminate him from the enquiry completely it would be a big step forward. I'm not here to fit anyone up,' Eva insisted, 'but somebody is systematically killing people who work for Seifert, and I'm trying to find out who.'

Gala still looked furious. Tal seemed less so. 'It can't be him.'

'Good,' Eva said. 'Why?'

'He's sick. It's why he experiments. His wife died of a degenerative disease. He couldn't help her. They met when they were both in the early stages of treatment. Some things that worked for him didn't work for her. I don't think he physically could kill anyone.'

A disabled researcher suffering from a degenerative disease? It didn't exactly feel like a prime suspect. Eva leant forward and rested her head in her hands. 'I guess that's another dead end,' she told them. 'It would have been good if I could have eliminated him completely, but if you don't even know his real name then that's not going to happen.' It was starting to look as though the trip had been a waste of time after all. Sutton would have her pound of flesh for that. 'Is there anything else you can tell me?'

Gala looked uneasy. 'There's someone who might know who he is. Another practitioner in a different field, a transhumanist at least.' Tal shot her an angry glance, but then he nodded. 'Derzelas mentioned him once or twice; I think he had worked with him.' When Gala gave her the name Eva's eyebrows shot up. 'Be careful of him though.' When she explained why, it was as though one small curtain at least had been lifted.

It seemed as though there wasn't anything else to say. Eva needed to find Crane, and then she needed to grab a couple of hours sleep before her flight. 'I can't say it was pleasant to meet you, Detective Inspector,' Tal said as he actually shook her hand, 'but I accept you have a job to do. A word of advice though.' Eva thought he was going to say more about the contact Gala had named. 'There are people in this club who are aware there is a police officer in the building,' Tal said. 'I think they may be looking for you by now. Did you know you had been followed from London? When you leave this room I suggest you get out of the club, as quickly as possible.'

–

Followed from London? Who the hell would do that, Eva wondered as she slipped out of the side room and edged her way around the club. The answer to that question came to her in less than a second. Duncan Webb, and through him Semion Razin's people. Did they have the resources to follow her to the airport and then on to Berlin? When she looked back over the steps she had taken en-route, Eva realised it would have been ridiculously easy for Webb to arrange.

Nobody had followed her from London. Nobody had needed to. Webb's people would have watched her board the plane and then contacted Razin's people in Berlin, because Alastair Hadley had been certain Razin had equivalent organisations in most major European cities. Follow her, work out her approximate destination, and then put a price on her. It was easy if you had the phone numbers of enough people prepared to kill for a couple of thousand Euros. Maybe, she thought as she slinked around the side of a dance floor, they even had a WhatsApp group.

Where the hell was Crane? Why had he abandoned her with Tal and Gala? Where was she supposed to go now? Again, the answer came to her quickly. She needed to get out of the club as Tal had said, and then back to her hotel. Would she be safe there? It didn't matter, she was thinking too far ahead. Crane had been aware of Ultras hanging around the club. Now she had to assume at least some of them were looking for her.

Would she be able to get out without being noticed, she wondered as she pushed the doors to the stairwell and started to make her way down to the ground floor. The doors swung closed behind her. It was at that point the question suddenly seemed academic.

–

Five of them, hard bodies, eyes wide, pupils presumably dilated by coke or amphetamines, but as they were all wearing mirror contact lenses, she couldn't be certain of that. Covered in tattoos and grotesque horned implants, all of them stripped to the waist, torsos slick with sweat. Studs, impaled in their skin, everywhere. She started to back away, but they surrounded her, there on the stairwell. 'Well,' one of them said in heavily accented English, 'Eva. We've found you.'

Cold fear that had swept over her the instant she saw them turned to outright terror. There had been a few other people on the stairs, but they had moved away quickly when this group showed up. She looked at her assailants in turn, eyes darting between them. 'You like the club?' one of them asked. 'You haven't seen the best bits yet.'

Suddenly she found herself being dragged, one on each arm, pulling her up the stairs to the next floor. She opened her mouth to scream, but another of them grabbed her by the jaw and squeezed. It hurt. 'Careful,' he told her, 'it's easy to slip on these stairs.'

Drunk, stoned high. Five of them, she knew what they had in mind. That terror gripped her as they dragged her up to the top floor, pushed their way through double doors and took her to a room with a window that looked out over the city. Doors closed behind her, but she could still hear the repetitive thud of a bass line from a PA system. Nobody would hear them in here.

They shoved her into the middle of the room, then formed a ring around her like a pack, circling. One said something to another; she didn't recognise the language, but it sounded Slavic. The other burst out laughing. Hysterical laughter, crazed, maniacal. She knew then why they had brought her up here. They were going to rape her. Then they were going to throw her out the window.

She knew them, from intelligence reports anyway. Conscripts in somebody's army. The kind they sent to ethnically cleanse villages and scorch earth, killers from teenage years still looking for the thrill of war. Psychos, too broken to care. She knew she was going to die.

Which one of them would make the first move? They all wanted a go. She could see that. She couldn't breathe. Tightness in her gut and her groin, she wanted to curl up into a ball and pray they would go away, but she knew they would not. All she could do was fight. She wouldn't win, she didn't have a hope in hell, but she didn't want them to find her easy. They were going to rape her and kill her. She was damned if she was going to let them enjoy it.

One stepped forward and shoved his hand onto her breast. He pinched, hard. She slapped his face, as hard as she could, so he slapped her back even harder and continued mauling her. *Screw you*, she screamed inside her head. One term of self-defence classes at uni, taught by a man with black hair and a black beard, in a white suit with a black belt. All she could remember. Eva straightened her fingers, almost bent them backwards then made a V-shape out of them. All her strength. She shot them forward, angled, landed them spread on either side of his nose, nails first, then scraped up into his eyes and scratched as hard as she could.

A yell made of anger, pain and hate. 'Fucking bitch,' he screamed as he let go of her and slapped his hands over his eyes. *Don't stop now*, she told herself. *You know what to do next.*

Right foot back half a step, then throw your hip forward. She could remember the man's voice, quiet and determined, telling the class where to hit and how. *Kin-geri*, the most basic karate kick. And the most dangerous. Bring the knee up first, foot pointed straight down, then snap it out like you're going to pull it back even faster; that's where the power really is. Total, cold terror, but she was committed now. She heard the words in her head as she threw the kick. Aim for the inner thigh, use it as a guide, a track, but keep going. Don't kick for. Kick *through*. Explosive release. Aim for a point a foot higher. Pull back just as hard.

The top of her foot hit his balls, and then snapped back as though it were on a spring. The sound was that of a cricket bat making contact, a loud, wet slap that brought with it the briefest instant of intense satisfaction. He froze for a moment as though unable to process the pain, then crumpled to the floor clutching his groin and gasping. She felt a second of elation, which quickly passed. The others would not make the same mistake.

A punch in the face. Hard enough to stun her. Two of them were on her now, one had his hands up her T-shirt, the other had her from behind and was dragging her jeans down around her knees. She struggled, but they were too strong. She looked down at the man on the floor as a third ripped her panties and tried to shove his hand in-between her legs. She squirmed, twisted and managed to pull away, but he grabbed her hips and turned her back towards him. He forced her legs apart, wedged himself between her knees, and then unzipped his fly.

A sudden crash. The doors burst open. *Crane*, Eva saw as she bucked and struggled. *Too bloody late.* He stormed into the room, light glinting on his prosthetics. One of the Ultras turned to jeer.

'Hey,' he barked, 'look, it's the tin man. You want to have a go too, tin man? Well, you got to join the queue. We're all going to fuck this bitch first, you can have whatever's left over.'

'Put her down,' Crane snarled. 'You've got three seconds.'

The man, pointed ears, tattoos across his face, silver eyes, sharpened teeth, studs and spikes on his knuckles and head, laughed. 'Or what? Or what, tin man? What you got up your sleeve? We gonna have to pull your arms and legs off too?'

Crane took several steps forward. 'I've got something you haven't, you jacked-up dog-faced pieces of shit,' he told them. Inexplicably, he was smiling.

Tattoo Face sneered. 'Yeah? What's that?'

Crane took a slow, sidling step to one side. 'A brain, obviously,' he said. 'What a bunch of total fuckwits. You didn't seriously think we'd walk into a spot like this on our own, did you?'

From nowhere, three men joined him. Clean-shaven, casually dressed, they looked almost painfully out of place for the club. Tattoo Face and the others tore their attention away from Eva. *A fight first, rape after.* Her chances had not improved. The man holding her dropped her. The guy trying to rape her zipped up his fly. She stumbled backwards and pulled her jeans up. There were five Ultras, counting the one on the ground still clutching his balls, and three of Crane's friends, whoever they were. The odds did not seem great. Then the men who had appeared behind Crane all produced handguns.

Stubby shapes, barrel that bit bigger than an automatic. Machine pistols, even she knew that. Tattoo Face scowled. 'You wouldn't dare.' He had barely finished the sentence when one of the three sprayed the ground in front of him.

Deafening, staccato fire, splinters ripped from floorboards sprayed the room. Tattoo Face and the others cringed. Crane wandered over, put his face in front of them and said: 'I've killed harder men than you.' He glanced at Eva then, where she was trying not to shiver uncontrollably. The slightest shake of his head, a movement that said: *time to go.*

*Bloody right*, Eva thought. She tried to pull herself together and walk straight, but Tattoo Face gave her a sneer and a nasty, contemptuous laugh. It should not have affected her, she knew that. Crane had played his card, she was getting out of there, but the sneer and laugh were like spit in the face. She snapped.

She couldn't hit Tattoo Face. She didn't dare risk that. Instead she stepped over to where the first guy lay on the floor, swung her leg as hard as she could and kicked him in the teeth. Then again. And again. She felt his nose break, then his cheek. He tried to shield his head, so she kicked in the ribs. Eventually the rage subsided, but the need for revenge did not. Looking Tattoo Face in the eye, she trod on the head of the man who lay at her feet as she walked towards the door. 'Tell Duncan Webb,' she said as she let the door swing behind her, 'I'm going to burn him alive.'

## Chapter Twenty-Eight

Crane and his companions drove her back to her hotel. She shook, but she still needed to know what the hell had just happened. 'Some friends of mine,' Crane told her, 'from the Kommando Spezialkräfte, Deutsche Bundeswehr. I first met their colleagues in Lashkargah, quite a few years ago now. I like to keep in touch.' He nodded his head in the general direction of the club. 'Those bastards were wise not to pick a fight with these gentlemen.'

The three of them gave Eva polite nods, as though they had just been introduced to her at a party. She was grateful, but the rage hadn't evaporated. 'Why did you leave me with Tal and Gala?'

'To open the back door for these guys,' Crane said. 'You were supposed to wait. Why did you not tell me a UK drug dealer in the pay of the Russian Bratva had put a price on your head?'

'Because I didn't know he had.'

But, she thought as she turned her head to stare out of the window, she bloody well should have.

-

Once Eva had showered, changed and in part at least pulled herself together, Crane and his friends drove her to the airport. Crane sat in the front and Eva sat in the back, sandwiched between what she now knew to be two commandos.

Crane had been Royal Engineers. He had told her that. She would have put money on him being involved in bomb

198

disposal at some point too; that wasn't a difficult guess given his injuries. She knew that was a job that required insane amounts of courage, and which earned appreciation and admiration even from men who were basically as hard as sodding nails. Of course Crane had friends. He could probably walk into a bar in any city in Europe or the US and never need to pay for a drink ever again.

'It's going to be a long wait,' Crane said, 'but you'll be safest there. Will you be okay in London?'

'Kingston,' she told him, pointlessly. 'I don't know, but I know what I'm looking for now.'

'I'm going to be back in the UK soon,' Crane told her. 'I'm there to help if you need me. Did Gala and Tal give you anything of any use?' The car pulled into the airport short stay lane.

'Honestly, I'm not sure. They gave me something I have to follow up on; it's still a bit confused at the moment. I don't understand where it fits, if it fits, but,' she shrugged, 'I'll let you know.'

Crane nodded. The car stopped and they all got out and stood in front of the departures lounge. 'What about this Webb character?' Crane asked.

That was another problem that would not go away. 'We're after him; we should have him soon. My team will have him banged up any day now, I'm certain of it.'

Crane raised an eyebrow. 'And will all this stop because he's in prison?'

The same question was preying on her mind. 'Best I can do,' is all she could tell him. Eva nodded at the three others. 'Please tell them, I can't thank them enough,' she instructed Crane, but by the looks on their faces she knew they all spoke English.

'Be careful,' Crane told her as she walked in to the departures lounge.

Eva smiled, even though the smile felt fragile, and nodded. *Be careful*, she thought as she went looking for security. *What difference would being careful make?*

She spent the next nine hours stretched out on hard, uncomfortable airport benches like a tourist who had missed her connection. At one point she relented, went to a duty-free shop and bought an inflatable pillow, eye mask, earplugs and a travel rug to complete the picture. She set an alarm on her phone and tried to sleep, as secure as she could be in the knowledge that Webb's contract killers would be unable to reach her on this side of the security gates.

Webb wasn't going to go away. He was almost certainly Razin's manager in Surrey, and she had convinced him that it was her fault that Jeffrey Cowan had taken his own life. And the problem with that was that it was true.

Cowan too had tried to kill her. It seemed standard practice for whoever was seen to be in the way of Razin's operations. Cowan, as a corrupt police officer, was rightly terrified of exposure though. He would not have survived prison. Webb was just an estate agent, and yet protected by Razin's magic circle. Prison would be little more than an inconvenience for him. And all of those indisputable facts brought her inexorably back to the person she still loathed and despised most in the world, Chief Superintendent Alastair Hadley.

If he was in fact a CS. Who knew what role Hadley really played? Cowan himself had thought Hadley to be a spook, one whom no one trusted. Untrustworthy he might be, there was no denying that, but Hadley was also unquestionably well connected. Eva did not know to whom he was connected, or what his network looked like, or where it touched, but his influence was indisputable.

Hadley was not a cop. He didn't have a cop's perspective. Hadley was something else. He burbled on about 'national security' and 'existential risk' as though the ridiculous phrases actually meant something. As far as she was concerned, Hadley was some prince of darkness who believed the only way to confront Semion Razin's rigorously hierarchical brutality was by fighting fire with fire. Lying there on a bench in Berlin Tegel airport, having only escaped gang-rape and being thrown to her death by the grace of a trio of soldiers who were not above freelancing for friends of friends, she began to wonder if Alastair Hadley might actually be right.

What did that mean? Specifically, what did that mean for her? Webb wouldn't let her go. When he found out his attempt in Berlin had failed, he would try again. And again. It was the way of Razin and his people, the ethos by which he operated, how he had grown his operation from a few hundred hard-core drug dealers to a structure that reached halfway around the world. *Always finish.* Nobody ever escaped.

The implications of that slowly began to sink in. Even if Raj succeeded, even if he and HMRC found the imagined link between Delta V and Cowan, it would not be enough. Webb could reach out from inside prison. He could buy thug after thug to try and kill her because Razin would soak up the cost. There was only one thing she could do to stop Webb. She knew that now.

But, try as she might, Eva couldn't bring herself to do it.

—

London. The plane bounced as it touched down at Heathrow; a crosswind had been building all the way across the Channel, and although the rain was still light, it blew in her face and stung her cheeks as she stabbed at the taxi app on her phone. She just needed to get home now. The club had looked so close to hell as made no difference; the five men who had been prepared to kill her for the fun of it were as near to any vision of demonic savagery as she had ever imagined. She needed to be back in her flat, somewhere safe. Eva glared at the Uber driver when he tried to make cheerful conversation and buried herself in her phone. Soon after that, he gave up.

The sky was dark again. It felt as though the only daylight she had seen in over a day was when she had peeked out from under her eye mask and travel blanket on the bench at Berlin Tegel. Even then the sky had been iron grey. Now all she could see was streaks of rain falling diagonally through sodium streetlights and an incessant pattering on the windscreen. It should have felt good to be home. Instead, the sight of those streetlights flickering on the water as they drove over the bridge that crossed the Thames brought only fear.

The cab dropped her off outside of her block of flats, in the shallow arc of a lane where taxis were allowed to stop. The concierge didn't look up as she entered the foyer and crossed it, headed towards the inner courtyard. At the back of the entranceway the door swung open onto a small garden paid for by a maintenance fee. In daylight it could be pleasant. Tonight she only wanted to be locked up indoors.

Eva was halfway across the garden when she heard footsteps. All around her, tower blocks looked down, fenced-in walls of brick a dozen stories high that each contained a hundred apartments. She saw lights on at most windows. The gardens were lit as well, but heavy clouds rendered the night dark. Footsteps. Someone was running towards her.

She turned, almost paralysed with fear, convinced she was going to have to fight again. She dropped into something like a combat stance that in reality was awkward and ridiculous. When she turned, though, she recognised the figure immediately. Fear turned to something else: a concoction of relief, bemusement and irritation.

'Kyle,' Eva barked into the darkness, 'what the fuck do you want?'

## Chapter Twenty-Nine

Kyle Shaw skidded to a halt. Even with his hood up, rain ran down his face. 'You cops are just all charm,' he grumbled at her. 'Not like, hi Kyle, how's it going, or how you been? Is that what I get? Oh no.'

She had been harsh, she knew that. 'I'm sorry,' she started to say, but Kyle didn't let her continue.

'Forget it, I got more important stuff. Listen,' he said, stepping closer, 'I think some bloke's been watching your flat.'

It felt like a punch in the stomach. Although she had half expected something like this, she had managed to put it to the back of her mind, but hearing it from Kyle brought reality crashing back in. 'You sure?' she asked, trying to keep the tremor from her voice. 'Just one guy? Same person?'

She saw the look on his face change. 'You expecting something?' Eva didn't need to answer. 'One guy,' Kyle confirmed, 'he just hangs around. Jeans, black hoodie, kind of big. Never lets you see his face. Except,' he reached into his pocket and dug out his phone, flicked through his photos, some more quickly than others, then stopped and held the screen up to her.

An awkward angle. It looked as though Kyle had taken the shot through the railings of the next flight of stairs, camera angled; the photo was blurred, but she recognised the corridor. It was a man, as described; Kyle had caught his face, a profile at least. She couldn't swear to it, she wouldn't have stood up in court and said so, but something about him reminded her of the face she had seen behind the wheel of the truck that had tried to run her over.

'Is he there now?'

'He was there,' Kyle confirmed, 'about twenty minutes ago. I figured I'd come and let you know if I saw you.'

She wanted to hug him. 'Thank you,' Eva said as she took out her phone. 'I want you to do something for me.' He didn't respond, so she continued. 'Go home. Get inside, shut the door. I'm going to go and find him and ask him what he thinks he's doing.'

Kyle looked horrified. 'What? Are you mental or something? You're going to go and try and talk to that bloke on your own?'

Eva shook her head. 'No,' she told him, 'not alone.'

–

She climbed the stairs to the fourth floor. Perhaps she should have waited, but by now she was just eager to get everything over and done with. Another of Webb's bastard thugs coming after her. This one either hadn't heard about Berlin or had been hanging around for over a day. Either way he was going to be sorry, she thought as she looked out onto the stretch of corridor that ran between apartment blocks. Before heading for the stairs Eva had phoned for an Armed Response Unit.

*Too tired to let it drag on.* There was only so much fear she could take. After a certain point it became like a toothache, a persistent pain that permeated every thought, pressed on her like a ceiling in a gothic horror story, winding inexorably down to crush her. *Screw that*, she decided as she stepped out onto the landing. *Time to start shooting back.*

Jacks had texted her, two words only. *On way.* The brevity of it felt refreshing, like the moment she had seen Crane's friends pull out machine pistols in the club, that sudden realisation that big guns were on her side. She felt vindictive, remorseless. If this bastard had come to try to kill her he was in for a nasty surprise.

The corridor was empty though. Had Kyle just been mistaken? He was a bright kid, she had to give him that, but he wasn't anything other than that – a kid. He could have got it wrong. She tried her old trick though, turned the logic upside down, inverted the circles in her mental Venn diagram. When she looked at it from the opposite side, considered the chance that Kyle might randomly spot someone when she knew Webb was after her, it seemed astronomically unlikely. Ergo, Kyle was almost certainly right. Somebody was watching her flat.

Just not now. Eva walked the length of the corridor glancing into doorways and windows as the entrances to the flats turned and faced out onto a covered walkway, but she saw nothing. He had been there, the photo was enough to convince her, but he wasn't there now.

She understood how people like Duncan Webb worked, how Razin's people tidied up inconveniences like her. Coming from Webb, with his slick hair and regimental tie, his veneer of unctuous respectability that ran barely even skin deep, it wouldn't be anything sophisticated – no hired contract killer would be given her photo. It would be a message, a word put out on certain streets and a couple of estates, around a handful of pubs and in car parks while talking about other deals. Twenty K for whoever makes this happen, no questions asked. *Market forces*, Eva thought as she raised her phone to make the call that would cancel the ARU. *Let the market work it out*. The phone connected. Eva opened her mouth to speak to the control room, but the words stuck in her throat.

He stepped out from behind a door, from a cleaner's cupboard filled with mops and detergent, saw her and froze. She saw the look in his eye: confusion and surprise. He hadn't been expecting her, not at that precise moment anyway. Maybe he had been about to give up for the night; it didn't matter. She could almost see the thought processes that ran through protracted if-then loops inside his head. Then, as though the programme had suddenly reached its end, his eyes widened as he realised his opportunity. Eva turned and ran.

He was behind her, she could hear him, a dozen paces. She sprinted the length of the corridor, slammed her way into a fire escape door and jumped the first half dozen steps down the stairs. She stumbled, leapt so as not to fall, crashed against the wall of the landing below but didn't stop. Next flight. The slap of his feet on the stairs. When she glanced behind her, she saw the knife.

A carving knife, nothing sophisticated, just enough to cut her guts out. It swung in his hand as he ran, fluorescent lights flickering on its serrated edge. She careened down another flight, hit another wall. She would have bruises all over her if she lived. A thud, closer behind her now. He had jumped the last flight. She couldn't get away.

Eva turned, bunched her hands into fists, snarled and screamed. It wouldn't do her any good, she knew that. She might land a punch or two, but she could almost feel the blade slamming up into her gut so hard it might pierce her back. Anger and frustration, the certainty again that she couldn't win.

Except she could. Another crash, a sound from above. A yell, high pitched and strangulated, something out of control. Kyle, almost falling down the stairs, fire extinguisher in hand. He slammed it into the man's back.

The man arched, jaw open in surprise and pain. Eva punched his face, not well. It hurt her hand, but when his eyes went wide, she did it again. It wasn't enough. He would recover in a few seconds, but it was enough to let them get away. 'Move!' she yelled at Kyle, but he was already moving.

They clattered downstairs. She didn't have time or breath to berate Kyle. Even though he had almost certainly saved her life, he had now put himself in danger. She would chastise him later. If there was a later.

A roar like a wounded animal. He would be behind them again in a moment. Something weighed in her pocket. Keys. She had taken them out of her bag when she had been expecting to just open her front door and collapse into bed. Now they slapped against her thigh, an inconstant reminder of the way the evening should have been. The front door keys were of no use to her now. The car keys might be.

As she kept running downstairs, Kyle brushed her shoulder. If they could get to her car they had a chance. Get in, slam the door, ram him into a wall, crush the bastard to death. She was past the point of trying to uphold the law. If she didn't kill him, she knew he would kill them.

Kyle. She didn't want to be responsible for him, but there he was, right behind her. Would he cut Kyle's guts open as well? The kid was a witness now; he had seen the man's face. Of course he would kill Kyle. Together they slammed on the door of the car park and burst through.

*Get to the car.* It was all she could do. She sprinted forward, keys out, squeezed the fob. Lights flashed. She was about to grab the door handle when something boomed in the echoing silence of the underground car park, so loud it hurt her ears. *Christ*, she thought as she flinched, crouched, dragged Kyle to the ground. *The bastard's got a gun.*

The knife had been to make the killing look like a mugging gone wrong, or maybe even right; it didn't matter now. Whatever it was, he had given up on that idea now that there were two of them.

*Not just two.* The shot had been deafening; anyone standing near the flats would have heard it. Eva shoved Kyle under the car then crawled across the floor. Rough concrete scraped her hands; the stink of petrol made her gasp.

She could see his feet. His footsteps were slow and deliberate. Why? He didn't know where they were, she realised. He was worried about them getting behind him and making a run for the fire escape, or the sloping ramp that gave access to cars. Minimum fuss, Eva thought as she watched him search. This was where he wanted to kill them.

A sudden scraping. *Kyle*, she realised. *You bloody idiot!* He had caught himself on the underside of her car. He was struggling to release himself. The man turned, walked forward, gun raised, steps more deliberate now. She couldn't let him get to the kid. Annoying pain in the arse he might be, but he was her responsibility. She darted between cars, made enough noise that he had to look away.

Suddenly she was out of choices. The doors to the refuse bins were closed, padlocked; there was no way back to the street, and he was behind her. Half a dozen metres. Eva turned. Saw him raise the gun. Aim it at her chest.

Then his head exploded.

And she thought the handgun had been loud. The screech of Jacks's automatic rifle filled the garage – two bursts, just to be sure. Head ripped to shreds, the bullets hit like a succession of hammer blows that caved in the left side of his skull and splashed viscous residue over nearby cars. One round struck the top of his spine. For a moment she thought the force of it would decapitate him, but before that could happen, he fell to the floor, unambiguously dead. Jacks trotted from the shadows as two of his team caught up with him.

'You okay?' he barked at Eva. She nodded, too shaken to trust herself with words. Jacks stood over the body and looked down. 'One more second,' he told her, as if she didn't know. He nudged the gun out of the dead man's hand with the tip of his boot, an action that looked as though it were some matter of habit. When he was satisfied, he stepped away from the body.

'This is getting out of control,' Jacks told her. 'It's got to stop now.'

# Chapter Thirty

Later, after she had thanked Kyle while specialist officers flocked and fussed around him, after she had given her statement to an officer from another station and had fresh DNA swabs and fingerprints taken, after her team had descended and insisted on running the crime scene, Eva finally crawled into bed.

She couldn't tell which was worse, the exhaustion or the fear. She had thought there would be a break, some respite between attempts on her life, but Webb was clearly intent on burying her as quickly as possible. Perhaps she could run. Get a new identity, disappear from view, use the resources of the witness protection programme to keep her out of sight for a while at least. She lay and stared at the ceiling, but as exhausted as she was, sleep would not come. Was that what she wanted to do? Run away, give up on her team, abandon the victims that Wren, and she too, believed were being held somewhere by some madman with a bizarre agenda she had not yet understood? Did she really want to admit that Webb had won?

*Consider the alternative.* She already had. Maybe there was a solution, one final approach she could make. She knew there was, but like giving up and going into hiding, she didn't know if she was ready for it yet. *If not now, then when?*

Christ. The crew in Berlin had been bad enough, but this time an actual innocent had been involved. Maybe Kyle Shaw wasn't innocent, for all she knew he could be bonking half the girls in his school, but he had looked out for her. He had taken responsibility, acted when he didn't need to act, and risked his own life when he had seen she was in danger. That counted for something more than GCSEs, or at least it did in her book. Which, of course, made it all the worse.

If Jacks hadn't arrived; if she hadn't made the call before she went upstairs and summoned the ARU, both she and Kyle would be dead by now. Kyle was a witness. There was no way he would have been allowed to survive.

More than anything else, that made her mind up for her. The screen of her phone glowed as she raised it. She had thought she could look after herself, and that might or might not be true, but it was no longer a point worth debating. What was incontrovertible was that, sooner or later, innocent lives would be lost, and that was something she had a moral duty to try to prevent. Through whatever means were expedient.

Eva typed with her thumbs. *Duncan Webb is the owner of a property investment firm, Webb County Partners, which has links to Saudi Arabia, Russia and China*. The light from her phone blotted out everything around her. She hated herself for writing the message. She kept typing anyway. *Webb is connected with a number of fatal incidents and money laundering that is into nine digits. When you first sent me to Kingston you were after the fixer in the station and Semion Razin's manager in Surrey. I got Jeffrey Cowan. Webb is almost certainly the other individual you were looking for.*

She paused, hesitated. The idea of helping Alastair Hadley made her feel sick to the stomach, and yet what could she do? If Kyle had died tonight and she had somehow survived, that would have been on her conscience. She could not allow that possibility to present itself again. Eva took a breath and wrote one more sentence. *We can't touch him*. Then she hit send.

She tried to sleep then. She lay on her side, knowing that she had done all she could for that night, and she started to drift away. She was almost there, had almost sunk into oblivion, when her phone pinged. When she looked at the screen, she saw it was half an hour since she had sent her message. The ping had been the reply.

Two words. Enough to chill her to the bone.

I understand.

—

She avoided the station the next day. It wasn't that she needed to. It was simply that she didn't want the undoubtedly sincere concern Flynn, Newton and Chakrabati would heap on her. They meant a lot to her, she counted them as friends, but the message she had sent to Alastair Hadley the night before had been like lighting a fuse. It weighed on her conscience. She didn't want to be around when it burned to its end.

Instead she descended on Kingston hospital, and Judy Wren's office. It seemed tidier now, as though Wren was finally catching up on the backlog caused by the inundation of body parts. 'Anything new?' Wren asked as she poured her a coffee from a pot that sat on top of a filing cabinet. She pointedly did not ask about the night before, although she must have heard about it by now. That was Wren, Eva thought. Sensitive and intuitive, even though she only ever worked with the dead.

'Plenty,' Eva told her, 'although I'm not sure what to make of it yet.' She told Wren about the Berlin trip but left out the detail of how it had ended.

'Body modification,' Wren mused. 'I've never even been that keen on tattoos, so it's a bit beyond me. I do know the techniques are getting more sophisticated. You say these people mix it with CRISPR?'

Eva nodded. She had needed to check the acronym, although she had read about the technique a couple of times in the past. Clustered Regularly Interspaced Short Palindromic Repeats – it didn't readily trip off the tongue. She knew it referred to sequences in the four chemical letters that made up DNA, which marked the places where 'edits' could be made with a particular enzyme, most often something called Cas9. CRISPR was a bit like sprockets in a piece of old movie film, and Cas9 was like the blade once used to cut it. 'They used the same process that made mice glow in the dark. What freaked me was how casual it all seemed.'

'And so it should,' Wren said. 'Freak you, I mean – because it's not casual. It's complicated, even though it's something you can do in your kitchen now. Biohacking' – she actually shuddered, Eva saw – 'yes of course it's just fine and dandy to cook up genetically modified plague on your Aga just to see what happens.'

'That bad?'

'Jennifer Doudna thinks so,' Wren said, 'and she invented the whole thing.'

'But CRISPR is a powerful tool for developing new medical treatments, right?'

'It is, by far, the most powerful in decades. It's still a work in progress, but yes, I can see why your body modifiers took a chance. It's just early days. All new techniques are risky at first.'

Wren's description echoed everything she had read. 'The glow-in-the-dark thing,' she started to ask.

'If the subject under discussion was computers,' Wren complained, 'I'm certain you would be a damn sight more rigorous with your terminology. Don't go all woolly on me just because this is biology.'

She had a point. 'The messenger RNA needed to induce bioluminescence,' Eva corrected herself, 'engineering that isn't a straightforward thing, is it? As in it would require a great deal of skill, just not necessarily a large laboratory.'

'Right,' Wren agreed, 'that's really the point of CRISPR. Technically anybody could do it, providing they had the depth of knowledge.'

'Okay,' Eva said. She stood. 'I may be getting somewhere.'

Wren laced her fingers. 'I really hope so.' She pursed her lips for a moment. 'I don't know why, but I'm absolutely convinced he has people out there he's experimenting on. I think he keeps them sedated. I think the first round of experiments are genetic, not surgical.' She gazed at Eva. The look on her face was sheer despondency. 'I know it's not fair to pile all this on you, but I really believe that if we can find them, we can save them.'

Another punch in the gut, but this time from a friend. The problem was she couldn't disagree with Wren.

'I know,' Eva told her. 'So do I.'

–

The underground was empty now that the rush hour had passed. She stood on a tube on the Northern line and reflected on Wren's intuition. Eva didn't have any proof either, but she was as certain as she could be that Wren was right.

Whoever was abducting Seifert personnel had the whole process down to a fine art. Someone was following them, watching them; it was the only possible explanation. When Flynn and Newton checked with the last person to see each of the abductees and went back over their movements, it seemed every single one of them had been in an isolated location, however briefly. A run on an almost empty common, eating lunch in secluded gardens, parking in a quiet street where they didn't have to pay for a meter – and none of those places covered by CCTV cameras. Somebody had known that. Someone had known where they would be alone, because the behaviours were habitual, the kinds of things the victims did nearly every day. Even so, the effort and planning would have been considerable. Like Wren, Eva couldn't believe that anyone who took that amount of care would be so cavalier as to discard their victims casually.

*Ergo*, she thought as she changed to the Bakerloo line and exited the tube at Oxford Circus, *ergo*. The one fact she had managed to uncover in Berlin seemed like a tantalising yet dubious key. It had the potential either to unlock everything or to be another false lead, interesting yet irrelevant to the disappearances. Whichever it was, that morning she was determined to find the truth. She would jam the key in the lock and force it if necessary. One way or another, she would get an answer.

# Chapter Thirty-One

*Cold storage.* Eva had first come across the term in a training session on cryptocurrencies at MPCCU. At first it had seemed like a contradictory concept, but after a couple of hours she had realised how powerful and simple the approach was.

Bitcoin, Altcoin, Zcash, Neo, dozens of others, all of them competing to be an international means of exchange, and all of them being exploited by criminals. Like gene editing, the science of blockchain was complex and confusing, but the power of it when used as a virtual currency was undeniable. Cryptocurrencies were supposed to exist online though; that had been the entire point of them. Why anyone would want to take them offline, to put them into cold storage, had initially escaped her.

And then it hadn't. Dealing with offline cryptocurrency, stored on especially prepared flash drives or USB sticks, was like wandering around with your pockets filled with gold bullion, only an awful lot lighter. You could circumvent the usual exchanges with it, avoid the places where hackers and scammers and even government agencies lurked and add yet another layer of obfuscation to the trafficking of illegal money. No wonder organised crime groups loved offline cryptocurrency. Now there was a whole new way to both conceal it and move it around, as Tal and Gala had explained to her. All you had to do was implant those drives under the skin of data mules, people willing to travel between countries with millions of dollars of cryptocurrency buried inside them. And all you needed for that, she thought as she knocked on a black door on Harley Street, was a skilled surgeon who was familiar with the practice.

Eva pushed on the door of Aaron Rose's waiting room and stood in silence. She counted seven people now: four men, three women. They were not wealthy people, she could tell that from the pallor of their skin and the dark circles under their eyes. They stared back at her, disliking her scrutiny. She sighed, loud enough that they would notice. Then she took out her warrant card.

She lifted it up, pointed it at them so each of them could see. Eva grasped it in her left hand. In her right she held the door of the waiting room. It was open. She made sure it stayed that way. The message was clear enough; she didn't need to back it up with threats, and anyway, she didn't want to. One by one the people who had been waiting to see Aaron Rose processed her message, understood it, then stood up and left.

Ten minutes later Rose himself stepped into the room, a look of confusion and alarm painted on his face. 'What's going on?' he demanded, but he did so quite quietly.

'I think you know,' Eva said. 'I know what your other business is. Some people in Germany told me. I'm curious as to how many Bitcoins you can smuggle on an implant, although I don't suppose that's a matter of physical space, is it? Do you want to talk about it now or would you rather I just arrested you?'

They sat in Rose's consulting room. He looked as though he was in pain. He should be, she realised. In the space of a couple of sentences his world had unravelled around him.

*Not a criminal*, Eva thought, as she scrutinised him, *not really*. An opportunist, probably foolish, almost certainly greedy, although she had no information at all about Rose's personal circumstances. Who knew what pressures he was under? She didn't need to understand, she decided as she watched him. She simply needed him to stop. That, and to confirm what Tal and Gala had told her.

'I'm not doing anything illegal,' he began as Eva sat in the chair in front of his desk and stared. 'I'm just… facilitating.'

'It's who you're facilitating *for* that's the problem.' She folded her hands in her lap. 'Fortunately for you, you have the opportunity to wind this side of your business up gracefully, as I think they say in bankruptcy courts. A legitimate reason to decline new customers and the chance to step away from old ones. That's the police breathing down your neck by the way. Don't worry. Your customers will understand that. Some might view this as a narrow escape.'

It took a few moments for that to sink in, but when it did Rose quickly made a choice. 'Yes,' he told her. Then, shamefaced, he said: 'Thank you. I'm assuming there is a catch?'

She had already worked out it would be almost impossible to identify Rose's previous clients, so all she could do was make trouble for him, albeit lots of it. Perhaps Rose had realised that too. She kept her counsel and smiled.

'It's not as bad as you might think. I need information, and I don't want to have to wait for it. It really is,' she leant forward to assure him, 'a matter of life and death.'

She saw his pronounced Adam's apple move up and down on his throat. 'I'm still a doctor,' he insisted. 'If I can help, I will.' He had been caught, but now he knew he wasn't going to suffer whatever consequences the courts might have eventually decided on. He damned well should at least try to appear magnanimous.

'I want to talk to you about human experimentation,' Eva said. 'And Anna Seifert. And,' she said as he opened his mouth to speak, 'Derzelas.' Rose closed his mouth again. 'You know the name?'

'I know of it,' Rose admitted. He shrugged. 'Not much, but I don't need to. I can guess.'

'Guess.'

Rose rocked back in his chair. 'I don't know what this has to do with your investigation, the other one I mean. I don't see how they connect. If you're talking about Derzelas then you're talking about Michael Sullivan, and I've got to tell you there is no way on this earth Sullivan would hurt a soul.'

Rose sounded adamant, more so than she had expected. 'Who is Sullivan?'

'A geneticist. An especially fine one, highly respected but ultimately tragic.' He frowned, Eva noticed, not so much at her as at himself. 'I met him a few times at various conferences. I liked him as well as admired him. It came as a shock when I heard he was sick. A degenerative disease; he went for the usual treatments. That was where he met Susanne. Both were at early stages, but her condition was more aggressive than his. When he realised traditional treatments weren't going to work, Sullivan started experimenting on himself to try to help her. That must have been especially bitter.'

'Why?' Eva asked, but she could already guess.

'He used gene therapies. They worked for him, but not for her. After a couple of years, she died.' Rose shrugged his shoulders, but he seemed far from dismissive. 'They seemed to encapsulate the phrase "love is pain" almost perfectly,' he told her.

'And Derzelas?'

Another shrug. 'Just a name. A Chthonic god of health and vitality in Dacian tradition; I think the point was two-fold. Both a god of health and an underground god. Concealment was the intention.'

'But why concealment?'

'Because Sullivan's work breaks rules, regulations and laws in half the countries on the planet. What he does is technically illegal, although it's hard to imagine him ever being put on trial for it. What's far more likely is that he'd be prevented from experimenting, which would be like a death sentence for him.' Rose shook his head. 'His cure turned out not to be a permanent solution, I know that much. Sullivan is not a well man.'

Eva watched him as he spoke, scrutinised every look and every word. She hated herself for how angry it made her feel, but she believed Rose. Another dead end, she thought as she waited for him to continue. Had Berlin really been for nothing? Rose's assertions seemed to match those of Tal and Gala's precisely.

'If Sullivan is performing experiments on cadavers then you can be sure they'll adhere to Human Tissue Authority guidelines. He's not some Doctor Frankenstein carving up corpses. Anna Seifert wouldn't allow that.'

She almost jumped. 'Seifert knows Sullivan?'

'I'm sorry,' Rose said, 'I assumed you'd know? Yes, the two of them are connected. I don't know to what extent, but is that a surprise? An exceptional researcher and the head of a pharmaceutical company? It's not that big an industry, Detective Inspector, not at the top anyway. People tend to meet like-minded people.'

Perhaps Berlin hadn't been a waste of time after all. 'But Seifert no longer deals with you?'

'Anna didn't approve of my other business. I'm not sure I blame her.'

Eva thought about that for a while. 'Then what do you do? How does it work?'

'It's not a problem,' Rose told her. 'I comply with the Human Tissue Act 2004, Schedule 1, Part 2, Section 12, quality assurance. Those people,' he waved his hand towards the now-empty waiting room, 'are in absolutely no danger from me. My devices are a hundred per cent safe. Seifert conducted tests using cadaveric tissue for me, but only to prove BioHeuristics devices continue to be safe to implant. That doesn't require the resources of Seifert. Another company, Scientific Support Services, provides Human Tissue Authority-approved testing at a fraction of the price.'

She took a cab to Waterloo from Rose's consulting rooms. The rain was incessant that morning, and although by keeping to the overhangs of department stores she would have been able to reach the Tube without getting drenched, the fact was she needed time to think. Anna Seifert had denied any knowledge of Derzelas, which if Rose was telling the truth was a downright lie. And yet, even assuming there was a connection between Seifert and illegal, or at least unregulated, human experiments, did that necessarily equate with murder? Could the body parts in the tanks of formaldehyde belong to victims of failed experiments? It seemed far-fetched, at least from the perspective of a respectable international company. If there was a connection, and both instinct and logic were now telling her there had to be, it would be something else.

The cab crossed Piccadilly Circus. Her phone pinged. A message, no sender ID. It didn't need one. She knew whom it was from. Her stomach knotted when she read it.

It now appears he has been syphoning.

Carefully chosen words. *It now appears.* Meaning it had now been made to appear. How had Hadley done it? It was probably a stupid question. He would have turned to his contacts in the security services and perhaps higher and said: we need to make this happen. Wheels somewhere would have turned. Bank accounts that would have been closed to the police would have been opened in the name of national security. Power without oversight. That was Alastair Hadley.

She slumped in the back of the taxi. She had not wanted to, but Kyle Shaw getting himself involved had left her no choice, or so she told herself. All she could do now was wait for the other shoe to drop, for a text or phone call that would presage the final outcome. She doubted it would take long.

Webb would be dealt with by Razin's people themselves. That was Hadley's plan, anyway. A long way from the letter of the law, but it undoubtedly smacked of natural justice. Fredrick Huss and New Thought would almost certainly have approved.

She tried to feel remorse, but found she didn't have it in her. All she could feel was the creeping certainty that, whatever the outcome, at some point in the future Alastair Hadley would demand his pound of flesh.

## Chapter Thirty-Two

She must be dreaming. Hazel Richards had thought that before, when the sharp pain had caught her, in the left of her back, just below the shoulder blade. She couldn't be having a heart attack; she knew that for a certainty. She had volunteered for the cardiovascular monitoring programme and had spent hours running on a treadmill with a spirometer covering her mouth; she had allowed dye to be shot into her veins just so the team could use her as part of the baseline of what a healthy subject should look like; she had even slept with an ECG monitoring her heart rate for twenty-four hours to be sure there were no abnormalities. Cancer, diabetes, even bubonic *sodding* plague – she could believe any of those. The one thing she could not be having was a heart attack.

So why had her heart felt like it was going to explode?

It wasn't until later that she realised the pain wasn't from inside her body, or at least not deeply so. Something felt like it had stabbed her in the back, just behind the heart. No wonder the pain had confused her. The sudden shock of it disordered her; she couldn't make any sense of it. Not a knife, she felt certain of that. Something else?

Or was it a dream? Had she had an allergic reaction to one of the drugs, was she now in anaphylactic shock, and had she only imagined that somebody had attacked her? Wasn't that the more likely scenario? Right now, was it not possible she was in a hospital somewhere with a line of adrenalin and God knows what else bringing her body functions back into normal range? Surely that made more sense?

Or, Hazel thought as she tried to open her eyes, was she still on the front step of her flat, lying undiscovered, some unknown chemical combination shutting down her liver, kidneys and brain functions?

*I'm dying*, she told herself. She tried to find the energy to panic, but the effort seemed too much. She clawed what she expected to be rough stone beneath her fingers, but instead of scraping, her nails slid over a smooth, soft surface. It gave under pressure. It felt like a bed.

*I'm not dying*, Hazel countered. She had been rescued. At least she was not in the street; she had to be somewhere under care. So why was there still a pressure on her chest?

A weight, pushing down. Something lay across her, something heavy and cool. It moved. Coiled, slithered over her, she felt the texture of it on her flesh. She had to be dreaming. Morphine, some anaesthetic, she didn't know what. This had to be reality mixed with hallucination. This thing, on her chest. It was moving.

A silhouette against a pale ceiling, something above her face. Suddenly she recognised the shape of the head, the flicking of a forked tongue, and the slithering pressure on her chest. She had to be dreaming. A nightmare. It had to be.

*A snake.*

Hazel tried to scream, but she could not. The head came closer to her face. Then, without warning, the weight was lifted from her chest. She felt something being dragged across her and the sound of an irritated male voice.

'That's enough,' the man said, but he wasn't speaking to her. She could see the man – his silhouette anyway. He held the snake's head in his hand. 'You can cut that out any time you like,' he told it.

# Chapter Thirty-Three

One thing struck Eva as odd. She was unable to find images of the person Aaron Rose had referred to as Michael Sullivan online. There were plenty of people called Michael Sullivan of course, literally hundreds of them on all the usual social networking and professional community sites, but none that matched the description given to her by Rose, and none that bore any resemblance to the portrait in Mathew Harred's painting.

He wasn't invisible though. When she searched back through academic sites, she found plenty of peer-reviewed papers, either authored or co-authored by him, from a number of academic institutions and commercial organisations. What was interesting was that the flow of publications seemed to stop around six years ago.

No images. No recent news. When she searched the Police National Computer, she could find no record of him but, more peculiarly, when she checked for mundane information like National Insurance and PAYE records, none seemed to have been filed for the past five years. He might have left the country, or like her abductees he might have simply disappeared. Eva couldn't make up her mind. Was he the abductor, however unlikely Aaron Rose thought that, or was he now just a collection of body parts disposed of in a tank or even a black bag somewhere?

She had no way of knowing. But she knew someone who might.

Anna Seifert sat with her back to a window that framed her in grey. Heavy, turbulent clouds filtered through tinted glass formed an impressionist tableau behind her. The clouds, churning and disrupted, were as unreadable as her face.

'Yes,' she admitted finally, after Eva had let the question hang. 'I know the name.'

Another, pervading silence. 'And?'

Anna snapped. 'I don't know what to tell you.' Her annoyance with the questioning finally showed itself.

'Well, try and think of something useful,' Eva barked back. 'There are six people missing from your company and there's at least a chance some of them are being held alive somewhere. At least try to appear as though you give a fuck.'

She saw Anna's jaw drop. 'Jesus,' she spat, 'what the hell do you take me for? I don't know anything about these abductions. Haven't we already sent you everything we have? What else can I do?'

'Tell me about Michael Sullivan,' Eva demanded.

'He did work for us,' Anna said, looking as though she wanted to punch Eva in the face, 'but it was years ago. I'm just not sure what else to say. He was an exceptional researcher, his work was excellent and insightful, he was at the University of Cambridge's biochemistry research group and Seifert collaborated with them on projects; we still do. Sullivan isn't there anymore.'

'Where is he?'

'I don't know.'

'Why did he leave? Was it because of his wife?'

Anna hesitated. 'Possibly,' she admitted. The fact that Eva already knew about Sullivan's wife obviated the need for further explanation. 'There were rumours, suggestions that Sullivan had crossed the line. Not,' she added, 'that anyone who actually understood these things would have blamed him.'

For a moment it almost sounded like an admission. 'Why?'

Another, longer hesitation then. 'There are rules we have to follow. You know what they are. For the most part the rules make sense. They're made to protect people and companies. Sometimes though…' Anna paused, seemingly making up her mind, deciding how far she could trust Eva, then continued, 'those rules become an impediment. They stop us giving treatments we believe will succeed because they haven't been subjected to procedural tests. I really don't want to sound arrogant,' she said, watching Eva's face for a reaction, 'but there are times when we just know better. I'm not deprecating those procedures or authorities, but sometimes you just know when something is going to work, because you've been involved with the process day after day, and waiting years for approval only means more lives are going to be lost. I know how that sounds coming from the MD of a pharmaceutical company,' Anna said, wringing her hands, almost as though pleading, 'but it's still the truth.'

'Michael Sullivan tried unlicenced treatments to save his wife,' Eva said. No, she couldn't blame him for that, but she had heard the same thing from Aaron Rose. Anna nodded, but said nothing. 'But you don't know where Sullivan is now?' Eva asked.

'He disappeared off the face of the earth,' Anna said.

—

Anna was lying. Eva could sense that, even though she didn't understand what she was lying about. Perhaps just half the facts, commercial secrets, projects she no longer wanted to admit to, but she hadn't given Eva the entire truth. Did it matter? That, she thought as she drove away from the crystalline building hidden in the Surrey countryside, was what made it so *bloody* frustrating. Whatever Anna was concealing could be either pivotal or of no significance whatsoever.

That frustration felt as though it was going to consume her. Whichever route she took she ended up in seeming cul-de-sacs, dead ends with more information just tantalisingly out of reach. She had been doing this for days now. What were the chances Michelle Barnes and some of the others were still alive? God, she had to believe they were. If not, the chances of catching Amanda Tyler's killer seemed almost non-existent, and she could no longer stand that possibility.

She had just reached the main road when Moresby called. 'Where are you?' he asked. The tone of his voice made it sound as though he was being circumspect, Eva thought. For a hulking uniform sergeant who could probably rip off arms and legs in a fight he frequently showed surprising degrees of tact.

'Just on the way back,' she told him. 'Something up?'

'Incident,' Moresby said. 'I think you need to see it. Becks and Raj are on their way. I told them I'd let you know. How far away are you?'

Eva glanced at the clock on her car. 'About twenty from the station?'

'Keep going,' Moresby instructed her. 'It's St Jude's Hill.'

—

Half an hour later Eva showed her warrant card to the guard on the Weybridge gate of St Jude's Hill. A gunmetal sky glistened behind wet, fractal branches as she drove down the narrow, winding lanes of the private estate. It was here that she had first met Moresby, some five months before, on her first day at Kingston station. A crime scene, of course. A grotesque and bizarrely premeditated murder that had seemed especially out of place in amongst the multi-million-pound houses that hid behind high rhododendrons and mature English oaks. A woman with her blood, and her eyes, removed with almost surgical precision. A clinical murder, Eva thought, one that by its nature and method had given clues as to the motive behind it. She knew she should be gaining the same insights from body parts submerged in formaldehyde, but try as she might those eluded her. And now, what would presumably be another killing. Moresby would not have disturbed her for anything less.

Eva didn't need directions. She simply followed the procession of police cars to the house where she knew she would find the body. Behind a line of blue-and-white tape that twisted and spasmed in a chill breeze, she found Will Moresby standing and waiting for her, quite still, almost monolithic in the broad driveway.

'I'm not going to like this, am I?'

Moresby raised his eyebrows just a little. 'Well I can't say I did. Wren's here, she's just setting up shop. Raj and Becks are inside too. None of them know exactly what to make of it. It seems like somebody is sending a message.' Moresby turned and walked with her to the front door of the property. 'Problem is it feels like they've written it in Sanskrit.'

Inside, scene of crime officers and forensic investigators knelt and scraped, took photos and marked out polythene-covered paths where it was safe to walk. Eva put on the required coveralls and followed Moresby to the body. What remained of it.

It sat in a chair, hands tied, feet bound. A man in a suit, a lounge suit, tailored, dark blue. Shirt, well, she assumed it had once been pale blue; there was just enough of the original colour on the cuffs to make that assumption. The rest of it was soaked in blood. Whoever it was, his head had been removed.

Brutally. Eva could tell that from the jagged tears of skin that circumscribed the neck. Wren would doubtless give her chapter and verse, but if she had been asked for her own opinion, she would have said a power tool had been involved. Brutally, she noted as she forced herself to look more closely, but still carefully. Whoever had decapitated the body had taken care not to touch the collar and striped, regimental tie.

'The house is on the market,' Moresby told her, mouth covered by a surgical mask. 'An estate agent found him. She'd been asked to meet a potential buyer. You can guess the rest.'

'Did the buyer show?'

'Of course not.'

'So, she was meant to find the corpse?'

'It looks that way. Most especially as she knew him.'

Eva stepped away from the body. 'I'm guessing we knew him too.'

'Yep. Don't you recognise him?' Moresby wasn't trying to be flippant, but there didn't seem to be any reasonable way to ask the question.

'I think so,' Eva admitted. 'Have we found the head?'

'Yes,' Moresby grunted, 'of course we found the head. We were meant to find the head. Want to see?'

'What do you think?' Eva retorted, but Moresby led the way anyway.

The dining room. Somebody, someone with a particularly twisted imagination, had seen fit to make a show of things. A mahogany table, large enough to seat a dozen. In the centre of it, a plate. Blood had seeped from the severed head and dribbled onto the table, trickled along it in a thin stream and dripped to form a soaking patch on the carpet.

'Jesus Christ.' Eva breathed the words quietly as she stared at the tableau, but Moresby nodded his agreement.

'He really must have pissed somebody off,' he said as he looked down on the face of Duncan Webb. 'Why else shove the apple in his mouth?'

Why indeed? Duncan Webb, head on a plate, mouth open and an apple wedge between his teeth. Either a message, or somebody's idea of humour. And something else. What seemed like wooden boarding placed in front of him. It looked as though it had been scorched in a fire, although not recently. There was something written on it, barely legible, covered in soot and moss. Hesitantly, she brushed her hands across it. When she did, when the fine layer of earth had fallen from it, she could read the words.

Eva gasped. She couldn't help it. More than the sight of Webb's decapitated head, the name on the sign chilled her to the core.

There were only three words: 'Winter's Gate Farm'.

# Chapter Thirty-Four

In the garden behind the house, in a quiet, secluded corner not overlooked and not being searched by scene of crime officers, Eva put her hand against a wooden fence panel to support herself, leant forward and threw up.

*Dear God in heaven*, she asked as she spat acrid bile into the grass, *what the hell just happened?*

Duncan Webb was dead. That much did not come as any great surprise to her. Eva loathed and despised Alastair Hadley; she thought of him as a lazy, entitled individual who saw himself as a law unto himself, but one thing she knew for certain was that Hadley had contacts. And whatever she might think of Hadley, she knew Hadley's contacts would be competent. Eva had told Hadley the truth, because Jonathon Crane had been right.

Duncan Webb in prison was just as great a threat to her life as Duncan Webb out of prison, and apart from running to some witness protection programme, there was nothing she could do to protect herself so long as Webb functioned. *Ergo*, she had to take Webb out of the picture.

Dealing with Semion Razin's people was not like police work anymore. It was like war. The tactics used anywhere from Mexico to Albania were those Razin would deploy in London and Surrey if he felt the need. Webb had known that when he tried to kill her. Why should she feel guilty?

*Because you're an officer of the law*, the predictably dutiful part of her mind told her.

*You're an officer of the law who's still alive to think that thought*, the perversely logical part of her retorted.

*Divide by zero error*, some esoteric third segment of her brain interjected. *Dump it. Move on.*

She couldn't touch Webb, but Hadley could, so she had told Hadley. That would cost her, but that was not the point right now. Hadley's cryptic message had meant he intended to set Webb up, to make it appear as though he was taking money from Semion Razin's till. That at least seemed proportionate, if not even vaguely legal. *Bad guys killing bad guys*, Eva thought as she dabbed her mouth with a handkerchief. *Pragmatically it's not the worst possible outcome.* So, where in God's name had the sign come from?

Her darkest secret. Alastair Hadley knew it, because Hadley had worked it out. The night Colin Lynch flipped the light switch at Winter's Gate Farm, and a coalbunker filled with industrial explosives had turned the farmhouse into a smouldering crater, that had been down to her. Another untouchable criminal, this one protected by Hadley himself, eliminated with the unwitting assistance of Semion Razin's organisation. But Razin's people had never known about her involvement. As far as she was concerned, apart from Cowan and Webb, Razin's people barely knew she existed. Had she been wrong about that too?

Before she had left the room, in large part to avoid awkward conversations with Moresby, Wren, Raj and Flynn, Eva had taken a photo of the head on the table and the sign, now uncovered, in front of it. She had it on her phone. She texted it now, sent it as a message to the number she had for Alastair Hadley. She wrote a question beneath the photo, a deceptively simple one, but she knew he would not take it at face value. *What does this mean?* Eva asked him.

She waited. Had Hadley set her up? What would be the point? How would he benefit? It didn't make sense, because she knew he wouldn't imagine there was any profit in simple revenge. It took less than a minute, but Hadley replied. When she looked at the message her stomach sank.

*I have absolutely no idea*, was all he said.

–

Webb was dead. The consequences would present themselves to her in due course, Eva had absolutely no doubt whatsoever about that, but right now she needed to get her head out of her arse. She stuffed the handkerchief back into her pocket, turned and walked back to the house.

Raj found her first. He seethed. 'This is our fault.'

Eva almost flinched. Raj couldn't know about the text she had sent to Alastair Hadley. She lied to him. 'I don't see how?'

'The investigation. I mean, the pretext for it. We said we were looking into potential discrepancies in the Delta V fund to get HMRC onside. HMRC started an inquiry. Duncan Webb was ultimately responsible for Delta V.'

'So?'

'With Webb dead there's no chance of getting a prosecution. HMRC won't pursue it any further. They'll drop the case.'

That stopped her in her tracks. Her mind shot into overdrive. 'But that means—'

'There really is something wrong with Delta V,' Raj hissed. 'Some of the money really must be bent. That's why Webb was executed. There's no legal basis to proceed now. It shuts down any investigation of the fund, kills it stone dead.'

She felt as though she had been slapped. Both right and wrong, Eva thought as she let Raj's theory tumble around inside her head. Wrong in that it was not their investigation that had triggered the killing, it was Hadley's. As soon as Hadley became involved somebody had realised it was more than a mere police investigation. Right as well though. Webb had been sacrificed to protect Delta V. And that could only mean the fund had been created with laundered money. She reeled. So why the sign? Some quid pro quo perhaps, Razin's people telling her they would stay off her back if she stayed off theirs? A promise and a threat? It didn't matter, Eva decided. Right now, none of it mattered.

'I haven't got time to think about it,' she snapped at Raj. 'You're off the case.'

His jaw dropped. 'What?'

'Listen to me,' Eva insisted, face in his. 'I don't know what happened here except it's got to be gang related. Webb was a criminal, now he's dead. All this,' she waved her hand at the room, 'can wait.' Raj looked both dumbstruck and furious. He didn't bother to hide his anger from her. 'For Christ's sake,' she hissed back, 'we've got a duty to the living. They're more important than a dead money launderer.'

Raj ground his teeth, but she could see he understood. 'You think the abductees are still alive.' He didn't make it sound like a question.

Eva shook her head. 'I don't know, but we have to act as if they are. We have to presume so until proven otherwise. Webb can wait,' she told him, jabbing a finger at the dining room. 'He's not going anywhere.'

'So, I drop this? For now? Jamie and Becks have been going snow-blind searching through the files Seifert sent. I don't know if I can help them or if I'll end up getting sucked under too.'

Eva took a gamble. 'Screw the files,' she said. 'You, Jamie and Becks, I just want you doing one thing. All three of you chasing this down, I need an answer. Long shot,' she added, looking him in the eye. 'You up for that?'

Raj scowled. 'Come on Eva,' he demanded quietly. 'Do you really need to ask? What the hell have you got?'

One weight off her shoulders. 'A name,' she told him. 'Michael Sullivan. If I'm right he's the figure in the painting. He's also connected to New Thought and Seifert, and it's almost certain he's been involved with illegal human experiments.'

'Sounds like our man,' Raj said. 'Where do we start?'

Another damned good question. 'Let's go and talk to someone who knows a thing or two about death,' Eva said.

Judy Wren turned to face her computer screen and scraped a browser window to a comfortable height. When she typed, she tapped the keys on the keyboard slowly and deliberately, as though even after many years the process was not something that came naturally to her. Eva pulled up a chair and sat down next to Wren. Raj leant in the doorway and watched.

'Antony Naeku's going to perform the first pass on your friend Webb,' Wren told them as she typed. 'He's turning out to be a gem.'

'It'll be interesting to know what the cause of death was,' Raj said. Wren ignored him. Eva turned to stare. 'What? I mean like, was decapitation the cause of death or was it post-mortem? It's not like I'm asking if he died of pneumonia.'

'Decapitation was the cause of death,' Wren muttered as she typed. 'You can tell by the pattern of blood spatters. There was still force in the arteries at the moment they were severed; the heart was still going. That much was unmistakable.'

'Jesus,' Raj said. 'He was alive all the time?'

Wren shook her head. 'A couple of seconds at most. As soon as the blade hit the artery, blood pressure dropped through the floor and everything would have shut down. I guess technically he might have been alive, but there was no way he could have been conscious. Systemic shock would've taken care of that.'

'Let's leave Webb to Naeku,' Eva insisted. 'Right now, I want to know what you make of Michael Sullivan.'

Wren arranged the browser so that she had a string of tabs open. 'There's quite a lot online if you know where to look. It's mostly academic material though. As you said, there doesn't seem to be anything of a personal nature that's survived. I think he's done a fairly good job of cleaning out social media accounts and the like, but I imagine if one of your computer forensics people at MPCCU went looking they would turn up far more than I have. I've stuck to the academic stuff, published papers and the like.' Wren turned to look at them. 'Is that okay?'

'It's more than we've got,' Eva said. 'Thanks for helping make sense of it.'

'It's mostly just impressions,' Wren told her, 'about the type of things he worked on. Sullivan was a respected geneticist. His focus was on epigenetic ageing. He was looking at it as a root cause of a lot of diseases. It's how we age at a cellular level,' she told them, 'as opposed to the kind of top-level biological ageing we usually think of. Many diseases are thought to be influenced by epigenetic age; cancers for example. As we get older our genetic blueprints become less clear when they're passed on to the new cells that our bodies produce to replace those that die. Those errors are sometimes compounded and result in what are effectively mutations. As cells get copied over time, the risk of that gets higher. That's what cancer is essentially, cellular growth that gets out of control because the cell design has gone wrong. It's like every day we photocopy ourselves,' Wren grinned, as though the analogy she had just thought of amused her, 'until one day we start running out of toner.'

'Epigenetic ageing,' Eva said.

'Yeah. Well, Sullivan was looking at ways of slowing it down, maybe even stopping it. You've heard of stem cells, right? Well, they have two categories of self-renewal, stochastic differentiation and obligatory asymmetric replication. I won't bore you with the details but whichever route you choose there's always an accurate copy of the original in the various versions that get created. That's a big deal,' Wren said. 'It means that in theory a pristine copy of your original blueprint always exists, if only we could find a way back to it. That's why the transhumanists are so keen on stem cell therapy.' She pinched the skin on the back of her hand and showed it to them. 'Look. Liver spots, UV damage, discolouration and wrinkles, all courtesy of badly transmitted DNA blueprints. Same on the inside as on the outside. As we get older, we get everything from arthritis to Alzheimer's, and that's just the A's. Addressing epigenetic ageing using stem cell therapy and similar in theory gives us a way back, a chance to reboot.'

Biology was not Eva's strong suit. 'What does that actually mean?'

'It means,' Wren said as she gazed at them, 'the fountain of youth. Anti-ageing, the reversal of epigenetic decay. Not today, obviously, but maybe not so far into the future as you might expect. People have been looking at anti-senescence for a hundred years. It's only in the past decade there's been any real progress.'

Eva frowned. 'I thought that was all crank stuff?'

'Mostly,' Wren agreed, 'like those miracle-cure anti-age face creams cosmetics companies charge an arm and a leg for. All they're doing is basically re-inflating cells by pushing water into them, which of course evaporates after a few hours. Some research though,' Wren swiped through tabs on her screen, 'is most certainly not crank stuff. It goes back to what's called the Hayflick limit, discovered in the 1960s. A cell divides, then those new cells divide and so on, but Hayflick discovered they stop at around fifty generations. They become "senescent". Current thinking is that doesn't have to happen, because certain organisms have "negligible senescence", meaning they show no signs of ageing. There's some serious money being put into research by pharmaceutical companies into anti-senescence.'

'Including Seifert?'

Wren shrugged, 'Big Pharma is less inclined to publish their best work than academic institutions because it gives away commercial advantage. But yes, they'll have a programme, and it's pretty obvious from the papers that Michael Sullivan was a part of it at some point.' A look of distaste settled on her face then. 'Genuine anti-senescence. Imagine the can of worms that would open.'

Raj shoved his hands into his pockets. 'Why? Longer, healthier lives, wouldn't that be a good thing? Isn't immortality what we've been looking for since Gilgamesh tried to learn the secret of eternal life?'

Wren all but leered at him. 'Gilgamesh was two-thirds god, oppressed his people and got to sleep with every bride on her wedding night. Immortality isn't something you're ever going to find on the NHS. Eternal youth will be reserved for those who can afford to pay for it, for your loose affiliation of millionaires and billionaires. Maybe those people in St Jude's Hill with their multi-million-pound mansions, perhaps they'd be able to afford the upkeep. Can you imagine how that would feel? A community of Methuselahs living right in your midst, perpetually youthful while you grow old and die.' She laughed, a bitter sound. 'Talk about inequality.' Wren said.

'But this is speculation,' Eva insisted. 'It's like next-century stuff, right?'

'Probably,' Wren agreed, 'but there's work underway right now to try and get there, and a lot of money being spent on it.' She nodded at Eva, 'like at that fancy spa you went to.'

She thought back to Savini's blood cleansing treatment. 'But still,' she said, pointing her finger at Wren's screen, 'this isn't there yet, because if it was everybody would have heard about it.'

'But a conspiracy theorist would say otherwise,' Raj countered.

Wren smiled. 'Perception is the only reality.' She folded her arms, implacable and defiant. 'Don't ask whether it exists. Ask whether somebody sufficiently paranoid or deluded could *believe* it exists. Isn't it a good enough reason for murder?'

–

Michelle Barnes. Paula Francis. Hazel Richards. Daniel Beale. Graham White.

The incident room was empty now. It was late. The others had all gone away. She had spent the last three hours piecing together every scrap of information she could glean from Seifert's personnel files, missing person reports, work attendance reports, consultancy timesheets, sickness records, disciplinary notices. She had cross-referenced it with everything she knew about the bodies in the tanks. Then she had gone to work.

238

On the whiteboard she had drawn a Hoffman graph, 4-regular with 16 vertices and 32 edges, a circle of points essentially, each point linked to another by rules based on angles. At each node she had set a criterion. Eva had narrowed the criteria. Age, gender and ethnicity didn't seem like good fits, but work area, location, time in service, time missing, proximity to identified bodies and a handful of other measures seemed more useful. She weighted them, calculated standard deviations, gave notional values to each parameter. Then she compared them with her list.

Michelle Barnes. Paula Francis. Hazel Richards. Daniel Beale. Graham White. Those were the names her divining lay before her. Perhaps it was mad, maybe it was as ineffectual a means of identifying the abductees as tarot, or casting runes, or consulting the hexagrams of I Ching, Eva couldn't know. All she did know, as she stared at the list of names, was that these were the individuals who matched her criteria. Five that gave her perfect scores.

She turned to her laptop and sent their photographs to print, and then she erased her workings out, photographing the diagram and her scrawl with her phone before she wiped them, and overlaid the whiteboard with their images. Under each photo, she carefully hand-printed their names.

Michelle Barnes. Paula Francis. Hazel Richards. Daniel Beale. Graham White. Somewhere, based on her statistical analysis, they were alive. She believed that, because she simply had to.

In the silence of the incident room, she made a promise. 'Be patient,' Eva whispered to the photos that stared out at her from the whiteboard. 'I'm coming for you.'

# Chapter Thirty-Five

Eva knew something had changed the moment she drew up to Seifert's security gate. The barrier was down. It stayed down. The guard on the gate came up to the driver's window with a firm but apologetic look on his face. 'I'm very sorry,' he told her, 'but access to the site is currently being restricted.'

She took a moment to process the information. 'Why?'

The guard shrugged apologetically. 'I'm sorry, I really can't say. I'm going to have to ask you to turn around and leave, please.'

Eva stared. 'That's not going to happen.' She took out her warrant card and aimed it at him. The guard looked almost pained. 'Sorry Detective Inspector,' he told her, 'I haven't a bloody clue what's going on up there, but the whole place is in lockdown. Nobody gets in or out.'

In the distance she saw men in the woods that hid the building. They were searching, that much was obvious. 'Seriously? I thought you had CCTV covering those woods?'

She saw the guard swallow. 'CCTV is down.' The alarm bells that had already started to ring inside her head became a cacophony. Eva shoved the door open and climbed out of the car. 'Look,' the guard started to say, 'I'm sorry DI Harris,' but Eva held up her hand. She was not about to give him a hard time for just doing his job.

'I'm going to make a phone call,' she told him, and thumbed the contact for Seifert's reception. The number rang for longer than usual, but eventually somebody picked up. 'Arnaud Seifert,' Eva said.

'I'm sorry,' the voice began.

She all but snarled. 'This is Detective Inspector Harris of Surrey police. I'm standing at your front gate but your very efficient man here is refusing to let me in. If you don't want to find yourself obstructing a murder investigation, you're going to put Arnaud on the line, right now.'

It took a few moments but eventually she heard Seifert's voice. 'DI Harris,' he began.

'I don't want any excuses Arnaud,' Eva told him, 'I want you to tell your man on the gate to let me through. Then I'm going to come and find you, and you are going to tell me just what the hell is going on.'

Another pause. 'Yes,' Arnaud Seifert agreed eventually, 'perhaps that would be for the best.'

–

She didn't bother with the speed limit. In the grounds that surrounded the site, in amongst the re-wilded fields and copses of trees, she saw Seifert security staff searching in what looked like a grid pattern, almost like scene of crime officers carrying out an area sweep. *What the hell is going on?* she wondered as she slowed her car to a halt in front of the reception area.

The smart brunette woman in the dark suit who had met her before was already waiting, but now she seemed distraught. Eva resisted the temptation to interrogate her in the lift. It didn't seem as though she would get much sense out of her anyway.

Seifert was in an office she hadn't seen before. Sumptuous, modern, a billionaire's control room filled with tastefully designed translucent screens showing elegantly laid-out graphics, but still Seifert was reduced to a laptop and phone, the last of which he clutched to his ear. When Eva entered, he waved at a chair. 'Thank you, George,' he said to the person on the call, 'I know you're doing everything you can. DI Harris from the Surrey police has just arrived.' He glanced at Eva. 'A coincidence I think, but perhaps now is the time?' Garbled speech from the other end of the line. All she could get was the sense of urgency. 'Very good, I'll tell her that: Let me know.' Seifert hung up. 'George Sommers, our head of security.'

'Tell me,' Eva demanded.

Arnaud took a long, uneven breath. 'Anna has disappeared.'

No wonder the site was in lockdown. 'When?'

'We think about three hours ago. We can't be sure. It's all a little hazy.' Seifert was clearly as distraught as the woman who had brought her to him, although he seemed to be keeping things together somewhat better. That could change, Eva thought as she watched his face. She took out her phone and thumb-typed a text to Flynn. *Anna Seifert missing*, it said, *around 3 hours ago. Start looking now please. More to follow.*

'I'll need to speak to Sommers,' Eva said. 'What alerted you?'

'Everything went down,' Arnaud said. 'CCTV, RFID monitors, all the systems that were supposed to protect us. Who could have done this?'

Either he didn't know, or he was keeping up a pretence, but that seemed unlikely, Eva decided. 'Okay,' she told Arnaud. 'Let's start with CCTV.'

—

Sommers met them in a windowless room on another basement level. The location seemed more familiar to her. She saw server suites and racks of computers, network switches and stacks of UPS batteries, the kind of kit she felt at home with. The security hub felt like any well-maintained corporate security facility, and Sommers was a bald-headed man with a precise, unambiguous manner about him. 'We were at the point of calling the police,' he explained.

'Why hadn't you?'

'We needed to confirm this was an actual disappearance, not some chronic systems failure on our part. The problem is,' he glanced at an IT support person who had joined them, 'it seems to be both.'

The name on the IT person's lanyard was Jo Foster. Redheaded and wearing glasses, like Sommers, she seemed precise and serious. 'The first indication we had that there was a problem was when the CCTV server went down, just over three hours ago. All the camera feeds died, which is not supposed to happen. What's worse is the recorded video for the last 24 hours appears to be deleted.'

A million questions sprang to mind. Eva tried to ask them in the right order. 'You offsite after 24 hours?'

Foster nodded. 'At midnight. Secure backup in a co-location for 60 days, then archive to tape. That's not the problem. Local storage is on triple-redundant RAID arrays; we do everything in threes. Something wiped the drives.'

Eva imagined the schematic. 'That's not an external attack,' she told Foster.

'Correct. Somebody had a root-level script, full admin permissions. They nuked the bloody lot,' she almost spat. 'Full-on sabotage.' An interesting reaction, Eva thought. Foster was taking it personally.

'Who has root permissions? As in, who knows the accounts and password?'

'Me,' Foster told her. 'My team. Anna Seifert.'

'Logs?' Eva demanded.

'Gone,' Foster said.

'Jesus,' Eva swore as she looked over Foster's shoulder at a screen. 'You're having to rebuild the OS?' Without the operating system the server's only useful function was as a paperweight.

'It's junk,' Foster told her. 'And that's not all, is it?' she turned to look at George Sommers.

Sommers looked anguished now. 'We should have been able to follow Ms Seifert by means of some personal location technology,' he ventured.

'You mean RFID chips inserted under her skin for tracking in the event of a kidnap,' Eva said. 'Don't worry. I've already had the conversations with Anna and Aaron Rose about her implants. I'm aware of how extensive they are. So, what, you can't pick the chips up through phone networks?'

'We can't pick them up at all,' Foster interjected. 'They were shut down just before the security systems were trashed.'

Sudden alarm, as what Foster had just said sunk in. 'Hang on. Those chips are *inside* Anna Seifert. The only way you could shut them down is by incineration or electromagnetic pulse.'

'A Taser might do it,' Sommers said.

Foster lost her temper. 'Come *on*, George,' she shouted at Sommers, 'that's just bollocks, we both know it. There's only one way both of these systems could have been deactivated.'

'Which is?' Eva demanded.

'Anna had to do it herself.'

–

'Yes,' Eva said as she stood in the cavernous reception area, 'Anna Seifert's disappeared. Let's assume abduction for the time being.'

Flynn's voice grated. She was on speaker in the incident room. 'You don't sound certain?'

'It's bizarre,' Eva admitted. 'Can one of you get on-site down here? I need every member of the IT team questioning. I think Anna Seifert must have had help. Only internal IT could have known how to write a batch file that would so completely wipe the security systems. Anna could have run it just by executing the script with root permission, but I don't think she could have written it for herself.'

'But the chips she's got implanted,' Eva could imagine Flynn's shudder, 'how would you turn those off?'

'I think Anna has full control over her RFID implants. She was able to tap combinations on them for security key codes, I don't see why one of those combinations wouldn't include an on/off switch for the tracker. Question is, did she switch the chips off voluntarily or did someone have a gun to her head?'

'Either is weird,' Flynn agreed. 'We'll start searching traffic cameras in the area.'

'How long do you think that will take?'

'Could be hours,' Flynn admitted, 'or even days.'

'Thought so,' Eva said.

–

Her next call was to the Metropolitan Police Cyber Crime Unit's technical hub in Vauxhall. She made it from the conference room in which she had first met Anna and Arnaud Seifert. Arnaud was there. So was George Sommers.

'Leticia North,' she said as the control room picked up, 'DI Harris, Surrey police.' She heard the call being transferred. If she had to choose, if somebody had asked for a straight answer, Eva would have told them Tisha North was probably the person she felt closest to in the world. Colleagues at MPCCU, they had formed an immediate friendship, the kind that did not diminish merely because they might not see each other for months. Perhaps even more importantly, they saw eye-to-eye. She understood Tisha, and Tisha knew everything about her. A slender black woman with spectacular cornrows, she was one of the few people whose technical competence Eva actually respected. Tisha was the kind of person you could call at four in the morning, ask for help and actually receive it. Eva knew that for a fact.

'Tisha,' she said before the technical team lead could make some flippant comment, 'you're on speaker.'

'Understood,' Tisha North said immediately. Eva could imagine the grin on her face. 'What can I help you with, DI Harris?'

'Abduction. Female, mid-thirties, blonde, about five-nine, about sixty kilos. Within the past three and a half hours. Tisha, do you have access to Surrey traffic and ANPR cameras?'

'We've got access to traffic cams right across the country,' Tisha said. 'We've also got town centre CCTV. I'm guessing you want us to run a face match?'

'Can you?'

'Yes. Are you at the scene of the abduction?' Eva checked her phone and gave her latitude and longitude from the map app. 'I'll use that as the centre. We've got access to the fastest face-matching algorithm available, but it needs feeding.'

Eva knew what that meant. She told Arnaud and Sommers to email her recent pictures of Anna and waited while they dug through their phones. 'Who does that belong to?' she asked Tisha. She meant the algorithm.

'Not on speakerphone,' Tisha replied, but it didn't matter. Eva could guess. The request would be relayed to the servers in Benhall in Cheltenham, to the clusters of Cray Shasta super-computers that sat in bunkers capable of surviving a megaton nuclear blast. Cooperation between government technology departments had become a priority, and Tisha of all people would know how to make best use of that opportunity.

Eva emailed around thirty photos to Tisha as they spoke. 'I'm ingesting them now,' Tisha told her. Somewhere, an algorithm would be running through the photos and building a model of a face from them. 'Subject's name?' Tisha asked. Eva told her. Tisha swore. 'Is there going to be a ransom demand? I can ask the country folk to start listening.' She meant GCHQ and automated monitoring of phone calls.

'I don't know,' Eva said, 'but please, just in case. Have you got enough?'

'I've got good face geometry and real-time feeds from every traffic camera within twenty miles of your location, plus I'm downloading the past four hours stored footage from everything I can find. If she's even glanced at a camera in the past four hours, this algorithm will find her.'

'Thanks Tisha,' Eva said as she went to hang up. 'Let me know.'

Anna Seifert was not on site; that much was obvious. Sommers was doing everything practical to identify her means of exit and soon he would have help from some of Moresby's men and a scene of crime team.

She headed back towards the station. On the way she dialled the incident room again. As she had expected, Rebecca Flynn answered the phone. Flynn just had a way of getting to it before anyone else.

Eva briefed her. 'Anything you need us to do right now?' Flynn asked.

'Has Raj or Jamie left yet? Uniform can deal with security, but I want one of them to talk to Jo Foster. She's in IT. I don't know her job title, but she knows what she's doing. She thinks the systems were sabotaged from the inside, and I agree with her. Tell whichever one of them is coming I need anyone with network admin privileges to be interviewed. They're all suspects.' She took a breath. 'So is Anna Seifert.'

'She could have staged this?' Flynn asked. 'Why?'

'Don't know,' Eva admitted, 'staged or something else. I'll tell you more when I get back.' Eva tried to make a calculation in her head, but whatever route she based it on thirty minutes was the number that kept coming up. 'Listen,' she told Flynn, 'one other thing I got from Aaron Rose that I haven't had time to follow up on. He mentioned a company called Scientific Support Services. Rose said they do HTA-compliant tissue testing for allergens and the like.'

'You got anything else on them apart from the fact they exist?'

Eva grinned. Acerbic she might be, but sometimes Flynn's frankness was a breath of fresh air. 'Not much,' she admitted. 'Mind you, right now anyone who cuts up body parts for a living is suspect as far as I'm concerned.'

Eva had only just got back to her desk when Tisha North called. 'Got a match,' she said. She was speaking through a headset, Eva could tell. She would be following the feeds from the ANPR and traffic cameras at the same time as speaking. 'But it's only a 68 per cent probability.'

'Let me see,' Eva said. She turned to her laptop, unlocked it and waited for Tisha's email.

'This was caught about forty-five minutes ago,' Tisha told her, 'from a traffic camera on the A24. I'm finding it hard to work out a route. My best guess is they were following country lanes but had to cross the A-road because of a diversion.'

'That's a fast result?'

'Money is being thrown at this stuff,' Tisha said. 'There've been a couple of near misses in the last year, scary ones.' She meant terrorist attacks that had been foiled, but it didn't take any great insight to work that out. 'We get to play with the big boys' toys so long as we don't make a nuisance of ourselves.' She was referring to GCHQ and the security service, Eva knew. Everything was becoming more like war, everything. It had even disturbed her, when on a recent day off she had seen armed police with H&K assault rifles casually wandering through the arcade of a shopping centre.

'You said they.'

'A black pickup truck with IC1 male driving. If it is Anna Seifert, she's in the passenger seat. There may be someone on the back, but it was hard to be certain. Got to tell you, she did not look as though she was under duress.'

'Hard to tell,' Eva echoed. A quiet sound, an alert note telling her a new email had arrived.

It seemed a large-enough file. Good resolution; one of the newer cameras, Eva thought. It took a few moments to unwind its way down her screen. She had to pan around the photo for a second, but when she did, she eventually found the car Tisha was referring to. Eva pinched the track-pad of her laptop and zoomed in. An impressive match, she thought as she screen-grabbed the picture, because in the passenger seat of the pickup was a woman, undoubtedly Anna Seifert.

'You said IC1 male driving?'

'You won't see it from that,' Tisha said. 'I had to mess with the image gamma. Sending that one now.'

Another email. Grainier this time, Tisha had played around with the contrast curves of the picture to tease out a result. White male, Eva agreed, although she couldn't see much in the way of detail on his face. Something about him though. She tracked across the image, then gasped.

'What?' Tisha demanded. The left hand on the wheel, Eva saw. It was prosthetic.

'I know the driver,' Eva told her. 'His name is Jonathon Crane.'

## Chapter Thirty-Six

When Eva reached the A-road, she put her foot down. Before she did so she fumbled for a button under the dash, and blue flashing lights in the grill of the Audi flared into life. The 3.2 litre V6 Quattro was not the fastest unmarked car the station had, but it was fast enough for her, she decided.

The speedometer read one hundred and twenty miles an hour, but the car stuck to the road like glue. Eva had been required to cover advanced driving techniques in training, but at the time they had seemed as abstract as a cycling proficiency test. Now she actually needed to make use of them, the big Audi made driving at speed feel as straightforward as pointing and shooting. Cars ahead of her eased onto the hard shoulder to let her through. She kept her distance and made sure the vehicles in front were aware of her before she overtook. Then she put her foot all the way to the floor.

Jonathon Crane had abducted Anna Seifert? The impossibility of it pressed down on her. She knew Crane, Seifert knew Crane; that simply did not compute. *Ergo*, she thought as she slowed for a roundabout, there was another explanation. And when she considered that, she found she liked the conclusion even less.

She should have taken Flynn or Newton. Either of them deserved to be there; technically she needed witnesses, logically she needed support. But this was Crane, she told herself as she took a chance and passed a row of cars, hurtling down the wrong side of the road; he had saved her life. Try as she might, she couldn't find it in herself to go in mob handed. And anyway, Eva thought as she followed the sat-nav away from the main road, to do so just did not feel right.

She had to slow to more sensible speeds then. Thank God she had still been on the line with Tisha when she recognised him. The pickup truck was obviously converted so he could drive it, but the number plate was false. When Eva did a PNC search, she found Crane did own an identical truck, but it was a year newer than the registration of the vehicle in the photo. When she checked the registered address, she found it was in the Lake District. Crane was covering his tracks.

'I can help,' Tisha told her, but Eva already knew that. Tisha scanned NHS records, National Insurance, bank details and then movements from traffic cameras of the car that was actually registered to Crane. 'I think he has a place on farmland in Sussex,' Tisha told her. 'His family own it. Want the grid reference?'

Of course she did. Eva had left her office without speaking to anyone and headed down to the garage, where she had signed out the unmarked car. The sergeant on duty had raised an eyebrow. 'No need to make a fuss,' Eva had told him.

No way on God's green earth had Jonathon Crane abducted Anna Seifert, absolutely no way. Yet CCTV at the office had been wiped and Anna's tracker chip had been disabled, and the only person who could have done both of those things was Anna herself. So Anna was not being abducted, Eva thought as she screamed along a lane that passed through open fields. Either Anna was the abductor, or Anna was trying to escape from them.

Which was it? If it had been Anna on her own, then she could almost have flipped a coin. She didn't know her well enough to formulate a conclusion. The woman was glacial and unreadable in both a studied and an intuitive way. Another straight stretch of lane. The needle nudged ninety.

Crane though. She trusted Crane. She had to trust Crane, it wasn't logical that Crane was untrustworthy, unless there was some insanely convoluted game in play, one in which Crane, Seifert, Savini and even Mathew Harred were participating, and she simply could not believe that. That narrowed it down to the last possibility, but if that was the case, why had Anna chosen Crane to run to?

The answer presented itself a few seconds later, as she half expected it might. Eva slammed on the brakes. Two men with rifles aimed at her head tracked her to a halt.

—

'I don't have a gun,' Eva told them. They ignored her. One of them patted her down while the other searched the car. 'I don't have an invite either,' she told them, trying to sound reasonable, 'but Crane said I could just drop by on the off chance.'

A black unmarked police car with blues flashing and doing just under a ton on a country lane didn't lend any great credence to her story, she knew that, but it seemed as though it was enough. 'Are there any others on the way?' one of the armed men asked her. He meant police.

She shook her head. 'No. Nobody knows I'm here.' Eva took a breath then, and told him her real reason for bringing the jet-black vehicle. It had been Tisha's idea, although it had struck her as the perfect solution. 'But the car has a tracker and I signed it out. Do you understand?'

Another soldier, obviously. She had given him not so much a threat as a positioning statement, but he didn't seem alarmed. Presumably this was why Anna Seifert had sought out Crane's help. She knew he would be able call on people who could protect her.

The soldier spoke quietly into a small, discreet handset. 'He says follow the lane up to the house,' he told her after he had received a reply. Then he added: 'He says slowly, please. There are horses in the fields, and they frighten easily.'

Eva did as she was told. Beyond a copse of trees, she found a single-storey house made from wood, well kept, neatly painted window frames and carefully varnished weatherboards. The pickup truck was in the garage next to it, and the doors to the garage were open. She slowed to a halt in front of the house and looked out. Natural materials under a grey country sky, a gently sloping roof with carefully recessed solar panels. There was a modest wind turbine next to the house, and the woods behind it were dense conifers that wouldn't have looked out of place in some Nordic setting. When Eva gazed at the house the word that came to her, completely unbidden, was *idyllic*.

The front door swung open and Jonathan Crane appeared. He stood for a moment, looking down at her as she approached; the trace of a question on his face. She wondered how he was going to react, whether or not he would be incensed by the intrusion. He didn't seem that way though. He half turned away as she reached the door.

'Black coffee okay?' was all he said.

—

She followed Crane into a living room that looked out over fields. The soldier hadn't lied, she thought as she was momentarily captured by the view. There were horses.

Anna Seifert sat, or more accurately curled, on the sofa. The look of confidence had disappeared from her face. Something close to desperation had replaced it. There was a puffiness around the eyes that, had Eva not been convinced of her almost cryogenic calm, would have suggested the woman had been crying.

She wore her grey suit, but the shoes had been kicked off and she had a black rug draped over her shoulders. She wasn't alone. Next to her, her hand in his, was a man whose face she recognised. Not Mathew Harred's finest work, but Eva suspected the material he had been given had not been first class either. The shadows on the painting's face had misled her too. Derzelas, she assumed, although the real significance of that name still escaped her. Michael Sullivan, in any event.

Aaron Rose had been right. He didn't look well; tall and lean, a bony face with dark straight hair marked by only a few flecks of grey. Eva guessed he might be in his mid-forties, although it would have been easy to mistake him for someone older. Sallow skin and sunken eye sockets, there was still something intriguing about the man, a frisson that said yes, I know I look like shit, but you really do not want to underestimate me. Eva glanced at Jonathon Crane. 'Black's fine,' she told him.

She sat in an armchair while Crane fixed coffee. 'How did you find me?' Anna asked. There was fear in her voice but curiosity as well, as though the puzzle had exceeded her anxiety. Eva explained, and Anna said, 'So the only people who know where I am are your colleagues?'

'Correct,' Eva told her. 'Even Arnaud doesn't know,' she said, pointedly.

'Father will work it out,' Anna assured her. She managed to make the noun sound both formal and intimate at the same time. 'He always does.'

'I haven't worked it out,' Eva complained as she took a mug of coffee from Crane. He delivered it to her in his prosthetic hand. It felt like a statement of his control over the limb.

'You worked out enough to realise Anna was coming here,' Michael Sullivan said. He had a soft voice, slightly clipped, a regional accent perhaps, or maybe by now a melange of more than one.

'Well yes,' Eva said, staring at him. 'I figured out all the obvious stuff.' For an instant Sullivan looked surprised. Then she saw the trace of a smile form around his eyes. 'I'm guessing this is a story that starts about five hours ago,' she told them. 'Anyone want to enlighten me?'

'This chapter does,' Sullivan agreed. 'But of course, it really started two years ago. That's when I began working with Seifert on an unofficial basis.' Sullivan had kept hold of Anna's hand, Eva noted. 'Working on an unofficial basis' was clearly a euphemism. It was why Anna had tried to protect him. 'I'm sick,' Sullivan told her, 'but you probably knew that. I won't bore you with the details, but it's a degenerative disease and I've been experimenting on myself, and others, to try and find a cure.'

'Others?'

'All willing participants, carefully selected, all fully informed,' Sullivan insisted. 'They have their own problems. They were willing to take some risks. In all honesty the greatest risk of all was failure, that the treatments I was working on would simply do nothing. I'm not a lunatic, DI Harris.'

She stared. 'Somebody is.'

'Yes,' Sullivan agreed. 'Somebody most certainly is.'

Another question came to her. She turned to glare at Crane. 'Did you know anything about this?'

'Nope,' Crane assured her. 'Not until today.' He nodded at Seifert. 'I've worked with Anna for years, but we don't exactly socialise. I'm not what you'd call a social animal.' Crane almost smiled. 'She'd told me she was worried about kidnapping because she knew I had contacts. I gave her some professional advice. I knew there was someone she was close to, but I hadn't met Michael before today, and I didn't know he was Derzelas.'

'I'm not,' Sullivan insisted quietly, 'but never mind that for now.'

Eva tried to ignore the interruption and thought again for a moment. 'So, you're responsible for Seifert's CCTV going down and Anna's RFID chips being offline.'

'Guilty as charged,' Crane admitted. 'With some help from one of Seifert's IT folk. It's a last line of defence,' he told her. 'The step beyond the panic room if you like, the point at which you have to burn all your bridges and do it pretty damned quickly. What do you do when your innermost barriers have been compromised?'

She stared. 'And had they?'

'Oh yes,' Crane said.

'How do you know?'

Anna started to speak, but Sullivan put a hand on her knee. 'Why don't I just go through this?' he said. 'I think things will be clearer if I do.' Eva didn't object, so Sullivan continued. 'I've used Seifert's facilities to experiment on human tissue. That's a crime, technically, because I haven't informed relatives or a Research Ethics Committee as to what I was doing. In doing that I came across a problem.' Sullivan paused, waiting to see if she would jump in.

Something clicked, inside her head. 'Too many body parts,' Eva guessed. Sullivan gave her a smile without humour.

'Yes. Seifert receives body parts and entire bodies from suppliers. They run their tests, then the human tissue is collected for disposal at an authorised facility. The parts and their containers are barcoded. What I noticed was that some deliveries were being made with a forwarding barcode assigned, so they would come into the tissue bank at Seifert one day and be collected for disposal a few days later without ever being touched by a researcher. It took me a while to imagine a reason. The problem was, I was wrong.'

Eva frowned. 'How so?'

'At first I thought the body parts were basically down to somebody running a body-snatching ring,' Sullivan said. 'It would have been disgraceful, despicable and I felt I was obligated to protect the evidence. Human tissue is expensive. There are facilities that would turn a blind eye to poorly completed paperwork if the price was right. That's why I preserved what I could. It took me a while to realise there was another, more likely explanation for them.'

'Which was?' Eva knew the answer to the question, but she wanted to hear Sullivan say it anyway.

'Somebody was using the disposal process to conceal murder.'

'There might have been other reasons,' Eva said.

'Yes. But over time the pattern became unmistakable, if you were looking for it that is. I started diverting body parts to a storage area of my own. I couldn't afford anything like Seifert's cryogenics, and I couldn't keep the parts on site, so I settled for formaldehyde.'

It seemed just about possible, Eva thought. If Sullivan had built up the tanks over a period of weeks. 'The waterworks. How did you get the tanks up to the roof?'

'The freight elevators the storage company had installed. I powered them with a portable generator. Luckily, I didn't have to cart the racks around. I had some help with that.'

Anna nodded. 'One of our industrial robots. You saw it in the morgue. Apart from other things it's designed to build optimised warehouse layouts. You were concerned by the aesthetics of the tanks,' she said. 'You should be. They were created by a machine.'

'Christ,' Eva muttered, astonished, although when she thought about it she realised she shouldn't be. The same machine that had laid out the body parts in Seifert's morgue, she realised; no wonder she had sensed a similarity. She knew how efficient the learning algorithms that drove industrial robots were. If Sullivan had simply marked out the space and told it to go to work, then the end result was bound to be optimal. That it also looked elegant was nothing more than a side effect. The implications of that disturbed her momentarily.

'My thoughts exactly,' Anna agreed. 'But it's not relevant anymore.'

Eva looked at Sullivan. 'You knew New Thought had used the facility?'

'I knew the connection would provoke interest from the police. The problem was I couldn't prove anything, and I couldn't do anything without incriminating myself.' He paused then. 'I make it sound as though I was confident about all this. I wasn't. Just sure enough to want to make certain evidence, if that was what it was, didn't get incinerated.'

'You didn't know about the abductions at Seifert?'

Sullivan shook his head. 'No. I only used the space for storage. I also needed to return the equipment I'd borrowed, the spectrophotometer and that. For a while I actually considered working there, but it was too bloody cold. I ended up leaving it there for a while. But the main reason I used the space was to preserve that evidence until I could figure out what to do with it.'

'A hundred tanks,' Eva said.

'It only took the machine a few hours to lay them out.'

She remembered the industrial robot in the morgue again, just as she recalled the robot arm Crane had been working with in Switzerland. Stupid devices that could perform brute-force tasks; it made no difference to them whether they were arranging cartons of apples or human hearts. 'So, what changed?'

'You did,' Anna said. 'When you came to us, we had to start digging harder. I think we provoked a reaction.'

'That came today?'

'This morning.' Anna took out her phone. 'We were going to contact you, I swear. I just needed to get to safety first.' Eva decided to reserve judgement on that. Then Anna showed her a video.

A room concealed by polythene. Sheets suspended from metal frames formed walls that hid the true nature of the space. It was impossible to tell if that was relevant, but it was a fact, a data point. In the room, a layout that looked like a hospital ward but somehow different, she saw trolleys with patients on them, but the trolleys were arranged in a circle. Not a circle, Eva thought as she studied every frame, a pentangle. There was something demonic about the layout. Five bodies – two men, three women – covered with tubes and electrical sensors, and beside each trolley a readout of the type you might expect to see in an intensive care unit. The camera viewpoint was from the centre of the room, but soon it moved. Against one wall was a whiteboard. On the whiteboard, printed in large type on an A4 page, was a message.

*I know you have the treatment*, the message read. *I've seen evidence of it in cellular analysis. I want Derzelas. I know what you*

*are, Anna Seifert, I want to be that too. Give it to me, or these five*
*people die.*

Finally. Finally, he had shown his hand and resorted to threats. She almost felt elation, although she knew it was too soon for that. 'I need to get a copy of this to digital forensics,' Eva told Anna. 'They need to rip it apart pixel by pixel.'

'There's more,' Anna said. Burbling paragraphs on the whiteboard told her something about the writer's delusions, their fears and their ravings. It needed a profiler to do it justice, Eva thought, but Anna was skipping forward. 'Look.'

Shots of Anna. Images from cameras with elevated viewpoints, looking down on her as though to emphasise the threat. Eva suddenly understood. 'That's Seifert's CCTV?'

Anna nodded. 'I knew I had to get out straight away when I saw it. I called Crane.' She inclined her head a little, Eva saw, a gesture of gratitude. 'We already had a backup plan in place, and he'd told me that the CCTV network wasn't difficult to compromise. I ran the script that trashed the servers. I expect Jo Foster is pretty pissed off with me.'

'She works in IT,' Eva assured her. 'She's pissed off with everybody, goes with the job. Why didn't you tell Arnaud?'

'Time,' Crane said. 'A video like that is a problem. Once it's sent, whoever sent it is going to immediately think: did I give too much away? By the time that thought is fully formed the decision to act is almost inevitable. I saw the video and was as sure as I could be that whoever sent it would change their minds and try to abduct Anna. I was right,' he added.

Crane's analysis had been spot-on, but Eva frowned. 'How do you know?'

Crane then disappeared, and a few moments later he returned carrying another prosthetic arm. 'I was wearing this one earlier. I thought I'd leave it as it was, so your forensic people could take a look.' He turned the arm over. Protruding from the plastic that covered the hand was a dart, about fifteen centimetres in length. 'It hit me as I was getting Anna into the car outside Seifert. He or she was going to try to take Anna.'

'Jesus Christ,' Eva swore. She knew Crane would understand.

He did. 'I don't know what to tell you, DI Harris,' he said as he passed her the prosthetic. 'Right now I don't give those people a cat in hell's chance of getting out alive.'

## Chapter Thirty-Seven

Eva kept to something closer to the speed limit this time. She didn't want to scare her passenger. Anna Seifert had objected, pretty damned strenuously, Eva had noted, but Michael Sullivan had insisted on going back to the station with her.

Anna was safe – or at least as safe as she could be in Crane's deceptively well-protected cottage with no fewer than four ex-special service bodyguards manning the perimeter. She hadn't seen Crane as the type to get involved with close protection, and to some extent she was right; he left that to younger men who were clearly damned good at it. What Crane was exceptional at, she had slowly come to realise, was threat assessment – the theory of protecting someone from danger, especially from clever and esoteric attacks. Crane's friends, the hard guys with big guns, they were the ones who executed the plans.

Sullivan though. For some reason as soon as she had met him, Eva had sensed in him the overwhelming urge to do the right thing. Not necessarily the legal thing (she understood his reluctance to adhere to rules that he felt were overly cautious generalisations), but the right thing. As she drove, she had to suppress a shudder. *Natural justice.* For a moment Fredrick Huss, Mathew Harred and the ethos of New Thought reverberated in her mind. *Do what thou wilt shall be the whole of the Law.* Was Sullivan cut from the same cloth?

'Mathew Harred painted you as Derzelas,' Eva said as they drove. Sullivan looked astonished.

'Harred painted me? I never sat for him. I never even met him.'

'But you knew of him?'

'By reputation,' Sullivan admitted. 'New Thought was interested in Derzelas and pointed some of its members, who were also investors, towards it. It was never anything more than a supportive relationship though, nothing except for overlapping interests.'

'And Derzelas?'

Sullivan actually smiled, but it was a smile of embarrassment. 'Let's be clear. I'm not Derzelas, as you put it. Derzelas isn't even really a thing, not in the way you think anyway. It was my idea unfortunately. It was just a designation to keep the auditors happy. There were costs that showed within Seifert's books that Anna didn't want to have to explain, so I came up with the idea of a code-name. A catch-all for commercially sensitive research, hiding everything in plain sight essentially. We needed a reason to keep from disclosing details of expenditure, because as I told you some of the activities were technically illegal. Technically,' he emphasised again, 'at least not the kind of thing a reputable pharmaceutical company could be seen to be engaging in. Derzelas just sounded suitably mysterious. But the name was never meant to be anything other than an accounting reference. Something for the bean-counters, a bucket to dump expenses in.'

She'd been torn between thinking Derzelas was either a person or a treatment. Now she knew it was neither. That was not the point, Eva realised. 'Somebody took it seriously,' she said.

'Yes,' Sullivan agreed. He was no longer smiling. 'We dumped the costs for a series of promising therapies that haven't met REC approval standards into the "Derzelas" bucket.' He took a breath. 'As I said, we went to human trials too. That's something Seifert could get into a lot of trouble over if word ever got out.'

Eva glanced at him, then back at the road ahead. 'But Seifert participates?'

'Yes,' Sullivan said emphatically. 'These are treatments we believe it's right to fast track into human testing, even though we haven't done the required years of clinical trials. They're treatments we believe in, but ones we can't legally put into people without years' more bureaucratic form filling. I know the rules are there for a purpose, but sometimes they're just plain wrong.'

The traffic in front of them slowed. The Kingston one-way system. For a moment Eva considered putting on the concealed lights in the grill and bullying her way through, but she felt no need to shorten the conversation she was having with Sullivan. Passengers in cars often felt more inclined to talk. She had frequently noted that.

'You're in a relationship with Anna.'

Sullivan shrugged. 'So?' He was right of course, the detail had next to no relevance. 'If you want to know my personal details, I have Familial Amyotrophic Lateral Sclerosis. Susanne, my wife, died of a neurodegenerative disorder, and I guess I've come to realise life is too short to be alone.'

That was a point that struck a little too close to home for Eva. 'And the involvement with transhumanism?'

'It's just the same questions we've been asking for thousands of years,' Sullivan mused, 'except now we like to think we have more sophisticated answers. What does it mean to be alive? Not in some spiritual sense, but what, specifically, is the difference between a lump of metal and a lump of wood? It's the ability of wood or any other living material to replicate itself of course; at the lowest level that's all that separates us from inorganic matter. But when you really examine it, that one difference is mind-blowing. It's almost as though one day three billion years ago some rock somewhere suddenly decided to grow legs. Why did that happen? Why did it keep on happening? It's like there's some hidden rule in the fabric of the universe that tries to keep a balance. There's entropy, the tendency for things to fall apart, but then there's emergence, the force that causes stuff to organise itself. The two stabilise each other like Yin and Yang. No wonder transhumanism gets caught up in mysticism. Life is pretty damned mysterious.'

His passion was obvious. 'But transhumanists are trying to supplant that natural process with a mechanical one?'

Sullivan swept the point to one side. 'What of it? What does it matter if we replace human organs with bio-engineered ones or even mechanical devices? Does it make us any less human? Would you say Crane was less human?'

'Of course not,' Eva said. Her answer sounded more vehement than even she had expected. 'But it makes me wonder what the end goal of transhumanism is.'

'It depends who you ask,' Sullivan said. 'I don't think there's any question as far as the lunatic who's abducting Seifert staff is concerned. He's deluded. He thinks Derzelas is some kind of miracle cure for everything. This guy wants to live forever.' Sullivan gazed at her. His look told her he understood exactly the mindset of the person she was searching for. 'And he's prepared to kill to fulfil his fantasy.'

–

When they arrived at Kingston, Eva took Sullivan straight to an interview room and left him there with a cup of coffee and a uniform officer for company. She had made plain to Anna that she had no intention of charging him because she was as certain as she could be that the only crimes he had been involved with were regulatory offences, and like hell was she going to use up police resources on those. The lawyers could fight it out, she told herself as she hurried to the incident room. Right now, what she needed was information, and Sullivan was the closest thing she had to a coherent source for that.

'So the New Thought connection was a dead end?' DCI Corrine Sutton demanded as Eva ran through the latest events in front of her and Eva's team.

'Honestly, it's hard to say, ma'am. Sullivan and Anna connected through New Thought, but that's tenuous. It's possible that whoever is abducting staff is a member of New Thought's transhumanist community, but I'm not sure that gets us anywhere either. Michael Sullivan is prepared to give us a formal interview under caution and provide what information he can, but I'm pretty damn certain it's nothing directly to do with him.' She took a breath. 'We do know two things now though. There are five people being held like lab animals in an experiment somewhere, but right now they're still alive. And although Anna Seifert may have been involved in the kinds of activities that might get her company a hefty fine, she's not a criminal per se, and she is most definitely at risk.'

Sutton folded her arms. 'But you're happy to leave her with Crane?'

'Frankly I think he can give her better protection than even we can,' Eva said. She turned to Newton. 'Jamie, I'd like you to do the interview with Sullivan. Don't worry about doing it on your own; he's not a hostile witness. Just get everything from him you can; you know the drill. Any detail, no matter how insignificant.' Newton nodded, picked up a pad and left the room. 'Becks,' Eva said, turning to Flynn, 'did you get anything on that company?'

'Scientific Support Services,' Flynn said. She curled her lip a little as she spoke. 'It's a legitimate company, nothing dodgy as such. I had Raj take a look at the financials, they're part of a group. There's the usual network of assets being shuffled around but nothing that goes beyond the "tax efficiency" level. At least,' she added hesitantly, 'that's what I think.'

Raj might have a different opinion, Eva thought. She would have to catch up with him later. 'Okay,' Eva said, 'but what do they do?'

Flynn's curled lip became an expression of complete distaste, as though the information was malodorous. 'They provide dead bodies,' she said. 'Like, they're the starting point of the process that ends up in that fancy morgue at Seifert. They go to hospitals and collect corpses that have been involved in accidents and the like, get all the release forms and documentation sorted, then deliver them to companies like Seifert on-demand. SSS are one of three that Seifert uses; the other two are based further away. One is in Scotland and the other in the Midlands. It's about getting the best human tissue, apparently.'

'So Seifert don't source corpses directly? I mean they don't have the relationship with A&E departments?'

'No,' Flynn told them. 'I guess it's not surprising. It's not an easy process even if somebody has a donor card. Somebody has to identify the body as being suitable for research and then get into the negotiations. SSS handle all that side of things, then keep the bodies on ice until somebody like Seifert can take them.' She wrinkled her face. 'Who knew there was a market for pre-owned bodies?'

'But they do their own testing on bodies too?'

'Yes.' Flynn picked up a sheet of notes. 'That's what Aaron Rose was telling you about. They'll put an implant into a body part, keep it on ice for a couple of months and then write a report on whether human tissue reacted to it. It's not cheap, but apparently Seifert charge a hell of a lot more.'

'And Anna Seifert doesn't want to deal with Aaron Rose and BioHeuristics because they load implants with Bitcoins into data mules,' Raj added.

'So SSS deliver bodies to Seifert,' Eva said. 'Do they collect the remains too?'

'For incineration,' Flynn said. 'That's another company, not connected. They just run the incinerators.'

Eva wandered over to a whiteboard and picked up a pen. 'It's almost clear now,' she said to no one in particular. 'We've almost got it. Derzelas is the key, even if it isn't really anything more than an internal code-name for a number of treatments Seifert doesn't want to go public with. Somebody thinks Derzelas is an anti-ageing treatment that works, one that Seifert is selling to the few people who can afford it. They have a scientific background of some sort, or enough to understand how such an imaginary treatment might work.' She thought about Tal and Gala then. 'And maybe it's not quite as far-fetched as it sounds. We know big pharmaceutical companies are chucking huge amounts of money at anti-senescence, and a conspiracy theorist might well imagine some of that work may have succeeded.'

Sutton looked over her shoulder. 'So they're looking for evidence of Derzelas in Seifert staff?'

'They think Anna is using them as test subjects,' Eva said. 'They know how to look for the biological changes Derzelas is supposed to bring.'

'But they're killing people in the process.'

'I never said they were sane. And look,' she said, pointing towards a diagram she had drawn on the board, one that followed the path body parts took from hospital mortuaries to Scientific Support Services, to Seifert and their experiments and then on to incineration. 'Pick up and collection are the exposed points. Somebody with the right knowledge could drop extra human tissue into deliveries but have it marked for disposal. Sullivan is right; it would be an almost infallible way of getting rid of victims.'

'Cold, though,' Sutton observed. 'Clinical.' She shrugged. 'So what do we do, raid Scientific Support Services?'

'I can't see any way around it,' Eva said. She stared at the diagram, trying to spot flaws in the process, but try as she might she couldn't find any. 'We don't know if whoever is doing this works for SSS or is, I don't know, a freelance delivery driver or something. We need to go in there for sure,' she told Sutton, 'but we're going to need some expert help.'

—

Jamie Newton finished with Michael Sullivan an hour and a half later. 'I ran out of things to ask him,' Newton admitted. 'I don't think he could have been more helpful.'

'You got everything on how he put the body parts into the waterworks?'

'He knew the space was empty,' Newton said. 'He'd been there plenty of times before, when the storage company had the place. He used New Thought's storage to keep records of tests. You know somebody had provided him with funding via New Thought before he began working with Seifert?'

Eva hadn't known that, but it made sense. 'Who?'

'Dominic Vance, the guy you said Arnaud Seifert mentioned. I don't have anything more on that,' Newton admitted.

'But Sullivan built those racks and moved the body parts he wanted to keep on his own?'

'With some help from an industrial robot. He said he had to put the racks together himself, but it did everything else.' She had seen videos of how warehouse robots could rearrange fixtures to provide the most efficient way of storing boxes. Tanks of formaldehyde filled with body parts didn't seem so very different. 'So do we go in mob-handed at Scientific Support Services?' Newton asked.

'Not far off,' Eva said. 'I'll need you, Becks and Raj for that.' She picked her jacket off the hook that hung on the wall of her office. 'Let's you and me get Sullivan back to Crane for safe-keeping though,' she told him as she headed for the door. 'There's one more question I need to ask Anna Seifert.'

—

It was evening by the time they arrived back at Crane's cabin. Wisps of high cloud caught the last rays of the sun. She stopped at the edge of Crane's fields to let one of his men check the car. Jamie Newton raised his eyebrows when he saw the weapon the man carried, but Eva paid it no attention. A few minutes later they drew up in front of the cabin.

Sullivan put his arms around Anna when he saw her. 'I said there wouldn't be a problem,' he said. They sat in the living room once more, and this time Jamie Newton took notes.

'I've got one more question,' Eva said. She directed herself to both Sullivan and Anna. 'There's one thing I don't understand.' They looked at her, expressions blank. 'Why has this person, whoever is abducting your staff, got it into their head that Derzelas is some kind of eternal youth treatment? Why don't they think it's a cure for Alzheimer's, or cancer, or the common cold for that matter? Why anti-senescence?'

Anna gave her the slightest of shrugs, 'Because technically,' she said, 'it is.'

'One of the treatments anyway,' Sullivan said. 'But before you get carried away, let's be clear. What we've seen is some positive results in reversing epigenetic ageing. That's categorically not an eternal youth drug.'

'Not yet,' Anna agreed.

'Not by a long way,' Sullivan insisted. 'We can reprogram certain cells to switch back on and revert to earlier cellular states. We adapted a protocol usually intended to regenerate the thymus. It's a major step forward, but it's years away from being anything more than a lab experiment.'

It took a few moments for the implications of that to sink in. 'But it *is* a treatment,' Eva said eventually, 'it isn't just a project name. It's something that could be given to a person to achieve a particular result?'

'Yes,' Sullivan admitted, 'but so what? Yes, it will make their cells a few years younger. Does that have an effect on lifespan? It's far too early to say.'

'It may be to you,' Eva said as she stood to leave, 'but somebody has jumped to all the wrong conclusions.'

## Chapter Thirty-Eight

Scientific Support Services sat in a small business park near Weybridge, along a road beside the European service office of a South Korean TV manufacturer and the fulfilment facility of a minor online shopping website. Not a big company, Eva knew, but a moderately profitable one. A small convoy of vehicles drew up in front of the building, and deliberately blocked the entrance.

She had elected to treat the offices as a crime scene. Eva had conferred with Sutton for the best part of an hour before settling on the approach. Sutton had spoken with lawyers and officers at Area before she had finally given her approval to apply for a warrant. 'We're effectively regarding them as suspects,' she had stated. 'We need to be clear we're justified in acting that way.' Eva already knew that, but she had a different perspective. Sutton needed every piece of evidence to be admissible, but Eva didn't really give a damn about trying to bring SSS to court. She only needed the one piece of evidence that would lead her to where the abductees were being kept.

Three cars, one for Moresby and his uniform officers, one for scene of crime officers, another for evidence. Rebecca Flynn, Jamie Newton and Raj Chakrabati were in the first car. In the passenger seat of the second, sat next to Eva, was Judy Wren.

'Do you know, I've never been on an actual raid before,' Wren said as they pulled up. 'I normally get called in later.'

'I don't think anybody's going to be taking battering rams to doors,' Eva said as she clasped the necessary paperwork in her hand and climbed out of the car, 'but there are going to be some very pissed-off people in there in the next five minutes.'

Moresby and three of his men went in first; another four went to the back of the building. 'I need you to stay where you are and listen to the Detective Inspector,' Moresby told two people who were talking in reception. Polite but firm, Eva noted. The two looked bewildered.

'I have a warrant to search the premises issued under Section Eight of the Police and Criminal Evidence Act, in connection with the murders of five named individuals,' Eva announced loudly. 'We will be interviewing everyone here today, and if necessary taking material as evidence. Nobody leaves the building until they've been interviewed.' She nodded to the two, a man and a woman who stood, mouths open, by a water-cooler. 'You might want to go back to your desks and wait,' Eva told them.

She had to repeat the announcement three times around the building before she was certain everyone in the company had heard and understood. When she found the office manager, he too seemed bewildered.

'We source all of our tissue from accident and emergency departments,' Phillip Kay assured her, 'as well as some bequests.' He looked like a pharmacist, Eva thought. The kind of person you might find behind a counter dispensing prescription medicine. Not a tall man, early forties, quite precise and clearly shocked by the presence of Moresby's officers.

'We're going to need to search your tissue bank,' Eva told Kay, 'as well as your records. Your staff will be interviewed. Once we're done with them, they can go home. We won't want them on site while we're searching.'

'For what?' Kay demanded.

'Body parts that shouldn't be here,' Eva said as she led him out of the office. 'I need to know where every piece of human tissue comes from, and where it goes.'

'It's all recorded,' Kay insisted, but Eva chose to ignore him.

She walked with Wren. The building layout seemed loosely familiar. She had seen the type a number of times before. A combination of office space and warehouse; the majority of the open-plan desk area was on the first floor above reception. Raj and Flynn had set up shop there and would be starting to open files that recorded movements of body parts. In the warehouse area, Eva and Wren found the chiller cabinets.

They stood in rows and were padlocked shut. Four large sets of double doors were the only opening on metal boxes that quietly hummed in the large warehouse space. The heart of it all, Eva thought as she approached them. They contained the human tissue that was the basis of Scientific Support Services's business.

Kay produced the keys that unlocked the walk-in cabinets. 'Temperature control is critical,' he told them testily. 'If you leave the doors open too long then the tissue starts to degrade, and we go out of business. You need to keep the doors closed.'

'It's only a couple of degrees above freezing in there,' Eva pointed out. 'How do we do that?'

He led them to a changing room where several sets of insulated jackets and trousers hung from pegs. They looked like the kind of clothes you might wear to walk around above the Arctic Circle, Eva thought. She picked up a parka with a nylon fur edge to it. 'It'll fit over your work gear,' Kay said. 'You need to put plastic gloves and overshoes on top of the thermal ones. We can't guarantee zero contamination given the nature of the tissue, but we try hard to get close.'

Once they were dressed, Kay unlocked the first freezer. 'These are the recent deliveries, whole bodies for the most part.' He swung the door open. They stepped inside. Cold fluorescent tubes lit the space; their breath made thin clouds in stale air. With a dull thud, Kay closed the door behind them.

'It's a shipping container,' Eva realised as she gazed at the interior.

'A standard forty-foot ISO container,' Kay agreed. 'They're usually used for moving fruit, meat and other perishables. We keep four on site, but the benefit of using them is we can get extra capacity at short notice if needs be. To suit demand,' Kay explained.

Racks lined one side. The container was forty feet long by eight feet wide, and eight and a half feet tall. Eva remembered the dimensions from her time at Southampton. Like a unit of international currency, the container could be sent anywhere in the world.

Wren had a clipboard. On the racks, more fluorescent tubes flickered into life. Four shelves ran the length of the container. Five body-sized black bags lay on each shelf. 'You have twenty intact corpses in this container,' she said.

'Correct,' Kay agreed. 'Average storage time is around two to two and a half weeks. We'll have most of the stock placed by then. We replenish as space becomes available.'

'The tissue comes just from this area?'

Kay shook his head. 'From anywhere in the south of the country. We also import from the US. There are around 9,000 fatal accidents in the UK every year though; in theory we have plenty of source material to work with.'

Wren pulled down the zip lock on the black bag nearest her. The plastic folded back to reveal the body of a man, mid-twenties, seemingly intact. 'Six thousand of those fatal accidents occur in the home every year,' she intoned, a wistful note in her voice. 'Thirty-eight per cent of those involve falls. I see plenty of them.'

'I know you do,' Kay told her. 'We deal with your hospital trust.'

Wren raised an eyebrow. 'I actually didn't know that,' she admitted. 'I suppose this process happens once they've left me?'

'Once the cause of death has been confirmed as not suspicious,' Kay agreed, 'then we make an offer for the body, or part of it.'

'Part of it?' Eva demanded.

'We have to be pragmatic,' Kay told her. The look on his face said he had heard the question many times before. 'If your

273

research is into brain diseases, then a liver isn't much use to you. We supply tissue components needed by companies; we always try and find the best possible match.'

In the cold light of the container, the implications of that slowly sunk in. 'So you do dissections on site?' Wren asked.

'Yes,' Kay told her. 'That's what container number four is used for.'

–

It didn't look much like an operating theatre, Eva thought as Kay showed them into the container. It felt more like a garage lock-up. It was painted white, and the same fluorescent tubes lit the space, but this time there was only a table and a single rack in the room, on the left-hand side of the metal box. On the right, tools hung from clips on the wall.

'You dissect corpses in here?' The idea made her skin crawl.

'We have a roster of qualified medical practitioners who do exactly that,' Kay sniffed. 'We have a standard template, if you will. Brain, heart, kidneys, liver and lungs are extracted first and put into containers. We then remove what we can, usually by body system. So muscular, digestive, respiratory, urinary, reproductive, endocrine, circulatory, nervous and integumentary systems.' He pointed at a circular saw. 'Sometimes though the requests are for more in the way of parts for mechanical analysis. We provide hip, knee and shoulder joints for both artificial joint manufacturers to test their devices and to medical schools for junior surgeons to practice implanting those joints on.'

The table was hard, Eva noted. A stainless-steel dissection table with a conveniently placed recess for draining fluids and washing the surface down after use.

'It's compact,' Wren admitted, 'but you have all the necessary equipment. How long does it take to reduce a patient?'

*To their component parts*, Eva thought.

'We can generally get everything that's useful and have all the residue tidied away inside three hours,' Kay said. 'Left-over material is sent for incineration.'

Three hours, Eva thought. Three hours to take a body and strip out the brain, heart, liver, lungs and kidneys, then to make decisions about what else was salvageable. Eyes, reproductive organs, stomach, glands, everything else. 'How do you keep track of the body parts?' she asked.

'We tag the bags,' Kay told Eva. 'We have a strict coding convention for storage and transport. And sometimes we stamp barcodes onto the components themselves, especially the limbs.' None of the limbs in the tanks in the waterworks had barcodes, Eva thought, which proved precisely nothing.

Wren waited patiently. It took until then for Eva to realise she was simply slowing the process down. 'Are you okay if I leave this with you?'

'I've inventoried tissue banks before,' Wren told her. 'Go and talk to the guys upstairs while I deal with the dead.'

–

Eva dumped the parka in the changing room and headed back upstairs. She needed to shower soon. There was a smell about the containers; the odour of flaccid flesh, and it had permeated her skin. She stank of bodies drained of blood, of particles of tissue that, despite cleaning, still clung to the blades of autopsy saws and hid in spatters behind light fixtures. Fragments of human meat sprayed by the electric spinning of circular blades, the incessant buzz as serrated edges sliced through muscle and bone. She could feel it on her. It made her sick, made her think of how close she had come to being just another corpse on Judy Wren's table herself.

Flynn and Raj were heads-down in files. 'What does it look like?' Eva demanded, more sharply than she had intended, as she slumped into a chair. Flynn glanced at her, eyes lit by an anglepoise lamp on the desk.

'A lot of work,' she retorted. 'How about downstairs?' Eva screwed up her face, and Flynn understood then. Raj ignored them both. 'Jamie's doing interviews with Moresby,' Flynn said. 'They're only getting the basics then sending the staff home.'

'Photos and DNA?'

'Yes. We can justify those for exclusion, the DCI made that clear.'

She looked across the desk. 'Raj?'

'I got livers and kidneys,' the detective sergeant assured her without raising his head, 'and pretty much anything else you might need replacing. I'm working backwards and putting them into actual people. As Becks says, it's a lot of work, especially once the bodies have been cut up. They send innards all over the place. The whole corpses are easier to track.'

'Where's Kay?' Flynn asked.

'I left him downstairs with Wren,' Eva told her. She let out a long, reluctant sigh. There was nothing for her to do here. Raj and Flynn knew exactly what they were about, Jamie and Moresby would have the interviews under control. She had effectively put herself out of a job. All she would do by monitoring them at this stage was slow everyone down. She felt like a spare wheel. 'I should probably get back down to Wren, then,' she said, but she wasn't convinced Flynn was listening.

–

Probably just as well, Eva thought after she pulled the parka back on and went to find which of the containers Wren and Kay were lurking in. Wren stood with her fists on her hips and an accusatory glare on her face. Kay was in front of her looking sheepish but defiant. 'They're not part of our inventory,' he was insisting. 'They're cleared by a non-UK Research Ethics Committee, so we can't touch them. They come from our sister company in the Netherlands. They're here because we have extra storage capacity at the moment. They're literally just borrowing space. We hold them for a week or two and then send them back. They do the same for us. It means between us we don't have to go to the expense of renting extra containers.'

'It's illegal,' Wren insisted.

'It's not,' Kay retorted, 'because it never gets used in the UK. We loan them space. It's like an extension of their freezers, that's all.'

'Where's the paperwork?'

'Rotterdam.'

Six white polystyrene boxes sat on one shelf of the now-open third container. Labels and barcodes covered them. Eva could see they had been re-used time and time again. Plastic straps held tight by padlocks wrapped them. She saw the look on Wren's face, and she understood it immediately. An unexpected rage swept through her. The implications of the boxes, their very existence, suddenly felt like a complete affront. 'Open them,' she hissed.

'I can't,' Kay insisted. 'I don't have the authority.'

'I have a warrant,' Eva all but yelled, 'and I'm bloody near incredulous you didn't mention this little side-line earlier. I'll decide if it's obstruction in a bit. Now either you open those boxes, or I get a uniform officer to rip them apart.'

'I don't have the keys,' Kay pleaded.

Wren stormed out. She came back a moment later with a pair of surgical shears that looked as though they could take off fingers, which was in all probability precisely their purpose. She nodded at the camera in the forensics kit. 'Record this please, DI Harris,' Wren asked Eva, 'I don't want any suggestion we interfered with the contents at a later date.'

Eva pointed the camera and watched Wren through the foldout screen. When the video icon turned red Eva nodded, and Wren slipped the shears under the plastic strap. She cut, and then did the same with the second strap. Inside the box Eva saw five packages tightly wrapped in black polythene. Wren cut into the package on top of the box, carefully, so as not to damage the contents. When she pulled back the plastic, she swore.

'Who the hell is responsible for this?' Wren demanded. Inside the plastic, completely intact, was a woman's head.

'It just comes to us from Rotterdam that way,' Kay insisted. 'The dissections haven't been completed. It's why they're being kept to one side.'

Wren placed the head on the rack, as respectfully as she could manage. She cut into the next bag, but by now Eva could tell what she would find. The torso, limbs and head, all detached. 'They take up less space this way,' Kay bleated.

Perhaps she had died in an accident. Maybe she had been hit by a car or drowned in her bath; there was no way of knowing without the attendant paperwork. Or perhaps she had been murdered. Eva fumed. She simply had no way of finding out now. 'Who is responsible for this?' she said, reiterating Wren's question, but with a cold threat in her voice. Kay couldn't fail to hear it.

'You need to talk to Darren Styles,' Kay gabbled. 'He owns the whole group of companies.' Eva felt her mouth fall open. The background work Flynn had done, the tracking of financials Raj had supervised: she thought she knew everything about the ownership of Scientific Support Services LLP. Clearly, she did not.

The sight of the dismembered head now sitting on the rack brought back images of Duncan Webb, the scorched sign for Winter's Gate Farm and all of the uncertainty that surrounded it. Something finally snapped.

'Who the fuck,' Eva screamed in Kay's face, 'is Darren Styles?'

# Chapter Thirty-Nine

'No,' Raj insisted as they drove towards Godalming, 'we didn't just miss him. This guy went to a lot of effort not to be found. There're loopholes in the Limited Liability Partnership structure that mean it's not difficult to hide actual ownership upstream in shell corporations. SSS and its sister companies appear to be owned by an investment group incorporated in the Isle of Man, but the reality is that group is basically Darren Styles.'

Eva ground her teeth. 'Is it dodgy?'

'As hell,' Raj confirmed. 'It's the kind of thing that sends HMRC into meltdown. Problem is, this company in Rotterdam, it's basically a mirror of SSS in Weybridge. I think Kay's technically correct. So long as they don't sell the body parts that get shipped between them they're in the clear as far as any Research Ethics Committee is concerned, but they're also dual-accounting. They don't include those parts in REC stock, but they do count it for tax purposes. It's only a preliminary look, but I reckon they shave forty per cent off their tax bill by shipping stock between countries and then offset the rest against offshore investments in the Isle of Man. Which means,' he said, shaking his head, 'for the past four years the group that owns SSS has actually been taking rebates from HMRC.'

'Shit,' Eva said. 'So this bastard is basically using the bodies of accident victims to amass tax-free cash outside of the UK?'

'Pretty much,' Raj agreed.

Her knuckles whitened as she gripped the steering wheel. 'I want to meet him,' Eva said.

A quiet road that looped away from the A283. A handful of houses, each separated by swathes of manicured lawns. She had probably become as astute as a local estate agent in giving approximate valuations to properties in the county. The houses in this little collection settled comfortably into the one and a half million bracket.

Eva slammed the car to a halt, threw the door open and climbed out. When she reached the front of the property, she kicked the gate and stormed up the path. At the front door she balled her hand into a fist and hammered, kept hammering, as though the door was a substitute for Darren Styles's face. She had no idea whether he was involved in murder or abduction, but the treatment of victim's bodies for profit felt like nothing short of abuse. Rage that had been growing within her for days finally spilled over. 'Darren Styles,' she screamed at the top of her voice, 'open this bloody door before I break it down.'

Nothing. Not a sound. If there was anyone inside the house, they had no intention of coming out. Raj appeared beside her. 'There's a battering ram in the boot,' he said. 'I could give it a go?'

Eva thought for a moment. When she had decided she could justify breaking and entering to Sutton, she turned to Raj. She was just about to say yes when a man appeared at the front gate of the house. 'I think you should leave before I call the police,' he told them.

Raj opened his mouth to speak, but Eva put her hand on his arm. 'Leave this to me,' she snarled.

The problem was, Eva thought as she and Raj sat with coffee served in bone china cups, that Ajit Singh was damned near impossible to dislike. She had wanted to vent her fury on someone, and a precocious neighbour seemed a good-enough target, but the instant she waved her warrant card, Singh, slender and certainly retired, had become irresistibly charming.

'I don't like to pry into other people's business,' Singh told them as they sat, 'but it's been difficult to ignore the ructions emanating from next door. The divorce has been hard; I'm not certain that ownership of the house has been resolved yet. It really is none of my business,' he said, although he gave them both a sideways glance as he said it, 'but I do hope Mrs Styles is the ultimate winner as far as ownership is concerned.'

'There have been fights?'

Singh almost winced. 'I had to let Dominique in one evening. She was in an awful state, wrapped only in a sheet. Styles was shouting and threatening; I called the police but they took a while to come. He hammered on my door, I felt threatened, what else could I do?'

Eva put her coffee down. 'What did you do, Ajit?'

Singh raised his eyebrows. 'I assumed you would know. I was cautioned for my actions.' He looked to a spot above the fireplace where a long sword she knew to be a kirpan hung. 'It's been in my family for two hundred years,' he told them. 'Not once has it let us down.'

She had suspected she was going like him as soon as she showed him her warrant card. 'You threatened Darren Styles with a sword?'

'Dominique had asked for my help,' Singh told them. 'And anyway, Styles was always an obnoxious son of a bitch.'

'It seems kind of extreme?' Raj ventured. He spoke cautiously, and by the tone of his voice made certain Singh understood he was reserving judgement. Singh's eyes flashed for a moment, but then he nodded his head.

'It might appear that way, Detective Sergeant,' Singh said, his tone grave, 'but there were other occasions when I had been tempted to call the police. She had run from the house with only a sheet to cover her that night, and I could tell from her breath that she hadn't been drinking. I was convinced she was in very real danger from Styles. When he came hammering on my door, I wasn't prepared to let him in. I told him so in no uncertain terms.'

'So Dominique never returned to the house?'

'Only to collect some things. She did so under a restraining order; Styles wasn't present.'

'Where is Styles now?' Eva asked.

Singh settled back in his chair. 'I have no idea I'm afraid. The house is in the hands of the lawyers now.'

She thought for another moment. 'And Dominique?'

Singh crumpled his forehead into a frown. 'I have an address for her,' he said, 'but I don't think she would be pleased to see you. The police were not especially helpful when Styles had become physically abusive.'

'That bad?'

Ajit Singh nodded again. 'She spoke to me that night, after he was gone. She told me what he was like. I'm glad she told me later.' He looked embarrassed, Eva thought, as though making a confession. 'If I had known before, I would have been tempted to skewer the bastard where he stood.'

–

Another hour wasted, Eva thought as they navigated the traffic between Godalming and Chertsey. More time spent chasing down leads instead of searching for victims. They were alive still, she knew that; or at least she believed she did. It might be self-delusion, an attempt to hide failure to progress from herself, but she felt convinced that whoever had abducted the latest victims had not yet killed them. Perhaps it was simply hope, but she found herself clinging to it. And as for whom, she thought as they parked in a resident's bay in an unremarkable modern estate, whenever the name Styles was mentioned now the hairs on the back of her neck started to rise.

Dominique Styles had rented a first-floor maisonette under her maiden name, Russell. Eva leant on the doorbell, but there was no answer. 'Could be at work,' Raj ventured. She could be, Eva agreed without speaking. Would they have to hang around all day?

They walked back down the stairs just as a car drew up in front of the flats. Nothing remarkable, Eva noted; a Japanese hatchback about six years old. The driver looked annoyed though, Eva could see that even from ten metres away. She glared, as Eva walked up to her. 'That's my parking space,' she said through the passenger-side window. Angry, resentful, but there was something else. A tremor in the voice that said something as trivial as an argument over parking might be the last straw. A tall, once-attractive woman with dark eyes and long dark hair, but now with shoulders slightly hunched and a hooded look of suspicion and fear on tightly drawn features. Dominique Russell was not in a good place; Eva sensed that immediately. She nodded, stood and turned to Raj. 'Do me a favour,' she said quietly as she threw him the keys. 'Move the car, would you?'

—

She followed Dominique Russell back up to her maisonette. 'I don't want to talk to the police,' Russell said over her shoulder. 'You've been sod-all use to me so far.' They stood at the front door while Dominique fumbled with her keys.

'I know,' Eva told her. 'Ajit Singh explained.' She winced when Eva spoke his name.

'I think I'd be dead now if it wasn't for Ajit.' The door swung open. 'Not that you bastards believed that.' She went to close the door in Eva's face. Eva stopped her. She put her hand against the door and pushed, firmly.

'I'm sorry Dominique. I really am going to have to insist.'

A look of incredulity. 'Are you arresting me or something?'

Eva kept her hand on the door. 'If necessary, but it really shouldn't have to come to that. We need to talk, Dominique, and you need to tell us everything this time.'

She saw the slow sense of realisation settling over Dominique's wan face. 'What's he done?'

'That's what we're trying to work out.'

They sat in the living room. Dominique had relented and offered them coffee, which they had both accepted, but Eva noted that Raj was only pretending to drink his. Dominique noticed too. 'Ajit just gave us coffee,' Eva admitted, by way of an explanation.

'You're on first-name terms?'

'He was very helpful,' Eva said. 'I don't think he likes your ex-husband.'

She sat opposite them. The maisonette was comfortable enough, but Eva guessed the furniture had come with it. A dense silence settled over the room. Raj looked as though he wanted to speak, but Eva ignored him. Eventually, Dominique gave in and asked the first question. 'What's this about?' she asked.

'Murder,' Eva told her, 'multiple murders. We found dismembered body parts in a disused building, but that's only part of the story. We think somebody is abducting people who work for a specific company and conducting tests before killing them. Does that sound the kind of thing Darren is capable of?'

The speed and vehemence of the response astonished even her. 'Yes,' Dominique spat, 'yes it bloody does.'

For a moment Eva floundered for the next question. 'Tell me about him,' she said at last.

'He's a vicious bastard.' Dominique hung her head for a moment as she spoke. 'He's a rapist and a pervert. If Darren wanted sex then that was what Darren got; there was no saying no. I tolerated it at first; I don't know why. I suppose the lifestyle was good. We always went to the best clubs, and money was never short. But after a while he never seemed satisfied, and his tastes started turning sadistic. It was just bondage to start off with, nothing wildly out of the ordinary. Then he started to get weird.'

Eva waited for her to gather herself. 'He started experimenting with implants,' Dominique said. 'Little devices he would put inside himself. He had one in a finger; it fitted under the nail. It was like one of those sparking things you find in lighters. He used to use it on me. I never knew when he was going to give me a shock.'

'He did this himself? He implanted them himself?'

'He knew how,' Dominique said. 'Darren used local anaesthetics; he had mirrors and scalpels. It seemed really weird, but it was like he enjoyed stitching himself up. Some of the implants contained drugs. He could get high just by pushing on them. He wanted me to try them too.'

'You said no?'

'I couldn't let him do that. That made him angry. I worried about the number of blades he kept around the house; he left them everywhere. I cut myself on them a couple of times. He just told me to be more careful.'

'What did you know about his business?'

'Only what he told me. I thought he was investing. I didn't realise what SSS did, or how deeply involved he was.' The strain of remembering showed on her face. 'There were so many moments that should have been the last straw: when I found out he took an active role in dissections, or when he insisted I should have a tracking implant inserted under my skin. But the actual last straw was the one where I ran out. We were in bed. He came at me with a scalpel, all the while telling me it wouldn't hurt. He would anaesthetise me, he said. It would be fun.'

Eva's skin crawled. What would she have done in those circumstances? How would she have reacted? Berlin came back to her then, the savage pleasure she had taken when her foot had slammed into the man who was trying to rape her. But how would she have reacted two and a half years ago, before Colin Lynch had tried to bury her alive in a ditch? She put the thoughts of her own circumstances to one side.

'How long had he been like this?' she asked.

'A few years,' Dominique told them. 'It was getting worse. His manic episodes were getting more bizarre.'

Raj leant forward then. He wanted to ask a question, even though at that point Eva wished he wouldn't. 'Did your ex-husband ever mention a woman named Anna Seifert?'

He asked the question quietly enough, Eva thought. His voice was soft and sympathetic. It wasn't immediately obvious why Dominique threw her coffee cup at him.

She screamed. Half doubled up, face contorted, every last breath of air exiting her lungs. Raj wasn't hurt, but his face dripped with lukewarm coffee. Eva grabbed Dominique and pinned her to the chair. 'Calm down!' she shouted. Dominique kept screaming.

Eva couldn't hit her, even though she knew it might feel like the right thing to do. Slap her face, slap her out of it: that's what Styles would have done, Eva told herself. In desperation, not knowing what else to do, she sat back down.

Raj, Eva noted, was sucking it up. Jaw clenched, handkerchief in hand, he quietly mopped his face. Eva remained implacable, or at least she tried to. After about a minute Dominique simply ran out of strength.

They sat in silence for several minutes more. Eventually Dominique raised her head. She stared at Raj. Eva thought she was going to apologise, but instead she glanced away and gazed at a small cabinet in the corner of the room. 'Top shelf,' Dominique told Raj, 'lawyers files. Fourth section, mental cruelty.'

Raj stood, walked to the cabinet, opened it, and took out the file she had mentioned. He flicked through pages for thirty seconds or so, and then stopped. 'Jesus Christ,' Eva heard him mutter under his breath.

'Darren was obsessed with her,' Dominique said by way of an explanation. 'Don't misunderstand me. He didn't want to fuck her. It wasn't like that. Or maybe he did, I don't know, but that wasn't the point.' Raj brought the sheaf of papers to Eva. When he looked at Dominique again, despite the fact he was dripping with coffee it was with an expression of empathy on his face.

Eva took the papers. There were documents and photos. In amongst the photos, some of which were images of the marks Styles had inflicted on Dominique, were pictures of Styles himself. She understood Dominique's reaction the instant she saw them.

'Why,' she struggled to find the right question to ask, 'does he look like that?'

Dominique hung her head. 'He thinks Anna is different, superior. It always seemed like something between Aryanism and the Midwich Cuckoos to me. I didn't realise how deep his fixation ran at first.' She raised her eyes to stare at Eva. 'He wants to be like Anna, a breed apart, or so he imagines. He kept on talking about eugenics and improving the species through intervention; he sounded like a fucking Nazi towards the end. Anna's everything he's not. Cold, dispassionate, intelligent. He altered his appearance, had plastic surgery, changed his clothes, dyed his hair, had the same implants.' She let her gaze fall again. Silent tears soaked her face. 'Darren had a twin, a sister. They were close.' Another pause. 'I sometimes wonder if they were *too* close.' A shake of the head. 'I don't know for sure, but it always seemed strange to me. But she died. I think something broke in Darren then.' Dominique pulled her fingers through her hair, then sat up to stare at the two of them.

She needed to talk, to explain. Less of an interview, Eva thought, more like psychotherapy. 'There's something unnatural about Darren's focus on Anna,' Dominique continued. 'He wants to possess her and to be like her, almost in equal measure. It's like he's looking for a replacement twin, someone to be a sister and lover both at the same time. Anna Seifert, successful and brilliant, who voluntarily had devices implanted in her. How the fuck could I ever be anything but a poor substitute for that?' She hung her head again. This time, when she started sobbing, she didn't stop.

Raj stood beside Eva and stared at the photos again. 'I think we may have a suspect,' he whispered.

'Sweet Jesus,' Eva whispered back. 'I would say so.'

## Chapter Forty

When they arrived back at Scientific Support Services, Sutton was already there. 'You think Darren Styles is a possibility?' she asked Eva before she had the chance to even take her jacket off.

'Absolutely, ma'am. If Dominique Russell is right, he just needs taking off the streets anyway, but he fits every profile we could imagine. Yes, I'm confident enough to switch all resources to looking for Styles.'

Sutton frowned and nodded. 'You called for a specialist support officer for Russell? Does she need that after this time?'

'Yes,' Raj interrupted, 'she bloody well does, ma'am. After what that bastard's done to her she needs psychiatric help. I'm just staggered nobody saw that before.' His shirt was stained and still damp, Eva noticed. She let her silence speak for her.

'So how do we find him?' Sutton asked.

'We're here,' Eva said, 'so we start with Phillip Kay.'

—

Kay sat in a chair in front of the desk in what until that morning had been his office. Sutton had pointedly taken the chair behind the desk. Eva perched on the edge of it and looked down on him.

'I can hardly begin to tell you how much trouble you, personally, are in,' Eva said as she stared at him. 'Not just the company, do you understand? This is a murder investigation and you have been obstructing it. You're aware you can go to prison for that?'

'I'm not being obstructive,' Kay insisted. The tone of his voice crept towards a whine. 'I haven't seen him for months. I don't know where he is.'

'But you did let him take the lead in dissections?'

'He owns the company,' Kay said. 'He told me he was qualified. What was the worst that could happen? If he'd messed up a dissection it was his cost.'

Sutton slammed her fist on the table and bellowed. 'Those are people you're talking about. How would the relatives feel if they knew you let any pervert with a chainsaw chop up their loved ones' bodies while pretending it was for research?'

'They don't have a say,' Kay barked back. 'We've purchased the bodies. It's a legal transaction. They don't have rights any longer. How is Styles practising on a body any different from some thumb-fisted junior surgeon ripping it open to learn to stick a hip joint in?'

'For Christ's sake,' Sutton growled.

Eva tried another approach. 'Look, we don't want you to take the fall for this. We don't think it's fair that you're the one who's going to get the blame when it's clearly down to Styles. Surely you can help us to help you?'

'But I don't know where the hell he is,' Kay pleaded. 'He's like that. He'll turn up out of the blue, hang around for a week or so, check the books, check the stock and then disappear. Have you tried the Isle of Man?'

Sutton shook her head incredulously. 'He doesn't live there. He hasn't got a house there. It's only a PO box. That's about tax avoidance, unless you're going to tell us he's a TT racer on the quiet?'

'Honestly,' Kay said, hands spread wide, imploring look on his face, 'I email him. I can email him, but your DS already got me to do that. I've got a phone number for him but as you heard, it just rings.'

'The phone is switched off,' Eva said. 'We can't track its current position, but its last position was in a private gym locker in central London. Not helpful.'

'I don't know what else to tell you,' Kay bleated. 'I've told you everything I know.'

Eva doubted that very much, but when she glanced at Sutton, she imagined the DCI had come to the same conclusion. Kay didn't know where Styles was. Kay might be hiding things from them, other little infringements of both regulations and decency, but he had no real idea of where Styles might be found. They could either arrest him for obstruction or let him go. She was about to raise that point with Sutton when the door opened.

With no apology for the interruption, Judy Wren walked in. She was holding something, Eva saw. It dripped. Wren positioned herself in front of Kay. It was clearly him she was looking for. 'What,' she demanded as she held the item in her hands up to his face, 'the hell is this?'

Eva slipped off the desk and took half a step backwards. It was a heart; that much seemed perfectly obvious to her. She could see where the aorta had been severed. It had been washed out. The liquid that dripped on the floor and now onto Kay's trousers was water, not blood. None the less, the sight and smell of it did little for her, and she could see Sutton felt the same way.

'What's up, Judy?'

'Another of SSS's little side-lines?' Wren seemed enraged again. She looked as though she was about to shove the organ into Kay's face.

'Judy,' Eva said quietly, 'could you please explain?'

'It's a heart,' Wren said. She kept staring at Kay.

'I can see that,' Eva told her.

'Just not a human heart,' Wren announced. Kay flinched, but then so did Eva and Sutton.

'Ah,' Kay said. 'No. It comes from the body of a mountain gorilla. From Uganda.'

'That's an endangered species,' Sutton spluttered.

'It died of natural causes,' Kay insisted.

Wren asked her next question through bared teeth. 'What is it doing amongst human body parts?'

Eva glowered too. 'It's from another sister company,' Kay said, wringing his hands with embarrassment. 'Northridge Support Services.'

'You didn't mention them,' Eva told him.

'There's a lot I didn't mention,' Kay said. He sounded exhausted now. 'I have no idea whether it's relevant or not. You asked me about Styles. I answered questions about Styles.'

She wanted to hit him, but she knew she couldn't. 'What does Northridge do?'

'The same sort of thing as SSS, but with animals. They provide animals for scientific research. Vivisection, basically.'

Eva curled her lip as she asked the next question. 'Dead?' she said.

'Alive,' Kay confirmed.

–

The office was quiet now. Sutton was downstairs talking to Moresby. Flynn, Newton and Chakrabati were wading through paperwork still. Wren was back in a chilled container sorting human body parts from animal. It wasn't a pleasant office, she thought as she sat in the fake-leather chair behind Kay's desk. It didn't belong to a company that had any aspirations, either for itself or for what it could provide in the world. It was a meat shop, pure and simple.

When Michael Sullivan had first discovered incorrectly labelled body parts in amongst the carefully managed morgue at Seifert Pharmaceutical, he claimed he had imagined them to be the by-product of body snatchers, individuals or a group who preyed on the reluctance of next of kin to give up the corpses of loved ones for research, and who behaved like modern-day Burke and Hares. In many ways that description felt right for Scientific Support Services. Sullivan had known something was wrong, just not what. He had rescued the incorrectly labelled parts and stored them, with Anna Seifert's help. Neither of them had known what to do with the remains; they had only known they needed to take care of them.

Styles knew Seifert. That much was obvious. Styles had encountered Seifert through Scientific Support Services, learned of Seifert's public research into anti-senescence, and somehow gleaned that something called Derzelas existed. That had to be through New Thought, Eva realised as she imagined the network diagram in her head, the links and nodes that connected events and people. Arnaud Seifert had let slip to Dominic Vance, who seemingly filled the role of New Thought's ultimate arbiter or decision-maker, that Derzelas was part of Seifert's research, and Vance had made the fact known to people with influence within New Thought. Eva knew precisely zero about Vance, but she could imagine that connection ended only in money and a belief that drugs could ultimately extend lifespan. That was where Styles came into the picture too, but instead of Vance's presumably cool-headed investment approach, Styles had built layer upon layer of fantasy inside his mind, and to some extent outside of it as well.

What was Styles? Another Mathew Harred, that much was obvious. It didn't feel like a coincidence that both Harred and Styles had in some way gravitated towards New Thought, because their ideologies felt liberating, although to Eva they also felt prismatic. They could be viewed through so many different facets, interpreted in so many different ways, from transcendentalism to transhumanism by way of Berta Nicholson's and Charlotte Savini's hedonists. New Thought attracted people with outlandish tendencies. Some more outlandish than others.

What could she discover about Styles? She had her laptop and an Internet connection; she could access the Police National Computer, HMRC, Companies House, the NHS and, of course, Google. Unlike Sullivan, Styles had not been especially careful about concealing his early years. But then there was very little to conceal. Styles had worked in the City, he had been a day trader, made his money, burned out by the time he was thirty. The trail became less straightforward after that. She found a number of companies for which he was registered as a director, but there was no real pattern to them. They simply told her Styles put his money anywhere he sensed an opportunity. That was not unusual, Eva thought. At first, nothing she could find online seemed especially unusual.

No wonder he had been able to hide. From a distance, Styles seemed as charismatic as wallpaper. It wasn't until she came closer that she started to see the pattern.

Over time the companies Style became associated with changed. They started to look like one another, in that they all had some therapeutic aspect to them. Pharmaceutical start-ups, medical device companies and some dubious restorative therapies – it was as though at a certain age Styles had suddenly become aware of his own mortality and sought to invest in businesses that might one day overcome it. He had become more actively involved in a few of the start-ups too. She found a small number of published papers online where he was listed as one of the authors, and it sounded like the accreditations were more than just a courtesy. Styles seemed to have become a practitioner in his own right, not formally qualified but seemingly competent. A researcher, capable of, amongst other things, analysing tissue samples and making calculations regarding anaesthetic dosages, albeit in the context of animal experimentation.

Eva checked his other records, the range that the government kept on file, the mundane information that for the most part focused on births and marriages, death and taxes. It didn't take her long to confirm what Dominique, his estranged and abused wife, had told her: that Styles was born one of a pair of twins.

Denise Styles looked like him. At least, she looked like the photos of Styles before he had tried to change himself into a sibling of Anna Seifert. There was nothing remarkable about Denise as far as Eva could see, except for one detail. Denise had died at the age of thirty-three. The cause was a heart attack.

She had died trying to catch an Underground train. A moderately successful lawyer, Denise had stayed close with Darren. The shock of her death must have been tremendous; Eva could at least concede that. An undiagnosed congenital heart defect, it had struck her down with no warning whatsoever. It was shortly after Denise was buried that Styles started putting his money in to medical start-ups.

She couldn't find much after that. The trail slowly cooled. Styles had become increasingly furtive in his business dealings. In all probability he was avoiding paying taxes so that he could invest even further. That was not her concern, Eva decided as she turned her attention to Northridge Support Services.

Kay had said the company was based in the North Downs. When she went looking for it on a mapping application, she found what appeared to be a large farm, several miles from the nearest habitation in the middle of agricultural land. There were no ground-level views of the location, and the website wasn't especially informative.

In fact, the most useful website she came across was an animal rights directory. It had Northridge blacklisted, and gave its reasons in clear, precise details that made her queasy. It sounded like Styles, she thought as she read transcripts from whistle-blowers and examined photos of the facility taken with telephoto lenses. It had a brutal, uncaring flavour to it; even the name tasted sour in her mouth. Low, single-storey buildings stood behind a razor-wire perimeter surrounded by CCTV. Eva picked up her phone.

'Becks,' she said after a couple of rings, 'all three of you, drop what you're doing. Styles is at Northridge and so are the abductees. I'd bet my life on it. I need an armed unit working up plans to storm the place as soon as possible.' *The decision to act*. The phrase tumbled out of the past towards her, but she knew she needed to ignore it. Some hybrid distillation of logic and intuition told her that she had to act and do so immediately, because if one word somehow got back to Styles then he would act first. The flip side of that particular coin was that she felt certain he would act anyway, that the abductees were coming to the end of their usefulness, and that those particular loose ends would soon be tidied away permanently. She needed to convince the team. She had to emphasise just how critical the moment was.

'Listen,' Eva said, loud enough so that Jamie and Raj would be able to overhear through the phone, 'we need to go in really hard, treat it like an assault. I believe absolutely that the abductees are still alive, but as soon as Styles knows we're coming I'm damned certain he's going to kill them.'

# Part III

## All That Lives Must Die

# Chapter Forty-One

Dawn was grey. Grey sky and green hills interspersed with copses of trees. The landscape felt like death, Eva thought as she followed the ARU vehicles up a single-track lane. No, she thought again, not that. It was like limbo, purgatory, somewhere in-between. An undulating Hades populated only by police vehicles and flocks of carrion crows. A place filled with portent. Anything could happen here.

What if she was wrong? What if Darren Styles had learned of her uncovering of him and in some other location was even now cutting the throats of those he had abducted, simply as a precaution? Could she live with that? Everybody made mistakes, but if this were a mistake, she might have killed five people. Her career would not survive that, much less her conscience. Or her soul.

She tried to shake the mood and concentrate on what she could see, which was not much. Northridge was concealed, hidden from view by a dark wall of high trees planted especially for that purpose. When she looked for buildings, she couldn't see them. White pine and hybrid poplar grew in amongst older native stock and pushed it aside; dense swathes of ivy clung to boughs and branches; sharp tangled brambles covered the ground. The lane the police vehicles were following entered the copse at an angle, so none of the structures could be seen from it. Eva knew the natural concealment to be a deterrent against unwanted approaches from animal rights activists, who had threatened the place on a number of occasions but never managed to penetrate the security surrounding the site. As she gazed at the twisted snarl of branches, needles and thorns, she began to understand why.

A convoy of cars and vans approached Northridge as quietly as they could. Two vans carried Moresby's people; another van and two Land Rovers brought firearms officers. Moresby, Jacks and Kitson, the Specialist Firearms Officer's Bronze Commander, had spent the night working out tactics. Eva, Flynn, Newton and Chakrabati followed in two unmarked cars, and a Technical Officer in a van packed with equipment came behind them. After the TO, two paramedics followed in a 4x4 with green and yellow markings. At the end of the procession was a beat-up Volvo that looked as though it had already driven to the moon and back. Eva had requested a veterinary surgeon to take care of whatever animals they might find at the farm.

Farm. Another euphemism, one that made her sick in the pit of her stomach. A place where Styles conducted experiments on animals, or at least kept them caged, ready to be shipped to laboratories where they would be gassed or put under the knife. She knew the arguments,; that testing drugs on living things provided the most information, but it still seemed obscene. And although the logic didn't quite work, she also felt there was a world of difference between researchers trying to gather data for some new life-saving drug, and a company like Northridge that essentially acted as both zoo and abattoir.

The misdirection had started near the main road. The entrance to the area surrounding Northridge had looked like nothing more than a lane to another farm, protected by cattle grids, five-bar steel gates and 'private property' signs. There had been no indication of where the lane led; only an aerial view from a satellite map had shown her that. She could see that Northridge sat in the middle of one of the densely wooded areas that lay scattered across the Downs. It had once been a country estate, but there was no sign of a house there now. Her map told her it stood barely fifteen kilometres away from Seifert as the crow flew, but the land was old here. Seifert had taken to careful re-wilding of the grounds around their site for ecological reasons, whereas Northridge made her think of the forest of brambles and thorns that sprung up around the castle in the tale of Sleeping Beauty. Perhaps that was apt, Eva thought as the convoy of vehicles drew to a halt. Five abductees on the edge of death, waiting to be awakened. Or slain.

'Bloody hell,' Rebecca Flynn muttered as officers emptied themselves from cars and vans. 'What do we do, go and knock on the door?'

Kitson, a powerfully built man whose grandparents had arrived in England from the West Indies in the 1950s, didn't turn away from the Ordinance Survey map laid out on the bonnet of the Land Rover when he answered. Dressed in black body armour, he already had his helmet on. The cover on his sidearm was now unfastened. 'Nobody goes within a hundred metres of that place until my people have surveyed the site.' He paused and looked up at Eva. 'That's assuming we have authority to proceed?'

She nodded, keeping her voice as steady as she could make it. 'Yes, Bronze,' Eva told him. It felt as though she were handing down a death sentence. *The decision to act. The rest is mere tenacity.* 'You have authority to proceed.'

*I'm in charge*, she thought. But that was not entirely true. In matters concerning the SFOs she would have to defer to Kitson, but ultimately success or failure would be her responsibility. Live or die, if the abductees were in the farm it was down to her. Which was why, she thought as she looked around the convoy of ten vehicles that had lined up in the lane, she had brought damned near everything she could with her, including the kitchen sink.

'Ready?' Kitson asked the TO, a fresh-faced young officer called Mandel. Mandel nodded, opened a laptop next to Kitson's OS map, then took a step backwards and lifted a remote control. Behind them the mosquito whine of a drone started, and the screen of the laptop showed an image of the ground rapidly falling away. 'Keep it high to start off with,' Kitson instructed as the drone climbed vertically at speed, 'high enough to hide the noise. Then fly a grid pattern,' he told Mandel, who stood fixated on the smaller screen clipped to the top of the controller. 'Let's see what we're dealing with.'

—

Twenty minutes later the drone settled back to the ground. The sun had risen a few minutes before six that morning and they had arrived half an hour later, so long sharp shadows still concealed the site from the air. Mandel had needed to use a night-vision camera to look down on it. As the drone flew, he snapped still images, which software on the laptop composited into a monochrome map. Kitson, Jacks, Eva and Moresby stood in silence and watched as the picture revealed itself. After ten minutes Kitson had let out a lengthy sigh. 'It's a maze.'

Jacks stroked his chin. 'It's a trap,' he added, 'or more likely a whole bunch of them. This place was built to keep animal rights protestors out. I'm not seeing any way to approach it without setting off alarms and God knows what else.'

Eva jabbed a finger at the screen. 'What's that?' The main site comprised a dozen single-storey buildings laid out like a compound and linked by covered walkways. The drone had picked up two thin parallel lines that seemed to delimit the outer edge of the structures.

'Those will be razor-wire fences ma'am,' Mandel told her as he flew.

'Two of them? Why two?'

'The outer one is to keep people out,' Jacks said. 'The inner is to keep whatever it is they let loose in that racetrack between the fences out of the compound.' He glanced at Kitson. 'Attack dogs, I shouldn't wonder.'

'Three roads in and out,' Mandel said as he steered the drone around the perimeter. 'Three gates. I think they have double layers that block off the racetrack when they open. The foliage around the area is really dense. I don't see any way of approaching the fences apart from going down the lanes.'

'Which will be covered by CCTV,' Kitson said. He stared at Eva. 'DI Harris, this place is a fortress. Anything we do to try to get in is going to be a major risk. Are you certain this guy Styles has the abductees locked up in there?'

She stared at the screen as Mandel kept adding shots to the montage. A cluster of low buildings that looked for all the world like a prison camp, interspersed with a labyrinth of internal fences, surrounded by razor wire and in the middle of woodland so dense as to be almost impenetrable. She had never felt so certain of anything as she did of this. 'I'd bet my life on it,' Eva said softly.

Jacks gazed toward the wall of trees. 'It may come to that,' he told her.

—

She stood under the canopy of a larch with Flynn, Newton and Chakrabati. Drizzle fell from the grey, featureless sky. 'The SFOs think Kitson is properly worried,' Jamie Newton told them. 'He doesn't reckon we'll get in without ramming the front gate with one of the Land Rovers, and that'll give Styles plenty of warning.'

'Time enough to kill the hostages,' Raj pointed out.

'What does that buy him?' Flynn grated.

She had a point, Eva thought. Would Styles give up the hostages if confronted by a full-on assault by armed police? She had to close her eyes for a moment. Too much supposition, too little data. The network diagram in her head looked like a constellation on a cloudy night, a paucity of stars. The fear in her stomach, not the fear of failure but the fear of the *consequences* of failure, gnawed at her. 'We cannot assume Styles will behave rationally in any way,' she told them as she opened her eyes once more.

'He wants something,' Flynn said.

'He wants something that doesn't exist,' Eva snapped back.

'What happens if we go in?' Raj asked, hands stuffed in pockets.

She hung her head. 'Last night, when I was talking it through with Kitson and Jacks, it all seemed so much clearer. We had OS maps, satellite photos and the plans of the farm. It looked like the SFOs would be able to cut the fence and enter the buildings without being detected. That's partly why Mandel's here. He would disable the alarms and shut down the CCTV. Having actually seen the place, I don't think we'd even get up to the fence without being detected.'

'We knock on the front door then,' Flynn repeated. 'We've got a warrant.'

'And either Styles lets us in, or he doesn't,' Eva said. 'If he doesn't, we have to ram the gate, and I'd give it a seventy per cent chance Styles kills the hostages.'

'Based on what?' Raj demanded, although he did so softly.

'I'm guessing,' Eva admitted. 'But you met his wife. Do you think I'm wrong?' Raj didn't answer.

'The only other option,' Flynn said, quite reluctantly, 'is to negotiate.' Eva flicked a glance at her, then nodded ever so slightly. 'Question is,' Flynn continued, 'if, like you say, he's probably up for killing the hostages, what have we got to negotiate with?'

Eva pulled out her phone to check the time, and then looked towards the opposite end of the lane. 'I'm hoping the bait is going to show up any minute now.'

–

Ten minutes later an unmarked police car crept down the lane and came to a halt behind the veterinarian's impossibly aged Volvo. The driver and the officer in the front seat climbed out and opened the back doors. As they did so, another unmarked vehicle pulled up behind them. *Christ*, Eva thought, counting a dozen vehicles in the lane, *you had better be right about this.*

Two figures stepped out of the back of the first unmarked car. The officer offered them an umbrella, and they huddled together under it once it was open. Anna Seifert and Michael Sullivan. It felt as though the sky had sucked the colour from them too. Anna wore her ankle-length grey coat, and Sullivan's skin seemed to match it. The rain was heavier now.

'I can't thank you enough,' Eva said as she stood in front of them, mud speckling her trousers and rain trickling down her neck. Sullivan angled the umbrella so that it covered her as well.

'How could we not help?' Anna Seifert said. 'These are *my* people, as you so eloquently pointed out.' She shrugged slightly. 'I don't think we could have ever imagined a creature such as Darren Styles, but there's no doubt he's acted because of Derzelas.'

Eva needed to make certain Anna understood. 'If it wasn't that,' she said, voice quiet enough that only the two of them could hear her, 'it would have been something else. I appreciate you feel responsible, but it's not your fault, and I'm really grateful for you being here.'

'What do we need to do?' Sullivan asked. They had started to walk slowly towards the last car, to where one of Moresby's officers and a hostage negotiator were already deep in conversation.

She needed to exhaust all the other options first, Eva decided as they walked. 'If all goes well, then nothing. If we need to use you then it's going to get a little more free-form, but if that happens just being here and showing your faces is going to be an incredible help.'

'You think they're in there?' Seifert asked.

The same question she had been asking herself all night. The answer had become an act of faith. 'Nothing else makes any sense,' Eva told her.

Mandel had not been idle. When Eva returned to where Kitson and Moresby now stood, she saw he had taken his laptop inside one of the Land Rovers, to shelter it from the slow drizzle. Moresby waited as patiently as Moresby always did; Kitson was more fractious. Mandel politely ignored the two of them. Eva eased between them, pushed her way into the car next to Mandel and stared at his screen. 'What can you see?'

'The main wireless network,' Mandel told her without looking away from the computer. 'It's reasonably secure.' He was only a handful of years younger than her, probably not long out of university. She imagined him to be a recipient of one of the information security degrees that had started springing up in those institutions that also offered computer science. About her height, with scruffy blond hair that hung down over blue eyes, Mandel wore casual clothes that marked him out as a civilian support, even though his job title was Technical Officer. All regional police forces were recruiting TOs now; the rise in cybercrime had forced that move upon them. She had to wonder if the relatively modest age difference and the fact that she was a woman would present any problems. She decided to find out. 'Any guest networks?'

Mandel nodded, slowly, eyes fixed on data packets running down the screen of a Linux shell. 'Password-protected WPA2, but I'm running Pyrit and PMKID Hashcat to deal with that.' He said it as though he didn't expect her to understand. She felt the need to disavow him of that misapprehension.

Eva pointed at what looked like a small circuit board sat next to his laptop. 'ESP8266 Deauthers aren't police issue.' Her smile was glacial. She enjoyed the look of surprise mixed with alarm on his face. 'I was with MPCCU,' she told him.

'It's personal kit,' Mandel admitted, face colouring, not knowing how she would react. That was not explicitly forbidden by the regulations of cybercrime, but he damn well knew it was severely frowned upon. 'Should I disconnect it, ma'am?'

By his expression it seemed she had made her point. Eva guffawed. 'Don't you dare. Good to see a bit of initiative. What are you looking for when you're in?'

Mandel didn't try to hide his relief. 'CCTV. I'm assuming they'll be half-way competent and changed the default account password, but so many of these cameras don't implement account lock-out. It's criminal.' He risked looking smug. 'I've got Hydra and a dictionary ready to go; once I'm on the network I give it three minutes, tops.' He shrugged. 'Getting on the network might take a bit longer.'

For a moment she felt envious at the simple complexity of the task, one that came without the consequence of somebody dying if an error was made. Get it wrong, just go back and start again. Like a computer game, re-spawn in a different location. 'Quick as you can,' she told Mandel. She nodded towards Kitson and Moresby, to where they now stood under the branches of a tree, gazing through the rain at the road up towards the farm. The pressure of her next words weighed down on her. They felt like almost like a confession. 'Very soon I have to decide whether I'm going to order that lot to go in hard and shoot Darren Styles on sight.'

# Chapter Forty-Two

She wanted to wait until Mandel had hacked the CCTV cameras, but Kitson pre-empted her. The ground had turned to mud. Rivulets of brown water trickled past car wheels and spattered her shoes. Kitson, in his body armour and helmet, disregarded it. He pointed towards Northridge.

'I want to see if we can get up to the fence from somewhere in-between the lanes.'

Eva looked in the direction he was pointing, towards a dense tangle of briars and bushes that met the lower branches of trees. 'Why now? Why not wait?'

He took off his helmet to wipe a few drops of rain from his forehead, then replaced it. 'I know how this sounds, but it's too quiet. It's like there's nobody there.'

A gnawing in her stomach again. Did she have the wrong location? 'That's actually possible.' She couldn't keep dejection from her voice. 'Assuming I've fucked up completely, that is.'

Kitson grimaced. 'Honestly, I don't think you have. It's the perfect place to keep them hidden, except for one detail.'

'Which is?'

'Staff. Is this guy a lone wolf or are there others in that place who know he's been keeping people against their will and knocking them off when he's done?'

Eva shook her head. 'He's a lone wolf. A classic predatory psychopath with a fixated objective, except in this case I don't think it's sex – although his ex-wife might disagree. I don't see any evidence of him needing to work as part of a pack.'

'I agree. Which says to me he's the only person in that place.'

She shrugged, trying to see Kitson's point. 'Almost certainly. So?'

'I bet that makes him pretty bloody careful about people approaching the site.'

Realisation struck her. 'Christ. He's watching us.'

He looked around and nodded his head, slowly. 'This whole setup is too well planned. We've stayed away from the gates, but I can't see a bunch of cars coming within half a kilometre of that place and not setting off alarms.'

Eva understood then. 'You want another way in.'

Kitson lifted his shoulders slightly and then let them drop. 'The racetrack,' he said, using Jacks's term, 'is empty. Why? I think he's holding everything back. I think one of the Land Rovers could ram the gate, but I don't know what the hell would happen if it did.'

'You think your people can cut through?'

'I think there's a double-width four-metre steel fence topped with razor wire behind those trees. It's tough, but it won't stand up to a bolt cutter. I'd like to get a couple of my guys inside the fence quietly and have them ready to give covering fire before we go knocking on the front door.'

'You don't want to wait?'

Kitson turned his gaze on her. 'Thing is, DI Harris, I think you're right. Nothing else makes sense. I think Styles is in there with five sedated people and he's perfectly capable of cutting their throats or worse. The longer we wait the more likely he is to do that. We need to go, right now.'

–

She could hear the laboured breath of the SFOs as they hacked their way through the undergrowth. There were three lanes in, each leading to an entry gate. Two were designed for vehicles, one for pedestrians only. She had seen that from the close-ups Mandel had taken from the drone. The two vehicle gates were on roughly opposite sides of the compound, and the footpath was more or less half-way between them. Kitson's officers, three of them, picked the longest stretch of fence to hack their way towards.

One of them muttered over the radio, 'Bloody glad we brought gloves. We wouldn't be able to get through this stuff without them.'

Kitson spoke softly into his headset mike. Eva listened through an earpiece connected to her radio. 'How close are you?'

'Five metres.' More muted swearing. 'I can see the fence; it's about what we thought. Heavy duty, but we'll be able to snip through it with the bolt cutters. It'll take a while, but once we're through we'll have—'

Then someone screamed. Long and hard.

Eva didn't hear anything else. It felt like the sound would burst her eardrum; she had to rip the earpiece out. When she turned, she saw she wasn't the only one.

Jacks was already running, weapon raised. Kitson yelled. 'Blue team, what the hell just happened?'

A voice, panting. 'Wait.'

'Blue team, I'm sending support.'

Another yell. 'No! Not safe. Repeat, not safe.'

She saw the knot of muscles in Kitson's jaw. Jacks had skidded to a halt; two of the other SFOs stood beside him. All had weapons raised, safety catches off, pointing at nothing. 'Blue team,' Kitson hissed, 'report.'

Muttering. Sounds coming through a headset, but not that of whoever had issued the instruction. 'Keep it together mate, we'll have you out of there in a second.' Somebody groaning, trying not to scream again. Spitting and swearing, two people exchanging brief, unintelligible sentences. The sound of effort; of strain. Another screech, but some note of relief in it this time.

Eva looked at Kitson. Kitson ignored her. 'Blue team.' Voice quiet, steady, in control even though he wasn't. 'I really need a report, now.'

A pause. Then: 'Bronze, some bastard set mantraps around the fence. Davis put his foot in one. His leg's broken, but we've got him out. We need a medic on standby.'

The paramedics were already there, waiting. Barely a minute later she saw two SFOs carrying a third man between them stumbling out of the brambles. Eva, Kitson and the paramedics ran up to them. Jacks and his team surrounded them, weapons still raised. A compound fracture, Eva saw. Bloody bone poked through the skin. Davis, the SFO, bunched his hands into fists and clenched his jaw. Tendons in his neck stood out as he struggled not to scream again. The paramedics went to work.

Kitson snarled. 'There's no point in hiding.'

'None at all,' Eva agreed. Her decision. It didn't seem like a difficult one now. 'Get SFOs and uniform to move up to the gate.'

–

Two Land Rovers slid to a halt barely a metre away from the wire. Metal grills covered both their windscreens. The vans that had brought Moresby's officers to the farm stopped half a dozen metres behind them, at an angle to provide cover if needed. Jacks and three SFOs ran up to the gate, and Eva stomped behind them through the mud.

'Bolt cutters,' Kitson yelled. 'Get that bloody gate off its hinges.' If the bolt cutters wouldn't do it, she knew they had a circular saw in Mandel's van. If the saw wouldn't do it, they would use the Land Rovers, which had bull bars and wire grating over the windscreens, armoured for riot control, although what kind of riot anyone ever expected in Surrey she couldn't imagine.

Maybe she had already heard the sound. Perhaps it was like a dog whistle, ultrasonic but falling down into the audible spectrum like a locomotive hurtling towards them. She felt the hair on her scalp lift as she looked around, trying to work out where it came from. She could tell by their hesitation that Jacks,

Kitson and Moresby heard it too. After a second or so she was able to localise it, sense the direction. Eva turned her head. Wished she had not.

They came tearing towards them around the racetrack. Five distended shapes. Brown-and-black bodies but yellow eyes, baying, howling, teeth bared, foam flying from their mouths. For a moment she didn't know what she was looking at, but then they hit the fence like five snarling missiles, and she didn't care. Eva jumped back. Everyone did, including Jacks and the other SFOs. The animals attacked the wire, leapt, scrabbled and bit at it. Movements almost too fast to be natural. Jacks stared, gun raised, mouth open. He spoke for all of them when he said: 'What the hell are those?'

—

Tom Hallett, the veterinarian, stood just over an arm's length away from the wire and stared through the rain. Five frenzied shapes twisted and thrashed and sprayed saliva in front of him. Eva, Flynn and Newton waited just behind him. Hallett was about forty, with a grey beard and a mass of thick grey hair, and wore threadbare jeans and a body warmer over a russet jumper. His expression, Eva thought, was the picture of complete disgust. 'I cannot believe,' he muttered quietly, so as not to enrage the dogs any further, 'what someone has done to these animals.'

She moved beside him and kept her voice as quiet as his. 'What have they done?' Eva demanded. The speed of their movements was frightening. Spit spattered from their mouths. She wondered if Hallett was going to tell her they had rabies.

He did not. 'They've been pumped full of anabolic steroids like body-builders and dosed on amphetamines to make them behave like this. It'll kill them of course. Their hearts won't stand it. Normal lifespan for a European Dobermann is ten to twelve years. If these animals reach five it'll be a miracle. Christ, they must weigh sixty kilos each. Don't let your people get anywhere near them,' Hallett raised his voice so Jacks could hear. 'They'll rip through that body armour. Normal bite pressure for a Dobermann is about 310 PSI. Look at those jaws. I reckon these monsters could double that.'

'I don't want to shoot them,' Jacks complained. 'It's not their fault.'

Something else occurred to Eva. 'Could you shoot them? Through the fence, I mean?'

Jacks gave her a sideways glance, but the question was theoretical. 'Not without wire flying off like shrapnel. It might even be enough to deflect a round.'

She turned away then, to hide the snarl of desperation she had to let take hold of her face, if only for a moment. A couple of deep breaths. Eva licked her lips and composed herself before turning back, but when she looked at the small group in front of the fence, she saw she was not the only one who felt desperate. 'He must know we're here. We can't cut the fence. We can't risk ramming the gate. How the hell do we get inside there?'

Rebecca Flynn wiped rain from her swept back hair and stood beside her. 'It's like you said.' Eva's voice was almost a whisper. 'Time to go and knock on the door.'

—

Anna looked horrified. 'Will the officer be alright?'

They sat in the second of the two unmarked cars, windows clouded by their breath. Sullivan seemed cold, as though the rain had penetrated his bones. He had his collar turned up and his hands jammed into his coat pockets. Eva gave the slightest of shrugs. 'It broke his shin. The paramedics said he'll need the bone pinning, but he'll recover. I'm more worried about the dogs right now.'

'You're not going to shoot them?' She sounded almost hopeful, Eva thought.

'Not if I can help it. More than that, we don't know what other tricks Styles has in store. Hallett has tranquillisers with him, but he says he could do with more.'

'Seifert Xanazipan,' Anna said. 'Anything would do, but we have supplies at the office. I can have it on a motorcycle courier in ten minutes. It will be here in twenty.'

'Please,' Eva said, but Anna already had her phone out and was typing a text. Eva had to ask the next question, even though it didn't seem the best time. 'Did you know about Northridge? Do Seifert do business with Northridge Support Services?'

Anna finished the text and put her phone back in her pocket. When she answered, she looked Eva in the eye. 'No,' she said. 'I knew of Northridge of course, I was aware of it, but Seifert Pharmaceutical and Seifert Biotech do not conduct animal testing in any of our businesses.'

If she had been asked to describe the look on Anna's face, 'imperious' would have been the word that sprung to mind. Anna Seifert, blonde hair tied back in a ponytail, grey coat down to her calves, the epitome of corporate power. Despite everything going on around them Eva couldn't stop herself from asking, 'Why?'

She could see the knot in Anna's jaw where her muscles clenched. 'Because,' Anna said, hands bunched into fists, 'I will not permit it.'

Finally. She had finally drawn back the curtain and seen where the real Anna Seifert stood. And what she saw, she liked.

'I'm pleased,' Eva told her quietly. 'But now we have to deal with Darren Styles.'

—

They stood in the rain in front of the gate. Jacks and his officers had taken a handful of steps back, but they kept their weapons raised and aimed at the dogs. The animals had taken to prowling in interweaving circles, yellow eyes fixed on the humans beyond the fence. They had stopped barking but instead kept a low whine in the back of their throats, a persistent hum that wouldn't go away. Eva tried to ignore it, but it rang in her ears as a constant reminder of their presence.

Anna looked poised. She had the air of a company director ready to step into a hostile shareholders meeting, Eva thought. Maxwell, the hostage negotiator, stood next to her. A large woman with a round face, she spoke quietly and earnestly. Anna was looking down and to her left, eyes focused on the ground, absorbing everything Maxwell said. If anyone could get through to Styles, Eva thought, it was Anna Seifert.

She could sense Mandel behind them trying to get her attention. *Not the time*, Eva thought. She flicked a glance at Flynn, who stood quietly to one side, and then nodded in his direction. Flynn understood immediately and walked, not quickly enough to attract attention, over to the TO.

Eva turned her head the other way, towards Anna and Maxwell. Kitson was ready, Jacks and Moresby were ready; she could see that. After another few seconds Maxwell stopped talking to Anna, returned her gaze and nodded. *Time*, Eva thought. One more deep breath, slowly so it wasn't obvious. Then she stepped forward and pressed the entry phone button on the gate.

'Darren Styles,' she said, her voice steady, 'I am Detective Inspector Eva Harris of the Surrey police and I have a warrant to search these premises. Open this gate and let us in.'

Nothing. Absolute silence. The sound of emptiness, apart from the patter of rain. That and the muted whining of the dogs, which on its own told her the compound could not be empty. She waited twenty seconds, then thumbed the entry phone again. 'Darren Styles, let us in,' she insisted.

Rain and dogs, nothing else. Anxiety and fear turned slowly to frustration, then to anger. She felt ridiculous, standing dripping in front of the gate, uniform officers and SFOs lined up behind her with nowhere to go. Anger finally spilled over; she leant on the entry phone button and yelled, 'Final warning,

Darren Styles. Open this gate right now or we ram it and take you by force. What's it to be?'

She was ready for more silence. Eva glanced towards Kitson, about to give the order to ram the gate when light and sound inundated them, drenched them even more thoroughly than the rain. Arc lamps on high metal poles flared into life; a screech of feedback stabbed her ears as speakers from a concealed public address system squealed. She heard the sound of a microphone being picked up, an irritated scrabbling as though someone had grasped it in a moment of bored reluctance. Then the voice. Sneering, superior, condescending, each word laced with tedium and vitriol.

'What makes you think,' it drawled, phase-shifting through rain-soaked electronics, 'you're in any position to make demands?'

# Chapter Forty-Three

It was Flynn who drew her away from the gate. She led Eva from the lights and the PA system while Anna, Maxwell, Kitson and Jacks stayed. Eva was half tempted to ask what was so damned urgent, but she already knew. Mandel must have broken into either the guest WiFi or the main network, which meant he must also have cracked the CCTV cameras. He had a view inside.

'Quick as you like,' Eva told him as she slipped into the car. Flynn climbed into the back seat. Mandel turned the screen of the laptop towards them.

'So, I got past the password on the guest network.' He pointed at log files in the Linux shell, a window of white-on-black text filled with arcane system command lines. 'Problem was that led straight back to the primary router, and whoever set that up did a pretty fair job.' Mandel watched Eva as he spoke. 'It's taken me longer than it should. It's not an excuse ma'am. I thought this place would be a pushover, but it wasn't.'

'But you're in now?'

'Yes.'

Mandel tabbed through screens until he got to the one she had been hoping for. Thumbnail feeds from the cameras. When Eva saw it though, she spat, 'Shit. Is that right?'

He pursed his lips and nodded. 'Sorry to say it is. There are at least forty-three cameras around the place, twenty-five outside and the rest in the buildings. I say at least. I think there's another network that covers cameras further out. I can't be certain yet, but I think he's got another ten dotted up to half a kilometre away. He knew we were here from the moment we turned off the road.'

Eva frowned at that. 'So why didn't he run?'

Flynn leant over her shoulder and pointed at the screen. 'He couldn't be sure we hadn't left cars at the end of the lanes. It's good coverage, but it's a bloody big site. He can't see everywhere.'

It made sense. 'Close though. And the inside cameras?'

The screen cycled through the thumbnails. 'Thing is,' Mandel told them, 'it's like a zoo in there. Animals in cages, everywhere. I think there's one conveyor belt that feeds them and another that takes crap away, I don't think there's any staff.' He seemed reluctant to ask the next question. 'They don't use all of them for testing, do they? There's thousands of mice and dozens of dogs. Reptiles too.'

Eva would have sympathised, but she didn't have time. 'Where's Styles? What about the abductees?'

'I think he's avoiding the cameras. He must know there's a chance we'd break in. But one of them is turned off. I don't think it's been turned off long though.'

'Why?'

'The log files from it are almost the same size as from everywhere else. If it had been switched off for long, they would be a lot smaller.'

'But we still can't see?'

'We can't see what's going on right now,' Mandel agreed, 'but it's just standard CCTV and webcams. They record files to disk. There are backups.' He clicked to another window. She saw a green line moving, quite slowly, from left to right. 'I'm copying one down now.' She watched as the line reached the end and disappeared. Mandel went to where the video file had downloaded, double-clicked on it and scrubbed towards the last few minutes.

Even Flynn gasped. The room in Anna's video, but from a different perspective. A camera pointing down on what looked

317

like a small hospital ward, an ICU, but with five patients laid out in a star pattern, heads towards the centre and monitoring equipment plugged into each of them. Tubes and wires, in their arms, groins, and down their throats, over their torsos and limbs. And in the middle a figure, back towards the camera, covered in surgical scrubs. He had entered the room from under the camera so at no point did they see his face. When he left the room, it was in the opposite direction. Then the camera went black.

Eva yelled at Mandel, 'Back up thirty seconds!' Mandel complied. She reached across and tapped at the keyboard. The picture zoomed in. It was pixelated; there was no enhancement, just as if she had been scaling up a video shot on a phone, but it was enough. Styles, of course. It had to be. In his right hand she glimpsed the serrated blade of a surgical saw. 'Time-code!' Eva bellowed.

Mandel checked the file attributes. 'File was saved at saved at six forty-three, less than ten minutes after we got here.'

Six forty-three. Forty minutes ago. Forty minutes ago the abductees were here, and they were alive. She wanted to scream. Flynn put a stop to that.

'Why did he turn the camera off,' she asked as Mandel searched the other cameras for signs of Styles, 'and what the hell was he going to do with that saw?'

–

When she returned to the gate the PA had fallen silent. The dogs had formed a line, Eva noticed. Hallett studied the dogs as they studied him. One of the SFOs stood quietly by, automatic rifle aimed at the dogs, but his finger was off the trigger. Jacks and Kitson were waiting for her. Eva looked around. Only Anna Seifert had not moved.

Anna stood in front of the gate, head tilted upwards. Eva followed her gaze. After a moment she saw where Anna was gazing. When the arc lights came on, they had illuminated a number of pieces of electrical equipment near the top of the gate. Eva too could now see the shape of a small CCTV camera, lit from above, looking down on them. Anna wasn't looking at it, Eva realised after a moment. Water running down her immaculate skin, Anna was staring into it.

'He can see us and he can hear us,' Anna told her as she approached. 'Hello Darren,' her voice stayed soft and even. 'Do you want to talk to me?'

Eva heard the rustle of a microphone being picked up. His voice was quieter now too. 'Why would I want to do that?'

'Obviously because I have something you want.' It didn't sound like a boast. She could practically hear Styles sneer.

'And I have something you want too,' Styles said, disdainful now. In control, almost worryingly so. Eva glanced at Maxwell. The negotiator had heard it as well. 'Maybe I'll talk to you later.'

'Why not now?' Anna demanded.

'Now?' he said, sounding relaxed, Eva thought. Laconic, almost indolent. Indifferent, as though suddenly they bored him. 'I can't talk now, Anna.' Not relaxed, she realised. He sounded patronising, contemptuous. 'Now I have work to do.'

-

'He's going to kill them.' Jacks stood in front of Kitson, rifle hanging from his left hand. 'He's going to kill at least one of them. You know he is.'

Kitson waved at the fence. He may have been twenty years younger than Jacks, but he wasn't stupid. Jacks had decades of experience. Eva knew that for a fact. Kitson knew it too. 'You want to shoot the dogs and ram the gate? We do that and we provoke him for sure. We turn one death into five.'

'We try the fence again. This time we test the ground before we tread on it. Hallett drugs the dogs, we cut a hole and go in.'

'Cameras?' Kitson barked.

'Mandel takes the lot down.'

'So we're blind?'

'We're blind already,' Eva pointed out. 'Styles guessed we might tap them so he's following his own blind spots. Losing the cameras doesn't make any difference.'

Kitson fumed, caught between Jacks's logic and an SFO with a shattered leg. 'And what do we do while you're cutting the fence?'

She felt like the Devil's advocate. 'What we were doing before. Anna keeps Styles talking. Mandel doesn't take down all the cameras; he keeps the one on Anna live, maybe a couple of others if they work for us.'

Kitson turned his back on Eva and Jacks for a second. When he turned back, he had gathered his arguments. 'We don't know which building the abductees are in.'

Jacks shrugged. 'It's true. We have to go building to building like it's a hunt for a shooter. What's new?'

'More traps.' Kitson stabbed his finger at the compound. 'Inside the fence.'

'Doesn't make for a very practical working environment,' Eva pointed out. 'I don't think you'd put mantraps where someone has to handle animals.'

'Styles will have weapons.'

Jacks dismissed the argument. 'So have we.'

Kitson was almost convinced, she could see that. The Devil's advocate in her piped up again. 'One thing,' Eva said to the two SFOs. 'Hallett can dope the dogs in the racetrack, but we don't know if that's the only pack. He could set others loose once you're inside.'

'I know,' Jacks admitted. 'But what else do we do? This is our day job. We go in on the assumption it's a hostile environment.'

Another pause, but only a couple of seconds. 'Okay,' Kitson agreed, 'I'll sanction another attempt on the fence. That's assuming,' he turned to Eva, 'you want to go ahead.'

Down to her, but she knew that already. 'It's a risk,' she agreed, 'but we know Styles has killed people already and he's clearly unstable. I agree there's an immediate danger to the abductees, so yes, I want to go ahead.' Jacks nodded at her. Kitson didn't look so happy, but he acknowledged the decision. Eva continued, 'But we negotiate at the same time. If we can work a solution without anybody getting shot, that's what we do.' She looked at Jacks and Kitson to be certain they agreed, but neither of them complained. 'Okay,' Eva said. 'When do we go?'

Kitson checked his watch. 'Five minutes.'

A trio of women stood in front of the high gate and waited for the entry phone, sheltered under a black umbrella from a now dark grey sky that soaked a verdant landscape with fine rain. Firearms officers stood to either side of them, weapons raised, because none of them knew whether Styles was mad enough to just open the gate and let the dogs out. Eva could see Kitson, twenty paces away, monitoring the radios of the team of four SFOs approaching the fence once more. As she stared, Kitson briefly ran his finger over his throat. She understood the gesture. It meant Mandel had taken down the CCTV cameras.

'Darren,' Anna Seifert said, 'I wondered if you were interested in talking about Derzelas.'

Eva wondered how long they would have to wait, but Styles didn't disappoint them. She heard a click as somewhere a microphone was switched on. 'Derzelas?' A voice rang from the PA system. 'What's that?'

'Please, Darren,' Anna said, keeping anger from her voice.

After a moment Styles sighed. 'I'm not sure what I would want to talk about. I saw evidence of it in Michael Conroy. Before he died, that is.'

Eva saw Anna flinch. She saw the muscles of her jaw clench and saw her blink to force back tears. She opened her mouth to speak, but then closed it again. She wanted to tell her to steady herself, but she could see Anna already knew she had to do that.

All Eva could do was surreptitiously slide her hand into Anna's, and squeeze.

'What I saw appeared to be a seventeen-year reduction in epigenetic age,' Styles told her. 'Is that Derzelas?'

She felt Anna's hand ball into a fist. 'Show yourself,' Anna said, 'and I'll tell you.'

Styles snorted a laugh. 'Right. With a couple of cops aiming guns at my head; like that's going to happen. But you know what? Anna? Do you know what?'

'No,' Anna forced herself to speak.

'I will.'

It was a trick. Eva could see it coming. It would be some stupid ploy to show how clever he was and how powerless they were. She was right. The door to one of the nearer buildings opened. There, standing in the doorway, was Darren Styles.

Eva heard Anna's intake of breath when she saw him. A slender man, wiry but strong, about five-nine with pale blonde hair and wearing a grey suit with a mandarin collar. A mirror image or, perhaps more correctly, a male twin. Maybe that really was what he was seeking, Eva thought, both a physical and an intellectual equal, as he imagined it, and a replacement for Denise. Styles's face twisted into a smile that she could not have described as anything other than sadistic. 'Hello,' Styles said.

Eva saw a momentary flash of red light, barely a blink, and then it was gone. The SFO nearest her grunted. He must have flicked the laser sight on his rifle on and off for less than a second. Plainly he did not like what he saw. 'We can't shoot him through the fence ma'am,' he muttered. 'If we hit it, we'll have ricochets everywhere.'

Styles grinned. 'Glad we're clear where we stand. So Anna,' he said, rubbing his hands together like a gleeful child. 'Come on then. Tell me all about Derzelas.'

Eva turned her head slightly, angled it so she could see Kitson from the corner of one eye but still keep track on Styles. She put her hand into her pocket and thumbed the volume button on her radio. The bud in her ear clicked as it connected. 'That's the second mantrap we've seen,' Jacks was saying. 'We sprung them both.'

'How far?' Kitson barely moved his lips when he spoke.

'Ten metres. We're further round than blue team were. The brambles are denser here, but then the cover's better too.' She could hear the strain in his voice. The vegetation had to be a nightmare to cut through.

'Look out for trip wires or any other alarms,' Kitson murmured.

'I put money on a wire at the top to detect climbers, but we're not going near that. Five metres. Moresby, you ready?'

Another click. 'Almost. We're at the narrow gate, so I hope the cameras are down. Hallett's got meat and a dog whistle. You want us to chuck it into the racetrack?'

'Chuck it,' Jacks said, 'but don't blow the whistle yet. See if they catch the smell.'

'Here we go,' Moresby told them. He grunted as he threw the meat over the fence. 'Hallett says there's enough drugs on this stuff to put a horse to sleep.'

Eva watched the dogs. Slowly, one at a time, they turned their heads to their right as the scent of meat reached them. Saliva dripped from bared fangs, but they didn't move.

'Let's hope so,' Jacks panted. 'We're at the fence. Have the dogs taken the bait?'

'No,' Eva told him.

'Okay.' Jacks muttered something to his team. His voice came back a second later. 'Keep him talking. Use the whistle to call the dogs. Starting to cut now.'

## Chapter Forty-Four

Anna was forcing herself to speak, Eva could see that. The woman was in shock. Between learning of Conroy's murder and seeing Styles's appearance, even her glacial grip on reality must be loosening; but still she kept going. In that moment Eva thought of Dominique Styles and the way she too had suffered. It was a pity the SFO hadn't been able to pull the trigger.

'We started looking at cellular senescence a number of years ago,' Anna said. 'I guess you're familiar with the concept, and the limit on the number of times a cell can divide itself. What seemed strange to us was how it felt like an arbitrary number. There was no obvious evolutionary reason for it.' She had hit the right note, Eva saw. Styles was hanging on her every word. Then Anna shrugged. 'Or maybe there is. The Hayflick limit dictates that human cells can only divide forty to sixty times before they break down by programmed cell death. Maybe it's a mechanism to reduce mutations and help keep cancer at bay. Or maybe as animals we're only supposed to live for so long.'

'Why would that be?' Styles scoffed.

'Because the longer individuals live the more time it takes for the species to evolve.' She was hooking Styles. Eva could see it in the look on his face. 'But that means death is an evolutionary choice. Individuals die so the species can develop. Now though, we don't have to rely on evolution to advance. We develop drugs, medical devices, we can augment ourselves artificially.' She almost had him, Eva could sense it. Anna leant forward a little. 'Which means,' she said, soft and compelling, 'death no longer serves any evolutionary purpose.'

'That's easy to say,' Styles said, not scoffing now, 'but how do you get from epigenetic death to cell renewal?'

'Stem cells. You change the pointer on the blueprint. Instead of aiming at the last generation of cells as a template for cell division, you point it at the original, pristine copy that still exists in stem cells. Basically, you interrupt the cellular interphase and give it new directions. Or, to be precise, old directions.'

Styles glared. 'And you've done this?'

Anna still had Eva's hand. Eva felt the nails dig into her skin, and she almost yelped. 'You've seen it,' Anna said. 'You examined Michael Conroy yourself.'

Styles's face was unreadable. 'I need to think,' he told them. 'Just piss off. I need to think. Go away, I'll come back later.' The speaker cut out. The door closed.

'I need water,' Anna said.

—

When she returned to Kitson he had barely moved. 'Hallett did his stuff,' he told her without looking away from the fence. 'They came when he used the whistle. Maybe that's what Styles uses. Anyway, the dogs are down.'

'Are they in?'

'Through the first fence. Working on the second.'

Eva took out her radio and spoke into it. 'Mandel, any sign Styles has noticed half the cameras are dead yet?'

The TO came back a few seconds later. 'I don't think so. There's a screen somewhere that cycles through them. I've taken the offline cams out of the play list, so unless he's paying specific attention he shouldn't notice they're gone for a while.'

She let the information tumble around inside her head, then said to Kitson, 'So we're good?'

'We're only part-way there,' he told her. 'We'll know more when they're through the second fence.'

Eva knew exactly how long it would take. Anna clambered into the back of the car, and the next moment buried her face in Sullivan's coat, using it to choke a scream of pain. He held her, horrified. Eva sat in the front. 'What?' Sullivan mouthed.

'I'm sorry,' Eva said, voice low. 'It looks like we have bad news about Michael Conroy.'

Sullivan looked aghast. 'I didn't even know he was missing.'

'He was one of the people you were' – Eva paused, not wanting to use the word 'experimenting' – 'running tests on?'

'He was a friend,' Sullivan told her. 'A fellow scientist, just a decent guy with an illness. Are you saying Styles—' he couldn't bring himself to finish the sentence. Eva nodded slightly but said no more.

Anna pulled her face from Sullivan's coat. 'Water,' she said. Maxwell passed her a bottle and she drank almost half of it. Her eyes were red and her face wet. She wiped them on her sleeve. 'We're going to have to do that again in a bit,' she managed to say.

'What you told Styles,' Eva asked her when she looked as though she could answer. 'Was that true?'

'Sort of,' Anna groaned. 'I mean, I was mixing a bit of science with complete bullshit, but that's what he wanted to hear. It is one of the theories of why we die though, and yes, it's part of the treatment we gave Michael Conroy. But this work is going to take decades to complete. There's no magic bullet for longevity; we're not even close. We'll get there,' Anna said, as much to herself as anyone else, 'but not for a long time yet.'

Eva gazed at where the door had closed. 'He'll be on the Internet checking every word he can right now. We don't have long,' she told them. 'We have to convince Styles we can give him Derzelas or he's going to start killing people.'

Mandel turned some of the cameras back on. 'It's a pain in the arse,' he admitted, 'but I can go through and change the IP addresses. That takes them off the monitor's playlist.'

They stood under an umbrella with his laptop resting on the bonnet of a marked car. Two vans blocked the view to the gate, and the Land Rovers were on the other side of the vans. Kitson watched over her shoulder. Eva understood immediately. It meant they could see feeds from the cameras Mandel had shut down, but Styles couldn't. She pressed the bud in her ear, but there was no report from Jacks's team inside the racetrack. It was good news, but she tutted. 'Can we get to the camera on the abductees?'

Another window with white-on-black text. Mandel scrolled. 'Log size hasn't changed,' he told her. 'I think he's physically pulled the plug on that one.' The image of Styles with a surgical saw remained in her head. Eva clenched her fist but said nothing.

Kitson couldn't hide his impatience. 'But we can see where Red team is?' Mandel tapped the keyboard and tabbed quickly through a dozen cameras dotted around the site.

Eva saw them first. 'Back one.' The screen flickered as Mandel went to the previous camera. She aimed her finger at the screen. 'There.'

Top right of the picture. Not a great view, she thought, but four SFOs huddled together, one of them just now laboriously bending back a section of the inner fence.

'Red team.' Kitson spoke into his radio. 'We can see you.'

'Really?' Jacks whispered. 'Can Styles?'

'No.' As they watched, one by one the team pushed their way through the fence. When they were through, they crouched and waited.

Eva could see why. The first pictures from the drone had shown barriers inside the main fence. Now in close-up she could see more detail. Wire cages about two metres high divided the grass-covered space between the fence and the buildings. 'They connect to doors on some of the buildings,' Jacks told them. 'At a guess I'd say they're exercise pens.'

Kitson scowled. 'More dogs?'

'Maybe,' Jacks agreed. 'They butt up against each other; we might have to cut through them. It's like a maze. It's hard to see where each cage leads.'

Eva heard the reticence in his voice. 'If you've got reservations, you get out of there. We've got other options. We're working on giving Styles what he wants.'

'There's five people in there somewhere,' Jacks reminded her, as if she needed to be reminded. 'See if you can keep him distracted by all means, but if he pulls anything, I need to know you'll support decisive action.'

The words chilled her, even though she knew Jacks was right to use them. 'I confirm use of force would be reasonable in the circumstances,' Eva said, but she couldn't keep a tremor from her voice.

Kitson grimaced but nodded. 'I authorise you to make the assessment of absolute necessity,' he agreed.

'Understood.' Jacks took a breath. 'We'll do our utmost to capture Darren Styles without harming him, but if he poses an imminent threat to the abductees or my officers, we'll use force, including lethal force if absolutely necessary, to neutralise him.'

A form of words, but they needed to be spoken aloud and for the record. Kitson acknowledged them. 'Sergeant Jacks,' he added once the rules of engagement had been made clear. 'For Christ's sake, make sure he doesn't neutralise you first.'

–

Flynn, Newton and Chakrabati stood together under an umbrella, a group aside from the others. 'I feel like a spare cock at an orgy,' Flynn complained when Eva approached.

'We're waiting as hard as we can,' Newton agreed.

She sympathised with their frustration. 'Jacks and his team might still have to pull out,' Eva told them. 'If it comes to it and it's too dangerous to storm the buildings or they're too tightly locked down, he's instructed to fall back and let the negotiator try again.' She felt her shoulders sag a little. At least with her own team she could reveal what she really thought. 'Styles is deluded. He's psychotic and unpredictable. He's built a complete fantasy around Derzelas.'

'Just because his twin sister died of a heart attack?' Flynn's tone conveyed no sympathy.

'Christ, I don't know,' Eva admitted. 'Maybe he was dropped on his head as a child. His wife said he used drugs,' she added, looking to Raj for conformation. 'He even implanted them,' she said. It doesn't matter. He ticks all the boxes on the psychopathy checklist and he's like a case study for personal construct theory. He could do anything if it fitted his world-view.' Eva pulled herself up short then. *Enough wallowing*, she decided. 'I need you to work with Anna Seifert and Michael Sullivan. Give them any help they need coming up with a package we can pass off as Derzelas. It's the only thing Styles will respond to. He's already convinced it exists, so give him whatever he thinks he wants.'

'Then what?' Raj demanded. He wasn't criticising, she understood that. He simply wasn't convinced.

'At some point he has to leave the compound,' Eva insisted. 'He can leave with Derzelas if the abductees are alive. If not, we stop him on the way out.'

'We let him get away?' She hated the look of disgust on Raj's face.

'For now. If it keeps them alive.'

They stood in silence for a moment. 'Maybe it won't come to that,' Flynn said eventually. 'Jacks is bloody good. Maybe he'll top the bastard. It'd save on a trial.'

It wasn't as if Eva disagreed. 'He's got a nightmare of a job finding his way through the exercise pens,' she told them. 'Styles has a maze of them at the back of the compound.'

She could almost see the cogs turn inside Jamie Newton's head, but she didn't understand why. After a few seconds he turned and stared at her. 'The what?' Newton demanded.

They wouldn't have seen the latest images from the CCTV cameras, Eva realised. 'There's a bunch of exercise pens crammed in at the back of the farm, in-between the fence and the buildings. They're pretty tightly packed. Jacks and his team are having to cut through them to get to the buildings from the fence side.'

Newton had never grabbed her before. The shock of him grasping her shoulders and pushing his face into hers almost paralysed her for a moment, but the look of horror on his face felt even worse. 'Boss,' Newton gasped, voice almost strangled, 'when the hell did we start thinking Darren Styles gives a fuck about animal welfare?'

She ran. Newton was right behind her. Eva shoved past one of the SFOs, grabbed Kitson and spun him round. 'Where's Red team?' she hissed.

Kitson's jaw dropped. 'What? You know where they are? What is this?'

'I mean exactly,' she said, dragging him over to where Mandel monitored his laptop.

'They're cutting their way through the exercise pens.' Kitson said.

Mandel watched their progress, headphones on, though Eva didn't know if there was an audio feed. When he noticed them he pulled the headphones off. 'They've got through two of the cages. This stuff is easier to cut; it looks more like heavy-duty chicken wire.'

Newton couldn't contain himself. 'Get them out of there.'

'What?' Kitson glared at him.

'I said get them the hell out of there!' Newton yelled. Eva grabbed him by the shoulder. She pulled him away from Mandel.

'What is this?' Kitson demanded. He would have yelled back, Eva thought, but Newton's behaviour was so uncharacteristic it shocked even him.

Newton could barely speak. The look on his face was of pure panic. 'Christ's sake, it's not where he exercises the animals,' he almost screamed. 'It's where he kills them.'

Kitson went to yell into his radio, but Mandel got there first. 'Look!'

Eva stared at the screen. She couldn't do anything else. Inside one of the cages, in a run of what looked like chicken wire framed between sturdy metal poles, four SFOs stood and shook convulsively. 'Red team!' Kitson screamed.

The four figures in black body armour twitched and spasmed. Thin tendrils of coiling smoke had begun to rise from their body armour. 'It's electrified,' Newton stammered. 'He kills the bigger animals in there. Saves on drugs.'

Kitson turned on the SFO behind the wheel of the first Land Rover and bellowed an order. 'Get that gate open!'

The SFO started his engine and backed up ready to ram the fence, but then Eva heard another, more familiar sound. Staccato drumming, the beat of an automatic rifle. Rounds hit the ground inside the fence, dirt and mud sprayed them. Like puppets whose strings had been cut, the SFOs dropped to the ground. Then the camera snapped off.

'Get the gate open,' Kitson yelled again. Eva heard desperation in his voice.

'Negative, Bronze,' the driver told him. 'He's got a clear shot. He'll cut us to pieces if we do.'

She shook. The image of Jacks and his team fitting as hundreds of volts ran through them felt like it had been burned onto her eyes. Kitson's lips were drawn back high over his teeth. He snarled, half doubled over, as though he had been stabbed in the gut. Newton and Mandel were paralysed with shock. It seemed as though only Eva could move.

She ran to the gate, stabbed at the entry phone button. Screamed. 'Darren Styles.' Spittle flew from her mouth. 'What in God's name have you done?'

–

Now she knew Styles had a gun. She ignored the fact. Eva stepped back from the gate and waited for him to respond. From the corner of her eye she saw Michael Sullivan and Anna Seifert, partly hidden by the two vans. Flynn, Newton, Chakrabati. Kitson trying to bring himself back under control. Moresby, face like thunder. SFOs, uniform officers. All of them gravitating towards the gate.

A click. Echo and feedback. The PA system came to life. Darren Styles, contemptuous. 'I warned you. I told you. You're really not in any position to make demands.'

She stabbed at the entry phone again. 'Styles.' She wanted to swear at him, call him every name under the sun. She knew she couldn't. 'I want medical attention for my officers.'

He spat. 'You know that's not going to happen.'

Eva had to force herself to ask the next question. 'Are they alive?'

'I don't know and I don't care. Where's Anna?' Despite herself Eva glanced around. Anna Seifert stepped out from behind the police van. 'There you are!' He sounded like some deranged grandparent overindulging a bewildered toddler. 'Now shut the fuck up, DI Harris. It's time for the grown-ups to have a talk.'

She seethed. Anna stood beside her and took her hand once more. 'Ah, how charming,' Styles mocked. His tone changed. 'Anyway, I've made up my mind.' Eva waited. She clenched her teeth, glared at the camera, counted her breaths. Made herself ready to listen to every nuance in his voice. Eventually, Styles spoke.

'Anna says Derzelas exists.' He sounded rational now, clinical, if only in that moment. 'I've seen evidence of that myself. The trouble is, will she give it to me?' Now he sounded sly, conniving and deceitful both at the same time. 'I know you're not telling me the whole truth, Anna. I know you and your friends take Derzelas at that spa in Switzerland of yours. I know you think you're going to live forever.'

She could hear the madness in his voice then. The complete psychotic fantasy that had grown in his mind, a delusion based on New Thought's transcendentalism and layered with Anna Seifert's cosmetic perfection. In amongst us are the super-rich, who had bought immortality from this immaculate high priestess of illicit science. A drug-fuelled wet dream that had become his reality. Styles, a burnt-out trader who got his kicks torturing women and cutting up dead bodies. Now he had the chance to live out his dreams.

'Well, so am I,' Styles continued. 'Bring Derzelas to me, as well as the tools I need to make more. I know you're going to try to trick me, so I feel the need to give you an incentive.' Eva felt her stomach sink. What was the sick bastard going to do now?

From nowhere, from some door that they had not seen, a dog trotted up to the fence. It was a Dobermann like the others, over-muscled and grotesque, but this one seemed calm at least. It had something in its mouth. When it reached the gate, it dropped it. Eva walked slowly up to the wire and looked down. On the grass, behind the wire, was a hand.

'I'm letting you have the hostages DI Harris.' Styles snarled into the microphone, voice redolent with spite and hate. 'I'm just doing it one piece at a time.'

## Chapter Forty-Five

'You have to give him Derzelas.'

'There's no such thing,' Sullivan protested. 'Not in the way he means.'

'Make it up.'

'He'll know.'

'How?' Eva pleaded. 'Because in ten years' time he finds he's getting old after all? I can live with that.'

'She's right,' Anna told Sullivan. 'We've got to give him something he thinks is Derzelas.'

'He's a psychopath.' Sullivan stared at them, eyes sunken and skin grey. 'I mean, seriously, he needs putting down. He's a dog with rabies, there isn't any cure. I never thought I'd ever hear myself say anything like this, but the world is better off with this guy dead. That's not going to be on anyone's conscience. That's just humane.'

'We can't storm the farm,' Eva said. 'He's got an automatic weapon aimed at the gate and it's too easy for him to slaughter the abductees.' She didn't mention Jacks and his team. Were they still lying in the electrified pens, bodies burnt and smouldering, or had Styles cut the power before it killed them? 'We need to make him believe he can get something in exchange and then get away. We have to give him a way out. He needs to think he's won, even though that's actually impossible.'

'Not asking for much, are you?' Sullivan snapped.

'Please,' Eva said.

They sat in silence. It grew in density like a fog rolling in; even the windows of the car steamed up until the mist seemed to fill the space between them. 'He's really sick, isn't he?' Anna said at last. 'I mean, as in twisted. He's perverted and sadistic. Is that fair?'

'He doesn't deserve fair,' Eva said, even though she knew she shouldn't. 'He has a love for cutting and blood. He bought a company so he could dissect bodies. He tortured his ex-wife with scalpels and implants. Michael's right,' she agreed with a nod to Sullivan, 'shooting him would be a mercy killing. That's impossible right now, so we need to find another way.'

'Cutting and blood,' Anna repeated. 'So, we give him what he wants.'

–

'It's a question of trust,' Anna Seifert said as they stood outside the gate. 'How do I convince you I'm giving you Derzelas? I don't care by the way,' she added as she stepped out from under the umbrella and let the rain fall on her. 'It doesn't matter to me that you get it, so long as you keep your mouth shut for a while. Keeping Derzelas secret is about supply and demand. The fewer people who know about it, the more they're prepared to pay. The more they pay, the more I can funnel into research and development. You're a businessman Darren. You get that, don't you? It's not just about longevity. It's about being able to afford longevity.'

'Research?' Styles asked. Eva could hear the hesitation in his voice.

'Theoretical maximums,' Anna said, response as smooth as silk. 'We're as sure as we can be that Derzelas works, but what happens a hundred years from now? Is there another stage, some other step that's needed to extend lifespan to two, three, five hundred years? We just don't know right now. We do know one thing though.'

'Which is?'

Anna flashed her eyes for his cameras. 'It's going to be an exciting ride.'

'Okay,' Styles said slowly. 'So how do I trust you?'

'We'll give you Derzelas,' Anna said, 'along with the necessary information to replicate it. There will be a contract too,' she added, voice as sharp as a lawyer. 'We know the risks. We've thought them through. We can't stop you selling Derzelas to support your own future research or buying ours from us, that only seems fair. What you may not do is undercut us, because that would jeopardise our future research and put those other developments I spoke of at risk. This benefits you as well as me. Do you understand that?'

As a negotiator she was terrifying, Eva thought. No wonder Seifert was one of the top thirty pharmaceutical companies on the planet. Anna had taken Styles's delusion and woven a complete mythos around it. Now she was feeding it back to him.

'So how do I know?' Styles demanded. 'How do I know you're giving me Derzelas, and not some shoddy substitute?'

'Because,' Anna said, staring up at the camera, 'it's going to come directly from my body.'

—

Eva found she couldn't keep her mouth shut. Incredulity prevented it from closing. 'What,' she demanded once they were back in the car, 'the fuck are you playing at?'

Anna waved her hand dismissively. She was on her phone again. 'It's not like I'm going to give him my spleen,' she said as she settled next to Sullivan. 'Just a little blood. And some flesh.'

'In a field? You're proposing giving a blood transfusion in the middle of a field?'

'He's not going to come to a hospital with us, is he?' Anna retorted. 'Honestly, there's no risk. You've got paramedics in the team, right? They can help me.'

'I understand the blood,' Eva said, staring at Anna. Was this woman actually as mad as Styles, or was this some manic attempt at redemption? 'But a skin sample?'

'It gives him enough variation in progenitor cell types to make him think we can't be concealing anything,' Anna said, 'even if we are. I'll take it from my forearm. The paramedic can disinfect it first. I can use a local anaesthetic. We pack the wound and dress it immediately afterwards.' Anna paused. 'And you spoke to Aaron Rose. You know I've had chips implanted in me.'

'You told me,' Eva grumbled. 'What's that got to do with anything?'

'One is a locator. I've had kidnap threats in the past. I turned it off so Crane could get me out of Seifert without us being followed. I've turned it back on again.'

'So?'

'So Styles won't know what it is.' She put her phone back in her coat pocket. 'There. Seifert are sending a courier with all data pertaining to Derzelas and samples of the drugs we gave poor Michael Conroy. They'll be here shortly.'

'What's that got to do with your locator?' Eva asked the question even though she was beginning to understand.

'I'll tell him a backup of the data is stored on it. He won't have time to check it. He gets the drugs, my blood, some skin and a chip he'll see taken right out of my body. If that's not enough to convince him, what is?'

And she had thought her own logic was remorseless. 'When he gets out, we have the locator. He doesn't get away.' Eva tried to imagine holes in Anna's plan. It didn't take her long, but when she flipped the logic on its head and went looking for a better plan, she couldn't find one. 'This isn't your fault,' Eva insisted. 'You don't get to take the blame for Styles.'

'Not my fault,' Anna agreed, jaw set hard, 'but it is my responsibility. I'm here, now, and I have a chance to do something about him. How do you imagine I could live with myself if I didn't try my hardest?'

Eva had to close her mouth then. There was nothing more she could say.

'One thing,' Anna said. 'I'm going to hate myself for saying so, but I agree with Michael. This *deviant* should not be allowed to walk the earth. If your officers with guns have the opportunity to do so, I think they should kill him.'

—

A long night and a day. For a moment a wave of exhaustion swept over her as she realised she had been going for over twenty-four hours. Eva had to force herself to focus. She stood alone at the end of the lane and waited for the courier to arrive.

Was Jacks alive? Had Styles really killed all four SFOs, or had he left them stunned and smouldering on electric wires? Did the hand really belong to one of the abductees who lay prostrate on trolleys in Styles's ward, or was it from an earlier body, one he had already dismembered?

It wasn't something she could afford to think about. She knew there was only one way forward, to convince Styles he was in possession of Derzelas and to get him out of the compound. If Anna was right, they would be able to pick him up later, but the more important action was to get access to the buildings. Nothing else mattered now.

The bike would be there soon. Anna had promised that. When it arrived Eva would have to act quickly. The prospect terrified her, but she couldn't afford for her fear to show. She had a plan, a course of action, and she would have the tools to implement it. She had to push forward and ignore the doubts. *The most difficult thing is the decision to act, the rest is mere tenacity. The fears are paper tigers.* She had to convince herself of that once again. Only one nagging question remained. Eva tried to push it to the back of her mind, but it kept forcing its way into her consciousness.

Once Styles had Derzelas, why did he need to keep the abductees alive?

The motorbike arrived ten minutes later. Eva carried the small package to the car, and Anna almost devoured it when she passed to her. Sullivan reached into the container and pulled out a USB drive.

'Don't you resent giving that up?' Eva asked.

'I was going to publish it anyway,' Sullivan said with a shrug. 'Most of this is going to be in the public domain.'

There were other items in the box. 'What else have you got?'

Anna Seifert took out a pack of pads in a nondescript flesh-coloured pouch. 'That will cover the cuts until there's the chance for proper treatment. It's for battlefield trauma,' she added. Eva heard the note of pride in her voice. 'Our products do good.'

Eva bit her tongue. With that one slip Anna had revealed just how personally she was taking the situation. This act of self-harm in front of Styles was somehow wrapped up in a need for a redemption that, in Eva's eyes, was unnecessary and unwarranted.

'And some handy containers to put it all in,' Anna finished.

She waited in silence. She knew she should be pushing, but at that point she couldn't bring herself to. It didn't matter. Anna Seifert understood. 'Okay,' Anna said with a sigh as she gathered the contents of the box together. 'We should get this done.'

–

Anna stood at the front gate. 'So,' she called out to Styles. Eva stood on one side of her, a female paramedic on the other. 'Do we have an agreement?'

PA speakers squealed feedback. 'Be clear what I'm getting,' Styles demanded.

Anna corrected him. 'What we're getting. You get Derzelas, comprising the compounds you saw used on Michael Conroy and the data needed to recreate them. There are step-by-step instructions on the USB drive.'

'How do I know the compound used on Conroy is the same one you used on yourself?'

'You know damn well. You're going to watch me take blood and tissue samples and put them in a box. You also get the chip holding the Derzelas dataset. You can compare the lot with Conroy's samples. They'll be the same.'

Styles had nothing left to ask for. He managed to sound begrudging anyway. 'It seems acceptable.'

'And I get the people,' Anna told him. 'Including the police team. Are they alive?'

'Christ's sake,' Styles growled. 'I don't know. They made noises when I took their guns off them. I haven't checked them since.' Eva felt her heart literally miss a beat. For a moment she thought she was going to have to lean on Anna, but the moment passed. 'And I get safe passage out of here.'

'We're only interested in the abductees and the officers,' Eva told him. 'You give us them and you can go. For now.'

Styles sneered. 'What, no royal pardon?' Eva didn't answer. They waited in silence for another handful of seconds. 'Well,' Styles said eventually, 'what are you waiting for?'

The paramedic's name was Steff. Anna turned to her. She slipped off her jacket and stood with her blouse sticking to her skin as drizzle slowly soaked it. Maxwell took her jacket. Steff passed Anna an elastic tie, which she wrapped around her bicep and pulled tight, then turned her forearm outwards so Styles could see her search for the vein on the inside of her arm. Anna flicked the skin, hard. She took a needle from Steff, held it up to the camera, and forced it into her arm. Steff passed Anna a length of clear plastic tube that she screwed into the green tap on the end of the needle, and then attached the other end to a clear plastic bottle. After a few seconds the bottle began to fill with blood.

'You can have 300 millilitres,' Anna told Styles as she watched the blood flow. 'That's enough to run hundreds of tests.' They all watched in silence as viscous fluid pumped in time with the beat of Anna's heart. After a couple of minutes Anna pulled the needle from her arm and Steff taped a plaster over the pinprick. She stood for a moment and took a sip of water. Eva knew she would be feeling light-headed, but after another minute Anna seemed to regain her concentration. She took a marker and drew on her forearm. 'It's about five centimetres square, dermis and epidermis. The chip comes with it. Okay?'

Eva heard disbelief in Styles voice. 'And you're going to do that yourself?'

Steff wiped Anna's arm with iodine. 'You can watch,' Anna said.

Was she actually teasing him, Eva wondered? Was she playing it like some sadomasochistic version of video sex? Maybe she thought Styles wouldn't be able to resist that. Anna took a syringe from Steff and shot it into the corner of the square, then went around and made three more injections. 'A couple of minutes,' she told Styles. Then she took out a scalpel.

The edge of the blade glinted in the glare of the arc lights. Eva winced as Anna probed the edge of the marker line with its needle-sharp tip, waiting for the anaesthetic to numb the skin. 'Okay,' Anna said after a while. 'That'll do.'

She held her arm in front of her, braced it across her stomach. She laid the blade against the outermost edge, and then drew down in one long, steady cut. Eva heard a hiss of breath, as though she could still feel something through the local anaesthetic. Blood oozed from the wound. Steff reached across and wiped what she could away. Then Anna cut again.

This time the skin parted. The blade had gone deeper. Eva could see the striations of flesh that lay beneath the surface. Then, more quickly, Anna made two horizontal cuts. She staggered. She might not be able to directly feel the pain, but the shock of the incision was making her weak. Anna looked into Eva's face. 'I'm having trouble focusing,' she whispered. 'I need your help.'

She suddenly realised what Anna meant. The hair on her scalp crawled. She wanted to protest, to refuse, but she knew she couldn't. 'Just cut a slice about three to four millimetres deep,' Anna told her. 'And mind your fingers.'

*Mind her fingers.* Christ's sake; that felt like the least of her worries. Eva held Anna's arm out so Styles could see. She steadied herself, forced herself to look into the bleeding incisions, tried to visualise the careful slices she would need to make to pare the top layers of skin from the flesh and muscle beneath them. Then, with a deep breath, she slipped the blade into the cuts Anna had already made.

Eva sliced upwards. What she hoped was a smooth, even motion. The skin felt like uncooked meat, which was exactly what it was. The blade slipped through it easily enough. *Like pork*, Eva told herself. She tried to distance herself from Anna Seifert. *Like raw pork.*

Thirty seconds later Eva lifted a section of skin away from Anna's arm and with it the bloody metal sliver that held the chip. Steff took both items from her with a pair of tweezers and placed them in a clear plastic container. She passed the container to Eva and then went to work on Anna, who was sweating despite the rain. Steff sprayed the skin and covered it with the patch Anna had requested. Anna looked at Eva through eyes that could not focus. 'Thank you,' she said. 'Now I've got to get all this stuff to Styles.'

Eva shook her head. She put the container in a small box along with the rest of the material Styles had been promised. 'You've done more than enough,' she told Anna. 'I take it from here.'

# Chapter Forty-Six

Eva waited at the gate. Kitson, Moresby and the SFOs watched her. So did Styles.

'No bloody way,' Kitson had gasped when she told him what she planned to do. 'We've got enough officers down already without giving him another one to dissect.'

'That's why we've got to get inside.' She needed to reason with Kitson, she knew that. She needed his support, even if he was only ever going to be reluctant. 'Jacks and his team have got to get medical assistance. Styles has the hostages; maybe some of them are still alive. The only chance any of them have is if we do what he says. He needs to believe he's got us.' She had frowned then. 'Let's face it, he pretty much has.'

'Christ's sake,' Kitson hissed, 'you'd be like a lamb to the slaughter.'

She shook her head, sure that she was right. 'No. Because we're giving him everything he wants. God almighty, I know he's insane, but he actually thinks this is his chance at immortality, or at least the longevity he's convinced himself Anna has. Do you think he's going to throw that away just to have a go at me? It's everything he's worked for. I'll just be the courier. We make this transactional, conditional, a straight swap, but we keep the pressure on him. We have to force him to act quickly, to make him take the samples and then get away. He needs to think he's up against the clock now, that you're getting ready to ram the gate and shoot everything that moves if we don't resolve this fast.'

'Trust me,' Kitson had assured her, 'that won't be difficult. Because first sign of trouble that's exactly what's going to happen.'

Was she fooling herself? Standing alone in front of the gates, she began to wonder. She'd run through every other strategy she could think of in her mind, but this was the only one she could imagine Styles agreeing to. She knew she wouldn't be able to live with herself if she left Jacks and his team to die in Styles's cages. And when it came down to it, she believed completely everything she had said to Kitson. It was her talisman. More than anything else in the world, Darren Styles wanted what he believed was Derzelas.

'I suppose this is meant to be some gesture of trust.' Styles's voice screeched and squealed over the speakers. 'But I don't trust you, of course.'

'I can leave the package at the gate for you if you want,' Eva called back. She knew he could hear her.

He scoffed. 'And have one of your thugs shoot me as soon as I pick it up.' He sounded dismissive. 'We both know that's not going to work.'

'Yes,' Eva agreed. 'It's your decision.'

Silence. It dragged on for almost a minute, but she knew better than to push the point. Styles had to go through the same process she had gone through, to work through the alternatives in his mind. Only then would he reach the same conclusions she had, that this was the only way for them both to get what they wanted most. For her it was Jacks and the hostages, for him it was Derzelas. Everything else, her arresting him, him killing her, became secondary. Surely he would see that too? She kept waiting. The silence kept dragging. Then, when she thought he might have actually gone away, the gate finally buzzed.

The outer layer began to pivot open as the inner one swung to meet it. The two were designed to lock together and block the racetrack, but she already knew that. 'Bear in mind,' Styles called to remind them, 'I have a gun. Several guns now in fact.

Anyone apart from you tries to come through the gate and I'll use them. You do believe me, don't you?'

The question didn't need an answer. The gates locked in place. She didn't look at Kitson or Moresby; she didn't dare. The path up to the first building was a narrow belt of slick tarmac; rain had formed shallow puddles on it. Eva started walking. When she had passed through the gates, she heard the whine of their electric motors once more and sensed them closing behind her. She didn't turn around. There was no point.

*I'm in charge.* When it came down to it, when all was said and done, it was her investigation, her responsibility. Anna Seifert had tried to shoulder the burden, but she wasn't an officer of the law. Eva had chosen that path, had made that choice five years ago when as a trainee analyst at MPCCU she closed down a child porn site and made the mistake of letting herself see the contents. She knew then what she had done in destroying the site had made a difference. Knowing that, she could not stop then. She certainly could not stop now. Of course she had to deliver the samples to Darren Styles. It was her duty.

Styles's threat stayed with her all the way up the path to the first building though. He had a gun aimed at her. She could almost feel his stare. He knew how to pull a trigger, but was he even vaguely competent with a weapon? He could even shoot her by accident. Or one of his other dogs, perhaps the one that delivered the hand, might turn on her. Or she might stumble into another of his mantraps or roast herself on electrified wires. Her fears didn't feel at all like paper tigers. When she reached the door of the first building, she found it was open. She pushed on it and stepped inside.

Eva had thought of the buildings that made up the farm as huts, but that didn't do them justice. Metal framed, the construction was breeze blocks covered with weatherboard, painted green and carefully maintained. The low roofs sloped on a pitch. On the south-facing side she saw solar panels. Huts they might be, but solid energy-efficient huts big enough to hold a lot of animals. And other things, she thought.

345

A low-level background hum; she heard it now. An unnatural melange; the sound of tropical birds mixed in with the squeaking of rodents and the low whining of small dogs. Almost more than Anna's wound, it sickened her. She saw cages, stacked up against walls on shelves divided only by litter trays. Despite herself she walked towards them.

'I think I'd like you to stand where you are.'

She almost turned, but the image she glimpsed from the corner of her eye made her freeze. Styles, of course. He had crept into the room silently, or perhaps he had been there all along. Whatever his method, he was there, and he was about a dozen paces behind her and to one side. In his hands, held almost casually, was a gun. A military assault rifle that had no place in English fields, Eva thought. It was not one of the SFO's weapons. She had no idea how he might have obtained it.

'I'm not moving,' she said.

'Put the box to one side for a moment,' Styles instructed. She did as she was told. 'Now take off your coat.' She did that too, looked around, and dropped it on the floor. 'Jacket.' Reluctantly, she complied. Eva stood in the cool interior of the hut in white blouse and black trousers. The cold wasn't immediate, but she knew soon she would be shivering.

'Arms up,' Styles said. 'Turn around slowly.' He peered at her as she rotated. 'Okay,' he said finally, 'doesn't look to me as though you have anywhere to hide a gun. You can come through.'

'Can I get my jacket?'

Styles gave her a glare. 'No.'

'It's cold,' Eva complained.

'I don't care.'

There was something obscene about him. Something unnatural. He had altered his features with injections and plastic surgery intending to make himself appear like Anna's twin, but the result had made him almost reptilian. His skin seemed stretched, as though pulled too far. His eyes, set in sockets

346

without lines or creases, were like those of a dead fish. His body was taut though. He had a nervous, neurotic energy that made him physically dangerous.

She followed Styles into a room with a stainless-steel sink and a metal bench, in an area divided by polythene sheets and lit by fluorescent tubes hung in metal fixtures from a low ceiling. It took her a few moments, but then the purpose of the room came to her, and she felt her stomach knot. 'Okay,' Styles told her as he sat on a bench across from her, 'let's see what you've got.'

She glared back. 'No,' she told him.

'Oh,' Styles complained, 'don't get clever. You're not that clever, so don't act that way. This,' he said, shaking the rifle, 'is a big gun, and it only takes one little squirt to rip your guts out.'

Her turn to scoff at him. 'Which immediately brings the rest of the SFOs down on you. Maybe you can hold them off, maybe you can't. Do you want to put that to the test?'

She could see Styles understood. 'So what do you want?'

Had he really even needed to ask the question? 'To see the abductees and the SFOs, obviously?'

He almost seemed disappointed. 'There was me thinking it was all about me.' His head sunk a little, but his eyes rolled up to stare at her from under hooded brows. 'You sure about that?' Styles leered.

'Yes,' Eva insisted. 'Why?'

That deranged cackle again. 'You'll see.'

–

In another building, adjacent to the first, Styles showed her the SFOs. She smelled them before she saw them. Four bodies in cages. An acrid stink of nylon seared to flesh hung in the air. They didn't move, but Eva could tell they weren't dead. Jacks lay on his side. Burnt skin, hair singed, eyes open but pupils contracted, unmoving. They were wet. There were puddles of clear water under the cages. 'They kept whining,' Styles complained. 'I had to turn the hoses on them.'

Animals in cages lined the walls. Mice, guinea pigs, hamsters, rats. Somewhere there were birds. She heard the echoing chirrups of canaries, finches, parakeets. When she tried to approach the SFOs Styles shoved the assault rifle at her. 'You wanted to see them. You've seen them. Move on.' He nudged her forward. As they left the room, she cast a glance over her shoulder.

Jacks blinked.

They followed a narrow corridor. Heat and humidity hit her when they entered the next building. Sweat burst from her skin almost straight away. Trees in black planters dotted the room. Wide, sharp fronds tangled with vines brushed the ceiling. Rainforest trees. Leaves scattered over the floor. The sweat on her skin pricked and crawled. In the corner of her eye, something slithered.

Styles watched her. Anticipated. She knew it would be there somewhere, whatever it was Styles wanted her to see. She stood still, turned her head slowly. On the ground, in the trees, between her and the next room. When she knew what she was looking for, they were impossible to miss.

'Careful Eva,' Styles whispered. 'Don't piss your panties.' She felt her eyes go wide but forced herself not to make a sound. That strange eight-legged scuttering, the tap of chitinous exoskeleton against man-made floor. They were huge. Bird-eating spiders almost a foot across, a dozen of them at least. They scuttled toward her, pedipalps raised as though tasting the air. 'Well look at that,' Styles cackled. 'They want to say hello.'

She needed to scream. She bit her tongue, felt blood in her mouth. 'They want feeding you idiot,' she spat at Styles. 'Are you going to keep screwing around or do I have to stamp on these fucking insects?'

'They're not insects,' Styles began to lecture, but Eva held the box out in front of her at arm's length.

'What happens if I drop this on them? Lots of broken test tubes? I wonder if they'll like the taste of Anna's blood?'

Styles's face clouded like a petulant child. He muttered. 'Stupid bitch.' He opened a container on the wall, reached in and pulled out the body of a dead mouse. He threw it over the heads of the spiders. They reared, forelegs waving, then turned and scurried towards it, fighting, climbing over each other. Styles threw another. 'Watch out for the anaconda next door,' he told her as he stomped past them. 'If she catches you, she'll eat you.'

—

Eva forced herself to follow Styles past the spiders into the next room. More trees, more stifling humidity. She saw the snake immediately. She couldn't miss it. It had to be close to six metres long, twenty feet of coiled muscle. The body was thicker than her thigh. The colour of rainforest mud, it had looped itself through several branches and watched her as she passed, forked tongue tasting the air.

'She likes you,' Styles chuckled. 'I can tell. She could swallow you whole, did you know that? It's fascinating to watch. I can sit here for hours while she digests the rescue dogs they send us.' She wanted to swear at him, to call him every name under the sun. 'She can be quite affectionate providing you keep her fed. She does love crushing things though. Can you imagine her just wrapping herself around you and squeezing?' Styles thought again. 'Hey, we could feed her if you like. I just had a couple of stray spaniels delivered the other day. You should see her technique; it's fascinating.'

'Stick to the job at hand,' Eva hissed. The snake edged closer.

'If you insist.' A sick grin. 'But you don't know what you're missing. Oh,' Styles said, as though another thought had just come to him. 'You should tell Anna she enjoyed Michael Conroy very much.'

—

The door to the rooms where Styles kept his pets closed behind them. A wave of cold nausea swept over her. Was it true? Could he have left Conroy's body for the anaconda to consume? It could have managed it, Eva thought, but she had the sense the idea had only just occurred to him, another mind game to taunt her with. Styles enjoyed dissection and, according to Phillip Kay at Scientific Support Services, had become skilled in it. Would he have given up that pleasure just to feed a snake?

They were near now. She could tell by the way polythene sheets hung from metal poles, the same sheets she had seen on the video, draped ceiling to floor like a quarantine area. The lighting was different here, the room darker. Low lights on tables lit the space unevenly. LEDs glowed in the gloom, and even from here she could hear the muted bleeping of heart monitors. 'Here we go,' Styles told her, drawing back a polythene curtain, 'my little laboratory.'

It wasn't that small a space. You could have stretched the damn snake out in it, and it wouldn't quite have reached either wall. Benches with laboratory equipment scattered across them edged around two sides of the square. In the centre, arranged as she had seen them on the video, lay the five abductees.

She tried to put faces to the names, the list that with Flynn, Newton and Chakrabati she had gleaned from missing persons reports and from Seifert's own human resource records. Michelle Barnes. Paula Francis. Hazel Richards. Daniel Beale. Graham White. She thought she knew them, three women, two men, but with their drawn, inert faces and unnatural pallor she couldn't be certain. Five low, unsynchronised beeps echoed in the room as monitors at their feet measured vital signs. She saw electrodes covering them, tubes that took blood and waste and others that provided food. They looked thin, Eva thought.

He must have been feeding them on a liquid diet for weeks now.

There would be plenty of other complications too. Bedsores, pooling of blood through inactivity, muscle atrophy, a build-up of toxins in liver and kidneys; the list went on. But they were alive; she could tell that from the steady bleep of the monitors. And, she saw as she scanned the sedated bodies, they were also intact.

Eva glared at Styles. 'I thought you cut one of their hands off?' She kept her voice brusque, uncaring.

Styles grimaced. 'Cut the hands off a live one? Do you know how much of a pain in the arse that would be? I'd have had to stitch them up, give them a transfusion, all that kind of shit. Why bother when I had plenty spare? And anyway,' he added, as though at pains to point out something she hadn't thought of, 'the dogs would never have brought you fresh meat. They'd have eaten it straight away.'

So the hand had been chilled. She hadn't thought to check. 'Nice dogs,' Eva said.

'I have a pack,' Styles let slip. It seemed he knew what she was thinking. 'I exercise them half at a time.'

The abductees were there. They were alive; more she couldn't say. Eva held up the box with the various components of Derzelas and samples of Anna's blood and flesh in it. 'This works for me,' she told Styles. 'I get the abductees and you get free passage out of Northridge. Are we agreed on that?'

Styles looked at her as though she was an idiot. He flipped the safety catch on the gun, held it at waist height, aimed it at her body.

'No,' he told her. 'That's not how we're going to play this at all.'

## Chapter Forty-Seven

'You need more assurances,' Eva said. She knew what her next task was. To get Styles to accept the samples, and then for him to just leave.

'I want to shoot you in the head you stupid, annoying bitch,' Styles snarled. Then he regained his grip. 'But we are where we are. So yeah, I need more assurances.'

She tried to keep the exchange as calm as possible. He had to feel safe. She knew he wanted something else. He wouldn't pull the trigger yet. 'Tell me what you want,' she said.

He pointed at a chair. 'For a start, sit down. But before you do, put the box on here.'

Eva hesitated, but then she lifted the plastic box and placed it where he had indicated, on one of the benches. She backed away and sat as she was told, hands folded in her lap.

Styles watched her for a moment but then put the gun on the bench next to the box. 'Let's see what Anna's sent us.' He took out files, paper copies of material on the USB drive, and gave them a cursory glance. 'Synthesis methods for the Derzelas CRISPR component,' he read. 'Well, that sounds promising. They say this is the kind of stuff you can cook up on your kitchen sink now. And look here,' Styles drawled, 'some ready-made examples.' Although he tried to conceal it, Eva could sense his excitement. Anna had judged it perfectly. The box contained exactly what Styles had hoped to find. He lifted out a set of vials and put them to one side, then kept delving. 'Samples of Anna's blood. I'll test some of that later. Maybe along with this,' he lifted out the plastic container that held the square of skin Eva had cut from her arm. 'I don't need much for tissue analysis, I've got the hang of that now.' He ran his tongue over his lips. 'Maybe I can fry the rest.'

She couldn't tell if he was being serious or sick, if he just thought he was torturing her with more of his outlandish suggestions. Even if it were only mind games, she still felt the need to kill him. Styles took the small, bloody chip that had come from Anna's arm and set it on the bench without comment.

'Now,' he said, picking up the gun once more, 'honestly. We have a whole bunch of problems here DI Harris; you do see that, don't you? And you're going to have to help me out if we're going to get this done.'

He wasn't pointing the gun at her. She should feel grateful for small mercies. 'I knew that as soon as I made the decision to walk in here,' Eva told him. 'What problems?'

'Well, look at these.' He waved at the vials. 'I mean, who the hell knows what shit is in these things? Derzelas or hydrogen cyanide? How do I know?'

Eva shrugged. 'That's biochemistry. I can't help.'

Styles leered. 'Of course you can.' He pointed the gun at her. 'Roll up your sleeve.'

–

Eva froze. Anna wouldn't have done anything stupid. She wouldn't have laced the vials with strychnine or similar, however much she might have wanted to. Anna had instructed the preparation of the vials, therefore the vials had to be safe. It wasn't that which had made her freeze. It was Styles giving her directions. If he started and she complied, how far would he try to go?

He already had started, Eva realised as she thought back over the past ten or so minutes. Every single move, gesture and instruction had been about him exerting control over her, testing her, preparing her, seeing how far he could push her.

She had thought she was standing up to him, but in reality, whatever action she took was a reaction. She had become submissive, and she hadn't even noticed.

She wanted to kick herself, to scream, to tell him to go to hell, but also to yell at herself for falling for his tricks. Of all people, she should have known better. Styles kept staring at her. With a gasp of disgust, she capitulated again and rolled up her sleeve.

'I was starting to think there might be something wrong with the vials,' Styles said.

'Don't be a moron,' Eva spat at the man pointing a gun at her stomach, 'Anna Seifert had them prepared. There's no way she would knowingly allow something harmful to be put into her drugs. I just don't like being your guinea pig.'

'No?' Styles grinned. 'Maybe you'd better get used to it.' He picked a vial at random, opened a syringe and filled it. 'You know how to do this?'

'It's not rocket science,' Eva grumbled. She took the syringe, squirted a couple of drops from it because she had seen doctors do that, then, without hesitating, jammed the needle into her arm and thumbed the plunger. It stung. She knew she had performed the injection badly, and she knew it would continue to sting for a while. Another reason to both hate and resent Styles.

They waited. Styles sat in smug, self-satisfied silence and watched the clock on the wall. Eva glared. After a couple of minutes he sighed, and put the vials back in the box. 'I was almost hoping Anna had put something lethal into the mix. You're very annoying. You deserve to die.'

The urge to curse and spit came back then, not that it had ever been very far away. Eva kept her mouth tightly shut to resist the temptation.

'So we have a working hypothesis,' Styles said as he dug into the box again. 'Let's say Anna Seifert has actually given me Derzelas. I can kind of see how she might not care too much; that stuff about the next stage makes total sense. This is like Derzelas version 1, the stuff that gets you to a hundred and fifty. But what then? How do you cope with a century and a half worth of memories, what about mechanical wear and tear, what about organs that need maintenance? It's a bigger problem, I absolutely get it. She believes this works, and she's as smart as they come, so that's good enough for me.'

Eva kept her face immobile. She watched him but gave nothing away.

'So cool,' Styles said. 'I've got samples, I've got the process, bring on longevity. Just one problem,' he said, waving the gun. 'You.'

The muzzle of the gun wavered, as though he were choosing exactly where to shoot her. 'When I say you,' Styles continued, 'I mean you and your nasty friends outside. Do I really think you're going to let me drive out of here?'

'In return for the safety of the abductees and the SFOs,' Eva said. 'You have my word.'

Styles sneered. 'I wouldn't piss on your word. I drive out of here and halfway down the lane I get caught in a crossfire, job done. Maybe it's a mile away. Maybe you wait twenty-four hours. Whatever the scenario, I leave, you follow, you kill me. Do not think I am as stupid as you, DI Bitch.'

She let the name-calling wash over her. She ignored it. 'I don't know what to tell you,' Eva said. 'I give you my word you can leave here with Derzelas, but you're right, after that all bets are off. You've killed people, Darren. You've admitted to it, so we will hunt you down and bring you to trial for that. Maybe they'll let you work on Derzelas in prison.'

Styles rolled his eyes. 'Oh, the good cop. What a tedious cliché. What happened to *Do what thou wilt shall be the whole of the Law*? I thought you'd seen enough of New Thought to understand. You should be wanting revenge; revenge is good. Take pleasure from killing, it's the ultimate expression of hunter over hunted. What's up with you Eva, or are you just that weak?'

'Natural justice?' Eva spat back. 'Are you sure that's what you want?'

'Well, some form of retribution.' He reached across the bench and picked up the blood-smeared chip cut from Anna's arm. 'Didn't you think I knew Anna had a kidnap tracking device implanted in her?'

Styles ambled up to her. Put the muzzle of the gun in her stomach. Used his right hand to slap her face.

Eva felt blood trickle from her lip. 'Put the gun down,' she spat at him. 'Pick up a scalpel, I will too. Let's see who bleeds to death first. I bet my life it's you, once I cut your dick off and feed it to you.'

He laughed. 'See? I knew there was someone more interesting in there. I just had to persuade her to come out. Wow, we're going to have some fun, aren't we?' He pushed again. 'How much do you know about Anna Seifert?'

She sucked her lip. 'Enough.'

'How old is she?'

Eva stared. Suddenly she needed to know. 'Mid-thirties?'

Styles kept his voice level. 'Fifty-three.'

She guffawed. 'Bullshit. You're lying.'

He smiled. 'You can check.' Eva couldn't answer. 'See? See what I mean? She's using Derzelas; it's the only possible explanation.' It wasn't, Eva thought. It was possible Anna had a combination of good exercise, good diet and an awesome plastic surgeon. If anybody knew how to keep herself in perfect condition, surely it would be the MD of a pharmaceutical company? Styles had shaken her, though. That one small fact had thrown her grasp of the case into turmoil.

'So,' he continued once he saw she was off guard, 'your problem is this. Are you prepared to come with me, to play the role of my hostage, just to save these five complete strangers and some toasted cops? Are you? I won't hurt you. All I need to do is get out of the country and then I'm gone. I get my freedom, you're inconvenienced, but these five get to live. How is that a bad deal?'

Could she say no? How could she say no? 'Or else?' Eva demanded.

Styles took a step back. Reached up to one of the shelves above the bench. Picked up a cigarette lighter. Sparked it. Held it to one of the polythene sheets that surrounded the room. The polythene began to wrinkle and melt.

He stared at her. He didn't blink. 'Okay,' Eva snapped when she saw a thin column of acrid black smoke starting to coil from a hole in the curtain. Styles snapped the lighter shut.

'There's a good girl,' he said.

—

She felt sick. Bile churned in her stomach, already acidic enough for not having eaten in almost a day. She had no choice. Eva gazed at five bodies laid out on trollies, helpless and oblivious. This was what it had all been about; this was her endgame. She had to go with Styles for the sake of these five Rip Van Winkles, sleeping Barbarossas who still had a chance at life. This, Eva told herself with almost more reluctance than she could stand, was actually what she had signed up for.

'Now,' Styles said as he fumbled around on the bench, 'it's not that I don't trust you, it's just that – I don't trust you. I think you're the good cop, willing to give up your life for the sake of the common people or whatever, but I wouldn't put it past you to try to cut my throat if you saw the chance. Fair?'

'Fair,' Eva agreed, before she had even thought about the answer.

'Good girl,' Styles taunted again. 'I can see we're really starting to get along. So, I'm going to take you with me when I leave, we'll hang out for a day or two, then I get the hell out of this godforsaken shithole of a country and go find somewhere with sun. I leave you here to die of vitamin-D deficiency. Joking,' Styles added quickly. 'But only so much. I need you to be a bit more compliant if you know what I mean, not ready to do something inconvenient at the wrong time. You understand?' He held up a syringe. 'So I'm going to sedate you.'

Panic hit her. She edged back in her chair. 'I didn't agree to anything like that.'

'Honey,' Styles purred, 'I don't give a rat's arse what you did or didn't agree to. This is what we're going to do.'

'How am I any use to you if I'm unconscious?'

'Ah,' Styles said, 'I see the misunderstanding. Quite understandable, that misunderstanding. This is just a mild sedative, it's more like a tranquilliser. I need you to be able to walk, I just don't want you jumping on my back or anything crazy. You'll still be able to talk, just a bit less than usual. You're right,' he agreed, 'I don't want to have to carry you around; you're enough of a burden as it is.' He waved the syringe. 'This is just enough that you'll do as I say,' he told her.

She stared at the syringe. Cold fear gripped her now. If she didn't do as he said he would kill the sleepers on the tables, and everything, everything she had done would have been for nothing.

'Now come on,' Styles screamed. 'Make your mind up time. Shoot the drugs or I burn the lot of them.'

Eva took the syringe. Stared at it. Shoved it into her arm.

## Chapter Forty-Eight

God, it felt nice. She didn't know what it was. Valium, Ativan, Xanax, Klonopin, Restoril, Rohypnol, Dalmane, Imovane, Ambien, Lunesta – she didn't know how the names came tumbling through her head. Just another advisory issued by some department somewhere, warning about what to look out for in opioid addiction she must have read and unconsciously absorbed. Whatever it was, it felt good. Warm, it touched every part of her body, from her fingers and toes down to her core. Nothing mattered now. She could just float away.

Styles was doing something. She didn't know what; it need not concern her now. They had reached an agreement. She had done her part. The abductees would be safe, and she could... she could just drift.

Spinning. She felt like she was spinning. Not round and round but over and over, tumbling. Sudden nausea, not enough to make her vomit but sufficient to upset her. A realisation, a familiarity. Whatever he had given her, she had taken it before.

Not taken. Been given. After Winter's Gate Farm, after Colin Lynch had rammed their car with his dumper truck, after she had ended up head down in a freezing-cold stream with a bleed from her femoral artery that had sent her into hypovolemic shock, the doctors had tranquillised her. They had put her into an induced coma, shaved her head and, like Styles's abductees, covered her with electrodes. They had read her mind, those unintelligible waveforms that glowed like jagged peaks of mountains on a horizon made of liquid crystal, and concluded they needed to wait for the swelling in her brain to go down before they allowed her to wake. And so, they had tranquillised her. And it had felt good then, too.

Had it been the tranquillisers? The dream of flying over an infinite landscape at incredible speed, the sensation of irresistible power that had filled her. Had it been the drugs? But it had happened before that, Eva told herself. Before Donna the lunatic paramedic had risked her own life by crawling into the car, before John, the equally insane firefighter had used his tender like a bulldozer and scraped the Scania P380 truck off them. It had been before that, during the time her heart had actually stopped, during the eight minutes when she had been, technically at least, dead. That was when she had seen what she had seen. And no shrink with a syringe full of tranquillisers was going to tell her any different.

Practical anger, something she could use. It felt like a tool, some mechanical gizmo with which she could loosen the grip the sedative had on her. After the initial euphoria the sensation seemed to fade quickly. The world was still something she viewed through a fish-eye lens. The warm sense of drifting hadn't gone away, but at least it hadn't subsumed her completely. She could still think, albeit slowly. And she could still act.

Styles was ignoring her. He was packing, Eva saw, putting his own transcript with the material Anna had provided and preparing to move out. He took piles of written notes and data drives too, some samples in sealed tubes and a handful of glass slides, then dropped them all into a pair of plastic holdalls. Styles glanced around the lab, checked the readouts on the five bodies laid out beside them.

His finger hovered over a power switch. She could almost read the thoughts going through his mind. What would be most useful, to leave the abductees or kill them now, cut the power and let them drown in their own fluids? Would cutting power to the intensive care systems actually kill them, or would their bodies simply take over for themselves? Was it better to kill them or leave them alive? He was trying to make a rational decision based on his chances of escaping; she could see it. After a few moments Styles took his hand away from the switch.

Eva would have to move soon. He would make her, she knew that. When she curled her hand, she found to her surprise that she hadn't dropped the syringe with which she had injected herself. It was empty, but it was still in her hand. For no rational reason she could think of, Eva slipped the syringe into her trouser pocket, pushing the needle out through the cloth so it wouldn't scratch her. She folded her hands in her lap then.

Styles looked down on her. 'Come on DI Bitch,' he said, grabbing her by the throat and forcing her to stand. 'Time to say bye-bye.'

—

Styles dragged her towards the back of the farm, twisting her arm and pinching her skin, unable to resist touching and hurting her even though he couldn't afford the time. Eva staggered. When she went to steady herself, tried to lean against the whitewashed breeze-block walls, she stopped. Stumbled again, deliberately this time, to seem more incapacitated than she actually was. Eva muttered something incoherent. Styles shoved her forward.

They paused in the next building. More cages filled with cowering mice. At the end there was another pen. Another five Dobermanns, lethargic, drooping and lounging. They too were sedated, she saw through the fog that permeated her mind. Poor bastards, Eva thought. She hung on the texture of the sedative in her head, braided the strands of it and dragged herself above it, like a night-time driver forcing themselves to stay awake.

He opened a cabinet by the pen and took out five pieces of meat, poured something on each of them from a plastic bottle and threw the pieces into the cage, making sure each dog received a slice. They ate, laconically at first, as though they were indifferent to food, but after a short while the feeding became more frenzied. He had laced the meat with amphetamines, she guessed, a dose that must be close to lethal, because after only a few minutes the dogs transformed. Yellow eyes, uncontrollable snarling, trails of saliva falling from their mouths, running in circles and throwing themselves at the wire.

Styles grinned his twisted grin and turned his back on them. He went to press a button on the wall, a green mushroom-shaped bulge she assumed would open doors to let the animals out into the grounds, but then he stopped. 'I think I'll leave them here,' he told Eva. 'I'll let them have the run of the place before we leave. It'll be a nice surprise for when your colleagues search the building.'

He shoved her ahead of him this time. Styles, holdalls slung over his shoulders, held the rifle held in both hands, and he used it to push her. Eva lurched and winced, making quiet complaining noises, but he ignored her and shoved her again. He wanted to really hurt her, to inflict pain he could take pleasure in, and he would soon; she could feel the sense of excitement growing in him. When they got to wherever they were going he would sedate her again, and then he would be able to do whatever he liked with her. He wanted to. She could sense it. He wanted to do to her the things he had tried to do to Dominique, to lay her out somewhere, tranquilised and unable to resist, and play his perverted games, the games he had played with corpses in the dissection room of Surgical Support Services. By the time he had finished with her there would be nothing identifiable left to find.

She knew she had to get away. She had no idea how. Even through the drugs, she knew the five inert people stretched out on tables in the other building were the priority. If Kitson could get a team in there, past the physical traps and past the dogs, she knew they would be safe. Once they were safe, she could get on with planning her own escape.

Styles would take her somewhere else, another property or warehouse, she could guess that much. Maybe she could grab the wheel. Pretend to be asleep, pick her moment, drag the steering wheel over and ram the side of some articulated lorry on its way to the Channel Tunnel. Take her chances. Hope Styles went through the windscreen on impact. She couldn't think of anything else just then.

The last building, next to the room with the dogs. Styles pushed her through a door that opened onto a garage. Three bays, only one of them occupied. A dark-green Land Rover, a working vehicle with scraped paint splashed with mud. Styles put the holdalls in the back. Then he turned to Eva.

He reached back into the room behind them and brought out a length of rope. 'You're going to stay here for a couple of minutes. I've got one last thing to attend to.' He grabbed her hands, forced them together and tied a crude knot. Then he threw the rope over a ceiling beam and pulled. She hissed pain. The rope burned her wrists. Styles pulled until she had to go up on the balls of her feet to take the strain off her arms. He tied it off on a cleat on the wall.

'Two minutes,' Styles promised her. 'Then we'll be on our way.'

'What are you doing?' Eva slurred.

He called over his shoulder to her as he left the garage. 'Just got to light a fire.'

—

Even before Styles returned, she could smell the smoke. Just a trace, the acrid stench of burning plastic drawn through the building by fans that took the stench of animal waste away. Only a wisp of it on the back of her throat, the slightest sting as particles invaded her eyes. From somewhere outside, she heard shouting.

From inside, too. Suddenly Eva heard a scream and shots. A sound she recognised, the triple report of an H&K G36 in controlled burst mode. But Styles had the only guns in the building; he had taken them from the SFOs when he electro-cuted them. If it was Styles, what was he shooting at?

A few moments later he crashed back through the doors, turned and let loose three more rounds. Face contorted with pain. He limped. She could see why. A sliver of wood like something from a smashed-up palette protruded from his leg. From inside the building somebody shouted something. The words echoed; she couldn't understand them, but she recognised the voice.

Jacks. The SFO was alive, or at least he had been until a second ago. Styles shot again. He stared at the chunk of wood sticking out of his leg, then with a scream ripped it out. Glared at Eva as if it were her fault. Aimed the gun at her.

She slumped again as though exhausted, dangled from the ropes even though they bit into her wrists. Still limping, Styles opened the door of the Land Rover and started the engine. He stumbled to the front of the garage and pressed the button to open the double doors. Grey light flooded in. The garage was at the far end of the farm facing the gates on the opposite side. It could be a minute or more before Kitson and the remaining firearms officers even noticed.

She had to stop him. Now was her only chance. If she didn't stop him now, this second, then she would be as good as dead and Styles would make her end twisted and slow just because he could. The sedative numbed her mind. It also dulled her emotions. She had to do something, she knew that, but in that moment she felt no fear. She could barely feel anything at all.

Engine running, doors open, all he needed was his hostage. Styles came for her. Punched her. It was a clumsy blow, his fist smearing blood on her face, and the sedative numbed the pain. Such hatred on his face. He was going to make her pay; that she could tell. He untied the cleat, grabbed her and shoved her at the car.

Eva stumbled forward, rubbing her wrists.

Doors wide open. The sound of shouting, louder now. In the distance, a crash. Metal tearing, engines revving. Kitson must have seen the smoke, realised what Styles had done. Maybe he had seen Jacks. Kitson had ordered the Land Rovers to ram the gates.

Shots being fired, at what she didn't know. Styles dragged her towards the passenger seat, the one place she didn't want to go. Eva stumbled. Put her hand in her trouser pocket.

He had her by her left wrist. Her right hand hung free. She took a breath. 'Stop a second,' Eva pleaded. Styles turned to glare at her, threaten her, lip curled in anger and disgust.

She clenched in her fist the syringe he had made her use on herself. Swung her arm up. Stabbed the needle into his eye.

–

He screamed. She pushed. The needle sank into the white sclera and scraped bone. Styles staggered back, not knowing what to do. The syringe hung from his eye. He seemed too shocked to touch it. Eva knew the actual damage she had done would be minimal, but Styles hadn't realised that yet. He lurched, swayed from one side to another, screaming all the while. The gun wavered. She was stunned. He hadn't tried to shoot her yet.

Eva crouched and stumbled around the front of the Land Rover. The engine ran. She could climb into the driver's seat, but something stopped her. He hadn't tried to shoot her yet, but if she took the car she knew he would. The rifle didn't require skill. He would just flip the switch, set it to automatic and hose the vehicle. She'd seen the damage Jacks's weapon had wreaked. Even the 4X4 wouldn't stop the spray of high-velocity rounds. If she tried to drive away, he would simply cut her to pieces. She couldn't use the car. She couldn't let him use it either.

Driver's door. She yanked it open. Slid behind it. Reached in, grabbed the key and twisted it out of the ignition. The engine stopped. She ran around the back of the car. Styles stumbled after her, syringe still hanging from his eye. With a final, demented scream he reached up with one hand and pulled the barrel of the syringe. It slipped out of the sclera with almost no resistance. Styles stood, dazed, wondering what to do now that he knew he wasn't blind.

Eva threw the key.

The world drifted in and out of focus. She aimed somewhere between grey and green, through the open doors of the garage. Styles bellowed his fury and shot at her, but she was already moving. Bullets skittered off breeze-block walls, most of them burying themselves in loosely packed concrete. He aimed the gun, searched for her, but then heard shouting from outside. Kitson and the SFOs had heard the shooting too.

He had to get the key. She knew that. He wanted to kill her, to cut her in half, to pump bullets into her body and watch her die, but he had to get the key. Did he not see it was his only choice? The key lay on the grass. Fifteen metres, she guessed. It had been a lousy throw. She knew he could be there and back in no time, key in hand, gun ready, finger on trigger, aimed at her head. Styles knew that too. He stalked out of the hut. Eva crouched, watched, held her breath. Then she tried to run. She almost fell flat on her face.

Her legs wouldn't move fast enough. She staggered like Styles, dragging her numb feet, forcing them to stay on the ground. Where the hell did she think she was going?

Styles limped across the grass to where the key lay, knelt down on his good knee, picked it up. Turned. Glared at her with a look of supreme hatred, as though imagining the things he would do to her. Stood. Started walking back, steadier now, towards the garage, blood still dripping from his wound and spattering the grass.

Her one chance. She had failed.

She tried to stumble back into the building, away from the garage, got as far as the door to the next room, but he could

366

still see her. Styles, almost back to the Land Rover, had his gun raised. Ready to shoot.

And suddenly, directly in front of her eyes, a domed, green shape. Before she even registered what it was, faster than she could think about the consequences, Eva slapped it with all the force she could muster. A click. Loud. Mechanical. Then the thud of muscle striking wood. A sudden brightness as daylight poured into the room.

She had hoped for a single shot, the echoing crack of a round as it buried itself in Styles's chest.

What she saw was a blurred flash of black and brown.

–

Two dogs hit him when he was less than five metres away. One rammed his side, sent him staggering. A third flew at his head, jaws wide and foaming, bit into his face. He screamed then, just for a moment, but quickly the screaming became something else as the second dog ripped open his stomach and buried its face in his guts.

She tried to tear herself away. She didn't need to see what was happening; there would be other witnesses at the far side of the farm who would be able to describe events, but she found she couldn't take her eyes off the scene in front of her.

Eva watched in silence as the dogs ate Darren Styles alive.

## Chapter Forty-Nine

Smoke drifted over the farm, although the fires were out now. It looked the way she imagined a war zone might look, after fighter planes had circled a village and dropped their bombs on civilian targets. The only consolation, Eva thought as she walked through the area marked out as safe by Moresby's people, was there was only one dead body here.

Two air ambulances had landed outside the perimeter. Six more paramedic units had been rushed in to give support. Rebecca Flynn stalked the fence with a camera, seemingly photographing every blade of grass in case they offered any iota of evidence. Raj was inside with Hallett making lists. Jamie stood with one team of paramedics, watching and waiting as slowly the abductees were brought back to consciousness. Eva walked over to another team who were attending to the SFOs.

'I thought you were dead,' Eva told Jacks. He had a drip in his arm; they all did. Burns and blisters covered his face. A paramedic was cutting away body armour where he could.

'I think we shorted the wires.' His voice cracked. He sipped at a straw placed near his mouth. 'I saw someone's boots on fire. The soles had melted, they were dripping flames. Then I realised mine were burning too. The electricity stopped. I think we burned through something. I don't imagine that piece of shit would have just turned it off.'

'But you got out? You cut your way out of the cage and stabbed him. I get the smashed-up wood, but how did you get out of the cage?'

His face cracked. A laugh, Eva realised. 'He used nylon ties to lock the doors. Thick, but you'd need to cut them to open the cages.' Jacks raised his hand. In it he grasped a small Swiss army pen knife. 'My wife gave it to me. I keep it with me. It was just a stupid anniversary present. I gave her a Japanese carving knife she wanted, so she gave me this in return.' He smiled. His lips bled as he did so, but Eva could see now he would recover. 'Rule one of digging yourself out of the shit,' Jacks reminded her. 'Work with the tools you've got, not the ones you wish you had.'

—

Anna Seifert hadn't left. Steff had given her a shot of something to help her with the pain from her forearm, but now that the shock had worn off Anna seemed almost dismissive of the wound. 'It's a surgical incision,' she said as she stood next to Michael Sullivan. 'I have people who can fix it inside a fortnight. One day skin grafts will be as commonplace as flu remedies.'

'Just not today,' Eva pointed out.

Anna gave her a wry smile. 'Just not today.' She looked towards where the five trolleys stood, out in the open now that the patients had been removed to the air ambulances. 'Will they be okay?'

Eva sighed. 'I hope so. They've been kept unconscious for quite a while. I've no idea what long-term effect that will have on them, but as of right now, yes, they're okay. Ordinarily they would be suffering from smoke inhalation, but Styles kept their metabolisms so low they hardly had time to breathe anything in. Longer term...' She could only shrug. 'Who knows how any of us will be in the longer term?'

'Not me,' Sullivan admitted. 'Do you think I'll be allowed to continue my work? I don't want to sound dramatic, but from my point of view it actually is a matter of life and death.'

Eva was about to answer when Anna butted in. 'All due respect to DI Harris, but the police will not have a say. Derzelas isn't harming anyone, so maybe it's time to get it out in the open. The police might want to express an opinion,' she added, gazing at Eva, 'but they better have a boat-load of lawyers with them if they do.'

Eva couldn't help but smile. Anna knew full well that the remaining level of police interest in Derzelas would be so close to zero as to make no difference, but she had earned the right to posture. Sullivan knew it too. She could see it on his face.

Nevertheless, Eva couldn't stop herself asking another question. 'How old are you?' she blurted.

For a moment Anna looked indignant, but after a few seconds she seemed as though she understood. 'Was that part of Styles's delusion? My date of birth?'

'Not thirty-five,' Eva guessed.

'Over twenty-one,' Anna retorted, but she seemed more amused than annoyed. 'I'm not going to tell you my age, Detective Inspector,' she said, a trace of a smile playing over her immaculate lips, 'because I think you would be shocked.' The smile faded. 'But not as shocked as if I told you how much I spent every year on keeping myself looking young.'

Eva felt her own face colour then. A stupid question, impertinent and unfair. In the aftermath she had simply let her curiosity get the better of her. She tried to make light of it to hide her embarrassment. 'Well, whatever it is, you look fantastic on it,' she told Anna. 'I'm definitely getting myself some of that.'

For a moment she didn't understand the expression on Anna's face: a look of sadness tinged with guilt. 'I'm sorry, Detective Inspector,' Anna said, as though making a confession, 'you simply couldn't afford it.'

–

Perhaps the conspiracy theorists had it right, Eva thought as she wandered back towards her team. Perhaps aliens do in fact walk amongst us. Creatures of light and magic, the super-rich for whom anything is possible providing that, ultimately, someone else pays. She had always known money was a zero-sum game, that for some billionaire to enjoy a gilded life a million others had to endure poverty, but the contrast had never seemed so sharp before. A linear correlation, but this time between life and death. Judy Wren's prediction came back to her then. *Immortality isn't something you're ever going to find on the NHS. Eternal youth will be reserved for those who can afford to pay for it.*

Anna Seifert's other dark secret. Not that she spent the aid budget of a third-world city on make-up and cosmetic surgery, but that what she had told Darren Styles about Derzelas was ultimately correct. There had been reversals in epigenetic ageing; there were huge advances being made in antisenescence. Perhaps the breakthrough would be thirty, forty, fifty years away, but whenever it was, it would come. The human body was just another machine, monumentally complex and in some ways hopelessly inefficient, but a machine nonetheless. And machines could be repaired.

*You simply couldn't afford it.* And there was the rub. The ultimate inequity. When the likes of Semion Razin built their empires based on the suffering of others, was it not in some way a quest for immortality? Just some vain attempt to push back the final curtain? She could feel her mood blackening, despite rain-smeared sunlight that even then was trying to ease its way through the blanket of grey. *Get your head out of your arse, Harris,* she told herself as she walked towards where her team now stood. *What's the matter? Did you want to live forever?*

–

A little while later a pickup truck she now immediately recognised crawled past the scattering of police cars and emergency service vehicles. Jonathon Crane, long coat covering Vantablack prosthetics and unnecessary sunglasses hiding his eyes, climbed out and sauntered towards Eva.

'Anna called me,' he said as he stood beside her. 'She told me what happened. It sounds as though you got the best outcome you could.'

'Just about,' Eva agreed, although if there was any sense of victory to be found in the day's events it completely escaped her. 'If only we'd spotted Styles sooner.'

The broad smile that cracked his face surprised her. 'Ah,' he beamed, 'if only. I remember that one.' He stared down at Eva. 'That's a game that's of exactly zero use to anyone,' he told her. 'I can say that with a very high degree of confidence.'

Jamie and Raj looked like kids with new puppies on Christmas Day. Rebecca Flynn seemed a whole lot more sceptical. 'You can't blame them for the amphetamines,' Jamie insisted. The Dobermann lying at his feet looked up with ridiculously pathetic eyes. They were from the five inside the racetrack, Eva knew. The dogs that had killed Styles were under heavy sedation.

It was Moresby's officers who had put the fire out, led by Moresby and Kitson, under cover from the SFOs. They had thrown themselves into the building the moment it became apparent what Styles had done. Hallett had accompanied them. Once the fire was out the paramedics had started working on the abductees while Moresby and Hallett had gone to check on the animals.

'It's curious,' Raj agreed. 'Maybe it's the steroids, but now the other drugs have worn off they seem more docile than any guard dogs I've ever come across.'

'But look at the muscle on them,' Eva said. She crouched down slowly and put a hand on the dog's shoulder, determined to try to make an unemotional assessment of the risk the animal presented. It responded with a grumble, turned its head and licked her hand. 'Oh bugger,' Eva said as she found herself compelled to scratch it between the ears. A second dog sat and stared at Jamie, as though hanging on his every word. Crane shook his head at them in gentle incredulity.

'So we got Styles,' Flynn mused. 'And somebody got Webb.'

Eva turned her attention from the dog's ears to its sternum. It rolled over, put its paws in the air and did a passing impression of an Internet meme. 'Somebody did.'

'And you know where Winter's Gate Farm is,' Raj pointed out.

'I know where Winter's Gate Farm was,' Eva agreed, 'but why somebody chose to put that sign next to Webb, I have no idea.' The coincidence hadn't escaped her. The transhumanist h-plus and the board for Winter's Gate, two signs had in their own ways come to represent the difference between life and death for her. The simple logic of it hadn't escaped her either. Though, now that she had the chance to think about it, there was only one person who could have possibly known the significance of the sign, she realised. Semion Razin.

'Sounds like you have some unfinished business then,' Jamie said. 'Maybe Jacks will be seeing you at Pirbright after all. A little CQB training never did anyone any harm.'

Jamie was right, of course. Razin's people hadn't gone away. Webb was dead, but the threat was still there. Jacks had wanted her to learn how to defend herself. Eva suspected Crane would recommend the same thing.

'Maybe he will,' Eva conceded, as she gave the dog one final stroke and stood up. 'I mean, what's the worst that could happen?'

—

Slow rain fell from a gunmetal sky and soaked green fields that crossed gently undulating hills. A mile from Northridge another copse of trees stood against the horizon. Cedars and oaks, birch and even the occasional ash, the copse was an island in an otherwise empty landscape. There were places where branch collars had been pruned and sawn wood had been gathered into neatly stacked piles. The path through the woods had been cleared and the bushes that lined it cut back. Somewhere high above, a carrion crow cawed a loud and grating companion call, which echoed in the trees and remained unanswered.

The hill the copse stood on looked down on the razor-wire fences of Northridge, but not from any great height. It was simply there, a part of the landscape, a minor feature that had existed in that spot for not less than four hundred years. Apart from its location, it was unremarkable.

A man stood under the shelter of the trees and watched. He had driven to the copse early that morning and had stood, or sometimes sat inside his car, watching what he could of the little drama unfolding a way across the Downs. He had watched and waited. And that was all he had done.

He was average height, slender, wore a broad-brimmed hat and a long dark coat. His skin was pock-marked. He wore small, round-lensed sunglasses. His hands were gloved. He gave the impression of being unwell, though he didn't cough or sneeze. He had watched all day. Now the little play beneath him had finished; it was almost time to go home.

One last indulgence. The man took a cigarette from his pocket and put it in his mouth. With his other hand he took out a lighter, raised it at arm's length, and sparked it. He watched the flame for a moment, before bringing it towards the end of the cigarette. A small flame, only an inch high, but still extraordinarily intense.

If anyone had been watching, if any of those scurrying around Northridge had happened to look up at the copse of trees in that moment, it wouldn't have been unimaginable that they would have commented on a distant flame, one that somehow seemed, just for an instant, to burn brighter than the sun.

# A letter from Carl Goodman

It's funny how the real world has a way of catching up with fiction. I wrote *Lifesign* before the pandemic, when for most of us biology was a long-forgotten and perhaps not especially loved school subject. Now it seems we're all far too familiar with messenger RNA and spike proteins. *Lifesign* isn't really about biology though. It's about what someone who is desperate enough might do if their delusions became more compelling than reality.

It's probably no surprise that some of the ideas for *Lifesign* came from articles on transhumanism. Others came from an absolutely stunning and heart-stopping exhibition by Canadian rock star-turned-photographer Bryan Adams at Somerset House called Wounded, which focused on young British Service men and women who had suffered life-changing injuries. In the middle somewhere were images of elective body modifications, the absolutely extraordinary extents to which some people will go to in order to remake their bodies as works of art. When you put all of those together in any order at all it's really hard to get away from our universal fear of mortality, and the idea that some things might actually be worse than death. *Lifesign* is most definitely a crime thriller though, so fortunately I had a protagonist capable of making sense of it all for me!

I've really enjoyed writing about Eva as a character. She can be more than a bit irascible at times and her relationship with the law can be fluid, but at heart she has a sense of justice and a conviction to do what's actually right, not merely what's correct. If that seems a bit like wish-fulfilment, it's because it probably is.

Pretty much all of the technology in *Lifesign* is drawn from real-life. When I wrote the book, I was working for a research company with a major multinational manufacturer for a client, using Virtual Reality amongst other things to measure how effectively new product developments worked on consumers. Eye-tracking, EEG recording, galvanic skin response, time-to-first-fixation, system one and system two responses – if you think some of the stuff mentioned in *Lifesign* seem a bit like science fiction, you're just going to have to trust me. It really isn't.

I'd just like to sign off by saying thank you to two people in particular. One is Keshini Naidoo at Hera, for giving Eva a chance. The other is Sandra Sawicka at Marjacq for, apart from huge amounts of patience and everything else, some really well-considered and nuanced observations. Definitely right about that surgical cap!

Carl Goodman

376